Sticks and Stones

The Barn Church Series

Book Two

by
SHELLIE ARNOLD

STICKS AND STONES BY SHELLIE ARNOLD
Published by Kaleidoscope Publishing
1738 Oak Trail St. NE, Massillon, OH 44646

ISBN: 979-8-9865367-7-4
Copyright © 2016 by Shellie Arnold
Cover design by Elaina Lee, edited by
Stephanie Arnold
Interior design by AtriTeX Technologies P Ltd
Available in print from your local bookstore, online, or from the publisher at
www.kaleidoscopebooks.net.
For more information on this book and the author visit: www.shelliearnold.com.

Library of Congress Cataloging-in-Publication Data
Arnold, Shellie
Sticks and Stones / Shellie Arnold 2nd ed.

Printed in the United States of America

Praise for *Sticks and Stones*

Shellie Arnold has done it again! I would recommend anything and everything Shellie writes ... and here's why: she understands people and what it takes to make a marriage work. She also is tenderhearted toward the Lord. Adhering to the biblical principle, "Speak the truth in love," Shellie cuts through the typical sugar-coated advice and gets to the heart of the matter.

I love the way Shellie puts solid marriage counseling into a story. The story she tells in *Sticks and Stones* is no exception. The struggles Rick and Julie Matthews go through clearly demonstrate the power our words hold--spoken and unspoken. But words don't merely hit the intended target. Collateral damage, in this case their children, is equally devastating. Healing is possible, but not typically achieved without intentionality.

As a pastor, I intend to purchase this series to have in our church library to use as follow up for the marital counseling I do.

~Tina M. Hunt, Pastor
Ashland First Church of the Brethren

Sticks and Stones offers readers an intimate peek behind the closed doors of the Matthews family and their pain—both past and present. This book has something vital to convey to every reader, no matter their circumstance in life. In a transparent and powerful way, author Shellie Arnold reminds us that it is both the things we say and the things left unsaid that matter most.

~Clint and Penny A. Bragg
Authors of *Marriage on the Mend—Healing Your Marriage After Crisis, Separation, or Divorce*

In *Sticks and Stones*, Shellie Arnold does a remarkable job of telling a captivating story that penetrates to the heart and soul of common marital blind spots and the roles we unintentionally adopt to deal with stress and conflict. Although merely fiction, the truths it brings to light about the complex destructive patterns found in many marriages are amazingly accurate. As a marriage mentor, I see these patterns all too frequently in marriages on the verge of collapse, and I'm thrilled to see a story that not only shows in meticulous detail how they develop, but also how couples can find resolution and reconciliation.

~ Linda Rooks
Author of *Broken Heart on Hold, Surviving Separation*

Shellie Arnold's *Sticks and Stones* is an exquisite portrayal of lost dreams. It's the heart-wrenching story of a fractured family finding their way back and learning to forgive. I wanted to sneak in a chapter during lunch and couldn't stop reading until I finished it.

~Ane Mulligan
Bestselling author of *Chapel Springs Revival*

Acknowledgments

A few days after God dropped this story idea into my heart, I had two prominent thoughts:

1) I don't think it's possible to write this book, and

2) I don't *want* to write this book.

I didn't think it could be written, because after asking several accomplished authors how I could make the storyline work, I was told I couldn't make it work. Having a main character who couldn't speak would kill the storyline. One prolific author shook her head, shrugged, and said, "Shellie, keep in touch with me. If you pull this off, I want to know about it."

So, my first thank you is to Loyd Boldman, to whom this book is dedicated. Loyd, you made me believe I could successfully write this book.

As far as concern number two mentioned above, I didn't want to write this book, because I didn't like the idea of sharing glimpses of a particular road I've been walking with God for many, many years. Being married, being a parent, and realizing you didn't learn a very important life skill is unnerving in itself. Being in a position to repeatedly repent to your family, then change and grow in front of them—baby step by baby step—that's even tougher.

So my next thank you is to my husband, who's lived in the fallout, benefited from the fruit, and loved me during God's work in this area of my life. Your eyes are my home.

Thank you to my agent, Tamela Hancock Murray. Your willingness to stick with me for round two shows your true bravery and character.

To the entire team at LPC, I'm only beginning to understand the tiniest bit of all you do and the dedication with which you do it. I count myself blessed to be associated with you all.

Endless thanks to the professionals and others who assisted in my research: the emergency responders at Lakeland Fire Department Station 6; Dr. Edward J. Meszaros, DMD; Eleanor Tracey; A.C. and J.C.; Kate Arnold, MA CCC-SLP (my daughter-in-love); Aaron Arnold (my firstborn and a terrific vocalist); Angie Brady; Mark Hancock.

To my son, Adam. When you read portions of this book and find some of your story, know that you were never defective, are always loved, and will forever be a miracle. Daddy and I love you so much.

As with the acknowledgments in *The Spindle Chair*, I must mention Larry Leech II and the "original" fiction group. You all helped me shape this story. I know we all miss Loyd.

To Dianna Love and Mary Buckham, attending your *Break Into Fiction* seminar helped me see I could indeed write this story.

To Dory Stewart and the Medina County Writers Club, you all rock!

To Eva Marie Everson, every person or marriage touched by anything I write has you to thank.

To my Biggest Fan, when I've fought discouragement, all I have to do is re-read your emails and cards.

To Jennifer Slattery, what a tremendous blessing you are!

To my children, who make me strive to be better. And again, to my husband, who loves me when I'm not.

To my God, Who gave me back my voice. Thank You for saving my soul from darkness. Thank You for saving me from myself. Thank You for demanding both transparency and obedience. In the beginning, You know I feared them both. I had no idea they contained the answers to many of my deepest, most painful prayers. I had no idea they were the soil where joy grows.

To Loyd Boldman

who told me he "heard" Julie, even when she couldn't speak.

Loyd, I know you're already singing in heaven, sometimes
I think I can hear you.

PROLOGUE

"I love being outside with you like this." Julie Matthews stretched under the blanket.

She slid a leg over her husband's thigh, slipped an arm across his trim waist, and rested her cheek against his shoulder. She smiled, grateful to enjoy sunshine after being practically housebound while taking antibiotics for an infection. Despite the August heat, a grown–up picnic was a fabulous way to start the next season of her life.

A balmy, south-Alabama breeze ruffled her hair, tickling her nose with the fresh pine scent of the woods behind them, and making the surrounding black-eyed Susans dance. Two dozen feet away from the old quilt she'd spread on the ground over an hour ago, two horses, his and hers, munched on tufts of clover. The creek nestled at the foot of the tiny floral hill trilled under the bright sun as if giggling with her.

She kissed Rick's damp skin. "You asleep?"

He took one of his signature deep breaths; her arm, draped across him, rose and fell. He felt around for his black Stetson, and smiling, laid it over his face.

"No one within a twelve-mile radius can sleep with you doing happy cartwheels in your head." He patted her bare hip. "Dozing certainly has its advantages, although I will need some sweet tea and a couple of those sandwiches in a minute. Seems I worked up an appetite."

"Do you think Rachel's okay?"

"Rachel's fine. She'll handle the first day of first grade better than Sean did." He waved a hand in the air. "And my cell's here ... somewhere."

"She's bigger than most of the other girls." Like Julie herself had been. "She's self-conscious."

"She probably will be for a while. Until she's a teenager and the boys start catching up. Then I'll handle the boys." He lifted his hat, shading both their faces, and looked over at her. "There's no blue like an Alabama sky, but I'd rather look into your pretty green eyes any moment of the day. They captured me when we were kids, but the way they shine when it's just me and you ... I'd give you the world if I could."

She brushed her fingertips over his lips. "Shhh." They'd just made love, her entire body still felt like it was covered with warm honey. "I don't want the world; I have you. You have what you want—the stables. We made a family—one boy, one girl—exactly what we wanted. Now the next part begins."

"You haven't been on stage since before Sean was born. Did you find a voice coach?"

"I found a great one. If I do the books for the stables, I think we can handle the expense. But I might have to hire a sitter some afternoons for the kids."

He raised to an elbow, donned his hat. "No reason they can't stay with me at the stables."

"Remember when we snuck out here at night? Was it last April?"

Rick grinned. "We spent time under a blanket then, too."

She grinned back. "Yes, we did. And I thoroughly enjoyed myself."

"Seems like I remember that."

She gouged him in the ribs. "You *better* remember."

He chuckled.

She sat up, knelt before him on the quilt as the blanket slid down, exposing her back to the sun's warmth. She stared toward the babbling water, cleared her throat against tears.

He linked his calloused fingers with hers. "I remember, too, what you told me that night."

"Do you?"

Her heart pounded as if she stood at the edge of a cliff. Why did she feel so exposed? They'd been married eleven years and had loved each other like they were the only two people in the world. But talking about this? She couldn't look him in the eye. How could she explain a childhood longing so deep she thought she'd drown in it?

He kissed her knuckles. "You can tell me again if it makes you feel better."

"I always loved going to bed at night. Not like most children." She shook her head. "Not like Rachel."

Rick chuckled again. "No."

"Regardless of what my mother said during the day about my aspirations, at night I could hide under the covers and dream about singing professionally. In my dreams, I was safe."

"You know, I've noticed you take naps when you're stressed. Maybe that's how you cope, you just go to sleep."

"I hadn't thought of that, but you might be right."

"And the angels?"

"The angels in heaven waited for me to fly up and sing to them. I'd fly up to a place so high and quiet, then sing a song I'd written for them. They smiled at me." She took a breath. "I sang for God, and He smiled at me, too."

During those dreams she'd felt so accepted by God, so very loved.

Rick sat up, drew her chin and eyes toward his. His patient, hazel eyes blinked slowly, then focused on hers.

"Julie. Your voice, I've never heard anything like it. When you sang the National Anthem before our high school football games, no one in the stands spoke. Even the jocks with me on the field stood quiet and listened." He paused. "Baby, you don't have to worry about being good enough. You always have been, always will be."

He kissed her.

She kissed him back. "Thank you for saying that," she whispered.

She hated being so uncertain, like a needy child desperate to be acknowledged.

"I heard you singing to Rachel last night. The song from the contest, right?"

"She loves that one."

"You won the scholarship; your mother should have let you go. It wouldn't have cost her one dime of your dad's death benefit."

Her father's death in a commercial aircraft crash had made her mother an extremely wealthy woman when Julie was only three. "I wish I could remember him."

"I know you do. If she had let you go to New York, I would have followed you. You know that, don't you? Ridden my horse right through Times Square."

She pictured him, her handsome, steady cowboy loping across lanes filled with irate drivers. She almost laughed.

"I think I'll start by rejoining the choir. It's not that I resent being a wife. I don't. Times like this with you are perfect."

"Baby." He took a long breath. "The choir's a good idea. You might decide that's as far as you want to go."

She pressed her lips together and stymied the impatience rising within like a desperate animal clawing its way out of a pit. She needed more than his support. She needed him to understand.

"We agreed before. After having children, it would be my turn."

He traced her throat with his rough fingers. "I know you can do it."

"Thank you." She grinned. "Tomorrow I'll call the voice coach and fire the accountant."

Chapter One

Eight years later

With her booted foot, Julie tapped a staccato beat on the scarred concrete outside her mare's stall. Seventeen minutes.

She rechecked her watch. Nope, make that eighteen.

Eighteen minutes wasted. Waiting in this sweltering May heat—what little makeup she had applied this morning was definitely melting into oblivion—while the local country radio station Rick insisted on piping through the stables whined in the background.

Who had time to write a song about setting a truck on fire? And furthermore, who would want to?

She checked her cell phone for a message from Rick. No message. She texted him *Where are you?* as she paced up and down the long corridor in front of thirty-plus, wooden, sliding doors. Above her, sparrows darted from the indoor arena on her right, to the hayloft above the horses and back, stealing tidbits for their nests. Swirling dust and the green scent of alfalfa tickled her lungs.

She coughed. A horse on the far end whinnied as if laughing at her discomfort, others down the line continued the heckling. She stopped again in front of Tempo's stall, plucking at her dampening blouse, as a twanging guitar joined a tortured violin.

"This is WCIK, where country is king! South Alabama's number one station right here in Rowe City. It's 4:22. Here's another favorite to help you pass the time."

Julie huffed. "Pass the time, huh?"

In the sticky air, she could actually feel the unused seconds scampering by, seconds that were already divided and delegated. With her oldest son graduating from high school in a month, then leaving for boot camp, there was a graduation party to plan. A guestroom to paint before her mother's arrival for said event. And she had three days—three short, already-spoken-for days—to perfect a solo in a fantastic new song for Sunday morning's service. Thaddeus Bartell, a record producer looking to branch into the inspirational market, was bringing his Nashville business partners to hear her sing with the choir.

She'd practiced so hard. Could she hit that high note at the end? If she nailed it, if the rough rafters of The Barn Church shook with it, Bartell's associates would surely be impressed. And finally, *finally* Julie would get her dream life of having a family and a singing career.

She closed her eyes, fanning her face. Sunday would be a great day. Sundays always were—the only day she felt close to her family *and* God. What more could a woman want?

But if her husband didn't call her, or show his face here at the stables in the next *two* minutes, she would have to skip the just-the-two-of-us ride that he wanted. She was already squeezing in taking Rachel out for pizza that evening—a reward for finally finishing a large science project, an incentive to buckle down on schoolwork through the end of the year, with the possibility of a little attitude adjustment thrown in for good measure.

Then, of course, choir rehearsal tonight.

She glanced at her watch. Twenty-five minutes and counting.

On second thought, no. With Rick late as usual, she simply couldn't fit the ride in, too. And she refused to endure another harmonica solo.

She turned to leave, just as Rick pulled up in his truck at the far end of the barn. He moseyed toward her with his Stetson on his head and a shopping bag in hand as if he didn't have a care in the world.

"Here ya go. Bought you some new riding gloves at Benson's."

"You've been in town? At the hardware store?"

He handed her the bag and she looked inside. "They're leather."

"They were on sale."

She checked the tag for chromium-free tanning, but merely touching them made her hands start to itch.

"I can't wear them." Like most leather products. *Remember?* No, he didn't remember. Just like he didn't remember he'd promised to never again loan her gloves to kids taking riding lessons.

"I'll just ... get myself another pair later. I've already got Tempo ready to go." She gave him back the bag.

"So you don't want them?"

"No ..." What part of I-can't-wear-most-leather-products didn't he understand? She used a synthetic saddle, synthetic reins.

He stood perfectly still. Watching her. Debating ... something.

While she waited.

And waited.

"You're late. You could've called." Something she'd been teaching their oldest son.

Rick didn't reply. No apology for being late and not calling, nothing. So there they stood, staring at each other.

Finally Julie turned. Behind her, he took a long breath and followed her into Tempo's stall.

He patted the brown and white Paint. "She's been moody the last few days."

The mare side-stepped and shuffled her feet, as if restless to get moving. Julie could relate. She grabbed the saddle horn. "Be still, girl."

From behind, Rick slid his arms around Julie and clasped his fingers over her I've-had-three-babies belly.

"Don't." She stiffened as he pressed his lips to her hair. She'd spent her young life trying to squeeze into her petite mother's shadow and had never succeeded. "I've asked you before."

Why didn't he listen to her anymore? Listen and *remember* things she said. He remembered everything about the horses—their diets, their owners.

She felt him freeze, but couldn't make herself turn in his embrace.

"Julie."

"*Don't.*"

She knew what he was going to say. That she wasn't fat, that she was still attractive to him, and being with her meant even more to him now because of the life they'd built, the storms they'd weathered together. Like her third pregnancy, which had added new dimensions to her full-figure. Like caring for Ben as a baby with his medical needs, which had left her no time to worry about fitness and exercise.

But Rick's weight gain in their nineteen years of marriage totaled a mere twelve pounds, all of which was perfectly-placed muscle. He couldn't possibly understand her insecurity and why his repeated requests to make love with their bedside lamp on were impossible for her to grant.

"Can we just go?" she asked.

"Want some help into the saddle?"

She felt her eyes widen. "No," she stuttered. Rick giving her a boost would certainly result in a hernia. For *him*. And wouldn't it be fun explaining *that* injury to family and friends. To her mother.

"All right. Have it your way." He slipped away.

She cinched the strap around Tempo and wiped the sweat from her brow with the back of her hand. Didn't Rick know that she was sick of repeating herself? To him? To the children?

Sean was the *easy* child—if there was such a thing—who mostly listened to her and followed her instructions, but he'd be leaving soon. Fourteen-year-old Rachel listened when doing so was to her advantage, but conveniently forgot chores she didn't want to do. And little Ben, well, Ben was only seven, a precocious seven, but still; with his health issues, his hadn't been and wouldn't be the easiest road.

If her music career finally flourished, Rick and the children would have to do more for themselves. Maybe then they'd appreciate her. Value her.

She led Tempo past a dozen stalls toward the searing sunlight. Placed a foot in the stirrup and tried to boost herself up. Her feet seemed stuck to the ground. Or her rear end was tethered to it. Where was a step-ladder when you needed one?

Something inside her flashed hot, and within seconds, boiled violently. She stomped her way to the fence. She tied off Tempo at a post, and fighting gravity, used the fence to climb her way into the saddle.

Dear God, something has to change—in my life, in my marriage. Please help me sing well enough Sunday that Thaddeus Bartell will offer me a contract. And I need my husband, my family, to hear me—really hear me—or me having a career outside the home isn't going to work.

"I'll be in the paddock walking Tempo," she called over her shoulder. Maybe that would hurry him up.

He didn't respond.

"Do you still want to do this?" she yelled. "We should have started thirty minutes ago."

***

Three stalls down, Rick unlatched the door and slid it aside, catching the tip of his thumb. A blood-blister formed. He shook his hand against the sting, and with the double-take, noticed and avoided a fresh pile of horse dung in the doorway. Win some, lose some.

With horses he almost always won. Folks brought him problem horses all the time. He could break them. He could teach them. He could turn them into whatever the owner wanted, for show, for farm work, for recreation.

Julie had been a different matter since Ben's birth. With her, Rick almost always lost.

He saddled Dutch, a burly old Morgan with wide hips. Dutch nipped at his front shirt pocket.

"I know, I know." Rick retrieved a peppermint ball and offered it to the stallion on a flat palm. Dutch crunched the hard candy with glee and blew sweet breath in Rick's face.

He rubbed the horse's jaw. "Yeah, you're a real ladies' man. Too bad a mint can't fix other mouth problems, huh, boy?"

There was a time when Rick made hurrying a habit, to appease Julie. And he used to answer her every question, when she fired them at him like a human machine gun. He had tried, in every way he knew since Ben's unplanned arrival, to make their life together something she could be happy about, rather than a reason for constant complaining.

But no matter what he did or how he did it, with Julie, he always came up short. Falling short all the time could eat at a man, wear him down until he didn't even try to reach as high as he once had. Like a volunteer coach who knows his team will be last place in the city league, sometimes a man simply needed to lower his expectations. Sometimes you just tried to make it through the season, so to speak, with as little conflict and aggravation as possible.

Yet ... a dying ember still had a little spark. And Rick had an idea for adding some much-needed fuel to his and Julie's fire. The two of them alone in a mountain cabin? The notion appealed to him on many levels.

He just wanted to make her happy. He wanted her to look at him the way she used to, before Ben was born. Rick didn't know why their marriage had deteriorated after his youngest son's birth. What he did know—what he'd only recently admitted to himself—was he didn't know how to get out of the rut.

He patted the horse's thick neck, led him out of the stall, then ducked into the tack room and grabbed a blanket and a rifle.

"Easy, boy. We're just going for a ride." Dutch wouldn't spook, no matter how skittish Tempo was today.

Rick latched a strap over the blanket and stowed his gun in the saddle's side pocket. He let the animal stroll out of the high-ceilinged barn and across the paddock, then mounted him. Julie was already astride Tempo, who paced the fence and whinnied like she was in a heated argument.

He passed through the wide gate, brought Dutch alongside, and bent forward to make eye contact with his wife.

"I won't lend out your gloves anymore." He thought of the vacation brochure hidden in his pocket. "Let's take the short trail through the woods, ride down by the creek. I have a surprise for you."

***

Julie nudged her impatient horse to a trot.

"Fine." She glanced at her watch. "Just make it quick. I've got to be back at the house in less than an hour."

She'd lost so much time already and time was the one thing you could never get back. Could Rick not wait until after Sean's graduation to spring something else on her?

She led the way in silence, finally exiting the woods with Rick close behind.

"Water's coming back up." He brought Dutch beside Tempo. "Been more showers this month than expected." They swayed together in the late afternoon sun and Rick reached for her hand. "Do you know what I'm thinking?"

His thumb caressed hers as she took in the lovely scene before her. Black-eyed Susans coated the gentle slope down to the creek. The same flowers, in the same place, where she and Rick had spread an old quilt on the ground eight years ago. Who knew strong antibiotics could counteract birth control pills? Nine months later Ben was born—complete with cleft palate, life-threatening sleep apnea, and chronic ear infections resulting in permanent hearing loss.

Her insides shuddered. This was the surprise? She looked at him and noticed the blanket.

"Are you kidding me? You can't possibly be serious." She laughed and pulled her hand free of his. What else could she do when picturing herself outside and *naked*. Only the birds and the bugs would see, still …

"Thank God I'm sterile—tubals cannot be overrated. But even if I had the time, there's no way I'm getting busy on the grass out here in broad daylight."

Her husband squinted at her, drew a long breath through his nose, held it, and finally exhaled as he adjusted his cowboy hat. "Then I guess it's a good thing I'm not in the mood."

She squeezed Tempo's reins. "Now wait a minute. You can't possibly be mad at me. If any of your surprise plans are ruined, it's not *my* fault. I was in the stables on time, waiting to ride as you asked. Which means I suffered through most of the thirty-minute classic country music sweep on WCIK. I'm giving you my undivided attention."

He shook his head. "You sure are. And your undivided mouth too."

"What did you say?"

A sleek, quick line surged out of the greening reeds beyond Tempo's feet. Julie locked both hands around the front of the saddle.

In a blur of movement, the hissing cottonmouth lunged. Its body whipped to strike. Recoiled, and lunged again.

The mare's piercing scream confirmed Julie's fear. Her horse had been bitten.

Tempo reared like Pegasus, kicked like a mule and took flight, racing along the river's muddy edge. Behind them, Rick's rifle fired once, twice, its blast echoing through the watery valley. The horse surged up the flowery bank to dry ground picking up speed.

Julie didn't dare let go.

"Not the trees!" Rick's voice spun through the wind-tunnel in her head. "Julie! Keep her in the open!"

She couldn't answer. Her grip slipped and she listed to the left. Desperate to avoid being thrown, she squeezed the horse with her thighs. Tempo took it as a command, turned again, and arrowed straight for the thick stand of trees. Ears back, the horse lowered her head and barreled through.

The low branch materialized from nowhere. Julie hit it full force. She flipped over Tempo's hindquarters.

The mare's rear hoof caught Julie's jaw; Julie heard it snap.

She landed on her left arm, and felt it snap, too.

CHAPTER TWO

Rick shoved his rifle back into the scabbard on the saddle. Heart cramping in his chest, he urged Dutch into a full gallop. His stomach pitched. The crazed, frightened look he'd seen in Tempo's eyes meant any prior connection between man and beast was null and void; the beast was now in charge.

Tempo wouldn't stop until something stopped her.

At the tree line Rick jerked Dutch to a halt. He jumped to the ground, looping the reins around a budding limb, and skirted through the dangling moss, swatting and ducking branches.

"Julie!"

The thick foliage muffled Tempo's quick cadence beating deeper and deeper into the woods. Panicked, Rick dodged down the battered path Tempo had forged, then stumbled into a clearing.

And lost the trail.

"Julie!!" He stopped, rested his hands on his knees, and gulped air.

Then he heard it. A high, faint sound like a wounded animal. He searched the open area, peering through crooked limbs and matted underbrush.

"Julie! Answer me!"

He almost stepped on her. She was balled up, lying in a shadow, clutching her arm. Blood streamed from her mouth, coating her neck.

"Oh, thank God." He knelt beside her.

***

From far, far away, her husband's voice told her to be still.

"Don't move, Julie."

But she needed to get up. Didn't she?

What was wrong with her eyes? They wouldn't open. And Rick was yelling at someone.

"Operator, you still there? We're in the woods about a half mile west of the north end of the stables. Matthew's Stables, that's our property. Tell them to come in off, um, Cloverdale Circle and cut across the open pasture down to Clover Creek. And tell them to hurry, she's breathing, but she's bleeding pretty badly."

Julie was stunned, far worse than the first day of third grade when Billy Bergman purposely stuck out his legs as she walked past the swings on the playground.

Aaah-ha, ha! Fat, fat Julie Pitts. She fell down and made a pit!

She needed to get up.

She leaned on her left arm. Pain splattered black ink across her mind.

***

Julie still couldn't open her eyes. And she was cold, very cold.

An unfamiliar voice faded in and out. "Looks like ... arm and ... problems."

A gentle hand squeezed her ankle.

"Julie." Rick. "Be still. I'm right here."

What happened? She'd been in the stables waiting for Rick. Then riding by the river ...

Her body started shaking. She wanted so badly to open her eyes.

"We need you to move, Mr. Matthews," someone said.

Gloved hands touched her. They were talking about her like she couldn't hear them. Something was around her neck. But no one held her hand.

"Mrs. Matthews, we put a collar on you. Julie, can you hear

me?" The voice that had told Rick to move was talking to her. "The brace will keep your neck straight."

She heard the metallic clang of buckles, the scratch-rip of Velcro.

"Julie. You're on a backboard. We have to belt you down for safe transport to the hospital."

The hospital. She was hurt, and they were taking her to the hospital.

Wide straps tightened across her body.

No. Please don't tie me down.

Fat Julie Pitts. Tie her up like a pig and she looks just like the first Thanksgiving dinner. Maybe we should put an apple in her mouth! Aaah-ha, ha!

"We're going to secure your head, ma'am. Are you with us? It will feel like a helmet with a chinstrap. I'm sorry, but it will be uncomfortable."

No, please. Don't put that on me. Don't put that on my head.

Now, Julie, each student in the class has to wear the hat she gets. It's just for a minute. Any boy here will trade you for that football helmet when I restart the music.

Aaah-ha, ha! Look at Julie Pitts. Maybe she'll be a 'Pitts'-burgh Steeler. She's already the size of a football player.

They secured her head. She tried to scream, but managed only a gurgled moan.

"Julie, we put an air-cast on your left arm. It's strapped down so you won't aggravate it further during the ride."

She was lifted. Somehow lifted and pushed into a roaring cave bright with eyelid-piercing light.

Ba-bam! Doors slammed.

Pain hammered through her face. The bliss of darkness returned.

***

The ambulance pulled away carrying Rick's wife, and left him at the edge of the woods beside his horse. All he could think as he watched the flashing lights shrink in the distance was that the paramedics hadn't let him ride with her. A gentle yet firm hand on Rick's chest had stopped him from climbing into the back of the ambulance. "Sorry, Mr. Matthews. Regulations."

The blaring siren shocked him back to the present. He needed to get home, get the children, go to the hospital.

He dialed Rachel's cell and untied Dutch.

"Rachel."

"Dad, did you forward the stables' phone to my cell? Some lady called, but I guess I deleted the number. Where's Mom? She's supposed to take me out for pizza and—"

"Listen, don't call anyone. Get Ben, both of you get ready to go to the hospital. I'll be right there."

"What? Why?"

"Just do what I'm telling you. Your mother's been hurt. We need to go to the hospital."

He ended the call. Vaulted onto Dutch and dug in his heels, spurring the horse to an instant gallop with commands and slapping reins. He pushed the horse faster, and faster still, all the way to the house. In minutes he loaded Rachel and Ben into his F-250 crew cab.

He called Sean. "Sean. Where are you?"

"With Lisa at the Downtown Diner. We're getting a burger."

"Tempo was bitten by a cottonmouth and threw your mother." Rick's heart skipped a beat. "Hang on."

"Yes, sir."

Rick handed the phone to Rachel. "Put him on speaker." He turned onto the highway and gunned the turbo diesel. "Your mother's being taken to the hospital in an ambulance. I've got Rachel and Ben. Meet us there."

"Is Mom gonna be okay? Is she like, paralyzed?"

Rick swallowed hard. "No, but she's hurt pretty bad." There was so much blood. "Just meet us there."

"Got it."

"And call the vet. Tell him ... well, I don't know where Tempo is, but Dutch is tied at the back of the house."

"I'll drop Lisa and take care of Dutch, then meet you at the hospital."

Rachel ended the call and dropped the phone onto the seat between them. "Ben, quit pushing your feet or knees or whatever you're doing, into my spine."

Rick glanced in the rearview mirror, caught Ben's eye, and gestured with his head. Ben adjusted his hearing aid and slid over. "Dad?"

"Yeah, buddy."

"Is that Mom's blood on your shirt?"

Julie's blood. On his shirt. Under his nails. In dark handprints on his jeans.

"Is Mom gonna be okay?"

Rick felt a rogue tear escape. "Yeah, buddy." He sniffed. "She'll be all right. But we might have to take care of her for a while. Okay?"

The seven-year-old leaned forward, reached one coltish arm over the seat, and patted Rick's shoulder. "What about Sunday? Will she be better by Sunday, so she can sing in church for that guy?"

Sunday. This was the most devastating thing that could happen to Julie, and it would not be an easy fix.

"Tell you what, buddy. We'll help her get better, and she can sing another day."

"Are we almost there?" Ben asked.

"About ten more minutes, buddy."

He sped to town as fast as he dared without risking a ticket. Slowed to the strictly-enforced twenty-five-mile-an-hour crawl as he drove on ancient brick streets past the courthouse, the Downtown

Diner, and Benson's Hardware. He eased around the bright red water tower near the railroad tracks. Finally he made it to the blacktop of the highway, and shot down 29. Would he find Julie dead or alive when he reached the hospital?

He followed the signs to Emergency Room Parking and held open the back door of the truck while Ben jumped down. Rachel exited the cab carrying her laptop.

"You brought your computer?" Rick asked.

"It's not for games." She rolled her eyes. "I have homework."

"We need to hurry. Let me carry it."

She looked almost embarrassed, then smiled a half-smile he knew would someday break a thousand hearts, including his own. "Okay." She handed it over.

His cell rang as they jogged across the parking lot. "Rick Matthews."

"Rick? Nathaniel Jordan."

Dr. Nathaniel Jordan, the OB/GYN who delivered Ben. Owner of Trident, a clever mustang, and the newest client at Matthews Stables. "Nate, can I call you back?"

"I'm on duty. Was in the ER, talked to the paramedics when they brought in Julie. You here yet?"

"Crossing the lot now."

"Don't waste your time in ER. Go to Surgical Waiting. She's being taken to the OR."

***

"Mrs. Matthews," a man said. "You're in the OR. Count backward in your mind with me. Squeeze my hand when I say the numbers."

Julie's body flashed cold, then hot.

"Ten. Good. I felt that."

A hand rested on her forehead. She blinked furiously, trying to focus.

16

"Nine. Good. Go ahead and close your eyes for me."

Her brain tunneled.

"Eight. Seven."

Her mind went dark ...

She was thirteen years old, standing at the squatty oak piano in her best friend's living room, running her fingers over the yellowed keys. Sharon entered from the kitchen and handed her a fizzing glass of Coke.

"Mom said she'd love to show you how to play. She'll be right here when she gets off the phone with your mom."

Julie was already taller than Sharon, everyone else in their class at school, even Sharon's mom. But something about the woman made Julie feel safe and protected.

She folded her hands in front of her. "But your dad and brother are gone, right? You're the only one who'll hear me mess up."

"Dad and Rick are hunting this weekend. They won't be back until tomorrow night. And everybody messes up the first time. You should hear some of my mother's students. Especially the boys who never practice."

"I can't believe my mom is letting me spend the night and stay tomorrow. How'd your mom get her to say yes?"

Sharon smiled. "She's pretty good at reading people. She told your mom what a sweet girl you are, and how you volunteered to help her with a project this weekend."

"A project?"

"Duh. She *needs* to teach someone—besides me—how to play the piano."

Julie's palms started to sweat. The secret notebook filled with songs she'd written waited in her book bag, right there on the floor under the front windows. If she learned to play the piano, to read music, she could write the melodies that flowed through her head. And maybe someday if she worked really, really hard, people might want to hear her sing those songs. Then God would smile at her all the time, and she'd get to keep the peaceful feeling she always got when singing to Him in her dreams.

Miss Grace—Sharon's mom insisted Julie not call her Mrs. Matthews—finally arrived, wearing the sweet, welcoming smile she always had whether greeting Julie or scolding Rick. She sat on the cushioned bench, motioning for Julie to sit beside her, and showed Julie how to position her hands over the keys.

"Here's middle C." She pointed, her voice patient. "It's in the same place on every piano."

Julie's heart soared with hope. "How long will it take me to learn all the keys? To be able to play anything I want?"

"You're a smart girl. If you work at it, learning won't take long at all."

"But we don't even *have* a piano."

Ms. Grace laughed. "You can practice here any time."

"My mom won't pay you," she blurted. Money was spent at salons, or on clothes and shoes at the new two-story mall in Birmingham. Julie's mom planned to move there as soon as Julie finished high school, to "finally start my life after losing your father."

But there had to be a way. "I could work. Here. Do part of Sharon's chores, or—"

"Oh, sweetie." She stroked a hand down Julie's thick hair. "Sharon tells me you have a lovely voice. Maybe you could sing for me some time."

Chapter Three

In the waiting room, Rick stood statue-still by the couch where Ben slept and Rachel sat typing. A Spanish-speaking nurse had just left after talking with the only other family in the waiting area.

He walked to the open doorway and peered into the hall, tapping his fingers against the doorframe as he looked in both directions, and willed someone, *anyone* to come and give him an update on his wife. No one came. Not even Sean, whom Rick had sent to the cafeteria for food and coffee.

Normally, Rick was good at waiting, a trait that often frustrated his younger sister. His patience habitually outlasted stubborn horses, and on more than one occasion, guided his bickering offspring to a truce, or coaxed a timid child onto a saddle for the first time.

He was proud to say he coached Julie through thirty-six hours of labor with Sean, a solid eighteen with Rachel. While Ben's birth was quick—a short, if not sweet, five hours from start to finish—the pregnancy had seemed endless to Julie. Rick had used every technique at his disposal to soothe her and lift her spirits. When she finally delivered their third child, he was as relieved as his exhausted wife. Sharon had hugged him, laughed, and said, "Vasectomy anyone?"

But tonight, now, while his wife was elsewhere in this hospital suffering from a broken arm, a broken jaw, and heaven only knew what else, his inherent tendency toward calm eluded him—like he'd scraped the bottom of the barrel during those awful minutes in the woods, while he waited with Julie for the ambulance to arrive. He had no reserve, no back-up resource from which to draw. With his parents half a world away in Germany helping his sister, Rick was on his own.

He tightened his fists as urgent demands scuttled through his mind like spiders. He wanted to know about his wife's condition, and he wanted to know *now*.

He glanced at his watch, used his thumbnail to scrape dried blood off the face. Almost midnight.

Sean rounded the corner with bags and a cup carrier in hand.

"The smell of fries will wake Ben. The three of you should eat."

"Yes, sir." Sean tossed Rachel a Styrofoam box. "Cheeseburger. Plain. Extra ketchup's in the bag."

"Thanks." She set aside her computer.

"Do we know anything yet?" Sean handed him a cup.

Rick gulped half of the large coffee. "Nope," he said, as Ben stirred awake. "Hey, buddy."

Ben signed *fries*, a hopeful expression on his face.

Rick nodded and pointed to his own ear. "Hearing aid." Ben sat up and adjusted the device. "And use your words, buddy."

A knock on the doorway drew Rick's attention. "Mr. Matthews?"

He straightened, setting aside his coffee. "I'm Rick Matthews."

"Dr. Chang." The stocky Asian man in scrubs shook Rick's hand and motioned for Rick to follow him into the hall. "Sorry about your wait; I was paged to the Pediatric ER. It seems tonight's the night for broken bones. I'm the orthopedic surgeon who repaired your wife's arm."

"How is she?"

"She's going to be fine. She should be moving to the recovery room momentarily."

Julie would be fine. The surgery was over, and she would be fine.

Rick felt the tremors begin in his own fingers—a steady, uncontrollable vibration as relief shook its way up his forearms. He shoved his hands in his jeans pockets and faced the doctor.

"She'll have a cast for a while, of course," the physician continued. "But the break should heal in about six weeks. Dr. Wyman, an oral surgeon, repaired her jaw before I worked on her arm. He had another emergency procedure immediately following your wife's. He asked me to give you this pamphlet about what she should expect after that kind of jaw trauma. He'll visit her tomorrow during his rounds."

Rick accepted the literature, stuffed it in his shirt pocket. "So, that's it? All that blood from a broken jaw? She didn't have any internal injuries?"

"No, Mr. Matthews. No other injuries. No evidence of concussion or head trauma, which is really good news."

Rick glanced back at his children and stepped closer to the doctor. "Will she still be able to sing? It's really important to her."

The physician's brow furrowed. "I don't see why not, after a full recovery of course. You can confirm with Dr. Wyman tomorrow. She'll be in Recovery for a while. A nurse will let you know when she's moved to the trauma unit. She'll be there for a day or so."

"When can I see her? Talk to her?"

"You can talk to her all you want after she leaves Recovery, but she'll most likely be sleeping until tomorrow."

Ben approached and wrapped his thin arms around Rick's waist. "Dad, can I have some of your fries?"

Rick returned the embrace, clearing his throat. "Sure, buddy." Ben skipped back to the couch as Rick offered a thankful nod to the doctor. "Appreciate you taking care of her."

Dr. Chang flashed a pasted smile. "I'll stop by tomorrow." He turned and left.

Rick sagged against a wall. Violent nausea churned through his gut as he remembered the pitiful whimpers from his wife's disfigured face. He knuckled a tear from his own cheek.

God, You know, in spite of everything, I love her. I thought I was going to lose her.

And he would lose Julie if she lost her ability to sing. The light that shone in those beautiful green eyes on Sunday mornings would be snuffed out. The peaceful smile—which illuminated her as she stood with microphone in hand, face raised to heaven, her brilliant voice echoing off The Barn Church ceiling—would be replaced with ... emptiness.

"Hey, Dad?"

"Be right there, Sean."

He reached into his back pocket for a handkerchief and felt the trip brochure. He *would* take Julie on a trip. He would help her recuperate, then take her anywhere she wanted to go. They'd be happy, as long as he had her, and as long as she could sing.

Rick returned to his children. "Your mother's out of surgery. She has a broken jaw and a broken arm, but she's going to be okay."

"Can we see her?" Ben asked around a mouthful of French fries.

"No, buddy. She'll be sleeping for a while. Sean, take your brother and sister home. I'll spend the night here or in Mom's room if they'll let me. Call my cell after you get up in the morning."

Rachel yanked her laptop's power cord out of the socket she'd plugged into when they first arrived in the waiting room. "So ... what? Mom's okay, and now you're sending us home with Sean in charge? It's like one o'clock in the morning. Do I have to go to school tomorrow?"

Rick sat beside his daughter and helped her pack her computer. He put his arm around her and looked at her. She was practically a duplicate of Julie at age fourteen. How long did he have before some love-struck young man put *his* arm around her?

"Yes, Sean is in charge. And no, you don't have to go to school tomorrow."

His reward was one of those heart-breaker smiles. "Thanks, Daddy."

***

Charlotte Church was singing.

Julie knew it was Charlotte Church. That soothing tone. The perfect vibrato. The lovely, clear sound like a sky so blue it might have been painted on glass.

Just like Julie herself had dreamed of singing since she was a little girl. From her soul. Full and flowing. Certain that God was listening, and pleased, and ...

Why would Charlotte Church be singing to her, in her sleep?

There was clanging—metal against metal. It echoed.

"We need a bed in Recovery," a male voice said. The same voice that had told her to count backward? "Preferably a half hour ago."

She heard beeps and a rhythmic whooshing like a vacuum turning on and off. The pinching scent of antiseptic stung her nostrils.

"Okay. I'm in soprano overload," a female said. With a click, Charlotte Church stopped singing. "And I have called for a bed in the Recovery Unit, sir. Twice," the woman continued. "Security's removing a drunken boyfriend. Former pro kick-boxer. Tried to kick down the entry doors to get to his girlfriend, and broke his own foot."

"I don't care what they're doing. This one won't stay under much longer. We have to move her or tie her hands. Or we'll have to extubate her here."

Julie strained to lift her eyelids. Through a slit she saw dark masculine eyes above a surgical mask. A gloved hand reached across her face.

Her lungs shrank. Something was filling her nose and throat. She couldn't open her mouth. Couldn't breathe. Couldn't speak.

She had to get what was in her nose *out*. She was *suffocating*.

She jerked her hand up and grabbed at her face. Her fingers wrapped around the tube sticking out of her nose.

Julie pulled.

"Shoot!" A large hand clamped over hers, while another stilled her forehead. "Ma'am! Let go! You're in the OR, and you're okay."

Razors! Her vocal cords screamed as hot blades lacerated her throat from the inside.

More hands held down her body. The masked man pried her fingers free and lowered her arm.

Tears bubbled behind her eyelids, trickled down the sides of her face, burning her skin.

What had they done to her throat?

"Mrs. Matthews, you're in the hospital and you're okay." The female spoke calmly, directly into her ear. "I'm Stella, your nurse. Your surgery's over and we're about to take you to Recovery. Hang in there another minute, and we'll get that tube out."

***

A warm blanket. Firm but gentle hands were tucking her in, rooting the soft, warm blanket under her torso and limbs. She felt snuggly, like when she was a child and she rolled herself in her covers before going to sleep.

Her body vibrated with cold, but her teeth weren't chattering. Thankfully, the blankets kept coming. Another and another. The wave of soothing heat penetrated her goose-pimpled skin, relaxed her tense muscles.

"Mrs. Matthews. You're in the Recovery Room now. I'm Stella, your nurse. That last blanket did the trick, didn't it?"

Julie wanted to answer, tried to answer, but sleep reclaimed her groggy mind. She didn't know how long she was out before she heard Stella's voice again.

"Sorry about all this bothersome monitoring, but that's how we get you out of here."

A band tightened on her arm. Almost too tight, then finally released. One eyelid wobbled open.

"Now that that's over, let's clean up your face a little before they move you to your room. Okay?"

A damp, warm cloth bathed her cheeks and throat.

"You know, sometimes I go to The Barn Church with my aunt. When I saw the name on your chart I knew it was you, and I had to say something. I've heard you sing, Mrs. Matthews. I'm not sure about God and all, but many Sundays I go to church just to hear you sing. Somehow your voice coats me with peace."

She wanted to say *thank you*, but the thought ended on a wince when pain surged from her injured arm. She could barely turn her head toward that side.

"You're getting feeling back, aren't you—I can see it on your face. I've got an icepack right here. Dr. Chang let your husband know you're out of surgery. You have such a lovely family; I've seen them sitting with you on Sundays. I bet they'll miss hearing your beautiful voice. But don't worry. You'll be singing again in no time."

***

Rachel Matthews, Mrs. Tate's third period English class: Thursday, May 1:

I have been told to keep a journal. To express my deepest feelings—like anyone really cares.

I've also been told that even though I have to turn this in at school, my mother will never see it. Otherwise, I wouldn't do it.

But it's either this, or my mother will be told how close I am to failing eighth grade English.

So, fine. Here goes.

I wish I wasn't built like my mother.

And I hate middle school. It's all of these girls who are prettier than me. Thinner. Or cute. There must be a farm that grows petite, bouncing blondes, and ships them right to my middle school, where they all become cheerleaders.

The boys are worse. Especially if they shave. Stupid eighth graders who think they can get away with anything if they're halfway through puberty and on the football team.

But at least when I'm at school I get away from my mother and all her demands and drama.

Hopefully I can spend most of the summer in the barn with my dad. Except I'll have more chores this summer, because my older brother is leaving. He's joined the military.

And next fall life will begin again. At HIGH SCHOOL.

Maybe I'll join the chess club; no one talks there. Or better yet, I'll join the debate team. Then everyone will have to listen to me for a change. Between the two, I could cut my time at home by five, six hours a week, maybe more.

No. No, wait. I know what I'll do. I'll try out for the High School Choir.

I wonder what would upset my mother more, if I actually make the choir, or if I don't?

She won't care. The only singing she cares about is her own.

Chapter Four

Pain, like none Julie had ever known, woke her from a fuzzy sleep.

Through squinted eyes—make that *eye* because her left one wouldn't open—she could see she was in a hospital room. And it was quiet. Too quiet for a jackhammer to be pounding in her head.

She flexed an ankle. Her right wrist. She could swallow, though her throat felt like someone had pulled a cheese grater through it.

She would have moaned, but could only huff.

"Hey, you're awake." Rick leaned into her partial vision. "I'll ring for the nurse."

His hand fumbled near hers on the bed. He pushed a button. Both ends of the bed seemed to rise simultaneously, sandwiching her in the middle.

Stop! was the thing to say. *Right now!*

But she couldn't open her mouth. Her arms were too heavy to lift, and she couldn't turn her head without feeling like she was giving birth out of her left ear.

She tried to grunt at Rick, as her one, useable eye widened in panic. She was caught in the unmerciful jaws of a torturous contraption that was about to make her face and knees meet for the first time since middle school gym class.

Ooohhh. The growl of frustration rumbled up from her lungs, but simply dissolved before hitting her tongue. The only option was to hold up a hand, the universal sign for "stop."

"I know," he said. "Hold on."

Rick pushed another button. Which lowered her head. The blanket stopped at her shins, so now her legs were raised, and her thighs barely covered by the thin, atrocious hospital gown. Could these things possibly be any uglier?

"Sorry, honey," her husband said. "I'll get the hang of this soon."

Hopefully. *Before* he broke her in half. Or she slid backward off the bed. Because she was indeed, slowly but surely, sliding off the head of the bed as the pressure in her skull built exponentially.

Oh, God, please *make him stop. Send an angel. Something.*

The curtain to her right ripped back. "Mr. Matthews, what are you doing to my patient?" The newcomer bustled to Julie's good side, wagging her finger at Rick, and pushed the correct buttons.

The bed continued to hum as Julie's feet were graciously lowered, her pillow lovingly adjusted, so that she was simply propped up in bed. *Heaven.*

"You're not really well enough to put on a show for your husband." The nurse jerked a thumb in Rick's direction. "Or was it his idea?" Her huge, black eyes danced in her equally dark face.

Julie glanced down with her good eye. The gown had hiked up to her waist, and her underwear was nowhere to be seen. Perfect. Now Rick and the nurse could see her fatty fatness.

What was it Grandma used to say? Always make sure you're wearing clean underwear when you go somewhere, because you never know when you might end up in the hospital. *You wouldn't want to be embarrassed by dirty underwear, now would you?*

How about *no* underwear?

She stared at the nurse, imploring for help with her working eye. *Please fix my gown.*

But it was Rick's hand that touched her flabby stomach first. She jumped. Or she would have if she'd been able. As it was, she could only tense her bruised body—which really, really hurt.

Her husband's hand stilled.

"Lift your bottom, sugar." Kindness shone in the woman's dark eyes. "Nurse Faye won't let you hurt yourself. Hold on to the rail with your good arm. There you go."

Rick pulled the gown down to her thighs. Then he patted her knee and leaned closer to her face. He took her uninjured hand in his. "Do you remember what happened?"

They had been riding—Rick's idea. Tempo went nuts, kicked her in the—

She couldn't open her mouth to answer him.

"I'll be right back," Faye said. "It's time for some more pain medication in that IV." She closed the curtain as she left.

Julie's left arm was in a cast. *What day is it?* She spelled slowly in sign language with her right hand, using what they'd both learned when Ben was small.

"Saturday," Rick said.

The kids? she signed.

"They came for a while yesterday, but I sent them home when we learned you'd be sleeping most of the day. Rachel's got some big assignment she has to finish, and seeing you like this upset Ben."

He held her gaze as he slipped around the end of the bed and moved to her good side. Then he carefully sat on the edge of the mattress. "I don't want to shake you."

Her entire body hurt so, so bad, it must have shown on her face.

"I think the nurse is bringing something for the pain."

He brushed his fingers across her forehead. It was the same kind of soft stroke he would give any horse's neck. Finally, here was the caretaker she needed, the one she had known and loved for nineteen years. The man was so gentle with horses. When he let that side of himself seep through, it simply melted her heart. Why didn't he ever stay that way with her?

He pulled back his hand. "How do you feel?"

In pain! And fat. She turned away. Her entire body felt like it had been twisted into a knot, then beaten.

Stinging tears leaked from her eyes. She had done everything right when Tempo was bitten. How, in this condition, would she be able to give Sean a going-away party? Or finish painting the guest room before Mother arrived?

The song. The *producer!* Disappointment quickened her tears. Truly, she hurt all over.

She raised her uninjured hand. The left side of her face felt extremely swollen, hence, the unseeing eye. Cold metal bound her jaws together.

"Your jaw is broken."

That's what happened when you rode into a tree and got kicked by a horse. You got your mouth wired shut, and you … couldn't … sing.

Please, God, this can't be happening.

Her nose started to run. She looked back at Rick, her eye conveying a desperate message. *Please wipe my face. Gently. Before snot runs into my mouth.* She closed her lips over the metal as best she could—how would she possibly clean *that* up?

Predictably, her husband simply sat there—waiting for what, she didn't know—as snot ran over her protruding lips.

Tissue she signed, and pointed to the box on a nearby shelf. Slowly, he handed them to her.

She wiped her face, knowing that some things didn't change. Rick moving quickly on anything was as likely as Julie's own mother offering an apology or an encouraging word; it would never happen.

She closed her eye and willed herself back to sleep.

***

Two hours. Julie had been awake in the hospital bed for all of two hours after drinking her pitiful lunch, and already she was willing to trade it for a nice, comfy bed of nails.

The sheets had surely been woven from sandspurs. The plastic-covered pillow crunched when she shifted her head. That ridiculous automatic blood pressure machine thing was still wrapped around her arm, a sadistic boa constrictor on a timer. Her choices on the television? Infomercials, Saturday cartoons, and news.

Thankfully Rick had stepped out to make some calls while Nurse Faye helped her use the bedpan. Yet another delightful experience.

"Your husband said you'd prefer red Jell-O to orange." Faye adjusted the sheets. "Something about you throwing-up orange juice when you were pregnant with your youngest, and that you haven't eaten anything orange since."

Julie nodded.

"Then I'll be right back," she said.

Night of the Orange Vomit. An event to remember.

Julie had been hugely pregnant with Ben and very unhappy about it. Totally hormonal. Too fat to get comfortable in bed and too emotional to sleep. She and Rick stayed up to watch late-night talk shows, and because she craved it, she drank almost a half-gallon of orange juice. Tall glasses filled to the top with ice—drinking it made her teeth hurt. But she hadn't cared. The feel of that chilled, thick sweetness going down her throat was so-o-o good.

Until about five minutes later when it decided to come back up.

She barely reached the bathroom before she hurled in the direction of the commode, but missed. Rick sat with her while she puked. Her hair was longer then, and he held it back for her while she wretched over the toilet. Then he helped her return to bed and tucked her in like a sick child.

He had cleaned the bathroom while she slept, but that was the last time she remembered him babying her. Even the numerous times she'd been up all night caring for Ben.

Rick returned to her room, pocketing his phone as he walked around the bed to her good side. "Hey." He started to sit, then watched her, as if debating. He leaned forward and gently kissed her forehead. "I'm so sorry you're hurt," he whispered. His eyes glistened as he pulled the chair closer to her bed and sat.

Did she have to be ill or injured to warrant tenderness from him?

"Here we go." Faye—what a sweetie—returned with two containers of red Jell-O water. "Hear about your horse yet?"

"Yeah." Rick accepted the plastic cups. "The vet's taking care of her."

"I know you don't want to leave your wife, but you should at least get something to eat. The crackers and ginger ale I brought you while she slept must be wearing thin."

He unwrapped a straw and met Julie's gaze. "I'm fine. Here, baby." He rested the straw against her lips.

She wished he would stay like this, just like this, close and gentle.

She sipped, laboriously sucking through her bound teeth. If consuming meals through a straw continued to be this difficult, she might actually lose a few pounds.

A loud whistling caught her attention.

"Hear that? It's Dr. Wyman, your oral surgeon." Faye raised the over-the-bed table and rolled it aside. "You can hear him a mile away. I'll get your chart."

Julie turned her head toward the door. A Mr. Magoo clone wearing a knee-length lab coat crossed the threshold. He strode to her bedside and happily shrilled the last few bars of Billy Joel's "You May Be Right."

"Mrs. Matthews! So glad to see you're awake." He clapped his hands and rubbed them together like an illusionist performing a magic trick. "And sitting up and drinking." He winked at her. "Always a good sign. Dr. Chang was supposed to have given your husband a brochure about your imminent recovery journey. Do you have any questions for me?"

She locked her gaze on Rick. It wasn't like *she* could ask the doctor anything.

Finally Rick cleared his throat. "Well, it looks like we've got about six weeks of liquid diet ahead of us. Which is about the same amount of time for her arm to heal."

"That's right." Dr. Magoo nodded. His saggy jowls shook after he nudged his horn-rim glasses back into place. "You two got a blender?"

She looked at Rick. A blender?

Rick took a slow-as-Christmas nose-breath.

She fought the urge to snap her fingers. Speak, honey. For heaven's sake, answer the man.

Her husband cleared his throat. "When will she get her voice back?"

"Get her voice back? Did someone take it?" He laughed, pounding on the bedrail with both hands.

Julie wanted to scream. Maybe she could be sedated for the next several weeks. Knocked out, so she wouldn't have to endure both the recovery and ... doctors like this one.

Her bed continued to shake as Dr. Comic repeated his question. He laughed so hard he started coughing and had to pound his chest to stop the spasms. Julie almost expected a camera crew to step from the privacy curtains and reveal themselves as part of a ridiculous reality show.

Dr. Wyman wiped his eyes with the backs of his hands. "I'm sorry," he said in a high-pitched voice. "I'm sorry, I've been awake almost thirty-six hours straight, and I get a little punchy when I don't sleep." He straightened his polka-dot bowtie. "Now. Where were we?"

Julie looked back at Rick, but he wasn't looking at her. His head was bent, as if he was staring at the floor.

The words "the answer isn't there, honey" itched on the end of her tongue, but she didn't want to try to sign that.

He raised his head as if it took all of his strength, met her eyes with pity and despair. And Julie knew—her inability to speak wasn't normal for someone with a broken jaw. Something was terribly wrong.

"Dr. Wyman," Rick said. "My wife can't speak. She can't make a sound."

The doctor's brow furrowed all the way up his bald head as Faye returned and handed him Julie's medical record. "What do you mean she can't make a sound?"

The nurse shrugged.

"Why wasn't I paged about this? Why wasn't I notified?"

Faye fisted her hands on her hips. "Many patients don't like to talk for a couple of days after surgery because their throats are sore from the intubation." Her eyebrows arched. "I figured the same for Mrs. Matthews since she's been using sign language to communicate through her husband. She didn't *have* to ask me for anything."

"Fair enough." He nodded again, then looked at Julie. "Mrs. Matthews, I have no idea why you can't speak. You should be able to, like a ventriloquist." He parted his lips and clamped his teeth together to demonstrate. "Shee whud I nean? But I'm not the expert on vocal cords. Let's call one in, shall we?"

Julie's heart sputtered, an engine that had run out of gas, choking out its last burst of power as Dr. Wyman told Faye he'd consult an ear, nose, and throat specialist for a possible laryngoscopy or swallow test. Julie didn't know what those were, but they sounded ominous enough. Tears came like a waterfall. Would she ever sing again?

She closed her eye. *God, please heal my voice.*

"Julie." Rick put tissues in her hand, placed the box on her lap. His stubbled jaw met the uninjured side of her face.

"I know you're scared." His words feathered down her neck. Her lips quivered, his tenderness making her lungs squeeze. He softly kissed her cheek—the gentle caress of a dandelion she wanted to hold forever but feared would die in her hand.

She didn't move. She couldn't think, could barely breathe.

"I know you don't want any visitors, including Pastor Pierce and Laurie, because you don't want anyone to see you like this."

He waited. Everything in her wanted to reach for him, but she was too afraid to move.

He pulled away.

"You go home and get some rest, Mr. Matthews. Or maybe find your favorite hat you said was lost when Mrs. Matthews was injured," Faye said. "We'll take care of her."

He pressed the TV remote into her hand. "The phone in the bedrail is turned off since you can't answer it anyway. Your cell's plugged into your charger on the nightstand—Sean brought it by this morning—in case you want to text me." His boot heels rapped the hard floor as he walked away. "Afternoon, Faye. I'll come back in the morning."

"Hmph," Faye said. "I don't know many husbands who would spend the night in a broken recliner like he did, just to be near their wife's hospital bed while she slept. Wish I had one like that."

Julie kept her eyes closed, and wished she had one like that all the time, too.

Chapter Five

Rick drove straight to the stables. Sean and Rachel had done the morning chores, fed and watered the horses, let several into the field to graze. Since his shirt smelled like rot and was ruined anyway—a two-day-old mixture of forest dirt, Julie's blood, and his sweat—he threw it in the tack room's garbage can and got to work.

He shoveled horse manure and soiled bedding, lugged mountains of it out of the stables using a wheelbarrow. He hosed down half of the thirty-four stalls. Dropped fresh hay into each from the loft as the gentle Saturday afternoon traffic of boarder owners passed below, and shared greetings with those who lingered.

As always, when he finished the last stall he hung the pitchfork and shovel in their places, leaned the wheelbarrow against the concrete wall in the little niche beside the loft stairs. Then he took his customary stroll past the tidied stalls, enjoying the scent of fresh hay on the floors. If only cleaning up the mess between him and Julie was as simple.

He took a break, grabbed a bottled water from the tack room refrigerator. Sucked it down while he straightened the racks of saddles along the side wall, and enjoyed the warm smell of worn leather. His shoulders fell and he shook his head as exhaustion turned his blood to sludge.

Coffee. He needed coffee.

In the small kitchenette, someone had laid a lead rope on the counter in front of the automatic coffee pot. He draped the line over a peg on the wall and noted the burner still warming a half pot Sean had obviously left. He grabbed a mug from the overhead cupboard and poured, then sipped it black and hot, letting the thick brew scald all the way down.

The vet bill for Tempo sat on his desk—since the bite hadn't been deep or into the meat, the horse would be fine in time. Rick didn't want to look at the charges; numbers were Julie's job. Or they had been before her accident. He flipped over the envelope, and remembered how she looked when he left her. Her skin pale against hospital sheets. Her battered face, and teeth stitched together with metal.

His stomach knotted at the way her limp body had sagged in his arms when he picked her up from the ground in the woods.

Rick drank the last drops, rinsed the cup and placed it in the drainer.

Despite their problems, despite their struggles, he was so very grateful she hadn't died. Yes, there would be bills. Big ones from the vet, not to mention the hospital. But having to worry about paying bills was better than planning a funeral. How could he have faced the rest of his life without Julie?

He should take some positive action. Do something to help his marriage instead of standing back and watching it disintegrate. He needed to show Julie he was still following their plan, still willing to help her pursue her career, even if that career was delayed, yet again.

So he would add another desk, right here beside his in the tack room. He'd have to air out the space, install a small air conditioner in the window behind him—Julie hated the smell of old leather and new hay. They could set up her new computer. It still sat, along with new unopened programs, in the box in the guest room closet.

When Julie was well enough, she could transfer their financial information to the new system, and show him how to manage the business finances. Something he'd put off learning every time she mentioned it.

Hmm. Julie, leering over his shoulder as he pecked at the keyboard with two fingers and tried to update spread sheets and balance sheets. If their marriage survived *that*, it could survive anything.

But relieving her of that responsibility would get her one step closer to pursuing her dream. If she got her voice back.

No, not if. *When.* God wouldn't let her voice be permanently taken this way, would he?

Rick reached for the radio and adjusted the volume as Johnny Cash sang about the line he walked. Loving a woman, being married, meant making adjustments and giving up some things, didn't it? But did the sacrifice always have to be his dignity?

"Mr. Matthews?"

Fully expecting to find a familiar client in the doorway, Rick reached for a towel off the shelf and turned, wiping down his face and chest. "How can I help you?"

The woman who stepped toward him was so stunningly beautiful, he almost stumbled backward. The flawless skin of a child, wide chestnut-brown eyes, waist-length black hair so shiny it looked wet. And a body built for modeling swimsuits. Her filmy blouse was cinched in perfect-fit jeans, which disappeared below the knees in what he'd bet were eight-thousand dollar boots.

She gave a shy smile. "I hope you don't mind my dropping by. I called Thursday and spoke to your daughter ... Rachel? She said Saturday afternoons are a good time to catch you here at the stables. I'm a Johnny Cash fan, myself." She gestured to the radio, her silky hair shimmering as it swayed, then stepped closer and offered a hand. "I'm Angelina Rousseau."

Rick raised both hands in surrender, and with thought, untied his tongue. "Ma'am, I smell, I'm filthy, and that's a really nice blouse you're wearing, too nice to wear in a barn."

Her smile grew. "Nathaniel Jordan told me you had a way with horses. He didn't mention that you charmed humans, too."

Rick cleared his throat. "Nate moved his stallion, Trident, here several weeks back." He rapped a knuckle on the stall wall to his right; Trident whinnied in response.

Rick retreated a step from his visitor. "I'm serious, ma'am. The stench over here is beyond rank. My wife was injured in an accident— uh, Thursday evening?—I've been wearing the same clothes and haven't had a shower since."

Her gaze slid over his bare chest, then locked with his as her brow furrowed. "Will she be all right?"

"Yeah," he said. "She, umm, she's still in the hospital."

"Then you have your hands full right now. Can we meet again, maybe Monday? Tuesday?"

Doctor bills, his brain chanted. New client ... *money*. "What exactly do you need, Mrs. Rousseau? You looking to buy?"

Again that shy smile surfaced. "Please. Call me Angelina." She tapped the wall as he had done. "Nathaniel said he couldn't be happier with Trident's care here."

"He's a fine-looking mustang. I think Nathaniel should stud him."

"Trident didn't wait for Nathaniel's permission. My mare is still at the stables where Trident used to be. She caught Trident's eye and she's due to foal late June. I wasn't ready to breed her yet, and certainly can't trust the people she's with to watch her closely. I want to move her before she's much farther along."

"And you want to know if I have space, if I'll take on a horse that close to foaling."

"Yes." She nodded. "Exactly that."

"Tell you what, call me in a few weeks, after I get my wife home from the hospital and things settle down here. I'll let you know."

"If I write you a check for three month's rent in advance, can I just bring her at the end of the month?" She pulled a gold-plated checkbook case and a matching pen out of an expensive-looking shoulder bag.

Maybe this was God's provision. So Julie's medical bills wouldn't take all of their savings. "Okay. I'll take the check, but I still won't shake your hand."

Rick wrote Angelina a receipt. She left, leaving behind a whiff of vanilla and musk that probably cost more than the check amount she'd just written. He downed two more cups of coffee, speed-dialed for pizza, stabled the few horses left in the paddock, and trudged back to the house.

Ben met him at the door in a blur of movement. "Can we call Mom? I want to talk to her."

"You know how to text using my phone?"

Ben stopped jumping. "Why can't I call her?"

"Listen, buddy, get your brother and sister, tell them pizza's on the way, have them come to the kitchen. I'm really tired, I need to tell all of you about Mom, and I only want to say it once."

Ben scurried away. Sean arrived quickly. "How long until the pizza gets here?"

"Soon. And it's two pizzas. One's loaded."

A grin spread like molasses across Sean's face. "Awesome."

"Tonight we eat like men." Rick rubbed a tired hand over his own exhausted face and called out. "Ben? Rachel?"

Ben pulled Rachel into the room. "Come on. Dad needs to tell us something about Mom."

Rick's daughter sat on the barstool beside him and threw her older brother a look of disdain. "I know that man-growl. It means I'll be picking onions and peppers off my pizza."

Rick stroked a hand down her thick brown hair. "No, it means I ordered a plain cheese for you and Ben, and another for Sean and myself."

"Thanks, Daddy." She smiled at him with her mother's face, jerking his heart. How different was his daughter's response to his touch, from his wife's. If only he could freeze time, freeze her, and transplant some of her acceptance and trust, to his wife. He kissed Rachel's cheek.

The doorbell rang, Rick paid for the pizzas. Within seconds, his children were moving to the table with drinks and napkins in hand. Sean tossed paper plates into place. They prayed and dug in.

Rick scanned their faces. "After we eat we're cleaning bedrooms." He paused, again looking at Rachel and seeing the Julie he'd fallen in love with so long ago. "And ... I'll be calling Grandma to let her know about your mother."

Sean choked on his drink. "Is that a good idea?"

"I don't think I have a choice."

Rachel's green eyes sparked with mischief. "Does Mom know you're calling Grandma?"

"Not yet."

***

Rachel Matthews, Mrs. Tate's third period English class: Saturday, May 3:

While cleaning my room tonight, I found a card my mother gave me last February. It says "My heart is happy because you're near. Happy Valentine's Day."

She never sounds happy when I'm near. She has endless complaints. Sure, sometimes she tosses a "Hello, how are you?" or "How was school?" at me, but she's never still long enough to hear my answer.

Other times she nags or criticizes me. She can be relentless.

It's like that gross thing the jocks did in science lab last Wednesday. They dropped some lizard they found into a beaker, turned on the Bunsen burner, then gradually cranked the fire higher and hotter. The creature squirmed, trying to climb out. But they cooked it mercilessly. The poor thing was toast.

Sometimes I feel like that lizard, dying a slow, painful death. I'm a carcass—but I'm not dead—and my mom's a vulture. I feel every jab and nick, every rip and tear as she chews me up. I get ready for bed at night, almost expecting to find fresh wounds and trickling blood.

Can a heart bleed? I mean, can a person bleed to death internally, from being stabbed by words?

I think so.

Or maybe just a soul, or personality, or whatever it's called that means the part of you that's very you. Maybe that's what dies.

And that's pretty much what happened to Jesus, wasn't it? After they beat Him and crucified Him, and stabbed Him with a spear, there just wasn't enough blood left to pump through His body, so He died.

Chapter Six

The 7 a.m. shift change brought Julie yet another new nurse. Mimi, a short Hispanic woman, loudly introduced herself as a recent graduate from nursing school.

"Time for some blood work. Gotta find a vein." She twisted open the blinds and turned on all the overhead lights. "You don't have to talk, Mrs. Matthews. I know you're mute."

Mute. It sounded like an awful disease. She has *Mute*.

God, please don't leave me like this.

If there was ever a time she needed to feel God smiling down on her, it was now.

"All done." Mimi turned off the lights and left.

Gloomy shadows filled the room. Julie flipped channels. Every televised church service seemed to feature a soloist.

Of course. This was Sunday. *She* should be at church, singing.

Yes, she still fought nerves before performing, still felt the prickles of apprehension creep over her skin. But the frightening nervousness and facial tics had faded once she learned to use her voice to fight the anxiety.

Singing always calmed her. Worship always made her feel better. So when she sang in public, she simply pretended those in the audience were the angelic friends from her childhood dreams.

She turned off the television. Right now she simply could not listen to others lifting their voices in song.

She stared out the window as morning rain pelted the windows. Checked her phone and re-read the sweet text Ben sent from Rick's phone last night. *Hi, Mom. Sorry you're hurt. Did you know Daddy killed the snake? He says when I'm big I can have a rifle, too. Love you, Mom.*

No message from Sean or Rachel, but they were teenagers. Hopefully Rachel wasn't getting away with too much during Julie's absence. More than once Julie had caught Rachel getting Rick's permission to do something after getting a "no" from her. Rick had addressed neither this habit, nor Rachel's snarky attitude after being caught. If Rick wasn't keeping Rachel in line, there was no telling what Julie would find when she finally got to go home.

Mimi returned with a wheelchair. "Time for your swallow test. Your husband called; he's on his way. I told him where to find us."

They arrived at a small, non-descript treatment room. A large chair in the center made the space resemble a room in a dentist's office. With Mimi's help Julie sat, then rested her head against the back of the chair.

"Good timing, Mr. Matthews." Julie's ears perked at Mimi's voice in the hall.

"Can I stay with her?" Rick asked.

"I don't see why not."

Rick entered the room. "Hey."

She touched her fingers to her brow, brought them away, *Hello,* then looked away, embarrassed at how awful she must look.

"You know it *could* be psychological." Mimi's voice outside caught Julie's attention again. "We learned about that in nursing school. She probably wouldn't be the first to have temporary vocal cord paralysis because of trauma induced stress, would she?"

Julie's cinched jaw clenched tighter as she stared at the institutional white ceiling with her one, working eye.

Did they think she was crazy *and* deaf?

A physician entered, pushing a computer on a cart. He parked it beside her and attached a long, black cord to the monitor. "Mrs.

Matthews, I'm Dr. Bradley, an ENT. Have you ever had this type of test before?"

Julie shook her head.

"You're unable to make any sound?"

She nodded.

He looked at Rick. "You're her husband?"

"Yes."

"Okay." He pushed some pedals on the chair. "I'm tilting you back, so just relax like you're taking a nap. You're not allergic to Lidocaine, are you?"

Julie shook her head again.

"Good. I'm going to spray Lidocaine in your nose to numb it a little. Be very still for me."

His eyes were inches away from hers, his blond beard almost touching her face. He examined her nostrils, each one twice. "I can see you've never broken your nose." He smiled and administered the analgesic. "This stuff works fast. See this tube?"

It looked like an earbuds cable, only a little thicker. Flexible.

"It has a fiber optic camera on the end. I'll be inserting it into your nose and lowering it down your throat so I can take pictures of your vocal cords. We do it this way for everyone, not just patients with a broken jaw. I'll warn you when I'm nearing your gag reflex. We'll have to work together, okay? Here we go."

Oh-*kay*. Her entire upper body convulsed at the foreign object entering her throat.

"Relax, Mrs. Matthews. Be still for me."

Relax? Was he kidding?

Panic pushed her back against the seat as he slid the tube into her nostril. She grabbed the right armrest, holding on as she watched more and more of the black cable disappear into her. It hit something. Dr. Bradley twisted it and jiggled it a little, then she felt it crawling further inside her.

Oh ... no ... oh ...

"We're nearing the gag reflex."

He was staring at the monitor, and talking to her like he was giving orders over the phone. Did he not realize she was near *freaking out?*

"Almost there. Breathe for me. Pant if you have to, but only for a moment. You can't relax if you don't breathe."

She tried the short breaths; they brought little relief. Her throat constricted, trying to swallow the tube.

"Okay, we're in," he said. "Fifteen minutes, tops."

Seconds dragged, as if in slow motion, marked by the doctor's tapping and clicking on the computer. She counted, trying anything to distract her mind as time stretched like a child's slingshot being poised to fire. Still the choking sensation continued.

God, please get me through this. Please let him tell me my voice is fine.

Rick? she thought to say the word, momentarily forgetting she couldn't speak. She wanted to reach for his hand, but he was watching the screen with Dr. Bradley.

"Say *eeee*."

She couldn't.

He gave her more sounds.

She couldn't make those either.

"Cough."

She tried.

He instructed her when to swallow and when to breathe. She followed directions as best she could, but the walls pressed in on her. Bright spots appeared before her one working eye, and her lungs seemed to shrink with the room. If her vocal cords truly were damaged, her entire singing career, her future, may have already ended.

"Breathe for me, Mrs. Matthews."

She concentrated on breathing and closed her eye. A memory flashed through her mind, the way she felt the last time she sang in The

Barn Church during a Sunday morning service. She'd ended the solo with a long note that faded to a quiet whisper. A holy hush settled over the crowd. No one clapped. No one moved. Pastor Crane walked to the pulpit. "Wow," he said. "Folks, let's just sit together in God's presence for a while, shall we?"

Gone. Those moments might be gone. Forever.

***

Rick had never seen his wife so stressed, not even when in labor with their children. She opened her unswollen eye; Rick watched her wither, like a deflating balloon.

"Relax for a minute, Mrs. Matthews." Dr. Bradley made a call on his phone and stepped into the hall. "You scheduled the swallow test to immediately follow my exam, didn't you?" He paused. "Well, the speech therapist isn't here yet and I can't stay. I'm covering ER today. Wait. Here he comes."

Rick heard murmurs, but he couldn't pick out exact words.

Another clinician entered. "Dr. Bradley had to go back to the ER. I'm Caleb, a speech therapist."

"Are you going to remove the tube now?" Rick asked.

"No. We'll use it for the next test. Then I'll remove it."

He opened a drawer in the cart, lifted out a tray, and sat it on a nearby table. "Mr. Matthews, you can hand her the cups."

A muscle in Julie's cheek started twitching. A tear dripped slowly down her face.

"Now, Mrs. Matthews. No reason to cry. You'll drink while I take pictures."

Julie's body tensed, as if ready to spring from the chair. Rick didn't know how she did it, but she made herself stop crying. In the quiet room, he heard her almost gag again and again, her body reacting to the tube in her throat.

Caleb pressed several buttons on the keyboard. "Okay, Mr. Matthews. Let's start with that first sample." He removed a stainless steel cover and motioned to Rick with his chin.

Eight tiny paper cups filled with different colored liquids lined a tray. "She has to swallow all these?"

"Afraid so."

Rick sniffed the orange one. Bananas mixed with … rotten eggs. "Do they have a taste?"

"Sorry. They're not exactly Jell-O pudding. I've been told a couple are a little bitter."

Rick handed Julie the first cup. Her lips trembled as she fought to swallow the dyed substances with the tube still in place. The continuous convulsing of her throat made his stomach spasm. He sweated through his shirt, willing her vocal cords to move, to work together and form sounds between swallowing. But despite her valiant effort, Julie remained silent.

As instructed, Rick handed her the second cup. She parted her lips, just the smallest of spaces, as she looked at him with one eye. Yet, she didn't drink. Instead she raised a shaky hand to his chest and flattened her palm against his heart. The tiniest shake of her head said *Give me a second,* and on her face Rick saw something he'd seen far too often since Ben's birth. Defeat.

He wanted to scoop her up, whisk her away, like a hero prince from a fairy tale. But he didn't dare wrap his arms around her. Not here. Not like this.

Her gaze flickered down then back up to his. Her fingers bunched the front of his denim shirt. For a moment, he thought the look said *need you.* Not like need-you-to-do-something, but need *you.*

He froze, then slowly lifted his free hand to cover hers.

Caleb cleared his throat. "Mrs. Matthews, we need to continue."

Her open eye went from bright green to dull and flat. She sucked a quick breath through clamped teeth and closed her good eye. She didn't open it again until after the test was complete.

"I'll add a report to your chart. Dr. Bradley will do that as well," Caleb said. "The specialist should come see you tomorrow with all the results."

"Results tomorrow." Rick watched him remove the tube, then leave.

Later, as Mimi pushed Julie back to her room, his wife stared straight ahead, her face expressionless. She climbed into bed and burrowed beneath her covers. Of course, she'd simply want to sleep after such an ordeal.

"I'll keep a close watch if you want to go home," Mimi told Rick. "If she wakes and wants you, I'll call. And so you know, her blood pressure's been up and down, up and down, and they're not sure why. It could be stress, but the doctor wants to keep her a couple more days. He might run more tests tomorrow."

Stress. He and Julie knew all about stress.

"Thanks for telling me. Call me if she has a tough time tonight, okay? Any time."

Rick stepped out of the hospital into the afternoon sun and headed home to work in the barn.

***

Night had fallen when Rick walked with Rachel from the barn to the house. She'd just spent five hours working with him, filling water buckets, moving heavy hay bales, and brushing horses on a Sunday afternoon. He opened the back door for her, and they shed their boots in the laundry room.

"You didn't answer when Grandma called," Rachel said.

"Nope." He'd forwarded Julie's phone to his for convenience, but he hadn't wanted to answer when his mother-in-law had called. "Didn't listen to her message either."

"Are you going to, then you'll call her back?"

"Yep."

"Do you think she'll come now?"

"Maybe. She was supposed to come anyway in a couple weeks for Sean's graduation. Now ... I don't know."

"Too bad Nana and Papa can't come. Guess they're still helping Aunt Sharon?"

"Yeah, they are." His sister was torn about moving back to the States so quickly after her husband's death since her children had lived their entire lives in Germany. "I'll probably call them in a couple days."

Rachel hugged him, her chin touching just under his shoulder. Another inch or two, and she'd be as tall as Julie.

"I love working with you, Daddy. When I grow up, I want to run my own stables."

"You'd be good at it." He returned the embrace, massaging her neck under the thick brown hair, which mirrored her mother's. "I love working with you, too, sweetheart."

A few more years, and she would leave just like Sean was about to do. Rick held her away to look in her face. *Julie's* face.

"Wasn't there a movie you'd rather have gone to see with your friends? Or shopping. Don't teenage girls want to shop all the time?"

"Daaa-dy. You know I prefer horses to people." A baby blush rose with her half-smile. "Except you, of course."

"Except me. Right." He kissed the top of her head. "Take a shower, bring your laundry. We need to start some wash."

She left him there, with the scent of worn shoes and fabric softener filling his nostrils. He didn't want to face another night alone in his bed, with Julie's side empty and cold. Didn't want to lie there trying to sleep, eyes closed, while the accident replayed through his mind—seeing the cottonmouth strike at Tempo once and again. Hearing the horse scream. Watching helplessly as the mare bolted away with his wife.

How he wanted to bring Julie home and take care of her. But would she let him? They never had much time together, but when they did, she hardly ever let him touch her.

And there was the issue of Trudey, his mother-in-law.

He had to call her. She'd want to know about Julie's accident. And yes, she'd probably come now to, um ... help.

Rick, an injured and very unhappy Julie, and her mother in the same house for at least two weeks. Things could get worse. A tornado could come through his property.

He took out his cell and listened as he made his way to the kitchen.

"Julie, honey, it's Mama." Trudey's sing-song voice blasted his ear. "I have *the* best news. I already called a bakery near you, ordered a cake. And I found a fabulous caterer. My new trainer at the gym, Jim—isn't that funny?—he has me doing these lunge things that have really toned my gluteus maximus, you know? I'd be glad to show you. I think they'd help you, too. Call me."

Rick hit erase and checked for any texts from Julie. The screen was blank. Walking to his bedroom, he took a deep, fortifying breath and dialed Trudey.

"I wondered when you'd call!"

Rick inched the phone back from his ear.

"I've been shopping. Got a dozen great new push-up bras, you won't believe the cleavage. I went to the Army-Navy store—met the *cutest* ex-marine, he wasn't single, so I don't think he'll call me—and picked up a camouflage half shirt and some matching BDU capris for myself," she said in her wish-I-was-a-teenager-again voice. "Anyway, I'll be wearing them to Sean's party. Really fit with the military theme, you know?"

"Trudey. It's Rick."

"Well, Rick, how nice. I should've known this wasn't my daughter. She never would've let me finish my story about the clothes. Has she roped you into helping with the party, too? Like you don't have enough to do with all those horses. She dreams up stuff but never finishes anything. What does the girl do with her time?"

Rick lowered himself to sit on the bed, ran a hand through his hair. "Yeah. About Julie—"

"I still can't get over that piano you bought her right after ya'll married. Didn't you make payments for years? Years? Could've bought a car for what you paid. You could buy *two* now if you sold it. Then Ben's born and *poof!*—she loses all interest ..."

That's probably how it looked to Trudey. His mother-in-law wasn't exactly one to gather all the facts before passing judgment. And if he didn't get a word in soon, she'd get her second wind, and he'd be stuck on the phone with her for the next hour plus.

"... it's not like I didn't offer to pay a professional to come and care for little Ben with all his problems. Poor thing. Having to nurse because he couldn't suck a bottle. Choking and turning blue all the time. And the way he'd quit breathing when he was asleep. What's that called? Apineum?"

"Apnea. Sleep *apnea*. Listen, Trudey—"

"*I knew* he should have been put in that children's hospital here in Birmingham until after his surgeries were over, so he could get the care he needed. But would Julie let me help? Let me pay for anything? Why, no. She said—"

"Trudey." Rick coughed loudly. Julie wasn't the only one who had refused to have strangers care for Ben as an infant and toddler. "I've got something really important to tell you. Can you listen for a minute?"

"Well, sure, sugar. I'm at the Starbucks drive-thru—gotta have a double-latte after the day I put in at the mall—in my new BMW Z4 roadster convertible. Handles like a dream. Very sexy. Winter blue to match my eyes."

"Right. Good." Rick steeled himself for the reaction he knew was coming. "Julie had a horseback riding accident Thursday night. She's in the hospital with a broken jaw and a broken arm."

"*What?*"

He turned the phone away as she screamed. The piercing, high-pitched noise always left him wanting to close his right eye.

"Why didn't you call me? I'd have been there in a heartbeat. I could've been at her side all this time."

Rick wet his lips. In his mind the sky was darkening. Clouds were gathering. Tornados forming.

"Yeah. She's been sleeping a lot. Doctors say she'll be okay, just a long recovery." He knew better than to mention the missed audition.

"How long?"

"About six weeks or so."

"But she'll be fine, you say. When's she coming home?"

"A few days, probably." He sure hoped his wife would be coming home in a few days.

"... you know we could do it before she leaves the hospital. She'd never notice."

"Do what?"

"*Sell* the piano. I've told you enough times I can get you a great price for it up here."

"Sell the piano?" He winced. The wind was picking up speed. "I don't think I can worry about the piano right now."

"She could use the money for self-improvement. A little lipo, a personal trainer, a new hairstyle, and she'd be a beauty. It'd really perk her up."

Lipo? Had his mother-in-law really suggested Julie have lipo?

"... and there'll be no arguments. I'll leave first thing in the morning, be there before noon tomorrow."

"Right. Okay." Rick sighed and ended the call.

The tornado was about to touch down. Right in his lap.

Chapter Seven

Truly, there was no sterile darkness, no alone-ness, which compared to being in a sealed hospital room in the middle of a black night. Buzzers and bells rang in muted tones outside Julie's door, phones shrilled in the off-beats. They invaded her personal space then ceased, leaving behind an eerie quiet and near-deafening silence.

Julie turned and laid on her side, staring with one eye at the faint red glow of the nurse call button in the bedrail. She took a slow deep breath through her nose and bound jaws, and tried a timid hum.

Nothing happened. No vibration in her throat, no rumble of any kind.

She tried again, ears straining to hear the slightest sound.

Silence.

She waited, listening as the round, hospital-standard wall clock ticked away the seconds. One minute. Two. She repeated the attempt.

Nothing worked. She couldn't hum, couldn't laugh. Couldn't scream or growl in frustration. She knew better than to try to whisper, that was the absolute worst thing a vocalist with vocal cord damage could do. And despite learning the language years earlier for Ben's sake, she'd have difficulty signing effectively with one arm in a cast.

She placed her right hand flat over her chest, moved it in a slow clockwise motion. *Please* she signed to God.

God was supposed to be listening, wasn't He? Always listening? And watching?

Surely He would hear her heart. Or see her hand.

She couldn't live like this. Without her voice.

A whimper dissolved in her throat. *Don't cry. Don't cry.*

Please she signed again and again, until her aching shoulder cramped as tight as her heart.

She chose an old hymn. *Blessed Assurance, Jesus is mine ...*

She focused on the words, trying to get the same close-to-God feeling thinking about the words as she did when singing. Remembering old hymns usually brought comfort. But not now. Not when her future was completely uncertain.

Rock of ages, cleft for me, let me hide myself in thee ... She concentrated on the lyrics. She wanted to hide, all right.

She pulled the extra blanket from the foot of her bed up to her chin, turned her back on the useless red button. No nurse could repair her voice.

Beneath the covers she put both hands together and signed as best she could with her cast. *When peace, like a river, attendeth my way, when sorrows like sea billows roll ...*

Julie knew the story behind the song. The husband and father who lost his children at sea reacted by writing the timeless hymn. How could anyone mean that after such a loss? And didn't he later completely turn his back on God?

She reviewed the lyrics again, trying to make the words her own. But they were simply a rug on the floor of her heart, hiding an awful, embarrassing stain.

If her voice was gone, she was ... nothing. The little girl inside her begged, *Dear God, I need You to heal me.*

Julie waited. Listened. No answer came from heaven.

***

Monday morning's dawn came, as bright and normal-looking as ever. Still Julie had no voice. Not now that she was awake, not even during last night's dreams. Rick arrived and sat by her bed as calm as he could be. Like nothing was terribly wrong.

She sat up, reaching for her minty mouth rinse and the small basin on the table by her bed.

Rick lurched forward. "I'll help you."

She didn't want to depend on his help. She hated the whole process of opening one side of her mouth, then the other, just to spray the rinse and swish it around. She knew she had buffalo breath. And she wouldn't be able to brush for weeks.

She avoided eye contact as Rick helped her use the rinse, holding the basin for her to spit. She was absolutely mortified over her swollen bruises and toxic breath.

"Better?"

She dried her mouth with a tissue.

How long did she have to wait for her test results? Didn't doctors make their hospital rounds early? Before they went to the office for the day?

Rick shifted in his chair. "You want a milkshake?"

She shook her head. Right now, she wanted the ENT to walk through the door and say that very, very soon she'd get her voice back. All Julie needed to do was endure the healing process for her arm, her jaw, her *face,* then she could again pursue her long-postponed dreams.

She just needed a plan. If she knew the plan, she would do everything necessary to speed up her recovery, and the nightmare would end. This injury was a blip, right? A little bitty bump in the long journey to her singing career.

Her voice would be fine. It had to be.

Shaking, she settled back against her pillow.

"Do you want that milkshake? How about more apple juice? I can go to the nurse's station and ask, so you won't have to wait."

She raised her eyebrows at him. *No* she signed. And again, no. She didn't want a milkshake. Or juice. *Using the straw is hard.* The insides of her cheeks were already sore from sucking through a straw for every little bit of sustenance.

Rick tapped his fingers against his thigh. He tapped. And tapped. *Stop!* She wanted to scream.

Dear God, I don't think I can take this anymore. How can almost everything Rick does be so irritating to me? And when *will the doctor be here?*

"Mr. Matthews, hello again." A young blonde glided into the room and gave Rick a lingering smile. She winked at Julie and wiggled her ring-less fingers. "Mrs. Matthews, I met your husband earlier in the cafeteria. The staff tells me you're the envy of every patient in this hospital. The only one with her own, private hunk seeing to her every need. Even I'm a little jealous."

Right. As if Miss Stethoscope, probably a size four like Julie's mother, in her perfectly-tailored, siren-red suit, couldn't get a date or find a husband. Who was she exactly?

The physician approached Julie's bed. "I'm Dr. Lilly, your new ENT. I've seen the results from the swallow test and looked back through your chart and surgical records. What you're experiencing is temporary vocal cord paralysis. Apparently you tried to extubate yourself—remove your breathing tube—right after your surgery. Since the balloon was still inflated, this caused trauma to both the cords, and the nodules which were already present."

Nodules? What nodules? Julie didn't have nodules. She'd *never* had nodules.

"You're a singer, right, Mrs. Matthews? I'm sure you know all about nodules or blisters. Cord paralysis, which can last for several weeks, will be like forced voice rest."

"Voice rest?" Rick stood. "We've done that, well, she's done that before."

"Right. After you get your voice back, the nodules may be gone, and of no consequence. If they persist and harden to nodes—callous-es—you may be forced to consider highly delicate surgery, or choose between speaking or singing." The physician backed away. "But let's think happy thoughts. You'll be discharged tomorrow if the cardiac tests are normal. Follow up with me in a few weeks if you haven't gotten your voice back and we'll recheck those nodules, get you hooked up with a speech therapist long-term."

"I have a few questions." Rick skittered into the hall after Dr. Perfect.

Julie's hand went to her throat. Nodules? The past several months had been especially stressful. Knowing Sean was going to leave. Dealing with Rachel's teenage moods, surly attitude toward her, and surreptitious behavior. The extra vocal exercises and careful warm-ups should have prevented blisters from forming, right?

She'd been so intentional, so diligent when practicing her solo, even without her voice coach. Yes, the notes were at the top of her range, but she had managed them even though she had to push. A little.

Julie slid down beneath the sheet, bent both knees, and huddled herself as she stared out the window at a perfect, cloudless sky.

A few weeks ago, she'd dreamt she was pregnant again. Not that she didn't love her children, but thinking of having another newborn to care for now made her almost as nauseated as her worst morning sickness episodes.

She had startled awake beside Rick, with that bottomless, *Oh, no* feeling you get when you've done something that can't be easily undone. She had tentatively placed a hand on her stomach, expecting to feel a confirming kick, and realized it was only a dream. At the time, she almost laughed aloud with relief.

The nodules—dare she think it?—possibly her fault. From misusing her voice? From over-training?

And the cord paralysis from trauma. Also her fault? Had she been fully awake when she jerked at the tube? Did she let go when they told her to stop?

Oh, God, please, please give me back my voice.

And if He refused ... if He *didn't* restore her voice, would she get to have that wonderful feeling of knowing He smiled at her, ever again?

***

Rachel Matthews, Mrs. Tate's third period English class: Tuesday, May 6:

Dad brought Mom home from the hospital today after picking up Ben at school. They came through the side door as if in slow motion with Ben holding her hand.

Mom looks like roadkill.

I guess some of the swelling on the left side of her face has gone down, but her eye and cheek look like a three-year-old waited until she was asleep then had some fun with purple and black Sharpies. Seeing her, I felt a little bad for some things I've written here.

She signed *Hello* to me. I motioned back and stayed at the bar pretending to study. She signed *Thank you* to Ben and went to the message board over the bar in the kitchen and sifted one-handed through the mail, throwing junk away.

Mom started signing to my dad, spelling P-R-O-, then hissed with frustration through her clenched teeth. She jerked open a kitchen drawer, dug like a frantic squirrel, and pulled out a notepad and pen.

Producer ???, she wrote, and held it up for Dad to see.

He started to answer, but Mom did her laser beam eye thing. With one eye. Freaky.

He opened his mouth again and she gave him her you've-just-done-the-stupidest-thing look.

Finally he placed his hands on the bar and faced the firing squad. "I called his office and left a message this morning."

This morning? she signed. *Not Friday?* My mother doesn't say four-letter-words. But I think she thinks them.

I knew enough to put two and two together. If Dad didn't call the producer on Friday or Saturday, it was possible he showed up to church yesterday and—oops!—Mom wasn't there to sing. Hopefully someone at the church told the guy what was going on, otherwise, there was no telling what the guy was thinking now.

Then my grandma walked into the kitchen. "Oh, my," she said. "But I guess everyone looks awful when they come home from the hospital, don't they?"

From the look on my mom's bruised face, I don't think Dad had told her Grandma was here.

"I let Sean use your car. Gave him cash to pick up sub-sandwiches," Grandma said. "Cooking for six is too much work for me and I just had my nails done."

I thought Mom was going to pop a vein. Instead she filled a glass with water, grabbed a straw, and stood at the sink with her back to all of us. I think her shoulders shook a little.

Grandma walked toward her, "Oh-my-baby. Maybe no one actually *saw* you on your way home."

For the first time ever, something made me want to protect my mother from *her* mother.

"Grandma, can we get pedicures while you're here?"

She came toward me. "Well, sure, sugar."

Mom never looked up. She just sneaked away behind Grandma's back. Dad spoke her name—it was the softest whisper I have ever heard. But Mom didn't stop. She kept moving, ever so quietly out of the kitchen. Dad just stood there drumming his fingers against his thigh, then walked out the back door.

"I'm so glad you care about *your* appearance," Grandma said.

I heard Mom's bedroom door click as it closed.

***

Rick skipped supper. By the time Sean reached the stables to do the evening chores, Rick had already finished them.

"I'm not late." Sean leaned into the tack room.

"You're not late."

Sean held up a small sack. "So, do you want me to hang your sandwich from the ceiling? Your desk is a wreck." He looked around, hands on hips. "Actually this room is a wreck."

Rick laughed. "I know, I know. That's why I did the chores. I need your help with something else." He grabbed the bag, inhaled the sandwich and downed half a cold root beer from the fridge, figuring Sean would eventually drink one, too.

They worked together in the dusty tack room, emptied it, slid and shoved everything onto the pitted concrete outside the stalls. Rick's desk, the file cabinets, piles of lead ropes, and stacks of blankets. They hauled out the tiny refrigerator and hosed down the floor.

When Sean popped the top on an A&W, Rick's eyes misted. He knew there wouldn't be many more moments like this. Just he and his oldest son, two ... men—yes, Sean was a man now—working together, sweating, and talking while Tim McGraw crooned in the background.

They sat together on the cool concrete, leaning against Dutch's stall.

"How does Lisa feel about you leaving for Basic Training?"

Sean belched like a bullhorn, pounding his chest with his fist. "Ah. Good one."

"Sean."

"Figure I'll hold my own in the barracks." He stood. So did Rick. "Are we doing this to keep you out of the house and away from Mom, or are we cleaning up so when Mom comes here you won't be in trouble?"

"A little bit of both, maybe." Smart boy. Smart *man*.

"We can use your truck tomorrow, move my desk from the house. I won't need it anymore, so Mom can use it. Save you from buying a new one." Sean leaned against Dutch's stall and reached in to rub the horse's thick neck. "Do you still love her?"

"Sean."

"Dad. I need to know. I won't give Lisa a ring now and expect her to wait to marry me in four years. She is ma-jor-ly unhappy about that." He paused. "I love her, but sometimes I don't like her. You know what I mean?"

"Yeah." The words snuck past his lips. "I know what you mean."

They continued working as sunlight faded to night. They loaded the room, arranging the space to accommodate both the second desk and Julie's new and yet unopened computer. When Rick released Sean to return home and call Lisa, his son grinned at him and trotted away.

So Rick closed up the stables, locking gates and double-checking both latches on Trident's stall. The stallion did indeed have the ability to open doors.

Rick walked home following his son's path, stopped in the mud room, and peeled off his boots. He found Julie in their bed. Her back to the door, facing his side of the bed, her cast-covered arm braced on a pillow. She didn't stir.

He supposed that for the kids, this would be like all the other times Julie had been on vocal rest to preserve her voice. He remembered instances when she'd used Ben's toy xylophone to get their attention. Sliding scales meant *stop* or *quit*. Later she'd used the sign language they'd all had to learn with Ben when he was small, having surgeries, and unable to talk or hear clearly.

He sighed as he stood face first in a blistering shower. Julie was irritated with him about not calling the producer right away, or warning her about Trudey being here. But he just ... well, he didn't know exactly why he didn't—as Julie would say—follow through on some things. Right now she couldn't speak. But after nineteen years of marriage, Julie didn't have to speak for him to hear the berating that was taking place in her mind, or read the exasperation on her face. Did she really think he didn't care about her? Or worse, that he was her enemy?

The house sat quiet. He exited the bathroom, turned out the lamp on the nightstand, and readied for bed in the dark. His hand grazed the knot of tissue below his shoulder, a scar he'd had since the night of Julie's senior prom.

He slipped beneath the sheets, facing Julie. The smell of her, the scent that had been missing those nights she was in the hospital, took his breath. He lifted a silent hand, feeling in the dark for her cheek, and brushed the hair away from her face.

He'd almost lost her. He could be facing an endless string of nights without her. Like his sister, Sharon, who'd lost her husband to a military training exercise just a few weeks ago.

Rick kissed her forehead, held his lips there, and whispered against her skin. "I do love you, Julie. I'm so glad you didn't die."

Embarrassment over not answering Sean's question had him closing his eyes. He should fix that. He didn't want Sean going to Basic Training wondering if his father still loved his mother. Rick did love her, even when her words sliced through him like a sharp blade through field hay.

"Dear God," he prayed aloud, "my wife needs her voice back so she can be happy."

Chapter Eight

Julie's bladder was screaming at her. It had been for the last five minutes.

She'd slept away much of the past five days—thank you, Percocet—except for early mornings and the brief moments required to drink her soup or a smoothie, while Rick held the straw. Now, if anyone heard her bumbling around in her room, someone would come to check on her before they all left for school.

Probably Ben would come first, that she could handle. Ben had the same caregiver tendencies toward her as Rick had for the horses. It was a sweet thing to see, a sweeter thing to experience, as he nightly read her a story or climbed in bed to snuggle before going to his room. The thought brought stinging tears to her eyes.

Still she didn't want to face—*with her face*— her mother until absolutely necessary. She simply didn't want to start another day hearing her mother say, "Oh, my. I guess it takes time for a face to return to normal, doesn't it?"

Ben's sneakers slapped on the tile as he raced down the hall. "I've got the grocery list, Grandma!"

Julie had written it last night, added a smiley face for Ben, and asked Rick to put it beside Ben's backpack. *There ya go, Mother. Happy Monday. You'll have to make several stops, so you'll have many new complaints about me.*

The raising of the garage door heralded her freedom and impending relief. If she'd been able, she would have chuckled at her mother's certain disgust over driving Julie's nondescript, four-door sedan. She tottered gingerly to the bathroom, refusing to glance in the mirror.

She'd been told her overall pain level would lessen now, so today she'd begin weaning off the heavy painkillers. Still, normal bathroom routines proved to be slow going and difficult—lifting her nightgown, looping it over her cast, then lowering her underwear with one hand. The whole process from start to finish was exhausting. At least she was now able to move without every inch of her body hurting. She washed her hand and rinsed her mouth, eyeing her reflection.

The bruises on the left side of her face had begun to fade, the black, purple, and yellow a smeared collage. The swelling around her left eye had lessened, a slash of Irish green peeked at her. Her bark-colored hair was matted on one side, and stood straight up on the other like an electrocuted cartoon character.

Her cheeks and mouth were the worst, still swollen and distorted. She parted her gums to reveal the metal laces binding her teeth. She looked like she belonged in a cheap remake of *The Bride of Frankenstein*, a far cry from the young freshman girl who turned the heads of her high school upperclassmen, a group that had included Rick.

Out of habit she stepped on the scales. Eleven pounds lighter—wouldn't Mother be proud? All Julie had to do was get kicked by a horse, break her jaw, drink her meals through a straw.

And possibly lose her ability to sing.

Julie shed her clothing and lathered a washcloth as fresh tears pricked her eyes. The sponge-bath soothed her skin but the process required looking at her body, and awakened the same uncertainty she'd had in her teens.

She hadn't understood the transformation she underwent the summer before starting ninth grade. Chubbiness and wads of fat had seemed to smooth out, stretching into long limbs, womanly curves, and full breasts. The weight was all there, it just ... moved. Like someone reshaped her in her sleep, molding her into a woman.

Thankfully Rick's sister, Sharon, had remained Julie's friend, despite the jealous competition among the neighborhood girls. Julie had spent almost every day at Sharon's house, listening to music in her room. Playing the piano and singing, or even swimming in the pool if no one was around. She'd felt stupid in her long t-shirt over a bikini, but she hadn't agreed with Mother that flaunting her assets was a good idea.

One particularly hot afternoon, Julie had let Sharon talk her into going swimming, even though Rick and one of his classmates, a boy named Tony Stafford, were already there.

Tony kept looking at her, watching her as if she were naked. Julie even heard him ask Rick about her in between cannonballs.

"How old is she?"

"She's like my kid sister. Thirteen, no, fourteen."

"She doesn't look fourteen. She's got a body like that model chick at school."

"You mean Charlotte?"

"Man, I'd love to get my hands on both of them."

Rick half-slapped, half-pushed Tony backward into the pool.

Tony surfaced sputtering, and flicked his long bangs from his face. "Dude! I was joking."

Rick glanced in Julie's direction, then glared at Tony. "Cool it, okay?"

Julie swam to the shallow end and whispered to Sharon. "Can we go back to your room now?"

She followed her friend up the pool steps and across the patio. Suddenly, there was Tony, blocking her path to the table, which held her towel, the towel she needed so she could dry off and go inside. He smiled widely, licking his lips, and looking at her as though he were touching her with his eyes.

"Three words. Wet. T-shirt. Contest."

Rick threw a Frisbee, beaning Tony in the head.

"Dude! What?"

"I said *cool it*."

Rick boosted himself out of the water, grabbed his own towel from a nearby chair, and wrapped it around her dripping frame. "Here. My apologies for Mr. Stupid. He simply can't control himself when he's near a pretty girl."

Her eyes had locked on Rick's, and her heart had flipped. It was the first time anyone had called her pretty.

Now, Julie rinsed the cloth and looked at her body. The stretch marks. Her sagging breasts. The belly that—courtesy of her lovely liquid diet—was smaller than it had been two weeks ago, but still heavily dimpled with cellulite.

A noiseless sob jolted her body. She pressed a wobbly hand to her mouth and tried to hum.

No sound came out.

Hoping for any sign of progress, she tried again, peeling back her lips and sucking air through her cinched teeth, trying to fill her lungs. She used her abdominals to force the air up and through her larynx.

Nothing.

Tears gushed, making her blind. She threw the cloth to the floor and stood alone, naked and weeping in silence.

***

The house was too quiet, Rick realized, peering into the refrigerator. Usually he heard Julie's voice as she talked on the phone, her beloved Andrea Bocelli or the younger Josh Groban providing background music. Sometimes it was Celine Dion who sang to him while he grabbed a late-morning snack.

Today there was nothing. No sound. No movement. He had never thought he could miss the snap of her words whipping through their home. "Rick! I can't find the receipt for *whatever*."

But there was no peace in this silence. The air didn't rest like it had the last few days when Julie slept. Instead, the stillness pulsed with pain.

A knee-weakening vision of his wife—limp, bloody, helpless after her accident—skirted through his mind, paralyzing him. What if he hadn't found her when he had?

He slammed the refrigerator door and rounded the breakfast bar. The family room was vacant. Both the couch and her favorite chair. The piano bench, as well. Calling her wouldn't help, she couldn't answer. He hurried down the hall to their bedroom, hoping he was over-reacting and making a fool of himself.

The room-darkening blinds demanded he turn on a light. So he walked to the closest nightstand and switched on a lamp.

Their unmade bed was empty.

He quickly scanned the floor and the open closet behind him. The hummingbird whine of their bathroom's exhaust fan beckoned him. He found the door closed but not locked.

He tapped. "Julie? You okay?"

He waited. If she were nude she'd want to cover herself. The knowledge stung, but now wasn't the time to try to fix that.

"Julie?" He turned the knob.

His naked wife stood at the sink with her beautiful back to him. The plum-like bruise on her left hip the only flaw on her soft skin. Tremors racked her body, her shoulders were slumped in utter devastation.

He risked an uninvited approach. He pulled a towel from a nearby rod and wrapped it around her from behind, turning her into his embrace.

He held her while she cried. Her entire being shook in his arms. He didn't know how she was silently weeping that hard, that deeply, without being able to open her mouth and gasp for air.

She slid an arm around his waist and gripped the back of his T-shirt. How long had it been since he'd felt his wife against him, clinging to him like this?

"Oh, baby. I know. This is so hard for you."

She burrowed against him, pulling her cast-covered arm in close, hiding in the cocoon formed by his body and the draping towel. He noted the wet rag on the floor.

"Do we need to cover your cast with a plastic bag so you can take a shower?"

She shook her head.

"Did you give yourself a sponge bath?"

She nodded, then lifted her gaze to his and scrunched a clump of her hair.

"You want to wash your hair."

She sniffed. Nodded.

"I can do it in the sink if you want."

She closed her eyes.

He felt like a beggar and it set his teeth on edge. An *Oliver Twist* figure in their relationship—*please sir, may I have some more?*—grateful for whatever crumbs she tossed his way.

He didn't resent *wanting* to do things for her. But he did resent feeling like he had to ask permission to do anything. And if he didn't ask permission, and then guessed wrong about what she wanted or needed him to do, the predictable chastising made the deed not worth the effort. Which resulted in Rick *not* doing many things he wanted to do, things for Julie that would make *him* happy.

Like wash her hair when she couldn't.

"Julie. Do you want me to wash your hair?"

She opened her eyes, gulped and nodded.

With one hand, he pulled back the shower curtain and placed both her shampoo and conditioner on the counter by the sink. He turned the faucets, testing the water temperature with his fingertips as he braced her against his side. His heart spasmed. Giving to someone you love, helping her, shouldn't be this difficult.

He released her, leaving only to grab two more towels. He draped one over the front of the counter and spread the other on the floor, motioning her to the sink. She inched forward, avoiding his gaze, clutching her towel to herself like her last cherished possession.

***

"Bend over slowly," her husband said. "So you won't get dizzy."

The caregiver was back—the Rick Julie hadn't seen for so long before her accident, the one she wished would stay even if she weren't ill.

Julie obeyed, arms to her chest. Out of the corner of one eye, she saw him reach for cotton balls.

"They'll keep the water out of your ears." He gently put them in place.

She tried lowering her torso while keeping herself covered with the towel. But gravity was her enemy, and with only one working arm, she had no choice but to clutch the towel to her sides with her elbows, hoping it wouldn't slide below her waist. She bent forward.

The warm water on her head, Rick's hands in her hair, were heaven. She breathed deep, and water ran in her upside-down nose. She had to abandon the towel to pinch her nostrils; it slid to the floor. A heated blush spread all the way to her toes, then a chill raced across her skin.

His hands stilled. "Do you want it back?"

She turned her head away from the faucet, raised her good hand and made a knocking motion. *Yes.*

Rick sighed and with both hands, draped the towel over her exposed back and hips. He took another long breath, waited.

Julie cringed. Could this be any worse? Her bruised and battered face, ghoulish wires protruding from distorted lips, a blown out body. Her appearance must repulse him. Rick was still so handsome, so *virile*. She ached to look good enough to be his wife. To be someone he'd be proud to claim as his when in public.

To enjoy being claimed as his, in private. Surely he regretted marrying her.

She ducked back under the running water. He took his time, working the lather through her hair as if he were massaging away a headache, then patiently rinsed the thick waves. He wrung out excess water and applied her conditioner, and gently patted droplets from her shoulders and upper arms while they waited to rinse.

He kissed her shoulder blade and held his lips there, whispering against her skin the same way he had on her first night home from the hospital.

Had he meant that prayer? And did he really know her that well, well enough to realize her ability to sing was as crucial to her as her ability to breathe?

She reached over her shoulder and rested her hand on his hair. If only he'd stay this mindful of her, this gentle with her.

He turned his head and kissed her fingertips. "Come on," he said. "Let's rinse out the conditioner. I'll bring in a chair. You can sit while I dry your hair."

Julie raised her head, the towel shifted. She strained to hold it in place with the fingertips of her uninjured arm. In the mirror's reflection, Rick stared at the shower, refusing to meet her gaze. Finally, he looked at her.

She felt exactly the way she had during the swallow test. Sitting in the chair, with a tube running down her nose, trying to swallow without choking, knowing her future would be determined by someone else's assessment of her condition. She was scared to death. And if she read her husband's expression correctly, he might be, too.

Neither knew where they stood with the other. Both expected rejection.

But she absolutely could not face her uncertain future alone.

She gave a weak, lopsided smile, and let the towel fall. Then she bent for Rick to rinse her hair, and for the first time in years let herself relax under his touch, her tears disappearing down the drain.

CHAPTER NINE

Rachel Matthews, Mrs. Tate's third period English class:
Sunday, May 18:

Dad took us to church this morning. During the drive, Grandma asked several times if we should turn around and take her back home, so she could be there in case Mom needed anything. Which meant Grandma really didn't want to go to church.

Dad kept rubbing his palm against his chin and assuring Grandma that Mom would be fine, and didn't Grandma want to go to church? Which meant he knew Mom did *not* want to be alone with Grandma.

Mom and Dad are somehow happier. They have been spending a lot of time in their room. More than once I've heard Dad laugh when taking Mom a milkshake or smoothie for her meal. They even hold hands and take walks around our farm.

Mom really can't talk. At all. It's fantastic—or it will be while it lasts. She can't yell at me about my chores or nag me about my schoolwork.

Before service started, Laurie Crane, our pastor's wife (she's one of the few, truly sweet people in this world) asked Dad if she could visit Mom this week. Dad scratched his chin again, said he'd have to talk to Mom about that, and suggested Laurie text Mom later this week. Then he introduced Grandma, who looked like she'd rather have her head shaved and eat goat liver than be in a church.

I have to admit, the choir didn't sound nearly as good without Mom. It's pretty weird that she doesn't like to spend time with Dad in our stables, but gets psyched about singing to strangers every Sunday in a renovated barn.

There was no solo today. Unless you count Deacon Floyd, this really tall black man, who prays like he's having an everyday conversation with God over peach cobbler at the Downtown Diner. He's very loud, especially when we sing "Amazing Grace."

At least the deacon can carry a tune, unlike Mr. Clyde Newman. He and his wife, Millie, usually sit behind us. Millie always tells me how nice I look even though I'm Amazon-sized compared to every other girl my age, and Mr. Newman winks at me. I sometimes wonder if God will put Clyde on the back row in heaven. Millie doesn't seem to mind his croaky voice; maybe because he says such sweet things to her she doesn't care how he sounds.

But Clyde *really* nailed us today, while everyone stood for the last song, "How Great Thou Art." Ben elbowed me, then the little twerp turned down his hearing aid. I nudged Grandma, whose eyes widened with each rising key change. I suffered through, along with Dad and Grandma, who nearly lost her balance and fell off her bright yellow high heels. Dad told me later he noticed Grandma swaying, and was very glad she didn't keel over, because there isn't a modest way to pick up a woman wearing a dress that's "painted on."

***

It was almost like before Ben was born.

Rick took a clockwise survey of his family around the kitchen table. Sean, his oldest telling a corny joke. Rachel, nudging her brother and laughing. On the opposite end sat his wife. Though they'd been taking walks together, once and sometimes twice daily, this was the first time she'd joined them at dinner since the accident three weeks ago.

She actually met his gaze and smiled at him like she was happy. With him. With her life.

To her left, the unexpected yet delightful Ben stirred ketchup into his mashed potatoes until they mimicked a sickly pink glob. The empty spot on Rick's right was meant for Trudey, but his mother-in-law stood with her back to them several feet away at the counter. She'd insisted Rick sit and eat before the Kentucky Fried Chicken grew cold.

Trudey, who brought home dinner and a brand new cappuccino machine because the nearest Starbucks was too far away, was trying her hand at making Julie a smoothie in the blender. She pressed the button, pulverizing ice and fruit. "This won't take but a minute," she shouted over the monotonous, horribly-loud grinding.

Rick looked at Julie, twirled an invisible lasso in the air, flung it in Trudey's direction. His wife stifled a silent laugh and shook her head, then smiled at him again. For another fantastic moment, childlike joy shone on her face and the corners of her mouth twitched up.

He pretended to reel Trudey in. Julie's eyes rounded and she wagged a finger at him. He blew her a kiss.

Her eyes flashed with surprise and delight. She raised a hand to her bruised cheek, her eyes darted away, then finally settled on the ketchup bottle teetering on the table's edge. She rescued it and sat it safely beside Ben.

Rick reached with his fork and tapped Ben's plate, motioned to his son's hearing aid, and pointed to the condiment bottle.

Ben recognized the prompt. "Thanks, Mom. I didn't mean to knock it over."

Under Julie's bruises, Rick thought he saw the remnants of a tender blush. Then she jerked back as Trudey placed a tall glass in front of her.

"Now. I used non-fat yogurt so, well, you know. And no peanut butter this time, there's too much fat in that. Instead there's protein powder and lots of blueberries. They're chock full of antioxidants. Can't be too careful when you're carrying extra weight. Higher risk for elevated cholesterol, diabetes, even cancer."

All the chatter and clanging at the table ceased. All eyes except Trudey's went to Julie, as Trudey clicked her way to her seat on ridiculous silver heels. Julie took the first sip of her drink, Rick stared at her until she finally raised her eyes again.

You are perfect, he mouthed.

His wife blinked rapidly. She raised straight fingers to her lips, drew them away from her mouth and toward him. *Thank you.*

Rick cleared his throat and addressed his children. "Eat up, you guys."

They proceeded with the meal. Julie finished her smoothie, but didn't leave the table.

Sean speared the last chicken breast. "Dad?"

"Split it with you." Rick breathed an inward sigh of relief. Dinner was nearly over, almost without incident. He raised the last bite of chicken to his mouth.

Trudey slapped her hand on the table. "Pineapple! I forgot to put some in your smoothie. Eating pineapple is supposed to limit bruising after surgery. This girl at the gym was talking about it." She cupped her hands over Ben's ears. "Boob job."

She released the little boy. "I bought cans of it today. Forgot it when I brought in the chicken. Julie, you have to have some every time you eat. Or those awful-looking bruises might stay until Sean's party."

Rick swallowed, looking at Julie. She was staring at the table in front of her. From four feet away he could feel her straining to keep her composure.

"Trudey. That's a nice thought. It truly is."

His wife's eyes lifted to meet his. They were dull, flat, exactly like they'd been during the traumatic swallow test.

"But Julie doesn't like pineapple." Rick held Julie's gaze. "According to her doctor, the bruises are healing normally. And those invited to Sean's party are friends who know she's recuperating from a serious injury. Folks here won't think twice about her bruises. They're glad she's going to be okay." He lowered his voice. "We all are."

Life returned to Julie's eyes like a steady moonrise over a pine forest. She gulped, and again signed *thank you*.

Beside Rick, Trudey puffed up. "Well, of course, we're all glad she's *okay*." She pushed back her chair and turned her attention to Julie. "You know, it's really too late to pursue your ridiculous childhood dream. I told Rick I'd help him sell the piano, it just collects dust and takes up the whole living room."

His mother-in-law rose from the table, walked to the sink. "And all your talk about God. Your accident and losing your voice might be a sign it's time you gave up singing and focused on a goal that means something."

Julie jerked like she'd been slapped. She stood slowly, signed *I love you* to the children, then *goodnight*, and walked to the master bedroom.

Rick tossed his napkin on the table, looked at his children who sat silent. "Sean. Horses are in, they've been fed. Check the barn and lock up for the night."

"Yes, sir."

"Rachel and Ben. Dishes. Kitchen. It's Friday, so you can stay up and watch a movie if you want. I'm going to take care of your mother."

He walked past the bar. "Goodnight. Trudey."

His mother-in-law didn't answer. Rick didn't care. He'd never known of anyone getting through to her.

He found his wife fully clothed, sitting on the edge of their Jacuzzi tub. After the last couple of weeks he knew what that meant. Still, the sheer joy of asking what she wanted, getting an answer, and giving it to her made their new ritual all the more fun.

"You want to soak?"

She nodded.

"Bubbles or salts?"

She lifted two fingers.

"Bath salt." He started the water. While it ran, he helped her undress. "Lavender or vanilla?"

She grinned shyly and pointed at him. "Oh, I get to pick this time." The game made him return the grin like a lovesick teenager. "Vanilla. And I get to wash your back."

She nestled against him. Reached for his hand with her good one and squeezed, then raised it between them. *I love you* she pressed into his palm.

His heart skipped a beat. "I love you, too," he said. "And your mother doesn't know what she's talking about."

Chapter Ten

The next day, late spring heat bore down on Julie as she and Rick finished their morning walk and made their way to the barn.

"You're sure you want to spend a Saturday morning in here?"

Julie nodded. *Want to be with you*, she signed.

They stopped at the tack room door. "And dodge your mother until she leaves to take the kids to the movies?"

She nodded again and stifled a noiseless laugh.

"Can't blame ya there. Especially after dinner last night." Rick opened the lock, smiled back at her over his shoulder. "I have a surprise for you."

She cocked her head. He opened the door with a flourish, flicked on the overhead light and the radio permanently set to Rick's favorite country music station. Phil Vassar sang about the last day of his life.

Her breath caught. The large room was spotless, the kitchenette immaculate. Beside Rick's desk sat Sean's old desk topped with her new computer—she'd thought it was still in the box, forgotten by Rick. In the far window, a portable air conditioner hummed, cooling the room.

"Come look." He motioned for her to sit in a chair while he braced a hip on the desk and leaned toward the screen. He turned on the computer. "I took it back to the store, had them load your accounting programs."

Julie's eyes welled with tears. She looked up at his face, that rugged, handsome face he liked to shade with his favorite black Stetson.

Did you find your hat? she signed.

"It's hanging behind you." He jerked his chin. "Why?"

He looked at her as if there was absolutely nothing wrong with her, nothing repulsive about her appearance. She remembered that look from their first date, their first kiss, from before she'd gotten pregnant with Ben. She raised a hand to his jaw.

"I would never sell your piano, baby. And you should never give up your dreams."

He'd been thinking of her when he'd fixed up this space. For the first time in a very long time, he'd thought of her, planned ahead, followed through and done something for her.

She raised a hand in a classic hold-on-a-second gesture. She clicked the mouse, brought up a word processing program, and clumsily typed with one hand.

You don't know how much that means to me.

"Yes, I do."

What I mean is—

He slid off the desk, grabbed his hat, and turned for the door.

"There's just no convincing you, is there? If you don't believe me by now ..." He shook his head and donned his hat. "Fine. I *don't* know how much you want to sing. Look in the desk drawer, your ear buds and the CDs you like just *happen* to be in there."

With her unbroken arm, she pounded her fist on the desk. *Thump. Thump-thump.*

He looked back at her. "What?"

Something was happening in her. It started like typical butterflies in her stomach, but changed to a flush of warmth. Of happiness. Of joy that grew and opened like a flower, filling her heart with love so fresh and young, so pure and hopeful.

If he really loved her like this, even when she looked the way she did—face bruised, mouth still swollen. If, when Rick looked at her, he really saw only beauty. And if he truly understood—not just knew how she felt, but understood how much she needed to sing ...

She rose on shaky legs. Her heart fluttered like those butterfly wings she'd felt a moment ago. Nervousness surged through her as it had on that long ago day she and Sharon swam with Rick and Tony.

She walked over, took his hand, and signed *I love you.* Then she pressed her swollen lips to his cheek and held them there, her face against his.

He didn't move. "I love you, too, baby," he whispered.

She eased back. *Tempo,* she signed awkwardly, gazing into his smoldering eyes under the brim of his Stetson, and had a delicious flashback. Eight years ago. She and Rick. Outside, naked, on a quilt. He'd looked at her then like he was looking at her now. They'd made Ben that day.

He cleared his throat. "Let's go check on her. She'll be glad to see you."

She held his hand as they walked toward Tempo's stall. They passed Trident, who was desperately trying to open his door. Julie jerked a thumb at the mischievous horse.

"Yeah. I had to double lock him. And put him between Dutch and the tack room. He smells a girl, he gets one thing on his mind. That's why I moved Tempo to the end, she's fixing to come into season."

Snake. Bite. Julie signed.

"The vet got here right away and treated her. He's put her on antibiotics and he's treating it as a puncture wound, being cautious of infection. She had some swelling and lost the hair around the bite, but she should be fine."

In the narrow stall, Julie inspected the horse's leg. Sure enough, two dark spots were visible just above Tempo's back right hoof.

Rick cleared his throat. "If you hadn't held on like you did, if she'd thrown you and the snake bit you instead ..."

Julie probably wouldn't be here. Maybe there were worse things than not being able to sing right now.

And, she realized with sudden clarity, if she hadn't had the accident, she wouldn't know about the nodules. She would have auditioned, possibly signed a contract, maybe begun performing, and caused permanent damage to her voice. Had the short-term setback of the accident saved her from failing in the long run?

She reached for Rick, placing her cast-covered arm between them, and held him tightly with the other.

Immediately his arms went around her. They'd held each other so much the last few days. Time and again she just walked right into his embrace, and he welcomed her without hesitation. She'd even gotten fairly comfortable with him helping her undress, bathe, and re-dress.

Last night, for a brief moment as she drifted to sleep, she actually forgot about the cast on her arm, the wires on her teeth. Yearning had spiked. She'd almost rolled over and kissed him, a clear invitation. But the reality of her condition stopped her.

What had stopped her in the weeks, months, years *before* the accident?

The tension between them, that's what. Over time it had stretched tighter, tauter, like an invisible high wire. And because of it, they hadn't been able to talk, to touch, to reach each other.

Julie didn't know where that tension had come from—maybe just residual stress from Ben's surprise arrival and ensuing health issues—but for now it was gone. As though the slate of their marriage had been wiped clean.

As if on cue, a music intro started; the DJ spoke over it. "Hope you're with the one you love, 'cause here's an Alabama classic. 'Feels So Right.'"

Space was limited between her horse and the wall, and they were standing in the only clean corner of the stall. She was surrounded by buzzing flies; the scent of fresh horse dung and soiled hay tickled her nose. But truly, there was nowhere else she'd rather be.

She pulled back, searched Rick's face. And started to sway.

His hold on her tightened. "You asking me to dance?" he asked.

She nodded, and watched the hungry lover in her husband push aside the platonic gentleman who'd been her caregiver since the accident. She inched her mouth forward and felt a lovely magnetic tug—the first in a very long time—as he began to move with her.

Feels so right, indeed, she thought.

He kissed her. Gently.

"I don't want to hurt you."

No, it was wonderful. Even with her mouth closed, even though she could only hold him with one arm.

She kissed him back with the slightest movement of her lips. He'd stopped dancing, but his hands were frantic, roaming over her back and shoulders.

His breathing quickened. "Ah, Julie. I've missed you so much."

And she'd missed him. Missed how good it felt to be wanted. To be touched. To be loved.

If only they weren't standing in the barn.

She broke the contact, pulled his arm from around her and raised his wrist to check the time. Twelve thirty. And Mother and the children were gone.

Bath, she signed, rubbing her one, working fist against her chest.

Rick's head dropped forward. "You want to go back to the house and take a bath." He exhaled through pursed lips and looked at her. "Okay. I was worried coming out here would be too much for you."

She shook her head. Pointed at herself, pointed at him.

Bath, she signed.

Understanding made him chuckle. He picked her up, though she wriggled in protest.

"Nuh-uh. No way am I chancing anything happening to you between here and the house."

Being carried both embarrassed and thrilled her. She half expected Rick to be winded and in need of a nap by the time they reached the house. Instead, he lowered her feet to the ground, held her against his side as he opened the back door. Then he carried her over the threshold and all the way to their bathroom, closing and locking doors as they went.

The sheer fun of it had her laughing inside. The look of focused determination on his face made her heart race with anticipation.

She turned on the faucets, suddenly shy over undressing as he watched.

"I'll be right back." As if reading her mind, he went into their bedroom, but left the door open. She heard the beep of his cell phone as she removed her clothes and slid into the warm water, careful to keep her cast on the tub's edge.

He returned and smiled at her. "I texted Sean. Previews are running. Movie's two hours. That means we've got close to three before they get back."

He flicked on the jets, shed his clothing, and joined her in the tub.

She pressed her hand to his chest—pinky and forefinger up, thumb out. *I love you.*

Rick kissed her. As best she could, Julie kissed him back.

***

"Daddy? Daddy."

Rick heard Rachel's call as she entered the stables—a solid three hours after he and Julie had started their *bath*. Julie was now sitting at her new desk, reviewing programs and making notes on a legal pad. Rick stood behind her, nuzzling her neck and dodging half-hearted swats from her hand. He watched as she clicked to the word processing program.

Aren't you going to answer her? he read.

"Daddy?"

"I'm in the tack room. With your mother." He nipped Julie's earlobe as Rachel came through the doorway.

"Gross. Almost as gross as the un-mucked stalls."

His daughter stood with arms crossed, glaring. His wife had leaned away, and was looking back at him over her shoulder, an eyebrow raised.

Rick laughed. He winked at Julie. "I got distracted earlier today."

"I bet." Rachel muttered and grabbed her rubber boots from the rack by the door. "Are all the horses out?"

"Yes."

"Then I'll start with Tempo's stall." She left.

Rick stole another kiss just below Julie's jaw. Her hand rose again. He caught it and kissed it, too, then backed toward the doorway as she wagged a finger at him.

"Type me a list, Gorgeous. Whatever needs to be done to make Sean's party happen."

Julie blushed, nodded, and shooed him away.

Humidity had joined the afternoon heat. Both slapped him as he exited the tack room. He grabbed one of several shavings forks hanging on the wall, and ambled down the concrete walkway past empty stalls.

As he approached Tempo's newest home, Rachel tossed a shovelful of manure into a wheelbarrow she'd placed outside the sliding door. Rick slipped inside before she reloaded her shovel, began working alongside his daughter.

"I guess you and Mom are getting along. Since her mouth is wired shut."

"Careful, Rachel. Your mom's been through a lot lately."

"Right. I guess being waited on hand and foot could make anybody pleasant."

She threw more manure out the door, turned back, and sank her shovel in again. Rick jabbed the tines of his shavings fork directly onto the blade, stopping her progress.

"When you've been sick, hasn't she taken care of you?"

Rachel ducked her head. "Yes. But I'm hardly ever sick. Ben's the one who needed all her attention."

"That's right. She nursed him because he couldn't eat any other way. She interviewed specialists until she found one who would give him the best chance for having normal speech in his adult life. She learned and then taught him sign language. *While* continuing to do all the wife and mother things—cooking, cleaning, taking care of the rest of us, even handling my company's books. How much time do you think that left her for herself?"

His daughter didn't look at him, but he could see her pressing her lips together.

"Well?" If there was one thing he couldn't stand, it was an ungrateful child. "This is the most rest your mother's had in years."

And it was probably doing her a world of good.

Rachel's head was still down. "Will she stay like this if she gets her voice back?"

Rick watched his daughter swipe the back of her hand across her nose. Using two knuckles he nudged up her chin. Tears swam in her eyes. He knew Rachel hated crying in front of anyone. Probably thought it made her look weak. She had no idea how his resolve buckled when she cried. And maybe that was a good thing. If she'd actually known how much power she wielded with her tears, well, *that* could certainly become a problem.

The question was, why was she crying?

Will she stay like this if she gets her voice back?

Honestly, hadn't the same thought crossed his mind? Earlier. While he'd been loving Julie, enjoying a welcome the likes of which he hadn't experienced in years.

He pulled a bandana from his back pocket, bent, and blotted rogue tears on her cheek. Finally she met his gaze.

"I remember what she was like before Ben, Daddy. She used to sing to me at night. Then Ben came and everything changed."

"That kind of happened for all of us." He took both tools, propped them against the wall. Wrapped his arms around her. He kissed her hair, noting its strawberry scent, her current favorite shampoo and conditioner.

"Listen. When your mom gets better, she's finally going to get to do what she's wanted to do her entire life. Think about how you'd feel, if every time you thought you were about to reach your dream, something happened that postponed it."

"I want to run my own stables. Like you."

"Not much longer and you can help me run this one. You almost know enough."

Rachel wouldn't need to leave or move away to have her dream. And maybe when she turned fifty, he'd let her date.

"Daddy?"

She whispered so softly, he almost didn't hear her. "Hmm?"

"I have a little problem."

"What's his name?"

She pulled back, rolling green eyes that matched her mama's. "Daa-ddy."

There was that knock-a-man's-knees-out-from-under-him half smile. Man, she was going to be a heartbreaker.

He winked at her. "I'm just making sure you're still my girl."

"I'm always your girl, Daddy." She paused. "You know how I struggled with those English assignments earlier this year?"

"But you've been working hard since then. I see you on your computer all the time."

"Yeah. About that. I'm sort of ... failing English."

He released her, checked the area around his boots, and stepped back. Scrubbed a hand over his face, then shoved both in his front pockets.

"The school year's almost over and you're just now telling me this." Although he tried, he couldn't keep the snap out of his voice.

"Shh. I don't want Mom to know. I don't want her to be mad at me."

"She'll know soon enough. Sean graduates in a week. Then you've got what ... two, three days left of regular classes? I figured I'd have to take you those last few days, but summer school's a different matter."

Rachel looked to the left, the right, the corner over his right shoulder. She crossed her arms. "I've been working hard. I really have."

"Sounds like it hasn't done much good."

"It has. I made a deal with my teacher. I've been writing like crazy to meet the word requirement. If I keep it up, they'll let me finish in summer school."

"No bus, right?"

"No." Misery coated her words. "I need a ride."

"Sean's shipping out, so he won't be here. I'll have double duty, because you won't be here to help with summer chores. The whole fence down the east side needs replacing, and your mother's got a broken arm. I guess you expect her to drive one-handed and with a broken jaw." He sighed. "When does it start?"

"The following Monday."

"That's almost six weeks after the accident. Maybe she'll have her cast and the wires off by then."

"I'm sorry, Daddy. I am. Please don't tell Mom yet. Please."

She looked at him with her mother's face, with that same uncertain expression Julie had given him a few hours earlier, right here in this stall.

"I can count on you, right, Daddy? Like always?"

The dilemma was familiar. His position, precarious. Here he was again, smack-dab in the middle between his wife and daughter, and he hated it. Absolutely hated it.

But what choice did he have if he wanted to keep them both happy, and protect the new, fragile intimacy between him and Julie?

Maybe, if he gave himself time to strengthen that bond. Simply delayed telling Julie and made as many new, happy memories with her as possible before anything else happened, they might get to keep the closeness they'd just rediscovered.

Rick reached for the tools, handed the shovel to Rachel. Began sifting soiled bedding. She took the cue; they worked together until the floor was clean enough to add fresh pine chips.

"Who else knows? Your older brother? Friends at church?"

Her eyes widened and she shook her head. "No one but my teacher."

"Good. Keep it that way. Don't tell your grandma, either. I'll figure out the best time to tell your mom."

"Not yet, though, right?"

"No, not yet."

"I have a paper you need to sign."

"Give it to me later." He handed her his shavings fork, exited the stall, and lifted the manure-filled wheelbarrow's handles. "Right now, I've got my hands full."

***

Rachel Matthews, Mrs. Tate's third period English class: Tuesday, May 27:

I feel like my life has been split in two, and each half has been turned inside out.

Before this year, school was my haven. Now I endure it.

Science is sooooo yuck. If my new lab partner Britney-the-blonde-bimbo (sorry, Mrs. Tate) says one more thing about me having a breast reduction and giving her my extra—I might just fail English on purpose and repeat eighth grade. To get away from her.

But Britney is Vice Principal Larl's granddaughter. Like I could tackle that one and win. I'd have an equal chance of winning an argument with Mom.

At home, I now live in an alternate universe. My grandma, who's been here four weeks and is staying through Sean's graduation, has somehow got me hooked on kiwi smoothies.

Kiwi. Because she read somewhere it prevents asthma. Not that I've ever had asthma.

It's also full of antioxidants and fiber, which I will need to prevent the weight gain I'm obviously at risk for, since according to Grandma, I'm "built like your mother, God bless you." Grandma is convinced my digestive tract is unhealthy, because I don't eat enough fruit.

Have you SEEN a kiwi? The seeds look like little black bugs. I spend, like, hours every night picking them out of my teeth. I simply cannot sleep feeling like critters are breeding in my gums.

My oldest brother—who's outta here, soon, anyway—has lost his mind. He's currently concerned about, what he calls, his *legacy*. He's cleaning out his room, and keeps giving our little brother weird stuff.

Every few hours I hear a throaty "Oh, man, that's awesome!" from Ben's room, that's how I know Sean has given Ben yet another treasure, like Sean's first teddy bear. The thing's missing both eyes and an ear. If you ask me, it's got a flesh-eating fungus.

And the camera. Grandma bought Sean a camera for graduation, but of course she gave it to him last week even though his party isn't until this Saturday. So now Sean's a bigger goofball than ever before. He pops out around corners, from behind doors, and takes what he calls "candid" shots.

Little Ben is the same old Ben, thank heaven. But my parents are like goofy, love-struck teenagers on an endless date.

They are kissing. ALL. THE. TIME. And hugging. Daddy is forever whispering in Mom's ear. She can't say anything back, of course, but she grins at him all the time.

Since the accident I have to knock on the tack room door before I enter. It was actually locked the other day when I went to find them. They were in there doing who knows what. I mean, I know. But I don't want to know.

Daddy laughs all the time. Mom gives close-lipped smiles, which is a good thing because she still has wires on her teeth. But I worry that she's just storing up all the snipping and harping she usually does, and it'll all come flying out when she is able to speak again.

I am a little worried, too, about Sean going to boot camp, though he says it's no longer called that. Now it's called Basic Training. Once you get there, you're stuck for ten weeks. It's grueling and you get yelled at a lot by a drill sergeant, even if you do everything right.

I asked him how he was going to cope. Being away from Lisa. Being away from home and having to eat whatever they gave him. Like the worst ten-week camp experience.

Sean laughed. "Rachel. No drill sergeant has *anything* on Mom. Basic will be a piece of cake."

Chapter Eleven

The sleeveless, shimmering-black pantsuit hung in plastic on the back of Julie's bathroom door. She was practically salivating in anticipation of wearing it.

Apparently the smoothies, the frequent walks with Rick, and the fact that she couldn't snack on sweets at night, had granted her a lovely byproduct of the accident. She'd lost eighteen pounds in four weeks and was positively tickled pink about that. The new outfit was three sizes smaller than anything she'd bought in years.

Careful application of foundation and concealer camouflaged the last remnants of bruising still present on her face. The swelling had finally diminished so she took special care with her eyes, applying a smoky shadow in the crease, adding depth. And employed a smudging technique she'd learned two days ago at the Lancome counter at Macy's when shopping with Laurie Crane. The effect somehow made her eyes look bigger, brighter, vividly greener.

The trickiest part tonight had been her hair. One-handed styling was almost impossible, but while she and Laurie were at the mall they'd popped into a salon and gotten some ideas from a professional stylist.

So earlier she'd had Rick wash and dry it when he'd come back from the stables for lunch that day. Then she set to work with a flat iron and small curling iron. Tendrils now framed her face from a side part, the rest of her often unruly mane lay in subtle waves past her shoulders.

If she were able to speak, she'd be squealing with delight.

She misted perfume on her throat, a hint of jasmine. Slipped on dangling silver earrings. Slid into her satin-lined pants and strapless heels, then carefully glided her cast through the left armhole. She pushed her right arm through the other, enjoying the cool material against her warm skin, checked her reflection, and opened the door, planning to have Rick zip her up.

"Wow." His hands stilled on the middle button of his stark-white dress shirt. His eyes sparkled with male appreciation, and he grinned like a man who'd just won an enviable prize. "Gorgeous. Gorgeous. Did I mention, *you're* gorgeous?"

His reaction was better than she'd hoped.

She knew she was blushing, but didn't care. A wave of feminine awareness washed over her, leaving boldness in its wake. She cut her eyes at him, turned slowly, gathering her hair and exposing her back. An unspoken "zip me" request.

"Gladly," he said.

He skimmed his rough fingers down her spine and up again. "I love your soft skin. Especially right here." He dotted kisses across her shoulder and up the side of her neck.

The temptation to turn in his arms and pretend they didn't need to leave for Sean's graduation was so strong, she almost gave in.

"I will definitely enjoy looking at you all evening. Problem is, I'm not gonna want all those people coming back to the house after. What time will the party be over and everybody gone?"

She raised her right elbow, swept her hand down, fingers together, pointed to the floor. *Late.*

She felt like the years had been removed. Like she was young and newly married. She was beautiful, or at least, Rick thought so. They couldn't seem to get enough of each other.

And the care. The gentle attention he gave her. Holding her hand during their walks. Neutralizing her mother's jibes ... she could practically feel an "in love" glow emanating from her face as he zipped her top.

"Not what I wanted to hear, but maybe you'll let me steal a kiss now and then."

She turned around, nodded, and raised her lipstick-covered mouth to his. Instead he kissed her nose, grinning, and chuckled when she tickled his ribs. He stilled her hand.

"I'm gonna drive up to the stables, check on things before we leave. Trident's been ornery. I don't know if he's kicking his water bucket off the hanger, or is lifting it with his teeth. But he keeps spilling it everywhere, then paws the wall until someone comes to give him more. It's too hot tonight to leave him without water, and I can't send Rachel as she's already in her dress and heels."

She tapped the face of his watch.

"I know, I know. Don't get my clothes dirty and come right back."

She watched him button his shirt, tuck it in black dress slacks, fasten a belt.

"Which tie?"

Three hung on the closet doorknob. She chose a black silk one, twirled it on a finger.

"If I wear that one, you'll meet me back here later?"

She laughed silently, shoulders shaking. Gave a knocking motion with her raised fist. *Yes.*

He left his shirt open at the collar, draped the tie around his neck, and left it dangling. She raised an eyebrow at him.

"Not 'til we get there, and only for you." He blew her a kiss and left.

She returned to the bathroom vanity. Checked her make-up and admired her reflection. Ran fingertips down her throat.

Despite the pain and uncertainty of the last four weeks, the forced voice rest had probably saved her career. Tonight their oldest son was graduating. Within a week, he'd leave for the military—that chapter of her life was ending. Days later she'd get her cast removed. The wires removed. Rick was making progress learning how to keep up his company books on the computer.

Her marriage had never been better. How wonderful it would be that when her voice returned—which she hoped would happen very, very soon—she could begin her career with Rick firmly at her side, rather than feeling like she was being pulled between her family and her dream.

A quick touch-up of lipstick and she snapped closed her small purse. Slid the strap of a satiny black sling over her head, the sleeve over her cast. Not perfect-perfect, but almost.

She raised her eyes to heaven, her fingertips to her lips and dropped her hand to her chest. *Dear God, thank you. Finally, every part of my life is falling into place.*

***

Rick peered through his truck's windshield, not recognizing the horse trailer parked by the stables. And he wasn't sure he knew anyone who could afford what had definitely cost upward of eighty thousand dollars or more. Whoever owned the rig had chosen it with comfort in mind.

Late May heat threatened to melt him before he made it down to Trident's stall and back, but if he moved fast, he might not sweat through his dress shirt. Determined to bypass drooling over the fine piece of horse trailer machinery, and hopefully save his dress clothes, he pulled up on the rig's passenger side, leaving the engine running and AC on. Julie would appreciate getting into a cool vehicle, especially on an evening like this.

He excited his truck and walked in front of the horse trailer, turned the corner at the stalls—

And ran right into Angelina Rousseau.

She swayed back, but the toe of her boot was under his. He caught her, barely, banding both arms around her waist, managing to keep them both upright by securing her against his chest. Her fingers gripped his shoulders. Her startled eyes—inches away—met his.

Steamy perfume wafted directly to his brain. Very ... potent.

Like her big brown eyes.

Carefully, he lifted his foot from hers. "Are you okay?"

She nodded, her waterfall of straight, dark hair floating around her face. "Yes," she said, breathless, eyes still wide. Then she seemed to focus. "My. You, um, clean up well."

"I'm sorry?"

She blushed. "No, I'm sorry. That came out wrong. You can let go now."

She stepped back. "I mean, you look dressed for an evening out. You must have plans. I should have called to confirm." Her voice dropped as if she were embarrassed.

He'd forgotten. Completely forgotten she was bringing her mare this weekend. A pre-paid boarder, referred by a friend, who hadn't crossed his mind since he deposited her check.

"You brought Godiva."

She nodded. "Yes. But I can take her back if I have to and return another day, if you don't have room."

"Hold on ..." His mind replayed the meeting from four weeks ago. "Godiva's due to foal, when?"

"Four or five weeks? That's the best estimate we have from the sonograms."

"Okay. She in the trailer, or did you already put her in the indoor arena?"

"I just got here, couldn't find you. I was about to call your cell. She's still in the back." She cleared her throat, blinking as if battling tears.

"Hey. It's okay. We'll fix it."

"I'm sorry," she said again. "But if you have a stall available, can I stay with her a while?"

"You'd be alone here."

"No." She sighed and looked away. "I'd be alone at home."

His cell buzzed. "Excuse me." He read the text from Rachel.

Mom says we need to leave in ten minutes.

He texted back. *Be ready at the door.*

"Rick." She shook her head. "I'll bring her back tomorrow."

"No, it's okay. Wait right here."

He walked to Trident's stall. Sure enough, the stallion had up-ended his water bucket. He motioned back to Angelina. "Want to help?"

"Sure."

While Angelina filled Trident's water bucket, Rick moved Dutch to the arena. He quickly shoveled the worst of two soiled patches into a nearby wheelbarrow, threw down some clean bedding.

"How's your memory?" He laughed at himself. "Better than mine, obviously. Remember this. M-A-T-T-8. It's the combination for both the tack room and the alfalfa storage room. Put Godiva in here. Get what you need. Call me if you have an emergency. I have to go," he said. "My son's graduating and my wife's waiting."

"She recovered from her accident? How fortunate for her. I'm glad."

"So am I," Rick said.

***

Julie craned her neck, just a little, as they passed the old, brick high school—now the middle school—and drove the extra half-mile to the new high school.

The new campus boasted a sloped-floor theater that, with the balcony seating, would accommodate all one hundred forty-two graduating seniors, their families and friends, and fellow students. Part of her missed the familiar concrete bleachers. The carefully maintained field where, eons ago, she'd sung the national anthem before football games. The place she'd won the statewide singing contest.

She'd never forget that night. Or the feeling she'd had as she closed her eyes; let the lyrics and notes she'd written flow out, knowing her voice soared over the crowd, out to the town, all the way to heaven.

How different her life would be if her mother had let her go to New York.

But, what would she have given up? She looked over at Rick.

They rolled into a parking space and stopped. He turned toward her and passed three tickets into the backseat. "Trudey, will you go ahead, take Rachel and Ben inside?"

"Well, sure, sugar. And I can't blame you, Julie, if you don't want to walk in, in front of everybody. Sneaking in after the lights are dimmed is so much better than having folks gawk at the cast and those awful wires right there on your face."

Rick crossed, then uncrossed his eyes at Julie. She grinned.

"Trudey, I need a moment to fix my tie." Rick spoke without breaking eye contact.

"Well, I can help with—"

"And I won't escort my gorgeous wife into our son's graduation ceremony until I look half as nice as she does."

"Oh. Aren't you sweet." Trudey slid out as Rachel and Ben exited from the other side. "Julie, I sure don't know how you nabbed such a good man. I guess you hooked him early on, before he really had a chance to meet other women." The back doors slammed.

Julie didn't need to grit her teeth; they were already locked together.

"Don't listen to her," Rick said. "She doesn't realize how ridiculous she sounds." He shook his head, laughed. "Or looks. *Where* did she get that getup?"

Julie's shoulders shook as she silently laughed, watching in the side view mirror as her mother traipsed across the parking lot in a black spandex jumpsuit with a faux-fur belt. She raised her right hand to her cheek, fingers straight, then flicked them toward Rick and shrugged. *I don't know.*

Her husband shook his head again, rubbed his chin. "Last

time I saw leopard print heels like that was ..." He adjusted the rearview mirror, tied his tie. "Don't think I've seen shoes quite like that before.

"Come here, Gorgeous." He reached for her, held her face with gentle fingers. Kissed her softly and pressed his cheek to hers.

She inhaled deeply, and smelled something different. She pulled back, with her middle finger made a dabbing motion at each side of her neck. *Perfume?*

"What?"

She sniffed twice, repeated the motion. *Perfume?*

Rick raised a shoulder to his nose, breathed in. "New client. She was at the stables when I went to check on Trident. We ran into each other, literally. I had to catch her to keep from laying her out. One of those women who carries her own atmosphere, if you know what I mean. The scent of her perfume stays behind when she leaves the room?"

He shook his head. "I should've changed shirts."

Julie patted his arm. Pointed at him and signed using one arm, hand up, palm facing him. *Great. You look great.*

She didn't want to ask. She didn't want to *need* to ask. But every insecurity she'd ever felt bubbled up. Something in her gut told her the woman might have been an ordinary client, but she was no ordinary woman.

Julie drew her hand across her own face. *Pretty?*

He took her hand in his. "We're going to be late."

She squeezed, stopping him. The look on his face told her she wouldn't like what he had to say.

He sighed. "As a matter of fact, she's a very beautiful woman. And she's obviously wealthy. And she's *married*, in an are-you-sure-you-want-to-wear-that-huge-diamond-in-a-barn kind of way.

"Baby. You're it for me. Your mother's an idiot. And this is our night with our son, whom I'm so proud of *I'd* sing at his graduation, if they'd let me."

She smiled at him around her wires. Signed *Thank you.*

"You're welcome." He scanned her face, lowered his voice. "But you're so gorgeous tonight, if we don't get in there soon I'll be very, very tempted to stay parked right here. Sean will not want to remember his graduation night as the time his parents got arrested for making out in the school parking lot."

She chuckled silently again, and studied his rugged face. The sexy laugh lines outlining his hazel eyes. The nose, which had been broken twice during high school football games. The mouth that had just said the right, absolute perfect thing she needed to hear.

She kissed him. Slow and sweet, running her fingers over his calloused ones.

He pulled back, raised his eyebrows at her, and held her hand still. "We're, um, going inside now, young lady. To see our son graduate. Don't move. I'll come around and get you."

He darted out, around the back of the truck, and helped her down with the same gentleness he'd used when they were dating, when they'd attended the prom.

Julie's heart melted into a puddle at his feet.

Arm in arm, they entered the auditorium lobby. Julie stopped, stunned by a wall covered with huge black-and-white photos showing the history of the school. She did a double-take. Amidst the shots of the first graduating class, championship sports and debate teams, was a picture labeled "Rowe City's Award-Winning Soloist." The picture showed her, standing before a microphone on a skirted stage, singing her heart out for the packed stadium. Heavens, she'd been so young. That night it had seemed the whole county had been in attendance.

After all this time, someone with influence who'd had input during the construction of this new facility, had remembered both her, and her accomplishment. They'd thought her a young, undiscovered star.

What wonderful things might happen when she got her voice back? Experience, training, even age would be her assets now.

Her heart galloped in her chest. Her dream was now only heartbeats away. *Heartbeats.* A few weeks, maybe months. But it was coming. She could envision herself standing on stages across the country. The world. And this time, her mother could do nothing to stop her.

"Well, look at that." Rick kissed her cheek. "Soon, baby. Soon."

Tonight is about Sean, she signed.

"Yes, it is."

Escorted by her husband, Julie walked into the auditorium to sit with her family. In her heart, she clapped and cheered for her oldest. She was *so* proud of him.

One down, two to go.

Chapter Twelve

Sean's schoolmates, other parents, and family friends from church, rolled in and out of Julie's home in waves. Heart-felt congratulations and the rising hum of chatter from those who mingled filled her house and spilled into the front yard. From her chosen seat in the kitchen, she heard laughter. Her son's rich, almost-a-man laughter. More than once she glimpsed his girlfriend taking his hand or wiping away tears. That Lisa loved Sean was obvious. Maybe that love would endure during Sean's absence.

Julie had planned every party detail with careful orchestration. She'd purposely let her mother handle the food—finding the caterer, planning the menu, ordering the cake—because those were the things her mother couldn't bungle. Much.

Each instruction she'd given Rick via typing at her computer, had been followed to the letter. Right down to Ben being assigned to stay near Julie. She could sign, greet folks, carry on simple conversations, with Ben as her voice. He took to the job with the seriousness of a soldier charged with a critical task.

She even heard snippets of occasional praise for her efforts. "She must have had everything in order." And, "What a feat to pull this off after that terrible accident."

Rick was the perfect host. For once, Rachel was a dream. She greeted folks at the door and directed them to the kitchen for refreshments.

To Julie's surprise, her mother didn't mingle, but actually stayed put and managed the kitchen. Stocking and re-stocking snacks, drinks, and punch, cutting the cake as needed. Considering what she wore to the ceremony, Julie was glad her mother had changed before guests arrived. Although the camouflage half shirt, matching BDU capris, and four and a half inch heels she now wore were still a little much.

And most thankfully, Trudey hadn't offered her phone number to any of the men in attendance. At least, Julie was fairly certain she hadn't.

About an hour into the party, Pastor Pierce Crane and his wife, Laurie, arrived. He walked in first, carrying their chunky, blue-eyed baby daughter like the proud father he was. Laurie followed, diaper bag in hand, and sat at the kitchen table with Julie while Pierce made the rounds showing off their daughter. With Laurie's dirty-blonde bangs and prominent freckles, she might have passed for a student.

"Julie, everything looks wonderful. We wanted to be here earlier, but Hope changed her schedule on me. I guess with having three children, you know how that goes."

Julie nodded.

"Did I ever do that, Mom?" Ben asked. "Did I change your schedule?"

She nodded again. Had he ever. Adjusting to having a healthy newborn was one thing, but a baby with a cleft palate, sleep apnea, and constant ear infections—that was a different animal.

Laurie looked around. "No telling where Pierce is. Guess that gives me a few baby-free minutes. How did you do it? With three? Some days I barely get my teeth brushed before lunch, and she's only six months old." She waved her hands. "Never mind. I know you can't talk, I don't know why I'm sitting here asking questions like this. Maybe we can e-mail each other."

Julie answered with a knocking motion.

"Yes!" Ben translated. "She said 'yes.'"

Julie placed a finger to her lips. *Shhh.*

"Sorry," Ben said.

Julie patted his arm then signed a message for Laurie.

Ben's brow furrowed in concentration. "The cast and wires come off in about ten days. She doesn't know when her voice will return. Email's good."

Laurie clapped. "Well done, sir. Well done." She rose. "I better find Pierce. He'll let Hope catnap on his shoulder, then I'll be up all night with her. You know he's going to honor the graduates in tomorrow morning's service, right?"

Julie nodded again. Laurie hugged her and walked away.

Ben snuggled close, wrapping a thin arm around her shoulders. He rubbed his cheek against hers and planted a sticky kiss there. He'd eaten way too much cake. "I love you, Mom. Hope I wasn't too much trouble."

Julie shook her head. *Never* she signed with her working hand. *Never.*

Someone knocked on the back kitchen door. Julie signed to Ben, *Go answer.*

He scampered off, leaving her alone, then lumbered back, pulling a strikingly lovely woman by the hand. Shimmering dark hair flowed over a model's body, stopped just below a tapered waist in tailored jeans. An expensive, obviously pheromone-infused scent permeated the air and seemed to hang beside Julie's chair.

That scent. The new, *female* client she'd smelled remnants of on her husband all evening.

As if the meeting had been planned, Rick and Rachel materialized in the kitchen doorway, stopping directly in front of Ben and the visitor.

"Don't think I've seen that one at church since I've been here." Her mother spoke, the standard you'll-never-be-that-beautiful expression on her face. Julie had received the same look from her PE Coach during the first week of middle school.

Sixth grade. Julie remembered being in the girl's locker room. Stripping down naked in front of other girls. Those huge concrete block shower rooms, which held several evenly-placed shower poles sticking up from the tile floor. Bathing beside five or six other girls at a time. Julie had been the only sixth grader who'd already started having periods. And wouldn't you know, she had been menstruating that week, of course.

She knew she smelled. Hated knowing that after she ran the track with the others at the end of class she'd smelled even worse. Hormones, yes, but also her weight. She'd come out of the shower room, and discovered her clothes inside out and spread on the benches in front of the lockers, the armpits and breast areas plastered with super-size maxi pads. She'd turned to see the teacher standing there with that exact, sympathetic expression.

"Julie, bring your clothes and come on to my office, honey," Mrs. Bixby had said.

Julie held the towel tightly to her chunky self. She followed Mrs. Bixby past a snickering herd of pretty and popular older girls. Mrs. Bixby led her into the office, shut the door, and closed the blinds.

Mrs. Bixby looked at her with that pitying look. "Julie, do you know who did this?"

Julie wrung the edges of the towel still in her hands. The perpetrator could have been anyone, but was probably several anyones. "No, ma'am."

"I *will* get to the bottom of this."

She swallowed hard, lowering her gaze, holding the towel ends together with one hand, reaching for her clothes with the other. "It doesn't matter."

"You can use my private restroom in the corner to change."

"Thank you."

"... Angelina, this is my daughter, Rachel." Rick's voice drew Julie's attention back to the present. "She'll run her own stables one day."

With seemingly natural poise Angelina extended her hand to Rachel. "Nice to meet you. Are you as good with horses as your dad?"

Rachel glowed, as she always did when anyone mentioned her daddy. She crossed her arms, cut her eyes at Rick and smiled at Angelina. "No one's as good as my dad."

Angelina looked at Julie's husband. In that split second, as those model-perfect eyes swept over Rick's open-at-the-throat dress shirt, Julie saw desire and longing in the woman's beautiful face.

"I'm sure you're right," Angelina said.

Julie was almost certain she heard traces of that desire and longing, too.

There was no way for Julie to clear her throat, then barge in. She couldn't gracefully walk up and smile, introduce herself. She'd removed the black sling when they arrived home, because it was chafing her neck. Now the yellowing cast which she'd let Ben color on and color over, hung pathetically at her side.

Slowly she stood. Half-hoping Rick would remember her, half-hoping he wouldn't.

Ben took Angelina's hand again. "And here's my mom." He pulled Beauty behind him.

Julie swallowed. Angelina offered her hand.

"It's lovely to meet you. So glad you're recovering from your accident." Angelina glanced at Rick, Rachel, Ben, and finally back to Julie.

Nice meeting you, too, Julie made herself answer through Ben. *Welcome to Matthews Stables.*

Maybe, like most of the other owners, Angelina wouldn't be around that much. Or at least, Julie hoped that would be the case.

***

The Barn Church stood on a huge corner lot with its hundred-year-old, gray-brown exterior; its huge and heavy double doors, wavy-glassed windows, and slowly expanding cemetery on the side facing the woods.

Oh, she'd missed it.

Julie stepped down from the truck to the large, grassy parking lot. She'd missed this place; missed Sunday mornings. She really, really missed singing here. But today, at least she was alive and she could have two of the three. The bonus? Her mother had slept in after last night's party, opting out of going to church with them. For the rest of the morning, Julie would be safe from her mother's caustic remarks.

Rick held the door open for her to enter the remodeled, yet rustic interior. As usual, an instrumental rendition of an old hymn flowed through the vaulted space. A soothing, string version of "The Old Rugged Cross." Her heart hummed along, embracing it as an old friend, then beat frantically as if she were about to perform. Why was she so nervous? Of course, because she knew what was coming at the end of the service, and she wanted it to be perfect for her son.

Clusters of church folks dotted the sanctuary; laughter came from some, others blotted tears. As her family of five made their way to their seats, she offered waves and received greetings. And realized she'd missed the people as much as she had the place.

"Julie. It's great to finally see you back here." Laurie plopped down on the pew in front of Julie, a wriggling, ruffle-covered Hope in her arms. "This child is going to make me old. She cannot be still, unless she's asleep. She's either going ninety-to-nothin' or conked out like the dead. Her naptimes are getting shorter and shorter. I don't know what I'll do when she starts walking."

Julie remembered those days.

Would you trade them?

The thought came like the softest whisper, so still, so quiet she almost missed it.

For the life you thought you wanted, would you trade them?

"I'll take her." Rick wrangled the gurgling child from Laurie. "She's got nothing on an unbroken mustang."

"You can take her to the nursery. She doesn't exactly respect church services yet. If her daddy's talking, she thinks she's supposed to talk back." Laurie looked back at Julie. "Julie, what am I in for?"

Some of the best days of your life, Julie thought, then realized she meant it.

She patted Ben's arm, who sat beside her. Placed her cast-covered hand in her right palm. *Help me.* She continued signing and Ben cleared his throat.

"Mom says, 'Does she like taking a bath?'"

Laurie nodded. "She does."

"That can be your quiet time, too, Mom says. Stay with her, but read, make phone calls, relax. Don't try to work when she naps. You rest, too."

"I'm sure you're right. Listen, did Rick get your new computer set up yet?"

Julie nodded.

"Want to meet on Zoom?"

Julie nodded again.

"Great. I can talk and you can type back. Get it? What do you think?"

"Mom says sure," Ben said.

"We can text, too, of course. But Zoom will be much more fun. It'll be almost like talking, better than e-mail even. Lately, I get around adults and my mouth will *not* stop. I think I'm starved for real conversation."

Julie signed and Ben interpreted. "Mom says she can do it tomorrow."

"Great." Laurie stood. "See you later." She left, taking a seat closer to the front.

Ben leaned against Julie's shoulder. "Whew. Listening to her made me tired. And church hasn't even started."

Rick returned, baby-less. He draped his arm around Julie, planted a soft kiss on her cheek, and whispered in her ear. "All five of us together at church. Sean leaves Tuesday. It's our last Sunday like this."

Julie inhaled deeply, struck by the realization. She had two more days of living in the same house with her oldest son. Two days to see him, hug him, tell him how much she loved him, how much he meant to her.

And no voice with which to tell him.

She gulped at the threat of tears. Her son knew, didn't he? That her love for him had always been so big, she'd often thought her heart might burst with it. Surely, he knew.

The service began with the opening choir number "Jesus Paid It All." If Julie had been able to sing, she probably would've been asked to do two or three of the verses, solo. But this time, for the first time in years, she was standing in the congregation. And worse, she was mute.

Fighting frustration, she concentrated on the tune, and meditating on the lyrics as the congregation sang along.

I hear the Savior say,
Thy strength indeed is small;
Child of weakness, watch and pray,
Find in Me thine all in all.

Millie and Clyde Newman were behind her, singing. Millie, just-this-side-of-flat; Clyde, jack-hammering the notes as if pushing out his last breaths. Julie thought he'd surely winded himself by the end of the first verse, and would drop out at the chorus.

She was wrong.

She heard as much as felt Clyde take a deep breath. Behind her, against the back of her legs, the pew vibrated as Clyde's fist pounded out every other beat, every other word.

Jesus paid it all,
All to Him I owe;
Sin had left a crimson stain,

He washed it white as snow.

Stanza after stanza she choked back tears as the congregation sang all six verses. By the time the song was over, she would have given almost anything to have her voice back, to join right in with Millie and Clyde's off-key efforts.

After the song, Pastor Pierce stepped to the podium. "You may be seated," he said. "We have some special folks to honor. Many of you were at the graduation ceremony yesterday evening. We have several graduates here this morning. I'd like to recognize them and their families, then have special prayer for each one."

Down the pew from Julie, Sean stood when called. He made his way to the front, where Pierce shook his hand and gave him a quick guy hug.

"We're proud of you, Sean."

"Thank you, sir."

"From what I hear, you'll be using 'sir' a lot over the next few years. When are you leaving for Basic Training?"

Sean stood straighter. "Tuesday, sir."

The pastor turned to Julie and Rick. "Big change for you, big change for your parents. Before we pray for Sean, does anyone have a bit of advice for a young man entering today's military?"

Behind Julie, Clyde Newman stood. Everyone knew he'd served in the Marines in Vietnam. From his stiff, white, crew cut to his starched posture, Clyde oozed ex-military.

"I've got a scripture for him." Clyde barked, as if in command. 'And the tongue is a fire, a world of unrighteousness. The tongue is set among our members, staining the whole body, setting on fire the entire course of life.' You'll get the meaning of that one real quick, from your drill sergeant. No matter what you do, he'll burn you up at least once or twice a day, if not every hour. Don't pay no mind, don't take the cutdowns and slime slinging to heart. Just follow orders, and keep a good attitude. You'll get through it fine.

"You'll be on your own, so it'll be up to you to remember. Jesus paid it all, son. Even when you mess up, His forgiveness is right there waiting to give you a new start."

While the congregation prayed for Sean, Julie swallowed past the lump in her throat. *Oh, God, keep him safe. Wherever you send him, keep him safe.*

After the service ended, she watched as her son received more good wishes and encouragement. When the well-wishes were over, Rick helped her into the truck. His warm hand steadied her as she boosted up. He made sure she was tucked far enough inside, then caressed her arm before closing her door. He hopped into the driver's seat, inserted the key. Turning to her he winked while revving the engine like a teenager showing off for his first love. He reached over, slid his hand behind her hair, and massaged her neck.

"You look tired. Been a big couple of days. You should relax on the way home."

She sagged against the headrest as they left the parking lot, gazed out the window, while Clyde's grating voice and his shared scripture lingered in her mind. *The tongue is a fire ...* had she been burned?

In her experience—her long, seemingly never-ending experience with Trudey—the tongue had been a shotgun. A device for scattering damaging, careless comments, which her mother fired at will. Probably like what Clyde called a drill sergeant's slime slinging.

As a child, still as an adult, Julie lived in the crosshairs.

Wounds, she thought. They'd always been a part of her life.

She repositioned her cast on her lap, raised her good hand to her cheek, pressed and felt the outlines of the annoying metal bands binding her jaw.

Tiny wounds, gaping wounds. Always there. Always an irritation from her mother. A source of constant discomfort, because even a mild thump gets to a person after a while, when that thump hits the same spot over, and over, and over.

Clyde had encouraged Sean, "Don't pay no mind," when referring to cut-downs and name-calling most people envisioned taking place during Basic Training.

Had she ever stood up for herself? Not talked back in a disrespectful way, which would only have brought more trouble, but ... inside. Had she ever questioned, ever weighed the truth of her mother's words about her? To her?

As far as singing went, yes. Julie hadn't made it to New York, hadn't been able to take advantage of the scholarship. She had, however, ignored her mother's nay-saying and continued pursuing her dream. Doing so had taken much longer than she'd anticipated. Still she'd be well on her way, right now, if not for the accident.

But—she thought, as they pulled into the garage, as Rick removed his hand, as her stomach sank—what if her mother was right about her marriage? What if everything her mother said about Rick picking her because he'd been too young to pick anyone else, hurt her so badly because it was the truth?

Julie looked over at Rick. Her handsome, cowboy husband.

"What?" He shut off the engine as the children scuttled from the backseat.

She shook her head, scanning his features, trying to read his expression.

She'd wondered, hadn't she? Deep down? All these years, she'd wondered if her mother's notion was correct. If the reason Rick had picked her, married her, was because they'd wed at such a young age, before he really had a chance to meet anyone else or explore other options.

If she had gone to New York, left him, studied music, waited to get married—

He wouldn't have ended up with her. He wouldn't be hers.

The surety of her thoughts rushed through Julie's veins like ice water. Rick would have picked someone like Angelina.

And Angelina, or whomever, would have been happy without the obvious money pleasures she now enjoyed, because she'd have Rick and all the satisfaction that came with him.

Julie shivered, swallowed, closing her eyes against the woman's image, which only made the vision clearer in her mind. Even when looking her best, like last night, she couldn't compete with the Angelinas of the world.

"Hey, you okay?" Rick asked.

She nodded, opening her eyes but avoiding his gaze by opening her door.

During her entire marriage, some deep part of her had always felt short-changed. Had whispered to her how she'd settled for less than she should have, when she postponed her dream, got married, had children.

Now she realized she wasn't the one who had settled. Rick was.

Chapter Thirteen

Most Sunday afternoons, Rick preferred to rest. If NASCAR was on, he and Sean watched, slurping root beer and eating everything edible that wasn't nailed down. Other times if his work level allowed, he and Rachel rode their property, on daddy-daughter dates he knew would end once she caught some smart young man's eye. On occasion, he and Ben wandered down to the creek, threw in a cane pole, and chewed on blades of grass. If they stayed long enough, Ben might run out of questions; Rick always ran out of answers.

Never in a million years, would Rick have envisioned himself spending a Sunday afternoon sitting beside his silent wife in the tack room, while she wept and typed a letter to their oldest son, who was leaving in two days. Yet here he was sipping a root beer, while Julie pecked at the keyboard, her smoothie mostly untouched in the glass on the corner of her desk.

Something had changed in her. Between church this morning and when they'd arrived home. He thought he could almost pinpoint the moment, sitting there in the garage as his children tumbled out of the truck, leaving only him and his wife. The way she'd looked at him as if she'd suddenly learned a painful truth, then moved so quietly, so somberly from the truck to their room. Sure, he hadn't heard her voice in over five weeks. But this kind of silence was full of words, full of meaning.

He'd seen her elated and thrilled, like when they were young and she won the singing contest. He'd seen her determined, like when she'd fought with doctors over Ben's care or lack thereof. Seen her focused before singing on Sunday mornings. After the accident, he'd seen her devastated, shaken to her core at the thought she might never sing again.

But this, this was like sorrow mixed with grief, mixed with a desperation he could only relate to a dying man's last words. Because he knew her, he could see. The mother's heart in her held words for Sean that she absolutely, positively needed to get out. And because she couldn't speak, typing them was her only option.

Rick eased his hand under her hair as he had earlier in the truck, and again massaged her tense muscles. "Is it okay if I read over your shoulder?"

She nodded.

Dear Sean,

I wish I could speak to tell you all of this, but maybe this is better, because you can take it with you when you leave.

You have the best parts of your dad and me. In case I forgot to tell you, I'm more proud of you than you can know. Loving you has always been easy. I hope you know I do. And always will.

Julie's brow furrowed in concentration. Rick lightened his touch, caressing her neck as she continued typing one-handed. He read and his eyes watered.

Rick gently patted her shoulder to comfort her. And himself.

She typed a parenthesis, then, *You don't have to stay. Just come check on me in a little while.*

"You're sure?" Leaving her in this condition didn't feel right.

She deleted the last two sentences meant for him, then turned. With her fingertips she traced the shape of his cheek and jaw, nodded.

"Okay." His cell rang. He turned away and answered. "Yeah?"

"Daddy, do I *have* to work with you all afternoon? Ben said he'll muck stalls. He actually *wants* to get dirty. Grandma just started painting my toenails. She's teaching me how to do a French pedicure."

"And she just happened to start that now, when you've got chores?" Surely, sometimes Rachel could test *God's* patience.

"Daddy, please? Can Ben help instead?"

Rick checked his watch. "Send him now. You've got one hour."

"Oh, thank you, Daddy. Thank you." She lowered her voice. "You didn't tell Mom yet, did you? About, you know."

Rick rose, grabbed a handful of peppermint balls from a plastic container on a shelf, shoved them in his shirt pocket. He'd planned to tell Julie this afternoon, about Rachel attending summer school. He had figured sliding it in now, between Sean's party and Sean leaving, she'd be a little distracted. The anticipated explosion would be at least deferred, if not eliminated.

But looking over at his wife now ... no. This wasn't the time.

"Daddy? Is it still our secret?"

"For now."

"Whew. Thank you, Daddy. I'll send Ben. And I'll be there soon."

He ended the call.

The printer on the far end of the desk hummed to life. He handed Julie the first page, then the second. She took a pen and an envelope from the desk drawer, signed with a flourish at the bottom of the second page. *Love, Mom.*

She looked at him, placed her injured arm in her open, right palm. *Help.*

Rick folded the pages in thirds, placed them in the envelope, sealed and addressed it. *Sean.* He set it aside.

Julie rose and went to the sink, dabbed her eyes with a paper towel from the dispenser.

Rick walked to her. "Hey. Are you okay?"

She blew her nose. Nodded again. And balled herself up against his chest.

He wrapped his arms around her. "I'm gonna miss him, too. Like crazy." He pulled back, lifted her chin. "But it's time. At least we know he'll be happy. Some people pick a job and don't know they don't like it until they get there. Then they're stuck. ROTC, it's always been his thing."

She half-smiled at him, but it was possibly the saddest smile he'd ever seen.

"Now let's get you back to the house. Soak in the tub, or take a nap."

Julie shook her head.

"No?"

No, she answered, clamping her index and middle fingers against her thumb, and again shaking her head. She went back to the desk, opened a new Word screen.

I need to write a letter to my mother.

"But she's right here. You can use Ben, or me, to say anything you want."

I can't use Ben. This is between Mother and me. I'll need your help giving it to her later this week, like I'll need your help giving Sean's to him tonight.

She placed her palm over her heart, rubbed in a circular motion. *Please.*

"Sure, baby. Whatever you need."

She straightened her fingers, placed the tips against her lips, then moved them toward him and smiled. *Thank you.*

"I'll come check on you in a little while."

Julie nodded and resumed typing.

Rick ambled to the covered arena, where Dutch had spent the night. He stepped inside. The horse met him before he closed the metal gate.

"Hey, boy. How'd you like having this big room all to yourself last night?"

Dutch nuzzled his shirt pocket. Rick patted the horse's thick neck. Dust and dirt flew. "You've been rolling in the dirt. Need a good brushing."

He presented the candies one by one. "Think I'll have Rachel take care of that after we fix you a clean stall."

Rick heard Ben approach. Tennis shoes smacking the concrete separating the row of stalls and the arena. The boy arrived breathless and bright, like the sun-filled child he always was. And already seven years old. Seemed like just yesterday, Sean was that age. Where did the time go?

Ben poked his head and arms between the metal bars of the farm gate. "I'm here, Daddy. What do you want me to do first?"

Stay little.

"I could use a hug while I think about it." Rick felt the same sad smile cover his face that he'd just seen on Julie's.

"Sure, Daddy." He ran to Rick, face alight as though he was claiming a prize. He squeezed Rick's waist and looked up. "How's that?"

"'Bout near perfect. Had to move some horses around. You update the board while I fix Dutch a new space?"

"I'll make the boys blue, the girls red. How's that?"

"Good idea."

"Can I ride later, Daddy? If we get the chores done?"

"Sure thing, buddy."

"Okay." Ben raced back through the gate.

In the past, Ben had needed to stand on a bucket to reach the top of the dry-erase board hanging outside the tack room. So Rick followed, ready to place a steadying hand on his son's back. But this time, Ben stretched high, swiping the eraser's tip across the top line. "Look, Daddy. I can reach."

"I see that. Dutch'll be first this time. Double-check where everybody is, okay? Better to do it right than fast. There'll be time for you to ride."

"Okay, Daddy!" Ben took off running down the long line of stalls.

Rick poked his head in the tack room to check on Julie. "Need anything?"

She shook her head.

"I'll be starting at the far end, work my way down." He left, again closing the door behind him so the cool air inside didn't escape.

Rick mucked three stalls, and with Ben's help shoveled in fresh bedding after his son updated the board.

"You go check everybody's water bucket. I want 'em clean and I want 'em full. If one's slimy, scrub it out and refill it. You got that, soldier?"

Ben stiffened, puffing out his little boy chest and offering a grinning salute. "Yes, sir. Right away, sir."

Rick chuckled and started on the next stall. He was half through that one when Rachel arrived, wearing shiny sandals.

"Look, Daddy. Aren't they pretty?" She pointed to her freshly painted toenails

"Yes, they are. But not as pretty as you. Lots to do today, so they won't be that way for long."

"Daaa-ddy. I just wanted you to see."

"Right."

"I'll change into my boots. Be right back."

She returned quickly, having donned the boots she kept in the tack room. Together they shoveled horse manure, moving piles to a pair of wheelbarrows outside the stall doors.

"Mom's typing away in there. She wouldn't let me see."

Rick stopped, wiped his brow with a blue bandana from his back pocket. "She's working on something important to her."

"She didn't look mad. I guess you still didn't tell her."

"No, I didn't. Yet."

"Because you like her not being mad at you all the time."

"Because I didn't think her knowing today would help anything."

Rachel stopped working, too. "Please, can we not tell her until next Monday when we have to? All my friends are having a sleepover this Friday night. Mom said I could go, you know, before? If you tell her now, she won't let me do anything next weekend."

"Your mother might surprise you."

Rachel rolled her eyes so far back in her head, Rick marveled they didn't get stuck.

"You know she hasn't changed for real. Soon as she gets her voice back ..." She paused, mumbled. "Bet you're hoping she doesn't get her voice back for a while. I know I am."

"Singing has always been important to your mom. I don't want her to lose that."

But, the old Julie wouldn't have written the letter she did to Sean. She wouldn't be sitting in the tack room on a Sunday afternoon, air conditioning or no. She wouldn't smile at him, let him tease her, let him touch her. Wouldn't make love with him, frequently, with such sweet abandon. Oh, she might toss him the occasional crumb of affection, but he'd never know which returned gesture he'd pay for.

He wanted to keep this Julie, who was most like the pre-Ben Julie. But what was he to do? What *could* he do?

"We won't tell her until Monday."

"Thank you—"

He raised a hand. "But ... let's give your mom a chance, okay? People *can* change. She might surprise you."

A knock on the stall wall got Rick's attention. They both turned to see Angelina standing in the doorway.

"Hi, Mrs. Rousseau," Rachel said.

"Angelina. Please."

Rick shook his head, caught first Rachel's eye, then Angelina's. "Mrs. Rousseau," he said.

Rachel sighed. "Yes, sir."

"You keep going," he told Rachel. "Put fresh bedding in here before starting the next. It's hot out today. We gotta start bringing some of them in."

He walked to Angelina, exited the stall while re-pocketing his bandana. "Is there a problem?"

"No. Rick, I just wanted to thank you again for taking in Godiva last night."

Rick lifted a full wheelbarrow, motioned with his chin. "I gotta go that way."

Angelina stepped aside, brushed against the open stall door. "Oh. Sorry."

How she expected to keep from ruining those pale, silk blouses she always wore to the barn, Rick didn't know.

"Be right back."

He walked past, catching a full whiff of her hypnotic perfume. Somehow it wasn't too strong, but still covered the odor of horse dung. Bet she'd spent as much on that as she had those pretty boots.

Rick pushed the laden wheelbarrow down the walkway in front of the stalls, around the end of the arena, and out to the rapidly growing pile of manure. How would he keep up with all the chores around here, with Sean gone and Rachel in summer school? Ben just wasn't big enough yet for heavy work.

I'll make do, he thought, tipping the wheelbarrow up, the manure out. Rachel didn't know it, but she'd have to earn the right to go to that sleepover. The two days between the regular term and the beginning of summer school, she'd be driving the tractor and moving this manure pile out to the back pasture.

Rick returned to the stalls, parked the wheelbarrow outside the next one in line.

Angelina stood to the side. "I brought my own tack today. I have a locker in the trailer. Mind if I keep it here? Outside her stall?"

"Be safer in the tack room."

"It's got a lock. Unless keeping it here's in the way."

"Behind me, over against the wall will be fine then. So it doesn't block the sliders."

"Of course. Sorry. I forgot your doors don't swing open, they slide." She paused, stood fidgeting with her hands. "Maybe you could help me move it."

"Trailer unlocked?"

"Yes."

He motioned to Ben. "Hey, buddy, come help me get some stuff for Mrs. Rousseau's mare."

They moved the locker; Rick was happy to find it had sturdy steel casters. They pushed it in place across from Godiva's stall, locked the wheels. Ben dashed back to his stack of water buckets.

Angelina opened the locker. Her alligator, wingtip boots flexed as she knelt and reached inside. She pulled out a new, emerald green lead rope, and stood.

"You might want to keep some extra boots here."

She glanced down. "Why? Are these kind not allowed?"

"If you want to ruin $4,000 boots."

"Oh." She shrugged. "They're just boots to me."

Clearly he'd made her uncomfortable. Which wasn't his goal. So he changed the subject. "Which vet do you use? Ben's updating my board."

"Dr. Bohanan."

"Pete?"

"Yeah."

"Good doc. Oversees several boarders I've got here, as well as mine."

She gestured with the rope still in her hand. "Mind if I bring in Godiva?"

"Not at all. I'll walk with you. Show you which fences are on. They're all wired, just not all live. "

"That would be good to know." They continued to the corral. "Special morning at church today for your son."

"You were there?"

"Nicholas and I attend on occasion. When he's not traveling on business. We sit in the back."

"Sean leaves Tuesday for Fort Sill. He's going into artillery."

"Quite a step from southern Alabama, home, and The Barn Church."

"Big one, at that." They stopped at the corral gate. "The gate and this side are dead, the three others on this pen are live."

"Got it." She placed both pinkies in her mouth and whistled. Godiva meandered over, stretched toward her owner. Angelina stroked the horse's muzzle. "There's my girl."

Rick chuckled. "You've got her trained."

"I work her a lot."

"You don't mind my asking, yours that big spread, sits back off Plantation Road?"

"It is."

"Lots of land. Already fenced and cross-fenced. Why pay to board her? Why not keep her there? No stables?" Money like she obviously had, she could certainly afford to build them.

Angelina's hand stilled, then she looked over at Rick. "You know how horses don't like being alone, travel in herds? Call one another when they're in the stalls?"

Rick nodded. A breeze fluttered her hair, sending the scent of her perfume in his direction.

"Well," she said softly. "I don't like being alone either."

***

Her son would be leaving in two short days. How was that possible?

Julie sat beside Rick and opposite Sean at the kitchen table in their quiet house. Rick had dropped a bug in Ben and Rachel's ears,

128

and cash in her mother's hand, successfully sending them out the door and to the Downtown Diner for sundaes.

Eighteen years and nine months ago, she'd been pregnant and in labor with her firstborn. Rick had stayed with her through all thirty-six hours, napping only when she did. At 8:43 p.m. she pushed Sean Richard Matthews into the world, then cried for joy as she first held her screaming, dark-haired son.

Although she was thankful to have a healthy baby boy, the initial feeling of separation, the knowledge that he was no longer a part of her, had caused a grief that took her breath. And a tiny part of her heart mourned, as her imagination fast-forwarded to this season of their lives.

Now, she looked at her son. Her boy. Her baby, who was going into the military.

Dear God, protect him. Please protect him.

Tears pooling in her eyes, Julie nodded at Rick, then slid the letter to her son.

Sean glanced at the envelope, then at his dad. "You want me to open it now?" For a moment those male gazes locked with a look Julie had noticed passing between them several times before. But now wasn't the time to ask its meaning.

"Yes," Rick answered for them both. "Your mother typed it this afternoon. There are things she wants to say, that she obviously can't right now." He cleared his throat. "She wrote it, but it's from both of us."

Rick's calloused hand slid up her back, around her shoulder, and squeezed. "Go ahead, son. We both love you."

That look happened between them again. For a second, Sean cocked his head, as if trying to figure out something. He shrugged and opened the envelope.

Why did it hurt to watch him read the note? Why was she so uncomfortable?

Julie hadn't tested her voice in days, right now would be a great time to get it back. She needed to explain. She *wanted* to explain. To make sure Sean realized her love for him. How proud she was of him. And more. All the things her mother had never given her that she was only now beginning to grasp were crucial for every child.

Rick had that bond, that security with his parents. So did his sister. And wasn't that why Julie had loved going to their home when she was growing up? The love and acceptance she felt there had fed her hungry heart and soul.

She reached for her glass with its straw, and sipped. She set it aside slowly, took a quiet, slow breath, and pushed with her abdominals, hoping for any sound.

Nothing.

Sean switched to page two, where she'd bared her heart. Page one was heartfelt, but in a generic way. The second page, more specific. More personal.

I've always known you had strong protector/provider instincts. That you've chosen a profession in the military makes perfect sense. Your quiet nature—much like your father's—will be a tremendous asset in Basic Training.

I'm sure that same quality is part of what drew Lisa to you. If she's who you choose to be our future daughter-in-law, we will love her with our whole hearts.

Julie had labored over each sentence, each word, as she'd done years ago when writing her songs to God. How odd both endeavors provoked the same trepidation.

"Thanks." Sean looked at her with the patient, hazel eyes he'd inherited from Rick. "Thanks, Mom. This means a lot."

She couldn't read his expression. What was he thinking?

Her emotions were a mess, she knew. Between the accident, her mother staying with them, the changes in her and Rick's relationship,

Sean's graduation, her first service back at church—heavens, was that only this morning?—life had been upside down for weeks.

But something was there, behind his eyes. A shadow?

The little boy he'd once been was looking at her. The ever-excited, dependably consistent child, who'd held her hand wherever they went and trusted her implicitly. That face peeked at her from a hiding place, then slipped behind a door.

The child was gone.

Panic bucked in her chest. She wasn't ready to let him go. Wasn't ready to say good-bye.

I love you, she signed.

"I know, Mom. I love you, too."

She grabbed his hand with her good one, then turned hers over atop his and signed again. *I love you.*

Sean rose and walked around the table to her. She stood, and he hugged her, the stubble on his neck pricking her forehead.

"It's okay, Mom. It's okay."

She held on with her one working arm, listening to his heartbeat.

Rick wrapped his arms around them both. "Your mom means it, Sean. We'll always love you. You always have a home with us."

"I got it, Dad. Thanks."

Julie craned her neck. Pressing her lips to Sean's cheek, she kissed her son good-bye.

Chapter Fourteen

Rachel Matthews, Mrs. Tate's third period English class:
Tuesday, June 3:

Arriving at school fifty minutes early means I'm sitting in the library with the weird kids and nerds. And I don't know why I'm writing this. No matter how many words I type and turn in now, it won't be enough to avoid attending summer school.

My dad knows. But my mother doesn't. He's waiting to tell her. Between Mom losing her voice and my brother leaving this morning, Dad thinks my having to attend summer school will be more than she can handle.

Whether the cause is me attending summer school or some other little thing it's only a matter of time before the "old" Mom comes back. I know it will happen as soon as her voice returns. Only now, Sean won't be there to share the line of fire. From now on, it'll be just me. Ben has always been exempt.

We took Sean to the airport this morning, all the drama from his graduation and flying away to his military future is over. Tomorrow is the last day of regular school. Thursday and Friday I'll be moving the manure pile with the tractor, a chore that can't wait until next week because I won't be home. Summer classes start Monday, with Britney-the-blonde-bimbo (sorry again, Mrs. Tate).

Here's what I want to know: Where is my safe place?

It used to be school, in pre-Britney days. Home should be, but as soon as Mom gets her voice back I know the bombing will begin.

If I could, I'd spend every hour in the barn with the horses and my dad. Horses are so much nicer than people. They're grateful for everything you do for them. They don't twist your words. And they never, ever accuse, blame, or embarrass you.

My mother can do all three at once. It's like a talent she has, like her singing voice. Or maybe it's the flipside of her singing voice. I'm not supposed to think God would ever play jokes like that on people, but it would make sense, in a do-you-want-fries-with-that kind of way. You can have a beautiful voice, but it only comes with a side of something else. You might bless others, but you'll also hurt your family.

***

As soon as they returned home from the airport, Julie got out of the truck, leaving her husband and mother behind. Writing the letter to Sean and giving it to him was one thing, sending him to Oklahoma was another. But the thought of actually giving her mother the letter she'd written, a letter that waited in her nightstand, weakened her knees and turned her stomach.

She hurried into the house, through the laundry room and kitchen, into the family room where her glossy, black piano waited by the window. She stopped short then walked to the Baby Grand. Running her working hand over the lid, she trailed her fingers over the shiny surface. She hadn't played a note since the morning of the accident.

The padded stool drew her, offering a familiar place of comfort and communion. She sat, lifted the key lid and slid aside the red, felt key cover. With her right hand she played a sliding scale from middle C up one octave, then down again. Pushing middle C again and again, she closed her eyes, listening to the tone, reveling in its constancy. Middle C always sounded the same.

Mother's heels clicked into the room. "I wondered if you ever play that thing anymore."

Julie's eyes popped open, her hand freezing above the keys. For one delicious, pain-free moment, she'd forgotten her mother was near. Forgotten about the letter.

"I heard that run thing you did just now. Is that all you know after years of lessons with Rick's mom? If I were Rick, I'd be mad." She cocked her head. "You should sell that piano. It takes up too much room in here, and you could put the money toward your medical bills. I'm sure Rick would appreciate that."

Pulse thumping in her ears, Julie lowered her hand to her lap. Across the room Rick caught her eye as he approached from the kitchen. She nodded, giving him the cue.

He cleared his throat. "Trudey. Would you mind having a seat? I'll be right back with something."

"Well, sure, sugar. I've got all the time in the world." She sat at one end of the couch and crossed her legs, bobbing her petite toes with their perfect, French pedicure.

Julie's heart thundered in her chest. The wall clock chimed; she turned and looked at it. Only 9 a.m. and she already felt overwhelmed by the day's events. Though Rick had read the letter and given her brief feedback, she doubted he really understood how difficult writing it had been.

He returned carrying the envelope. Sitting opposite Trudey on the couch, he looked at Julie. "You sure about this?"

She nodded again.

"Trudey, this is addressed to you. But Julie doesn't want to just give it to you, she wants me to read it to you. And if you have questions after I'm done, she can answer with sign language, and I'll translate. Like Ben did at the party. Okay?"

Her mother's foot stilled. Her eyes narrowed. She glanced at Julie then focused on Rick. "Okay."

He opened the envelope. "Dear Mother," he read. "It's taken me a long time to figure out some things. As a child, I often wondered if I grew up in the wrong family. We've never liked the same things. My hair isn't like yours. My skin isn't like yours. You're petite and I'm not. Do I take after my dad?"

Her mother stiffened and uncrossed her legs. "I will not talk about your father. It hurts me too much. Why are you bringing him up like this? To hurt me?"

Rick read on. "I really want a picture of him. Just to have the memory."

"Memories only bring pain. I was shattered when he died. Simply shattered. You'd think after losing him in a plane crash, I'd be scared to fly, instead I can fly anywhere because of the settlement. Free airfare anywhere for life, where's the justice in that, huh? Where was God when your daddy died?" She crossed her arms, then uncrossed them. "Oh, just hurry up and get this over with."

"Since my accident," Rick continued, "I've done a lot of thinking. And I've realized what's most important to me. Like Rick's love and our marriage. My children and their happiness. My family is more important than anything else."

"And your daddy is a lost part of your family." Mother shifted, re-crossing her legs and bobbing her foot again. "Is that what this is about?"

Julie shook her head. Why didn't she understand?

Her mother waved her ring-adorned hands and glared at Julie. "All right. I'll find one and mail it to you. Satisfied? Shouldn't you be concentrating on something else? Like losing the rest of your excess weight?"

"Trudey." Rick spoke softly, but with authority. He rose and walked to Julie, stood behind her and placed a hand on her shoulder. Julie reached up with her good arm and laced her fingers with his. "Keep going?"

She nodded.

"You mean there's more?" her mother asked.

"There are things I need from you," Rick read. "Or I guess, don't need from you. Please don't say anything further about my singing. Or my appearance." Rick paused. "Or my piano, or my faith. I realize they have no value to you, but it hurts me when you say negative things about them and about me. Just because you can't see an injury doesn't mean it's not there."

Her mother stood. "I'm entitled to my opinions. I came here after the accident to help, and this is the thanks I get? So much for the Christian love and good will you've tried to guilt me with over the years."

Julie squeezed Rick's fingers, then looking up, released them. She made a thumbs-up sign, and placed it on the fingers sticking out from her cast. *Help.*

"Trudey. Will you please sit and let me finish?"

Julie's mother glared at her; Julie's heart raced like a thoroughbred's. She wasn't trying to start a fight; all she was trying to do was stop her mother from hurting her further.

She placed her open palm over her heart, moved it in a circle. *Please.*

"Trudey. Julie needs you to listen to all of this, and talk about it while the kids aren't here. Do you see what she's doing? She's saying please. As in *please listen to me.*"

Her mother lunged. "Give me that."

She snatched the letter out of Rick's hand and shredded it. Like tiny ashes, the pieces fluttered to the floor.

"I don't have to listen to this. And I'm not staying where I'm not wanted. I had planned to stay a couple more days to see the kids, but, no. I'll be packed in five minutes. If you won't take me to the airport now, I don't care how much it costs, I'll call a cab." She stalked down the hall.

"I'll take you to the airport whenever you want to go," Rick called after her, then squatted beside the bench. His hazel eyes found Julie's.

Tears bubbled in Julie's eyes. She continued circling her palm over her heart.

"I know. I know," he said. "You weren't trying to hurt her. But she can't hear that right now, and frankly, I don't want her hurting you anymore. She needs to go."

From the guestroom, drawers slammed. "Two minutes, Rick! I'm almost done!"

He raised Julie's cast-covered hand, kissed the exposed fingertips. "You know your body's going to crash now, from Sean leaving, and this deal with your mother. Take a nap while I'm gone. Just sleep." He shook his head and wandered down the hall.

Rick returned first, carrying her mother's huge, fuchsia suitcases. Julie watched her mother follow him back through the family room, the kitchen, toward the laundry room. She waited, but her mother said nothing to her. Didn't even look at her, just shut Julie out like she always did.

The back door opened, closed. The garage door raised. Out the front window, she saw Rick's truck back into the driveway, heard the wheels leave gravel for the highway.

She went to the kitchen, grabbed a high-protein shake from the fridge. Drank it through a straw on the way to her bedroom. Fully clothed she laid on Rick's pillow, and taking his advice, let herself fall asleep.

***

A slamming door woke Julie. She sat up. Her shoes had been removed and placed on the floor by the bed, her favorite afghan draped over her legs. Rick.

Smiling, she ran her hand through her hair. Someone knocked on her door.

Ben bounced into the room. "Daddy said I could wake you up if I knocked first. Tomorrow's the last day of school, and we're having relay races and water games and Free Play all day! I have to wear my bathing suit."

Julie raised her right hand, palm facing Ben, and pushed forward twice. *Great.*

"Mrs. Furley said I have to bring a towel and a bag lunch. Can I use my lunchbox instead?"

She nodded.

He bounded forward and kissed her cheek. "Thanks, Mom. Daddy said Grandma left, and I have to help with chores. Bet you're sad." He ran from the room.

Deciphering Ben's disjointed comments sometimes confused her, but this time she understood. Sad? Yes. And disappointed. If someone really cared about you, wouldn't she want to know if she was hurting you?

Julie went to the kitchen. She put a frozen lasagna in the oven, set the timer, and walked to the barn.

Rick met her outside the tack room, shovel in hand. He stepped close and kissed her forehead. "I almost joined you in bed after I got home from the airport for the second time today. But you were sleeping so peacefully."

She motioned for him to follow her into the tack room and turned on her computer. *L-A-U-R-I-E*, Julie signed.

"Want me to call her? See if she can Zoom?"

She made a knocking motion.   *Yes.* He called Laurie, but she wasn't home, so they chose to text instead.

Laurie: Did Sean leave today?

Julie: For Oklahoma.

Laurie: How are you?

Julie: Okay about Sean. Question?

Laurie: Shoot.

Julie: Is that "the tongue is a fire" verse Clyde Newman quoted in church really in the Bible?

Laurie: In James somewhere. Chapter 3?

Julie: But it means words, right? That words can destroy a person?

Laurie: Yes.

Julie: Today I told my mother, some things she says hurt me.

Laurie: What happened?

Julie: She left.

Laurie: My mom's been gone ten years. I miss her every day.

Julie: Because she was good to you and made you feel safe. I envy you.

Laurie: How can I help?

Julie: Book of James?

Laurie: Yes.

Julie: I'll read it and get back with you. Bye.

Laurie: Good plan. Bye. Oh! One more thing. Pierce and I were both talking last night about how much we miss you singing at church.

Julie: I miss it, too. You'll never know how much.

Laurie: Text me if you need me.

Julie: Will do.

Julie signed off and clicked onto the Internet, quickly locating a Bible site. The English Standard Version sounded like what Clyde had quoted and was easy to understand. Verse eight contained the phrase "deadly poison." She couldn't help but think of the snake bite.

Weary, she rested her head in her hand.

Dear God, I haven't talked to You much lately except about my voice. I didn't realize how much hurt I carry because of my mother. Please show me how to heal.

***

After a long shower, Rick towel-dried his hair. He'd spent that entire Thursday lugging alfalfa bales, off-loading them from the delivery truck and into the barn-length loft above the stalls. Hard work. Dirty work. And hot. At least the load would last well into summer.

Thankfully, Rachel hadn't griped about or tried to wriggle out of her assigned tractor work. Ben had managed the gates, making her trips to the back acreage easier. And he'd rotated horses in the pastures. Scrubbed then re-filled the water buckets like a pro. Even scampered up and down the stairs to the loft, bringing Rick water and root beer and Gatorade.

The little guy was so tired on his first day of summer vacation, Rick knew he'd never make it through a bath after supper. So after pocketing Ben's hearing aid, he hosed off the giggling child in the yard and sent him inside. That boy's laugh contained the purest, most innocent joy Rick had ever heard. A beautiful sound which set the world back on its axis.

Rick exited the bathroom. The bedside lamp cast a soft glow onto the bed where his wife lay, onto his pillow where an envelope

141

waited. Julie must have, at some point, typed a letter to him, too.

He smiled at her. This new Julie—which was really the old, pre-Ben Julie—was the girl he'd married. How he loved her.

He walked to the bed, lifted the envelope. It bore his name.

"You want me to read this now?"

Julie nodded.

He felt the grin spread across his face as he slid under the covers beside her. He drew her close and kissed her.

"I'm so proud of you." He looked into her eyes. "For not letting the injuries beat you. For sending our son into adulthood with the love and support he needs. For telling your mother the truth."

Her eyes left his. Using the envelope, he coaxed her to lift her chin.

"Look at me. I know how hard that was for you. But you didn't do anything wrong. The next move is hers."

His wife's brow furrowed.

"I know. She might stay mad for a long time. Or, she might miss you so bad she starts considering what you said."

Julie shook her head.

"It could happen." He brushed her hair back from her face. "Everything's going to be all right now. Next week your cast will be taken off, and the wires removed."

Her eyes lit with joy.

"I know the record producer hasn't called back yet, but maybe that's a good thing. You needed time to recuperate and take stock. Our family's been through a lot, especially these last weeks. This way there's no deadline. You set the priorities, you set the pace. You can call him when you're ready."

She placed a finger over his lips.

"You want me to stop talking?"

She smiled shyly, pointed to the envelope, and kissed him. Slow.

Soft. And needy.

He opened it, unfolded the single sheet of paper with two print-ed lines in the center. *I love you*. And below that, *Can we make love tonight?*

His wife loved him, wanted him, and needed him. What more could a man want?

"I know this ordeal has been awful. The accident. Sean leaving. You standing up to your mother. But I feel like it's a new beginning for us. One day after Rachel and Ben leave, it will be just us."

She flattened all four fingers of her good hand against his mouth.

"Right. Stop talking."

She grinned, her eyes sparkling like an excited child's. That look, that free, unburdened look usually preceded a laugh; how he'd missed it. And not just since she'd lost her voice. No, if he were honest, her laugh had been rare for weeks, months, even years before the accident. Ben's arrival had derailed her life so abruptly, so completely, and much more so than Rick's.

He laid the letter and envelope on the nightstand, then moved over her. Her right hand skimmed his left shoulder, her fingers grazing the scar. She reared up and kissed the mark. He nibbled her jaw, blew down the side of her neck, knowing she'd shiver at the tickle, and under normal circumstances would've giggled.

"Hm-hm-hmm."

They both went statue still. Her eyes filled with hopeful tears. "Did your voice just come back?"

"Mmmmmm." Her eyes rounded.

"Did you know?"

She shook her head. "It just happened," she croaked.

"Tell me," he said.

"I love you," she answered through her bound jaws.

"I love you, too." He kissed her face, her jaw line, working his way down. "I told you. Everything will be all right now."

Chapter Fifteen

Sunday morning at church Julie greeted people with waves and sign language, still depending on Ben's help in conversations. She didn't want to strain her voice, so she'd told no one it had returned. After church, she found Laurie in the nursery changing Hope's diaper.

"We've got to clean you up before we go eat with Grandma and Grandpa."

"Laurie." Julie spoke through her still-bound jaws, from the doorway.

Her friend turned, eyes wide in her freckled face. "Did you just talk?"

She stepped closer. "Yeah. It surprised me Thursday. I didn't believe it at first."

Steadying her child with one hand, Laurie grabbed Julie's arm with the other. "That's wonderful. This is wonderful, right? And means your vocal cords will be okay?"

"I think so. I'm trying to ease back into using my voice."

Laurie straightened Hope's yellow sundress and placed her child on her hip. "That sounds smart. I think I'd do the same. But, you don't look happy."

"I'm thrilled to have my voice back." Julie paused. "Rick says everything will be all right."

"But you don't think so."

"Something's wrong. I can't figure out what, but something's just not right."

"You mean other than Sean being gone and your mother leaving the way she did?"

Julie nodded.

"You *think* something's wrong, or you *know* it, like, deep in your spirit?"

"I think I know?" She laughed. "That doesn't make any sense, does it?"

"Sure it does. God's stirring up something. What do you think it is?"

"I'm not sure. What do I do?"

"Just listen. He'll tell you. You might not like what you hear—I know I sometimes don't—but He'll tell you."

"I've never felt like this inside before, so I'll take your word for it."

Her uneasiness increased when she left church. She thought about the scriptures Laurie had directed her to earlier that week, about what could be the true source of her disquiet, worried over it on the ride home, all afternoon, and into the evening.

That night, she sat in bed with her Bible in hand, again reading the small book of James, trying to figure out why she felt so unsettled. Was the problem inside her? Between her and Rick? She couldn't tell.

When Rick came to bed after checking the horses, she put the book aside expecting him to comment on her reading and reach for her. He did neither. He turned his back to her and went to sleep.

She awoke Monday morning with a throbbing headache, and sighed at the pain. Her husband had risen before her, which wasn't strange, but for some reason added to her apprehension. The shadow of a new issue had appeared, but she couldn't identify it.

She quickly dressed, hustled herself and Ben through breakfast, figuring she'd let Rachel sleep in on this her first Monday of summer. She opened the dishwasher and found a skillet and plates, evidence of Rick having already made himself an omelet.

"Mom, guess what," Ben said. "Bradley Huggins said the first day of day camp is the most important because that's when we pick teams."

"What kind of teams?"

"I don't know, but I hope Bradley picks me."

She ruffled his hair. "Go brush your teeth. We have to leave soon."

She poured herself a glass of apple juice. Standing by the counter, she inserted a straw and raised the glass to her lips. The back door opened. Rick and Rachel entered, obviously returning from the barn.

Julie motioned at Rachel with her glass. "You've already been helping your dad?"

Rachel avoided her gaze. "Sort of." She walked through the kitchen.

Rick washed his hands in the kitchen sink, barely glancing in Julie's direction. "We'll be ready in a minute."

"Rachel's going with us?"

Rick hesitated. "We'll be dropping her off on the way."

"Dropping her where?"

"I'll explain in the truck."

They now had two stops to make before meeting with the orthopedist. "Will we be on time to my appointment?"

"We'll make it." He strode after his daughter.

They left home a few minutes later. In the front seat, Julie flexed her left hand, anticipating the cast removal, as Ben chattered in the back about all the exciting things he looked forward to doing at day camp. "Daddy?"

"Yeah, buddy."

"Pick me up at three, okay? Not two-thirty because we'll still be playing soccer."

"Will do." He reached over to gently hold the fingers protruding from her cast. "You nervous?"

"A little. Where are we dropping Rachel?"

Julie glanced back to her daughter, who sat behind Rick, staring out the window. On the seat between her and Ben rested the backpack she'd used during the previous school year. What was going on?

She looked at Rick, who still drove one-handed. He took a long nose-breath, then blew it out slowly, something she hadn't seen him do in weeks. They pulled into the parking lot at their first stop.

"Ben? Got your lunch?"

"Yes, Daddy. Bye, Mom."

"Bye, Ben."

Ben exited the truck and entered the building. Rick pulled out onto the highway. He took another long breath.

"Our daughter had some difficulties this year in English."

Julie turned to Rachel. "You didn't say anything."

"She tried to fix it. She went to her teacher. Didn't you, Rachel?"

"When did you ask for help? If you struggled all year—"

"She didn't meet a writing requirement."

"*A* writing requirement?"

Julie looked around. "We're driving to the school."

In the rearview mirror, she stared at her daughter. "You failed English and now have to attend summer school?" She and Rick would be spending most of the summer taking Rachel to school over one assignment?

"She's been diligent, Julie."

How could Rachel have kept this from her? From them?

"She's been steadily working to complete a four-thousand-word journal. She's completed over half, and, yes, they're letting her finish in summer school."

"Rachel, how long have you known this?"

"Since the day of your accident," Rick answered for Rachel.

Then it dawned on her. *She* didn't know about Rachel's failure to complete her assignments, but Rick did. She looked at him. "How long have you known?"

Her husband cleared his throat. "That's tough to say."

"A day? A week?"

He placed both hands on the wheel. "Ah, a few weeks."

"You knew?"

And he'd kept it from her. Was she the odd one out here, too, like she was with her mother in regard to her father?

"Have you grounded her, given her any consequences at all?"

"I moved the manure pile last week," Rachel mumbled.

"That's it?" If her jaw hadn't still been wired shut, she definitely would've ground her teeth.

Rick pulled to a stop in front of the school. "She needs to go now, Julie. Rachel, go on inside."

Her daughter fled. Rick drove on.

"How can you defend her? I do *not* believe this."

She'd thought their marriage, their relationship, had changed for the better over the last weeks. Rick had been loving her and putting her first, even ahead of their daughter, like he used to. She'd thought they'd gotten back what they had in their pre-Ben years.

"You've been covering for her." Julie's voice caught, she could almost feel the tender seam they'd stitched between them rip. "Like you always do. And how is that not *lying* to me?"

***

They waited over an hour at the orthopedist's office. A silent, very uncomfortable hour, before finally being called back for an x-ray, then to an exam room. Dr. Chang had only visited her hospital room once, but Julie definitely remembered the husky Asian man with the kind, wide smile. In less than ten minutes he quickly removed her cast, gave her instructions regarding mobility and skin care.

"Call if you have any problems." Dr. Chang patted her now cast-free hand and left.

They made their way back to the receptionist, where Rick paid her co-pay.

"I'll be outside." Julie walked to the truck and stood waiting, stretching and turning her left hand.

Rick soon followed. He produced his key fob and unlocked the truck. Julie got in without his help as he slid into the driver's seat. "We have to hurry to make it to Dr. Wyman's office on time. But I can do it."

She didn't answer. She couldn't answer. How could Rick betray her like he had? How could he and Rachel have kept this from her, all year and since her accident?

Thirty minutes later Julie sat in a dentist's chair, hands folded, waiting for Dr. Wyman to appear. She heard him whistling his way through the office, hopefully coming toward her. But the Mr. Magoo-looking oral surgeon passed her room for another.

She looked at her husband. Rick hadn't uttered a word since they'd left the orthopedist's. Even now, he simply sat on the bench under the window, flipping through a hunting magazine.

"Aren't you going to say anything?"

His hands stilled. Long seconds passed, then he looked at her. "Like what?"

His hazel eyes weren't cold, exactly, but they were definitely veiled, certainly distant. A roommate look. As if she were someone he tolerated, because he was stuck with her. Where had the Rick of the last few weeks—the loving, attentive, caregiver and lover—gone?

A nurse entered the room. "Julie? Please follow me."

After a round of x-rays of her mouth and jaw, the nurse led Julie back to her room. "The doctor will be with you in a moment."

She climbed back into the dentist's chair. The whistling again caught her attention. She listened, straining to put a name to the tune. She looked heavenward. The theme from *Star Wars*? Really?

True to form, Dr. Wyman entered with a flourish, his knee-length lab coat billowing behind him. His bulldog cheeks shook as he pumped Julie's hand. "Mrs. Matthews. What a delight."

She smiled around her bound jaws. "Nice to see you, Dr. Wyman."

"And you're talking now." He winked at Rick and extended his hand. "Well, that puts a new spin on things, doesn't it?"

Rick stood and accepted the offer. "Sir."

The doctor turned back to Julie. "The films show you're progressing nicely. You've been a good girl, Mrs. Matthews. The bones are still perfectly aligned, exactly how I positioned them during surgery. Jawbones always break in more than one place, yours was broken in three. I'd rather be safe than sorry, so, barring any setbacks, we can probably remove the wires in two weeks. You can set it up with my receptionist on your way out."

"You won't take them off today?" She looked up at the doctor, then over at Rick. "We thought my jaw would heal the same as my arm."

The physician wagged a finger. "It's not that simple. Didn't you read the brochure? At least you've got two out of three problems solved. The cast is off and your voice is back."

He walked to a cabinet by the door, then handed her a brochure from a display.

"We need your jaw bone to be as strong as possible before we remove the wires. For two or three weeks after that, your jaw will only open a little." He reached into a drawer, produced a set of plastic teeth, and used them to demonstrate. "Your ability to chew will return gradually. But with exercises you'll regain full mobility."

He fished in his droopy pocket, and withdrew a set of red, clacking teeth, set them on the counter. Immediately they jumped their way across the surface. Dr. Wyman spread his arms in a grand gesture.

"Just like these! Aren't they great? Any questions?"

"No. No questions," Julie answered.

Rick stood. "Thanks, Dr. Wyman."

"See you in two weeks." Whistling an encore of *Star Wars*, Dr. Wyman left the room.

***

Rachel Matthews, Mrs. Tate's English class, summer session:

Wednesday, June 11:

My mother has gotten her voice back. Hooray, right?

School is now my favorite place again. Despite Britney-the-blonde-bimbo's constant remarks (sorry, Mrs. Tate) about my bra size. Yesterday as we filed out the door for lunch, she actually popped my bra strap from behind, and somehow unhooked it. No one's ever done that to me before, although a couple of stupid boys tried in seventh grade.

I quickly folded my arms across my chest and went straight to the restroom near the cafeteria, thinking I could go in a stall, fix the bra, and still make it to lunch. But plumbers were in there, and the girls' bathroom on this end of the building was closed. Which meant I had to walk all the way to the other end of the building. Only the doors that lead to those bathrooms *lock* behind you when you leave. (This I did not know.)

So I fixed my bra, but got locked out of the building. I had to climb the fence and walk back around the campus.

By the time I got to the lunchroom, lunch period was over. I grabbed some saltine crackers from the condiment table and ate them on the way to my next class.

I know I only have six more weeks of Britney to endure, so that makes it bearable. If I'm smart during these six weeks (like never again standing in front of Britney) I can avoid any further bra mishaps.

Not so with my mother. I'm stuck with her. I'm sure it's only a matter of time before she goes back to her old ways, lying in wait for me every day when I get home from school. She's always been the biggest hypocrite. Sure she sang and smiled at church. But off stage, I felt like she was a hunter and I was the target. I never did anything right. And now that I screwed up English and have to attend summer school she'll probably never be happy with me again.

Before Ben, she used to tuck me in bed at night and sing to me. Sometimes I even sang with her, softly, because I really wanted to hear her beautiful voice. Singing together was like our special thing. She taught me to play "Chopsticks" on the piano, and sometimes she played with me.

But after Ben came all of that stopped. And every time I tried to play the piano, Mom said I did it wrong. I played too loud. I played too fast. Or my hands were in the wrong position. Who cares?

So, I stopped trying to play the piano and started learning about horses from my dad.

No one knows this, but sometimes when I'm alone with the horses, I sing to them. They always listen. And they don't care if I mess up every note.

When Daddy and I talked weeks ago about Mom eventually getting her voice back, he said I should give Mom a chance to change. Now, they're not kissing in front of me anymore; I guess she hasn't.

Chapter Sixteen

The next morning, Rick entered the barn by predawn moonlight. Barn swallows chirped in the rafters, one darted past him, and the horses whinnied as he headed to the tack room then Dutch's stall. He brushed Dutch, admiring the black Morgan, who had one of the finest muscular builds Rick had ever seen.

"Good boy. Let's go for a ride."

He placed a blanket on the horse's back, lifted the saddle into place. Left the horse standing on the concrete walkway in front of the stalls, while he grabbed his hat and a handful of peppermint candy from the tack room. To Dutch, it was never too early to enjoy candy. Rick led the horse out, his hooves clopping. He gave the horse a treat and took one himself. The last few stars faded as he mounted.

They proceeded in near silence over damp ground. The gentle sway, that smooth gait, made Rick smile. The first rays of dawn shot up over the horizon. He adjusted his hat, watched the dew glisten on grass. He pulled the reins and turned south. Just like humans, horses didn't like having the sun in their eyes.

The red shift came first, casting a hazy glow over his land. *His* land. Gone were the high school days of Rick working as a hired hand on Junior Burch's ranch. The days of him and Julie living as newlyweds in an ancient, twelve-by-forty mobile home to the left of the driveway. When old man Burch died, his grieving, childless widow no longer wanted the main house or the land. She up and moved to Kentucky to live out the rest of her life with her spinster sister, and gave Rick the dream of a lifetime.

The red hue burned to an orange slash across the sky as Rick rounded the last fenced pasture. At his command, Dutch picked up his pace, and settled into a steady lope.

Last year, on December 28th to be exact, Rick had mailed the last payment on a fifteen-year mortgage. He owned this land. The home and barn with stables, the pastures, fields, and woods. He'd bought it with blood, with tears, with dreams.

But he'd never dreamed the terrain of his life with Julie would be as treacherous as a minefield.

The last threads of pink speared the sky. Sunlight flashed and the colors of sunrise disappeared. Julie's accident had been just like that, a flash. And everything changed.

Thankfulness that she hadn't died had flooded him. His love for her had surged to the surface of his heart. He'd reached out to love, to help, and she'd welcomed what he offered. Even the way she looked at him had changed. The exasperation that showed he'd been judged and found lacking, had vanished. Real love once again shone in his wife's eyes.

One week had passed since her voice returned. Only seven, twenty-four hour days in almost two decades spent married. Somehow they'd been worse than the last seven years of walking on eggshells. No, walking on shattered glass was more like it. He'd found himself waiting, just waiting and bracing for her to revert back to the person she'd been before the accident.

So he'd pulled back, he knew he had, from her and the closeness they'd regained. A silent Julie, well, he felt safe enough with her. But a Julie who could once again talk ...

"Dear God," Rick reached the corner of his property and spoke to the morning light. "I love her. I would never leave her. But I don't think I can tolerate her cutting me to shreds like she used to."

So where did that leave him? Keeping the peace had always been his goal. Let her talk, let her fuss, end the ruckus quick and easy with silence. If now that her voice had returned, she changed back the way he feared and he spoke up, he'd be forced to deal with the wars he'd worked to avoid for years.

He turned Dutch around. He pulled off his hat, slapped the reins, and spurred Dutch to a full gallop. The animal strained through the morning air, running faster and faster against an invisible competitor.

Rick leaned forward. "Go, boy! No one's holding you back."

He laughed aloud when they finally reached the barn. Dutch was panting and sweaty, his muscles quivering from exertion and delight. Rick dismounted and walked the gelding in. He untacked the horse. Hosed him down, and sweat-scraped him. After a few more candies, he sent Dutch into his stall and filled the horse's water bucket. A distinctive whistle echoed from the indoor arena. Rick strode to the arena gate and saw Angelina.

The dark-haired beauty stood near the far wall beside Godiva, massaging the palomino's huge belly. Rick opened the gate and walked to them, certain Angelina would hear him and turn. But she didn't. Her head was bent, her booted foot tapping the reddish sand as she hummed to her horse. Rick hadn't yet turned on the radio and speakers in the barn. Angelina must be wearing earbuds.

Trying not to frighten her, he made a wide arc and approached from the left. He looked at his watch and entered her line of sight. She glanced up and removed an earbud, but didn't maintain eye contact.

"Six-twenty a.m.?" He ran a hand down the mare's neck. "Anything wrong?"

Angelina shrugged. "No. Not really." She turned away, but somehow a delicate breeze of her perfume blew in his direction. "I just missed her."

"I know folks who sleep in the barn when a horse is close to foaling. Guess you could if you want."

She crossed her arms at her waist and her shoulders shook. Rick had a flashback to Julie and the day he'd found her standing in their bathroom, weeping.

"Hey. She's fine, right? Dr. Bohannon will check her every couple of days if you want."

She shook her head, squared her shoulders, and turned back to him. Her eyes shone with unshed tears. "He performed a sonogram the day before yesterday. Godiva's great, and so is the busy, healthy colt she'll deliver in a couple of weeks."

Rick smiled. Their gazes locked. He stepped closer. "Then may I ask why you're crying?" His hand rose as if on its own determined journey to touch her hair. He clenched his fist and lowered it back to his side.

"I ..." She rolled the gold chains at her neck between her fine-boned fingers. Her voice dropped to a whisper. "Have you ever left your wife?"

He recoiled, but her eyes didn't waver. "What?"

"Like on business trips. Do you leave her alone? Do *most* men leave their wives?"

"I guess a lot of folks travel for work, but I've only done so a few times. Except for sick kids and having babies, we'd spent only a few nights apart until her accident."

Angelina sighed and smiled wistfully. "That's what I thought." Her tone indicated a change of subject. "So, she's fully recovered? Everything's back to normal?"

Rick stepped back. "Yes. She's almost the same as before."

"How long before she can sing again? I've heard her at church. Your wife has a truly beautiful voice."

"Well, her voice is back, but the wires won't be taken off until next week."

Angelina shook her head, still looking straight at him. "Does she have any idea how lucky she is?"

His cell rang. "Excuse me." He strode a few feet away and answered. "Hey."

"You want me to take the kids?"

With her still-bound jaws, she sounded especially snippy. Wasn't that what he expected?

"If they're ready, I can take them," he said.

"I'll do it. See you when you come in for lunch." She hung up.

Rick pocketed his phone.

"I'm holding you up." Angelina led Godiva toward the gate.

He held it open for her. "No. You're not."

She took the mare to her stall, slid the door closed. "You need to go."

"Angelina."

She stopped, standing as still as a doe listening for a predator. What man in his right mind would constantly leave a woman like this alone? If he could, why not take her with him? "You're welcome to stay. *Always* welcome to stay. You're not in my way." He cleared his throat. "But I do have to work. I'll check on you later if you're still here."

He turned and went to the tack room, switched on the radio and the air conditioner. He booted up Julie's computer and checked first the records, then new emails for any changes in diet affecting morning feedings. Satisfied, he pulled supplements from the cabinets and started mealtime. Knowing Angelina would have already fed Godiva, he bypassed her stall. He filled water buckets and felt his mind settle down to daily tasks.

Rick spent the morning with the farrier. Several horses needed new shoes or adjustments to their old ones. Wanting lunch he walked back to the house, noticing Angelina's showroom-new, silver Cadillac Escalade no longer sat near the barn.

Julie stood at the kitchen counter, drinking a smoothie. "We have lots of leftovers."

"That's fine."

"I didn't know what you wanted."

He opened the fridge, removed several plastic containers. "That's okay." His phone rang. "Rick Matthews."

"Mr. Matthews. This is Vice Principal Edwin Larl. I'm wondering if you and Mrs. Matthews could come to my office?"

"Is this about Rachel? Is she all right?"

"Yes. She's fine. But this does concern her. I'm sorry to interrupt your day, but it's important."

"We'll be there shortly."

Rick pocketed his phone and looked at his wife. "That was the vice principal at the school. He needs us to come to his office. It's about Rachel."

"Is she all right? What happened?"

"She's fine. But he wants to talk to us." He slapped leftovers on a plate, heated it in the microwave while he poured a glass of iced tea. "I only need a minute to eat and change shirts."

***

Edwin Larl's office sat on the fourth floor of a hundred-year-old brick building. The old high school now housed the middle school, and as Rick and Julie climbed the "up" staircase, Rick felt as if he'd traveled back in time to his own school days. The same dingy, speckled brown floor tiles edged by the same cracked, black plastic baseboards. The same runny snot-green plaster covered the walls. He thought he smelled the coarse powdered soap that had filled the ancient hanging dispensers, soap which scraped the skin and stung like fire if one's hands were split from tackles or rope burns. Between football practice, 4-H competitions, and rodeos, his hands had been a source of constant aggravation during his entire high school career.

"Mr. Larl didn't say why he needed to see us right away?" Julie stopped at the top of the stairwell and looked at him.

Rick had already answered the same question twice while driving over. Persistence was one of his wife's strongest attributes.

"He didn't say why. He asked if we could come now and I said yes. I don't think he'd have called if it wasn't important."

160

Rick placed a hand at the small of her back and guided her down the long hallway lined with metal lockers, around the corner by the bathrooms—there was that distinct soapy smell—to room 416. The sign on the door said Vice Principal. Rick knocked.

"Come in."

Rick turned the antique, glass doorknob. The wooden door creaked as it swung on large, iron hinges.

From the top of his polished head, to his anchor-tattooed, bulging forearms, to the starched crease of his tan pants, Vice Principal Larl was the epitome of spit and polish. He greeted Rick and shook his hand, nodding to Julie. "Ma'am." He motioned to a pair of chairs directly in front of a battleship-gray desk, and waited until they were seated to seat himself.

"Thank you for coming so quickly." He looked directly at Rick. "Are you aware of Rachel's ongoing assignments? What I mean is, you know she has certain requirements she must meet to advance to ninth grade."

Rick opened his mouth to answer; Julie beat him to it. "Mr. Larl. Rachel spends countless hours on her computer. I'm sure she's completing all assignments."

Again Mr. Larl looked straight at Rick. "Mr. Matthews, your daughter is current with her assignments, one of which is a personal journal of several thousand words. She has almost reached the word length requirement. It's the content that's become an issue."

The vice principal's hound-dog eyes stayed focused on Rick's. Rick's senses perked. He saw experience, kindness, even understanding on the saggy face. The old man was trying to tell him something he didn't want to say in front of Julie.

Beside him, his wife leaned forward. "Mr. Larl. Our daughter doesn't use profanity, or—"

Rick raised a calming hand. "Hold on, Julie. Let him finish."

Mr. Larl leaned back and pulled at an extendable key ring attached to his belt. He unlocked a drawer in the metal desk, removed a large manila file, and handed it to Rick. Julie leaned across her chair to read along.

The first page was labeled JOURNAL. Along with Rachel's name, the teacher's, and the course title, all centered on a field of white. The second page started with the words "I have been told to keep a journal. To express my deepest feelings—like anyone really cares."

Rick felt his eyes narrow. He flipped back to the front to confirm this was indeed Rachel's work, then returned to the second page. The rest of the paragraph had been black-lined, like a top-secret federal document.

The words "I hate middle school. It's all of these girls who are prettier than me" leapt off the page. There was reference to boys on the football team and how boys that age can be such a nuisance. Then more black. The entire last page of that first entry was blacked-out, line by line by line. So was the second entry.

Rick thumbed to another, which referenced science class. "If my new lab partner Britney-the-blonde-bimbo says one more thing about me having a breast reduction and giving her my *extra* ..." The date indicated the entry was written during the regular school term. But Rachel had passed science without issue, so that class was over.

Rick looked up at Mr. Larl. "Rachel's only subject for summer school is English."

The vice principal nodded and his brow furrowed. "That's correct. But the student named there is completing her English requirement as well."

"They're in the same summer class."

"Exactly."

Anger on behalf of his daughter warred with restraint. There was more to this story, he could read it on the man's weathered face like he read fear or calm on a horse's.

"Tell us the rest."

Mr. Larl smiled apologetically. "Mr. Matthews, I appreciate your forbearance. I've heard talk about your way with horses. I had hoped that bone-deep diplomacy would extend to humans. Unfortunately, Rachel records many more instances of, well, harassment."

Julie grabbed the file from Rick's hands. "Someone's been bullying our daughter? For weeks? And it's carried over into summer school?"

"I assure you, the other girl, Britney, is being disciplined.

"Mr. and Mrs. Matthews." The old man addressed them both, but directed his response to Rick. "This is a very delicate situation. Britney is my granddaughter, if you read further, Rachel mentions this. I'm walking a fine line here trusting your discretion. There are private issues within the family causing Britney great distress. My and my wife's best efforts to fill the gaps aren't having the desired effect."

Julie leaned forward. "So she takes out her unhappiness on our daughter?" She turned to Rick. "Why wouldn't she tell us?"

Rick grabbed his wife's hand and she sat back. "Julie, please. Let's listen."

Because that wasn't all. From the look on the old man's face, his off-the-charts level of discomfort, Rick knew there was more. The blacked-out portions must mean something else entirely.

He took a deep breath, retrieved the file from Julie. One thing at a time. "Mr. Larl. Has our daughter retaliated in any way?"

"I'm happy to say, no. And embarrassed to say she tolerated it much longer than she should have."

"Then how did this come to your attention? Did Rachel finally complain?"

The old man paused. "Only in the journal. I admit I didn't want to think this of my own, hurting grandchild. It's taken time, but I've investigated, questioned students. Britney does pick on—"

"Bully." Julie interjected.

Mr. Larl sighed. "Yes, bully. Britney does bully your daughter, and demeans her in front of other students. The teachers in general weren't aware, but her English teacher brought the entries to my attention. Britney is good at being subversive. I'm so very sorry."

Now Rick leaned forward, tapping the file, which now sat on his lap. "Does Rachel know you're telling us? Showing us the journal?"

The vice principal nodded an affirmative. His eyes stayed on Rick's. "We met and discussed the terms of me showing you the journal."

"Do we need to read all of it?"

"That's at your discretion. The school board offers counseling for the victim and family in matters such as this. And, of course, the consequences to Britney are being handled."

Julie crossed her arms. "Why shouldn't we see our daughter's schoolwork? Are there more awful things your granddaughter has done to Rachel that you're not telling us? Is that what those blacked-out sections are?"

The man's eyes sparked, then pleaded with Rick not to question him further. "Mr. and Mrs. Matthews, you have my utmost sympathy. And you're free to examine the rest of the file."

Rick studied Mr. Larl. "We'll take it with us. You'll hear from us soon." He rose, offered a hand. They shook. He ushered a reluctant Julie down the hall. "Wait until we get in the truck to say anything. Then we'll talk."

She hurried down the stairs ahead of him, across the schoolyard to the truck and stood by the door tapping her foot. "Oh, I've got something to say, all right. We're going straight home, and we're going to read every word of her journal on that laptop."

Even on their daughter's behalf, Julie's take-charge tone made him shudder inside as he closed her door and rounded the hood. And Rick wished he could just keep walking. Through the parking lot, down the street, anywhere his wife wasn't.

Chapter Seventeen

Every protective instinct inside Julie was coming to life and flexing its muscles. She thought of the taunts she'd received at school for her name, her size, her weight. The awful experience in gym class when the older girls had marred her clothes. She could *feel* the Mama Bear within standing to her full height, ready to protect and defend.

"I don't think Mr. Larl is telling us everything," she said as Rick cranked the truck. "Don't you think he's hiding something?"

Rick pulled onto the street. "I think we'll have to talk to Rachel to get the whole story."

"Exactly." Julie rested the file on her lap, opened it to read. "She didn't say anything. She just suffered in silence."

She thought again of her own tormenting classmates, and of her mother's unsupportive responses the few times she'd complained.

"How long has she gone to school expecting to be a target?"

"Like I said, we'll have to ask Rachel."

"Did you know?"

He didn't answer.

"Rick, did you know?"

"No."

"Well, that's something at least, unlike her failing English. You two are *such* a pair, I believe that if she wanted you to, you'd keep this from me, too."

"What's that supposed to mean?"

"It means exactly what it means. And here I thought ..."

"Thought what?"

"Nothing. Just ... I can only handle one problem at a time."

She scanned the journal. More than half of the pages were black-lined. "Look at this. I don't trust that vice principal. You know Rachel's computer password, don't you?"

"I have an administrator password, and yes, she left her laptop at home today. I think Mrs. Tate is having them watch a video of a play. Why?"

"Because I want you to access her files so we can read them. That's why."

Rick sighed. "We're definitely back to business as usual, aren't we?"

They arrived home. Julie walked straight to Rachel's room. She sat on her daughter's twin bed and realized the furniture had been re-arranged. One long side of the bed was now pushed against the longest wall. The desk sat with its finished back against the footboard, creating a little alcove in the corner. The entire wall was covered in photos, posters, and magazine articles, all concerning horses. Two huge stacks of horse magazines and a flashlight occupied the nightstand by the bed.

Julie pointed. "Do you think she's read all of these?"

Rick sat at the desk, turned on Rachel's laptop. "Read them? She's memorized them. She knows more about diet and supplements than I do. Are you really going to make me do this?"

"Yes. It's important. We can't let this go."

"This might take a minute. She's got a lot of files in here."

Julie closed her eyes. If Mr. Larl was withholding the full extent of Britney's mistreatment of Rachel ...

She looked at Rick, who was obviously reading.

"Well?" She waited. "Did you find it yet?"

"Yeah." He wiped a hand over his face. "I, uh, found it."

She rose.

He read as she stepped to him, glanced at her, then turned the screen away from her and stood, raising both palms in surrender. "You're not going to be happy after you read this."

She leaned around him to see. "What? There's more, isn't there."

Rick looked at the floor and shook his head. "I'll go pick up the kids."

She glanced at her watch. "You'll be early."

"Yeah. But I think it's best if I leave now." He walked out the door. In the silence, she heard him go back through the house and out to the garage.

"Well, for heaven's sake. So much for follow-through and handling this together."

She took his seat. Turned the screen, read the opening she'd already seen.

I've also been told that even though I have to turn this in at school, my mother will never see it. Otherwise, I wouldn't do it.

Julie's brow furrowed. What did that mean?

But at least when I'm at school I get away from my mother and all her demands and drama.

What? Why would she write that?
She read on.

I could cut my time at home by five, six hours a week, maybe more.

She read on.

I wonder what would upset my mother more, if I actually make the choir, or if I don't?

She won't care. The only singing she cares about is her own.

Julie scrolled up, and reread the last lines. Did Rachel resent Julie's singing? But, Julie remembered singing to Rachel when she was little. Rachel had loved it.

The next entry started on a more positive note.

While cleaning my room tonight, I found a card my mother gave me last February. It says "My heart is happy because you're near. Happy Valentine's Day."

Julie remembered buying the card. The front had a picture of a mother horse and her foal.

She never *sounds* happy when I'm near. She has endless complaints ...

Julie clutched her stomach and stopped reading. This couldn't be true.

It. Could. *Not.* Be. True.

She thought of the file lying on the kitchen table. These were the parts Mr. Larl had black-lined. Julie returned to the beginning, studied the first paragraphs of the first entry.

Rachel had intended Julie to never see this. Ever.

Most of the printed journal was black-lined—

Most of the journal was about *her.*

Ill with dread, she scrolled through more entries. She read about the night Rick brought her home from the hospital. About Clyde Newman's croaky voice, yet kind words. The comparison between Julie's words and Britney's taunts. And Sean telling Rachel "No drill sergeant has *anything* on Mom."

She read to the end, and learned her daughter feared her voice returning, expecting the "old mom" to return with it.

Julie emailed the entire file to herself, then turned off the computer and ran to her room. She opened her Bible to James 3.

Old mom.

"The tongue is a fire ... full of deadly poison ... with it we bless our Lord and Father, and with it we curse people ..."

Deep inside she heard Laurie's words from Sunday. "You *think* something's wrong, or you *know* it, like, deep in your spirit?"

She read the Scriptures again, tears filling her eyes. Had she done to her daughter what her mother had done to her?

No. She loved Rachel. Her only daughter.

This was all a mistake. A misunderstanding between a busy mother and a hormonal, pubescent teenager. Wasn't it? Rachel hardly seemed to listen to her.

The phone rang. Julie answered. "Hello."

"This is Courtney at Dr. Lilly's office. I'm calling to confirm Mrs. Matthews' appointment for Monday morning."

To check the nodules and her vocal cords if her voice hadn't returned. "Actually, this is Julie Matthews. I've gotten my voice back."

"Well, good for you. Dr. Lilly still recommends a follow-up. Will we see you Monday?"

"Can I re-schedule later if I need to?"

"Yes, you could, but you might have to wait a couple of weeks. Dr. Lilly's schedule is very full."

"I'll be there." The nodules must be gone, the damage healed, or her voice wouldn't have returned, right? "And thank you."

She ended the call. A faint rumble vibrated the house, proof the garage door was rising. Which meant Rick, Rachel, and Ben were arriving home. Julie listened. And waited. How long did it take for them to get out of the car and come into the house?

Finally the back door opened and closed. Rick's boots clopped through the kitchen and down the hall. He walked into their bedroom and closed the door behind him.

"I sent Ben to the barn to start chores."

"Good. We can have a good, long talk with Rachel."

"No," he said. "Rachel is going to stay with a friend tonight."

"What? No way is she going to a friend's house when we need to talk."

"She already had your permission to spend tomorrow night with Amber. Amber's mom said she'll take Rachel to school tomorrow and pick her up."

"You didn't tell her we read the journal."

"She's upset enough about Mr. Larl talking to us about the bullying. She's getting her things and I'm taking her to her friend's. We can talk to her about this when she comes home Saturday morning."

Julie stood and walked toward him. "You're siding with her? Why am I not surprised? You always take her side."

Rick blocked her exit. "It's not about sides. It's about me having a couple more nights before my family explodes."

A knock sounded at the door. "Daddy? I'll be in the truck. Bye, Mom."

"I'll be right there," Rick spoke over his shoulder.

"Bye, Rachel. I love you!" Julie called, then lowered her voice. "This isn't right. You and I should have a united front."

"We haven't had a united front since Ben was born."

"What?"

Rick's shoulders slumped as if a heavy burden had just been placed upon him. "I've got to turn in early. I'm up at four tomorrow to deliver a horse to Tuscaloosa. There and back is over eight hours of driving. I'm sorry. I just can't do this tonight."

He opened the door and walked away.

***

She didn't want to think about it. But she couldn't *not* think about it. What Rachel had written in her journals kept Julie awake until the

170

alarm sounded for Rick. She dozed then, and after taking Ben to day camp returned home and went to her desk in the tack room.

She opened her email and re-read Rachel's journal. Fury bubbled inside her at being accused, at being attacked and not given the opportunity to defend herself. Then the anger cooled, leaving behind a bitter ache. How could her baby girl have written those things about her? Rachel didn't really feel that way about her, did she?

Ben was at day camp, Rachel was at Amber's, and Rick was on the road. The morning should have been a lovely, quiet break, a time for her to input more data so she could hand the bookkeeping over to Rick, once and for all. Grateful for the use of both hands, she began updating and double-checking spreadsheets and balance sheets for Matthews Stables.

Then nausea rolled through her stomach, breaking her concentration. Her mind, hard as she tried to keep it on her work, kept darting back to her daughter's journal. The words couldn't possibly be true. Not all of them, anyway.

She dialed the first few numbers to Rick's cell, but couldn't bring herself to complete the call. She swiveled to the stereo behind her, turned on the radio. Stood and grabbed a bottled water from the small fridge, and noticed two boxes of straws sitting there on the counter, just waiting in case she needed them.

How could Rick be so thoughtful about some things, yet seemingly turn off his affection for her without even telling her why? Without even giving her a chance?

She turned the radio off. Turned it on again and searched for a different, non-country music station.

The CD's. Julie opened the desk drawer and there they were, her favorites by Andrea Bocelli, Charlotte Church, Celine Dion, and Josh Groban. She reached back and switched to the CD player, inserted one of Celine's albums, and quickly chose "The Prayer," a duet with Andrea Bocelli.

As always, the orchestral intro was heavenly. Then came the first notes from Celine, the end of the verse, and Andrea's Italian lyrics followed by Celine's English.

Julie turned up the volume and let the notes soar to the rafters and loft. Without fail in the past, this song above all others had made her feel peaceful and calm. The blending of the voices. The build of the orchestra. The seamless beauty of the stringed instruments made Julie's heart sing.

But today she couldn't get past the lyrics. The humility of them. The yearning. The writer's quiet petition for help, as a trusting child would ask, obviously expecting a kind, compassionate answer.

Julie buried her face in her hands, remembering times when the trusting part of her heart had been brutally crushed by her own mother. The most significant time, when she'd been seventeen and only two weeks into her senior year in high school. The art teacher and choir director, Mrs. Dardee, had pulled her aside after a choir rehearsal.

"Julie," she'd said. "Can you come to my office?"

"Yes, Mrs. Dardee." She followed from the high stage on one side of the gymnasium. They walked behind heavy, gold curtains and down creaky, wooden steps to the storage room Mrs. Dardee shared with the band teacher, Mr. Gage.

Ever the southern gentleman, Mr. Gage stood when they entered. "Ah, Mrs. Dardee, you brought our prodigy." He motioned to a folding chair beside a row of four metal file cabinets. Julie sat.

"Did you tell her?" Although Mr. Gage looked at Julie, she knew he spoke to Mrs. Dardee. "Of course, you didn't." Behind his silver spectacles, Mr. Gage's eyes smiled. He leaned back against his desk.

Mrs. Dardee shuffled over in her polyester pantsuit, a piece of paper in her hand.

"I can only stay a few minutes," Julie said. "My mom will wonder why I'm not home on time."

"Of course," Mr. Gage said. "This is what we wanted to show you. We believe you can win."

Mrs. Dardee handed her a flyer about a singing contest. Participants were required to sing an original song. The grand prize was a scholarship to the finest vocal institute in New York.

Despite her mother's lack of encouragement, Julie spent the following weekend at Sharon's, sitting at Rick's mom's piano and working on her song. The final version spoke of how she knew God saw her, heard her, watched her, and paid attention to every detail of her life. And how that knowledge gave a feeling of safety, of security, of peace.

Desperate for her mother's support, for the first time Julie shared with her mother one of her songs, "When I Sing to You." *In my dreams I sing to you and watch you smile at me ...*

"The tune is pretty, but I don't think you'll win with words like that," her mother said. "I sure will be glad when you finish this God-seeking phase and face the real world. You'll never be famous writing and singing songs like that."

"I wasn't trying to get famous," Julie answered quietly then went to her room.

She'd known her lyrics were primitive and simple, but that was *her* on the page. She'd written her heart. Couldn't most people relate to wanting to feel safe, wanted, and loved?

With fluid grace Celine and Andrea changed keys, the song built further, then they sang the last perfect notes. Without doubt, the song wouldn't be nearly as beautiful with different words. Children and adults alike wanted to feel safe in their world, their lives. Did Rachel really not feel safe in hers?

"Did your taste in music change overnight, Rick? Where's Johnny Cash?"

Julie looked up. Angelina Rousseau stepped into the open doorway, looking like she stepped off a magazine cover.

"Oh, Julie. Um, is Rick here?"

"How long have you been here?" She'd thought she was alone.

"I'm sorry," Angelina answered. "Rick said I could come anytime, since Godiva's so close to foaling."

Julie stood. "Sure, sure. Rick's on the road. He sold a horse to a breeder in Tuscaloosa. He's delivering it today."

Angelina entered the tack room. "That's right. Yesterday he said he'd be gone today."

"Yesterday?" Had Rick talked to Angelina before or after the trip to see Mr. Larl at the school?

"Well, I did see him here yesterday morning, but he told me last night. I was here again when he brought in the horses just before sundown."

Rick had indeed brought the horses in a little early, then set the alarm clock for 4 a.m., and gone to bed without speaking to Julie.

"You know, Rick is just the nicest man. In the middle of all the chaos your family has been through, with your accident and you in the hospital, then your mother visiting and your son graduating, he still took the time to help me and my horse."

"I didn't think you boarded here before my accident."

"I didn't. I showed up the Saturday you were in the hospital, and practically begged Rick to let me bring Godiva here. Had to bribe him with a check." She smiled, showing perfect teeth. "Three months' rent. That's how I ended up here on the night of your son's graduation. But Rick just moved Dutch and made room. He really is the nicest man."

"My husband won't be back until late tonight."

Her husband. Who was out of town and not speaking to her right then, but was apparently very comfortable talking to Angelina. Julie knew she'd always been intimidated by beautiful women, but her current unease went beyond self-consciousness about her appearance. Considering the conflict between her and Rick, could this woman be a real threat to her marriage?

"He doesn't leave his horses quickly, even when he knows they're going to a good home. Ben and I will be doing the night feeding." Julie took a breath. "Is there anything I can help you with?"

Angelina backed away, playing with the gold necklaces dangling at her throat. "No. I only wanted to tell him Dr. Bohannon said Godiva should deliver in the next two weeks." Her eyes sparkled like buffed black onyx. "I'm so excited and nervous, like I was the one having a baby."

Julie looked at the enormous diamond on Angelina's left hand. "Do you and your husband have children?"

"No. We, Nicholas has a very demanding job."

Julie bet it was. "What does your husband do?"

"He's an efficiency and productivity expert. He consults for companies all over the world."

No children and her husband was gone a lot.

Angelina pointed to the stereo, from which Celine Dion's voice continued to flow. "You're working. I should go."

Julie sat, folding her hands on the desk. "I'll tell Rick about the foal."

Although Angelina left the room, Julie couldn't shake the feeling another woman was making herself at home in the stables.

Chapter Eighteen

Early Saturday morning, Rick lay awake by Julie.

They'd barely spoken the day before. She hadn't called him, and he hadn't called her until construction delays on I-65 meant he wouldn't get home when anticipated. When he finally arrived, he found her asleep on the couch with the television volume on low. He nudged her along to bed. His head barely hit the pillow before sleep claimed his mind.

Now daylight was just peeking in past their bedroom curtains. Rick heard a knock at their door. He rose and crossed the room. The knock could only come from Ben.

He opened the door. "Hey, buddy." The child greeted him with the cough of an eighty-year-old asthmatic.

Julie woke instantly. "That doesn't sound good."

In typical summer flu fashion, the little guy was too congested to breathe through his nose. Rick placed a hand on Ben's forehead. "I think he's got a low fever. You feel miserable, buddy?"

Ben nodded.

Wrapped in her robe, Julie bundled Ben back to his bed.

"I'll feed the horses." Rick went to the barn. Later he found Julie in the kitchen, drinking a smoothie, and cooking his breakfast.

"Pretty late when you got home last night."

"Yeah. They're redoing bridges from Montgomery down below Greenville. Complete stops with detours off then back on at the interchanges. Lots of upset truckers out there last night."

"I suppose so. Guess I won't be going with you to pick up Rachel at Amber's this morning." She paused. "I need a few things from the store. For Ben."

Oh, he hated this. The look from her that said the explosion was simply delayed, not diffused. "Maybe it's better to talk with her at home than in the truck."

"You mean, so she can go in her room and pout?"

"No, I mean so I'm not driving and trying to—" Rick took a deep breath. "Never mind. Give me the list. I'll get them after I get Rachel."

Twenty minutes later, he picked up Rachel.

"Did you have fun at Amber's?"

"I *always* have fun at Amber's. We take over the family room, dancing and singing with a game on her Kinect. Her mom dances, too." Rick glanced over, caught Rachel rolling her eyes, but smiling. "Amber's mom is a riot. She teaches ballet, so she can stand on one leg and put her other foot behind her head. It's a little freaky."

"I imagine so."

He shouldn't be thinking what he was thinking. That a part of him wanted to keep driving and avoid what awaited him at home. He could always move into the barn for a while, and pretend that's where he needed to be until Godiva dropped her foal.

"Ben's running a fever. Gotta make a stop."

The grocery store parking lot was a war zone, but at least the list was short: cans of chicken soup, a gallon of Gatorade, and two boxes of popsicles—but no "Family Repair Kit."

He placed the bags in the back floorboard and climbed in behind the wheel. He exited the parking lot and reached across the front seat to wrap her hand in his.

"Daa-ddy." She gave that half-blush, killer smile. "Are you missing Sean or something?"

"Or something," Rick said. He purposely hadn't brought up school or Mr. Larl. Rachel knew they'd been told about Britney's bullying her, but she didn't know they'd seen other parts of her journal.

"Me, too."

They passed Angelina's home on Plantation Road. "Back there's where Mrs. Rousseau lives," he said.

"It's already cross-fenced. Why does she board with us?"

"Don't know. I guess she's only got the one horse."

"She has really nice clothes."

They passed cow pastures and fields. Rick pulled into the driveway and stopped beside Nathaniel Jordan, who appeared to be leaving in his doctor-beige Volvo. They each lowered their windows.

Rick motioned with his chin. "You been up to ride Trident?"

"Yeah. First time I haven't had a Saturday morning call in almost a month. How's Julie doing?"

"She's okay. She's good." He shifted into park. "Got the cast off this week, but not the wires."

"Broken jaw is a nasty injury. Can't rush the recuperation there. Like after childbirth. Some patients push themselves too hard, do too much, return to work too soon. They always pay for it. Makes the recovery even longer."

"I guess you'd know."

Nathaniel laughed, scratching his receding hairline. "Seeing how I delivered half the kids in town, I guess so. Can't believe Sean's graduated and gone like that."

"Knocks me back sometimes."

"Saw the extra lock you put on Trident's stall. Good call. Do I owe you?"

"Naw. You sure could stud him, though. That boy's got one and only one thing on his mind."

Nathaniel leaned back against the headrest. "I hadn't considered that. Is there money in it?"

"Sometimes good money. Or, you could stud him with someone you know, have them train the offspring and sell them." Rick caught himself, then cocked his head, thinking of the pretty mares he'd bought at the beginning of spring. "You interested? We could have our own horse factory going up there."

"I just might be," Nathaniel said. "Hey, I gotta run. First day off with the wife in a while. Working together all the time just ain't the same as a date, you know?" He shifted his car back into gear. "FedEx truck delivered a while ago. Long, thin boxes. I had the guy stack 'em in the barn on the concrete rather than outside on the dirt."

"Thanks. I appreciate it."

"See ya."

Rick nodded. "Later." Nathaniel drove away. "Must be the stall mats. We've got our work cut out for us to change out all of those."

Rachel moaned. "Daddy, do we have to?"

"Yes, we do." And if that was the worst thing he had to look forward to for the next few days, he'd be a happy man.

He parked in the garage. Julie met him at the kitchen door, took the bags he carried as Rachel trailed behind.

"Ben started vomiting, so I won't fix him any soup yet. I have him settled in front of the television. He's half asleep. We should talk in our room."

"Daddy?" His daughter asked with panic in her eyes.

"It'll be okay, Rachel," he squeezed out the words as they followed Julie down the hall.

"But I didn't mean to get Britney in trouble. I wasn't trying to get Britney in trouble. Everything I put in there was true; a few more weeks of class and I won't have to see her anyway."

Julie ushered them in—Rick couldn't help thinking *executioner-style*—and closed the door behind them. "This is about much more than Britney."

Rachel backed against the wall beside the door and folded her arms. "Mr. Larl made Britney apologize. She even got suspended for three days, and she's not allowed to sit by me or talk to me. I didn't do anything wrong."

Julie seemed to soften. Her face relaxed, she walked to the bed, sat on the edge, and lowered her voice. "No, Rachel you didn't do anything wrong as far as Britney was concerned, except not telling anyone she was bullying you. Why didn't you tell us?"

Rachel looked at the floor, then again at Rick. "Daddy?"

"It's a good question, Rachel."

"I, Britney didn't come to our school until right before Mom's accident. I didn't want to bother you."

"Didn't you know we'd help you?" Julie asked.

"I thought I could handle it myself."

Julie turned to Rick. "Do you believe her?"

"Julie, please."

"No, Rick," she said through her clenched teeth. "I want to know if you believe that's the reason she didn't tell us what was going on."

"We read the other parts of the journal, Rachel."

His daughter's mouth fell open and she looked at her mother then back to him. "Mr. Larl promised me!"

"I have the password to your computer, remember?"

Her eyes widened. "You couldn't. You *wouldn't*." Tears bubbled in his daughter's eyes. "Mrs. Tate promised me no one else would see it. She said everything I wrote in my journal was safe." Her voice hitched. "And private."

"We could. And we did." Julie stood. "Now, Rachel—"

"Okay," Rick said. "Your mother and I will talk about this further later."

"We'll talk about this now, because Mrs. Tate and Vice Principal

Larl, and heaven only knows who else have read the horrible things you wrote about me. Rachel, why would you write those things?"

"Because it's true! That's how you make me feel."

"I did not change into a monster after Ben was born."

"I didn't say you're a monster, but you did change."

"That's ridiculous. I still loved you. I'll always love you. Every family makes adjustments after the birth of a child—"

Rick stepped between them. "Julie, that's enough."

"See, you never listen to me. Before Ben came you tucked me into bed every night. You sang to me. You were teaching me to play the piano."

"I would never hurt you on purpose. It wasn't like I rejected you—"

"Hey!" Rick yelled. "I said that's enough."

He looked from his wife to his daughter, knowing reaching for either of them, holding either of them would only make the rift wider.

Rachel wiped her face with her hands. "Fine. She's right, I'm wrong. I'm to blame. I'm always to blame."

Rick slid his handkerchief out of his back pocket, handed it to Rachel. "You are not to blame. But I do need to talk to your mother alone." He lifted her chin, looked directly into her eyes. "You're not in trouble."

"She's not in trouble?" Julie asked. "Of course not. It's two against one, and I'm the *one*."

He silently opened the door, sent his daughter out and closed it quietly. Then he rested his forehead against the cool wood.

He turned and looked at his wife, his back against the door. *Dear God, how did this happen to my family?*

"If I changed after having Ben, it's because I didn't have a choice. I had to change to survive."

Julie motioned between them. "We weren't supposed to have any more children. But once he was born, what was I supposed to do?

Give him away? Not care for him? Listen to the doctors who said he'd never have a normal life, put him in a special school somewhere and forget him? I did everything I was supposed to for him, because he was my baby. I love him. How could I not? I love all our children."

Now his wife was crying, too. To think before Julie's accident, Rick had thought all he and Julie needed was a little time alone, kind of a second honeymoon, to rekindle their love. Could he have been more wrong?

"I didn't mean to stop doing things for Rachel. But I did mean to do more for Ben than some mothers would. And somehow she's holding that against me?"

"Yes, you did do everything necessary for him and more." Rick used the same gesture. "And it cost us. It cost you."

"Don't put my dream of singing in the same column with a cancelled vacation or postponing the purchase of a new vehicle."

"I'm not. I said nothing of the kind. I know what singing meant to you then. I know what it means to you now. But we've got a problem here, and you starting a singing career won't take care of it."

"Rachel's surreptitious behavior and her journals are the problem."

"No, the problem is that I started defending you to myself."

His wife's eyebrows rose. "What?"

How could he even begin to explain that all three of them were right—probably—and all three of them were partially wrong, if he couldn't figure out the intricacies himself?

He raised both hands as if holding back a flood, although he knew doing so wouldn't hold off the disaster descending on his family.

"Think back, Julie. Think about the reason you wrote Sean the letter you did. The reason you wrote to your mother and the things you said to her in your letter. You want to know why Rachel didn't stand up for herself against that bully Britney? Everything you say to her is exactly like the things your mother says to you. She practiced being a victim by living with you."

And, God forgive him, Rachel might have learned to be a victim by watching his daily example.

Rick rubbed a hand over his face. Everything he'd done to keep peace, to be a buffer, had just come back and slugged him. Looking at his wife now, he knew he might have just broken her heart.

"I've got work to do." He left the room, because facing the conflict and her pain was something he simply wasn't strong enough to do.

He found Rachel sitting at the bar in the kitchen, eating dry cereal. She and Julie disliked milk.

"You'll need more than that for what we've got ahead of us."

Rachel's eyes rounded. "Is Mom right behind you?"

Rick removed the iced tea from the fridge, poured himself a tall glass, and drank more than half of it. "I don't know. How fast do you want to get out of here?"

She slid off the stool. "Pretty fast."

"Then help me pack food to take with us to the barn. We'll stick it in the fridge down there."

Rachel quickly dumped her cereal in the garbage and filled plastic containers with what they'd need—roasted turkey, lettuce leaves, slices of tomato. Rick grabbed two grocery bags, and stuffed one with a package of whole wheat sandwich buns, an unopened jar of salad dressing from the pantry, plastic utensils, and a roll of paper towels. The other he filled with Rachel's sandwich fixings, four garnet apples, and a family size bag of Cheetos, his and Rachel's favorite. They were messy, but who cared?

As he and his daughter strode to the barn, an atypically cool summer drizzle laced the air. With the overcast skies and clouds just heavy enough to keep the mist coming, working all day in the barn would not only be peaceful, it could be downright pleasant. Even though he'd lost part of the morning, they'd probably get at least a dozen stalls cleaned and scraped, and new mats laid before sundown.

They stowed their food in the tack room. Rick sat the Cheetos on the counter, opened them and helped himself. With a timid grin, Rachel slid her hand into the bag. They each popped the top on a root beer and chugged.

The sprinkle outside kicked up to a spattering rain, heavy drops plopped on the barn's tin roof, creating a soft roar of background noise. He turned on the radio, just as Blake Shelton's "Don't Make Me" begged the woman he loved to reconsider her way of thinking. If Rick remembered correctly, the song's music video showed rain pouring both outside and inside the couple's home.

"We'll start at the far end, work our way down." He licked orange powder from his thumb. On impulse he turned off his cell and sat it on the counter. If anyone needed him at the barn, well, he was already here.

Steady footsteps drew his attention to the doorway. Angelina Rousseau leaned against the frame. "Hi, Rachel. Daddy got you working out here on a rainy Saturday?"

"Sort of."

"Hey, Rick. I don't see Ben."

Rick wiped orange fingers on his jeans. "Ben's a little under the weather. Summer flu."

"How'd your trip go?"

Her subtle yet unique vanilla scent mixed with a fresh rain breeze, wafted past his daughter and right to him. "My trip?"

"The horse you sold. Tuscaloosa?"

Had that been only yesterday? Rick felt he'd aged a year in the past twenty-four hours. "Right. It was fine."

"I should've warned you, the interstate's a mess. Nicholas gripes about it every time he drives north of Montgomery. Which is pretty often."

Rick lifted his root beer. "Can I get you something? You know you can help yourself when you're here, right?"

"Oh, thanks. Good news about Godvia, huh? I came to give her another massage."

Rachel's ears perked. "You're certified?"

Angelina laughed, a long, husky roll. "No. But I learned from a certified therapist who often visited where I used to board her. I watched, asked questions, and I learned."

Rick caught Angelina's eye. "Sure you don't want anything?"

"No, thanks."

"What's the news on Godiva?"

"Dr. Bohannon said two weeks tops. He said I shouldn't worry unless she goes past the end of the month. I saw Julie yesterday, didn't she tell you?"

Rick shook his head. "No. She didn't."

Rachel donned her boots and gloves. "Are you going to do the massage now? Can I watch?"

"Sure."

Rick folded his arms. "Rachel, I need your hands today."

"Right." His daughter sighed so dramatically, he almost laughed.

Angelina bit her bottom lip. "Well, if I helped you two, maybe your dad would give you a break later and you can watch me massage Godiva."

Rick gestured at her clothing. Yet another silk blouse, perfectly tailored jeans, and boots priced about the same as a compact car. "You can't work in those. They'll be ruined."

She stepped into the tack room. "The boots are durable. You can't hurt alligator." She plucked at her blouse. "I have two dozen of these."

"Wait." Rachel dug in the cabinet behind Julie's desk, then held up a baby blue T-shirt that read *Matthews Stables*.

"Remember these, Daddy? From the parade we rode the horses in last year. Mrs. Rousseau can wear this."

She turned to Angelina. "You can change in the bathroom and drape your blouse over the desk chair. I even have extra gloves."

"I've got my own gloves in my locker, but since you insist I'll try the shirt."

Rick folded down the top of the Cheetos bag, pushed it against the back of the counter, as Angelina took the tee from Rachel.

"I'll go muck the arena." Rachel darted out the door.

Rick motioned to the cotton shirt in her hands. "You really don't have to do this."

She shrugged. "I've got nowhere else to be."

Like they had the other morning, those dark eyes seemed fixed on his. With sincerity and trust, rather than the judgment and anger he'd walked away from in his bedroom. Rick shook his head, shot his empty drink can over the desk to the garbage pail near the door.

"Two points." He jerked a thumb toward the back corner of the tack room. "You know where the bathroom is."

To his amazement, at his direction they easily established a system. Angelina led a horse out to the arena while he and Rachel mucked the stall. Together they removed the old mat and loaded it onto his flat-bed trailer. He hosed down the stall, the girls installed the new mat, and they started again.

At mid-afternoon they took a break for lunch, and settled in the tack room with filthy clothes but freshly-washed hands. WCIK serenaded them as they ate off paper towels and crunched crisp apples.

"Boss man," Angelina teased, "you've got orange-Cheetos lips."

"I'm not the only one." He pointed at her.

"Okay," said Rachel. "Worst country song ever."

"Bubba Shot the Jukebox," said Rick.

Rachel laughed. "Like the one at the diner?"

"Yes."

"That's dumb," answered Rachel.

"You asked."

She cut her eyes at him, then at Angelina. "Achy Breaky Heart."

Angelina wiped her mouth with a paper towel. "I have to admit, Billy Ray Cyrus did have some moves." She paused. "I rather liked 'Did I Shave My Legs For This?'"

Rick almost choked.

Rachel laughed so hard she hiccupped. "That's not a song."

Angelina smiled. "Yes, it is."

Rick's gaze locked with Angelina's again. She'd done something different with her make-up today, something shimmering that made her eyes sparkle. Her hair still had a silky shine despite their hours of sweaty work. The T-shirt fit her very nicely, too—

Stop it, he told himself. He closed his eyes in shame.

Later as they finished the tenth stall, Rick's back threatened to freeze up. Though he'd done the heaviest work, he knew the girls had to be hurting, too.

"Ladies, let's stop for the day." He leaned on his shovel.

"Finally." Rachel moaned. "I need another water. Anybody else want one?"

Rick and Angelina declined. Rachel went to the tack room.

"You didn't have to work like this," he said to Angelina.

"It was fun."

"I feel like I should give you a break on the boarding fee."

"Rick, stop. I would've been alone at home." She removed her gloves and seemed to look straight to his soul. "Your daughter's a treasure. And friendship like this, it's priceless."

"Sun's about to go down. I need to get started on the evening feedings. Rachel doesn't have to help me. She can watch you give Godiva a massage, if you still don't mind."

"I don't mind her at all."

"Goodnight, then." He left her standing by Godiva's now clean stall.

Later that night, Julie was already asleep when he showered off the grime of the day, and rid himself of the smell of sweat and horse dung. But more than once he had to shake Angelina's lovely scent from his mind.

Chapter Nineteen

In the grass parking lot of The Barn Church, Julie pulled her car farther into the implied space between two other vehicles. Rick had stayed home to tend Ben, and give her some time away from the vomiting and moaning. Of course, Rachel stayed home, too. Apparently she worked so hard yesterday she could hardly get out of bed.

The ancient double doors stood wide open. Wiry Clyde Newman stood on one side of the doorway offering his hand. Deacon Floyd—Clyde's polar opposite in appearance—manned the other side. The deacon's broad, welcoming smile shone brightly in his big, black face atop his bulky shoulders and frame. Julie had always thought him to be one of the kindest people she knew, with his quiet voice and steady rhythm of speech. How did someone get to be that calm? That patient and easy-going?

His children are grown, she thought. *And, he's not a mother. Or a wife. He has a wife.*

But Laurie was a wife, and mother, and she had a calm, caring manner. Was it simply personality? Would it last when Hope became a teenager?

Julie shook both Clyde and the deacon's hand as she entered the sanctuary. The choir rows were filling up. A few members spotted her and waved. She waved back, continuing up the side aisle. She scanned the audience for Laurie, but saw only Pierce. He motioned her over and shook her hand.

"No Matthews troop this week?"

Julie shook her head.

"Still not sharing about your voice returning?"

She hadn't realized she didn't answer him with words. "Guess I'm a little self-conscious about talking through gritted teeth. At times it sounds so mean."

"So that's what I've been doing wrong when I preach."

Julie laughed. "Is Laurie here?"

"In the nursery. Hope's teething and not liking it one bit. Laurie's trying to calm her before service starts."

"Thanks. I'll find her."

"Sure."

Julie made her way to the back of the building. The huge, old barn was open to the rafters in the sanctuary at the front. But the rear of the building had a ceiling of normal height in the nursery, classrooms, and offices.

She leaned in over the open Dutch door. Laurie sat in a rocking chair at the far end of the room rocking a half-asleep, sniffling Hope. "There's my angel. I know, those nasty teeth. But you can't eat pizza without them."

Julie reached over and unlatched the door. "Hey. Is this a bad time?"

"No, she's nursed and burped. We're in the home stretch now."

Julie walked over and sat in the rocking chair next to Laurie's. "Ben's still got the flu."

"It's going around. Probably won't be anyone else in here all morning. Isabella came in for a minute, just to use the changing table. She and Luke are getting married soon."

Hope blinked at Julie with her daddy's blue-glass eyes.

"Pierce said she's teething."

"Four at one time across the top. Her bottom's raw from diarrhea with it. Cries every time she pees 'cause it burns. I'm coating her with ointment, but she's just plain miserable." She kissed her daughter's blonde head. "Aren't you, baby?"

As if on cue, Hope took a stuttering breath. Julie watched as the child relaxed and finally let her eyes close.

"There she goes," Julie said.

"Thank heaven. I was up with her all night. She's been a pretty easy baby until now, but nothing comforts her. She has to wear herself out with anger and tears before she'll sleep. And she wants to be held all the time." Laurie laughed. "I practically live in my nightgown. I think this is the first time I've had on real clothes all week. But how are you? Bet you're enjoying life without the cast."

Julie flexed her left hand. "Definitely a plus. And the voice has stayed. Another plus. I'll have the wires for five more days, until Friday, but who's counting?"

"Life's a wonder, isn't it? You think you're sailing smooth, then *boom!* Nothing's like you expected. All my life I'd wanted to be a mother. I had no idea how I'd yearn for a dry bra and adult conversation." She laughed.

"Can I ask you something?"

"Absolutely."

"It's pretty personal."

Laurie stopped rocking. "Please don't treat me like the pastor's wife. We're friends. Nursing a baby is the most natural thing, but I wouldn't have had a clue how to survive those first few weeks of exhaustion and knots and bleeding scabs without you. I'm a little worried about her having teeth." She resumed rocking.

"There are ways to deal with that, too. Call me anytime."

Muted strains of the choir's opening song marked the beginning of the service. Laurie laid her hand over Julie's on the armrest. "Bet you're anxious to get back up there."

She was, but she wasn't. Rick's comment *we've got a problem here, and you starting a singing career won't take care of it* had her insides tied in knots.

"So," Laurie said, "you wanted to ask ..."

"Have you always been this nice? This caring and nurturing?"

Laurie smiled. "Pierce would say it's my personality, and that's what drew him to me when we met in college. Empathy's my strong suit, but the flipside is I can get my feelings hurt pretty badly if I had my heart set on something."

"Which is what happened when you got pregnant with Hope." Julie considered for a moment. "But you didn't know you had that weakness. I mean, until you found yourself in that situation, you didn't know your marriage could be that vulnerable."

"Oh, it was vulnerable all right. And you're a hundred percent correct that my pregnancy put both mine and Pierce's weaknesses in the spotlight, so to speak."

Laurie carefully stood. "Lower that bedrail, will you?"

Julie obliged. Laurie lay down her daughter, covered her with a blanket, and raised the side back into place. In deep sleep, Hope's baby-pink lips mimicked sucking and tiny bubbles formed at her mouth. Both mothers returned to their seats and rocked, each chair creaking its own, distinct rhythm.

"You've tip-toed around whatever's bothering you, and now you're stalling." Laurie closed her eyes. "If you don't start talking I'm likely to fall asleep and drool on myself like Hope is."

"You know about the accident. And the producer from Nashville. When I was in the hospital I was so angry and scared. I felt so alone. Then Rick started taking care of me." She felt a tiny blush rise. "It felt like when we were first married. It felt like before Ben was born."

"Every woman likes to be pampered and babied sometimes. Nothing wrong with that."

Julie looked down at her hands. "But this was more. There was distance between me and Rick that I didn't let myself recognize and admit."

Laurie nodded. "And during your recovery you saw the difference between the two."

"Exactly. But now I realize Rachel was as affected by Ben's arrival as I was."

She told Laurie about Rachel's journal. Her voice quivered as she shared Rick's reaction, and how her marriage seemed in worse condition now, than it had before the accident.

"Remember that feeling I had that something wasn't right?"

"Yes."

"This was the cause. Rick didn't know about the journal entries, but he knew Rachel felt this way about me. As soon as my voice returned, I felt the change in them."

Laurie looked over at her sleeping child. "Which must hurt you pretty badly. If I hurt my daughter that way, even if it was a misunderstanding, I'd want her to tell me. Although it would be hard to hear. I can't promise I'd take it well."

Julie stopped rocking. "But what if what she thought about you wasn't true? She's convinced I changed after Ben was born, that I stopped loving her, caring about her, listening to her."

"Forgive me, Julie, but you just finished telling me how different your marriage was before Ben. Isn't it possible Rachel's life changed as much as yours? Did you ever explain things to her?"

"I couldn't explain them to myself. I was barely *surviving*. Ben was a surprise—I think I told you that—but I did love him. Caring for him, doing everything to keep him alive and fed and healthy was never in question. But I was drowning."

Her eyes watered and she gulped. "Having a cleft palate, every feeding was a risk he'd choke and turn blue. With the apnea, he frequently stopped breathing while sleeping."

"I can't imagine the stress you were under."

"My entire life changed focus in a heartbeat. The goal of every day, every hour, every minute, was keeping Ben alive until the surgical reconstruction of his palate. After that, it was constant ear infections, learning of his permanent hearing loss. Surgery last summer to repair his eardrum. Rick's been building the business to pay for insurance and the bills. There's been no time to do anything else."

"Except what had to be done the very next minute." Laurie reached for her hand. "You didn't throw your daughter by the wayside. Life put you in an impossible position. That crisis is over, but you're still left with the fallout."

"According to her journal I constantly snap at her."

Tears, which had puddled in her eyes, spilled over. Julie let them fall as she looked at her friend.

"Laurie, I'm afraid she's right. I didn't think about it before, but now I see I barked orders to get our family through another day, sometimes another minute. I didn't even think about not tucking her in bed after Ben was born. And I did stop singing to her and teaching her how to play the piano. But I never said to Rachel the things my mother said to me."

Laurie's eyes shone with sympathy. "No, my friend, I think you say completely different things to your daughter. Yet you both have deep wounds from your mothers. If you don't heal the relationship, you'll lose your daughter like your mother has lost you."

"I used to get so angry, so frustrated with doctors and therapists who said Ben would never be able to function in the real world."

"Are you angry and frustrated now?"

"I'm ashamed to say part of me still is, because of the accident. And these stupid wires."

"The wires would frustrate any breathing person. Though you do look fabulous."

"Twenty-four pounds. I've lost twenty-four and a half pounds. I'm in a size fourteen for the first time since I got pregnant with Ben."

"Which should have made your mother extremely happy with you."

Julie laughed. "My mother's never happy with me."

"Because she's unhappy inside. There's a great verse in Luke. Chapter six I think, you'll have to look it up. Jesus talks about how we all speak from the abundance of our hearts. Your mom's unhappy inside, so unhappiness comes out of her."

"I don't like the frustration that's inside me, Laurie. The anger. I'm afraid over the years it's all come out at my daughter, and I didn't even realize it was there."

***

Julie eased off the gas and turned in at her driveway. Her stomach fluttered and her heart pounded, the way she imagined they would if she were on her way to perform at a sold-out arena.

She walked into the house. Rick sat at their butcher-block table, reading the Sunday newspaper.

"I thought you'd be watching the NASCAR pre-show."

"I'll have to listen to it in the barn. The farrier's on his way. Trident won't put weight on his back right hoof today." He continued reading, not looking at her. "Ben hasn't thrown up any more, but he hasn't eaten anything either."

"And Rachel?"

"Rachel's doing her homework in the tack room."

She waited, but he still didn't look in her direction. "Thanks for staying with Ben so I could go to church."

"What did Pierce talk about this morning?"

She walked over and sat directly across from him. He simply turned the page of the sports section.

"I don't know. I spent the morning talking with Laurie about the situation with Rachel. I needed another woman's perspective."

Finally he looked at her. "As opposed to my perspective. She's our daughter, but you'd rather get advice from a friend than listen to me."

"I didn't mean it that way." He knew how hard making friends was for her in the first place. Did he really resent her asking their pastor's wife for help?

Rick rose from his seat, went to the fridge, and refilled his tea glass.

"Rick, I didn't mean it that way."

He gulped the drink and set his glass by the sink. "I'll be at the barn."

"You don't understand."

"I understand perfectly. I'm an idiot, and we're back to business as usual."

"I'd like to talk to her tonight." She turned to watch him walk to the mud room, where he donned his boots and hat. "I'd like to talk to Rachel. Both of us, together."

He didn't answer. He left, closing the door quietly behind him.

"I'd like to fix this," she whispered.

"Mom? Mommy?" Ben sounded groggy and weak.

She went to the family room where he lay watching the pre-show for the race.

"Can I have some chocolate triangle toast?"

Julie knelt in front of him, brushed his matted hair and felt his forehead. "I think your fever's finally broken. You're hungry?"

"I didn't ask Daddy for chocolate triangle toast. Only you know how to make it."

A secret recipe, she'd told him after his last surgery. Bread lightly toasted, crust removed, covered with a light layer of Nutella, and cut on the diagonals.

Last summer, she'd have done anything to see him smile while they were stuck inside the house. He hadn't been allowed to play or swim or ride the horses, couldn't bend over or cough or even sneeze. And he'd hated the huge, earmuff-looking bandage on the side of his head. On a whim she'd created the special treat, and almost wept with gratitude when he gave a snaggle-toothed grin and asked for more.

"Let me take your temperature. We'll start with one piece and see how it goes."

She started a pot of vegetable soup and while it simmered, settled with her Bible in the family room near Ben. Luke 6:45 stated one's words indicated the contents of one's heart. But it was the preceding verses that most caught her attention. *Hypocrite,* the same word Rachel had used in her journal. The term for anyone who refused to see his own faults and instead dwelt on the faults of others.

She closed her eyes, swallowed against the shame rising in her throat. She'd known, for as far back as she could remember, that her mother resented being a widow and single parent. That she'd never forgiven Joseph Pitts for, as she called it, dying on her. Every word she'd ever spoken of him was laced with grief, coated with anger, and left Julie stockpiling guilt for being the tie binding her mother to "a pain worse than childbirth," losing a spouse.

If Rachel's journal was even partly true, Julie had indeed been painfully aware of her mother's verbal cruelty, yet had been acutely unaware of her own. The emotional subtitles she'd communicated with Rachel hadn't come from the death of a spouse, but the delay of a dream.

Fists clenched on her Bible, Julie shook her head. *Dear God, You know I didn't know I was doing it. I didn't know. I ask forgiveness. I need help—I don't know what to say to my daughter. Show me the truth. Show me the beam in my own eye.*

"Mom? Can I have more chocolate triangle toast?"

She rose on shaky legs, took the plate from his extended hand. "Absolutely. It won't take a minute."

"Thanks, Mom. You're the best mommy ever."

Her eyes stung at the sincerity shining in Ben's. At least she hadn't made the same mistakes with him she seemed to have made with Rachel.

She popped down the toast. Maybe it had happened as simply as Laurie theorized. However necessary at the time, Julie's careful and focused attention on Ben had left Rachel feeling neglected. An outcast of sorts, nudged aside by a baby brother.

But Rick had taken up the slack, hadn't he? Shuttling Rachel to the barn with him and teaching her about the horses. Father and daughter had a special equine bond.

Yet, was it a shared affection for horses that bonded them? Or, had Rachel turned to Rick because in her mind, she'd been abandoned by her mother?

Julie served Ben more special toast, and braced against a surging tide of dread. She read, thought, and prayed throughout the afternoon, brainstorming what to say and how to say it. Still, she jolted with apprehension when foot stomps sounded at the back door.

"Daddy, that's not how it goes." Rachel laughed as they entered the house.

"You better double-check. A karaoke failure at Amber's might end the world as we know it."

"Daa-ddy."

"Don't leave your boots in the middle of the floor. Put them on the shelf where they belong."

"Mrs. Rousseau said she's got some she never wears, my size and everything, that I might like to have. I told her I'd have to ask. Can I, Daddy? Can I?"

"I'm sure she'll be here when you get home from school tomorrow. We'll talk about it then."

"Yes, sir." Excitement bubbled in Rachel's response.

Julie watched and waited. Seconds later they squeezed through the doorway to the kitchen, like two best friends practically joined at the hip. They both saw her at the same moment. Their faces froze, the chatter stopped, their steps slowed.

Bile curdled in her gut. Jealousy? Was she jealous of Rick and Rachel's relationship?

She blinked, and studied their startled then wary faces.

Fear flashed in Rachel's eyes and she looked away. "I forgot my homework in the barn. Be right back." She fled like a threatened rabbit.

Rick walked to the kitchen sink and washed his hands. "Is what's in the pot for supper?"

"Yes. Vegetable stew."

"Great. I'll take a bowl in the family room and watch the end of the race."

She carried a bowl of soup to Ben, encouraged him to eat slowly, then let him crumble Goldfish crackers into his supper. When the race ended, she timed carrying Ben's bowl to the kitchen to when Rick and Rachel carried theirs. Taking a deep breath, she stepped into her daughter's path.

"Rachel, I want to apologize for saying things that hurt you."

Rachel stood rigid as if expecting a blow, her eyes on the kitchen ceiling. "Am I supposed to say anything?"

"Maybe accept my apology?"

"What about Daddy?" Rachel looked at Rick. He looked at the floor.

"What about him?"

Arms folded, Rachel stared past Julie's shoulder. "I have school tomorrow. Can I be excused to my room?"

Rick took a deep breath, exhaled slowly. "Yes, Rachel, you may go to your room."

Julie looked at him. "What? Why are you letting her go? We *need* to talk this out."

She scanned their faces. A look passed between husband and daughter, the same vibe lingering in the air as the night Julie gave Sean the letter.

She gulped. Had she been the odd one out that evening, as well? Is that what she'd sensed?

Rejection sparked hurt, which flashed to a flame of panic. *I don't have to listen to this. And I'm not staying where I'm not wanted.*

She heard her mother's words in her heart, ready to jump out.

No, she thought. No! And holding her hand over her mouth, she left the room.

Chapter Twenty

Four o'clock in the morning and Rick couldn't sleep.

His body was exhausted. The previous day after helping the farrier with Trident, he'd cleaned more stalls and placed more new mats while Rachel worked on schoolwork in the tack room. Pushing himself past the point his muscles shook with fatigue, he'd finished the last two stalls by sheer will, and a desire to leave his body tired enough that his mind wouldn't be able to think.

His plan hadn't worked. Though every joint and ligament ached, his heart and mind throbbed much like the torn callouses on his right hand.

He rolled slowly, from his side to his back in the bed. Fighting a groan, he raised a knee, draped a forearm against his tightly furrowed brow, and stared into the darkness. Beside him, Julie sighed and adjusted her pillow.

"Sorry," he said.

"Hmm? What?"

"I tried not to shake the bed too much."

"I didn't say anything," she answered.

Even with her sleepy tone, her still bound jaws made the words sound tense, forced, and spiked with disapproval. He'd expected no less, which was why he'd offered the apology before she even had the chance to fuss at him for disturbing her sleep.

Their normal. He'd been trained, or had trained himself, to express regret at any given moment, to feel remorse and freely voice it. Even when there was nothing to apologize for.

The bedside clock changed to 4:12 a.m. The quiet, middle of the night, but he knew sleeping was impossible. He slid aside the comforter. Slipped his feet to the floor. Pulled on a work shirt and jeans, then crept from the bedroom. He eased the door closed behind him, and stood in the silent hall of his home.

Ben coughed in his sleep. Rick looked in on him. The child had kicked off all his covers, and had balled up at the foot of his race car bed, mouth open. Rick covered him up where he lay, then peeked in at Rachel. How she favored her mother—her thick brown hair spread on her pillow—never ceased to melt his heart. Leaving her room, he ambled through the house and out the mud room door.

The moon appeared huge. Almost close enough to touch, if one were brave enough to stand on the barn's roof. It seemed to cast a filmy glow on the quiet earth as Rick trod to the stables. The horses heard him approach, they always did, and whinnied as he unhooked the first gate and walked past their stalls flicking on lights. He entered the tack room and, out of habit, reached for the radio switch. But the quiet seemed to have followed him to the barn, conquering the restless noise in his head. For once, he indulged in silence and was surprised to find it oddly comforting.

His body begged for sleep. He sat and leaned back in his chair, folded his hands behind his head, and told himself he'd close his eyes for only a minute or two. So his mind could reset and stop replaying every curt exchange that had taken place between him and Julie over the years. So he could remember what the previous weeks had been like, when it seemed their love had been reborn.

What would it take to start over in their marriage?

"Rick."

Was he dreaming? Drifting in twilight sleep, having wished she'd pursued him all the way out here to the stables, just to be near him? Just to be alone with him.

"Rick."

A soft touch on his arm. He felt a slow smile begin. He tried sinking into the dream with a sigh.

And smelled Angelina Rousseau's perfume.

Rick opened his eyes. Scrubbing both hands over his face, he sat up. How long had he been out?

He blinked to focus, and there she was. Angelina. "How long have you been here?"

She'd folded both hands at her waist. "Not long. The lights were on, but there was no music, so I looked in." She stepped back. "I shouldn't have disturbed you."

"No, it's fine." He rose. Sunshine speared through the tack room windows. "I didn't get much sleep last night. Came out here to get an early start on the day, guess I dozed off."

"I should've stayed longer yesterday and helped you again, rather than popping in for a few minutes to check on Godiva."

"You don't work here, Angelina. Your help Saturday was appreciated, but you pay boarding fees for a reason."

"I know." She moved to the window. "But I might as well have stayed. Nicholas had promised he'd be home from a job in Pennsylvania by noon. His flight landed at 11 a.m. That's why I came by for only a few minutes. I needed to be home when he got there. But, he never showed."

"Like, he missed his flight?"

She fiddled with the half-dozen silver chains at her neck and stepped back. "He didn't miss it. The job's not finished. I guess he'll come home later this week."

The horses neighed for his attention and their breakfast. He grabbed his black Stetson resting on the back counter. His gaze locked with Angelina's as it had last week when she'd referred to her husband's business trips. *Do most men leave their wives?*

And it hit him. After a full recovery, Julie's career might take off, and *he* might be the one left behind while she pursued her dream. He'd considered the logistics of running the stables without her, which was why he was spending so much time learning the accounting programs. But he'd not considered the abandonment he might feel every time she traveled to sing for others.

How could two people stay close if they spent little time together?

Or, would frequent times apart actually save their marriage? If she wasn't there to find fault, if he didn't have to run interference between her and Rachel ...

He placed the hat on his head. "I'm thinking you miss Nicholas pretty badly when he's gone. That's why you're here so much, right?"

She looked away, turned. "Can you, um, wait a minute to start morning feedings? I'll be right back."

He heard her boots click down the concrete walkway outside the stalls, heard her flip the heavy metal latches on the locker outside Godiva's space. She returned with a check, and both hands shook as she placed it on the desk between them. Again she folded her hands at her waist.

"Are you all right? What's going on?"

She cleared her throat and lifted her eyes to his. They glistened with unshed tears.

He skirted the desk and, as when he'd found her crying in the arena last week, his instinct was to reach for her in comfort. This time, he was forced to clench both fists at his sides.

"I lied to you." She gulped, obviously straining not to cry. "The first time I came here, when I asked you to take on Godiva."

"I don't understand." He lifted the check. Read the amount. "You don't have to pay extra because she's pregnant. Though I have wondered with her size, if she's farther along than you implied."

"It's twins."

"That almost never happens. Like, one in ten thousand."

"I know."

"And this is her first?"

"Yes."

"Why didn't you tell me?"

"I was afraid you'd turn us away. Another place I looked at didn't want the liability."

"Because having twins is pretty dangerous for the mother and the foals. But you knew that already, didn't you?"

She grasped the hand that held the check. "Please don't make us leave. I trust you. I trust you with her and her foals. I'm so frightened for them."

"What do the sonograms show? Are the foals whole and intact? I guess you told the vet not to say anything to *me*."

She squeezed his hand. "Yes, I did. Because I was afraid you'd make us leave. But the twins look remarkably healthy." Her face glowed with hope. "One is a little smaller, that's to be expected, but I know he's a fighter."

"You're taking a big risk with Godiva. With all three. Conceiving twins is rare enough, but having them survive is even less common."

"I know," she said. "But I won't submit her to a selective abortion. I want them all. I need them all."

She raised their joined hands to chin level, the check still dangling between them.

"Here's my bribe. Prepaid boarding fees for all three for a year, because Godiva should deliver in the next week or so. And until then, I do want to stay here in the barn with her as much as you'll let me. Nicholas isn't home anyway. I can throw a sleeping bag down on the concrete outside her stall."

"That's ridiculous." He waved off her idea. "Of course, Godiva can stay. Of course, you can sleep here at night. I think I've got a fold-up cot somewhere. We'll scoot my desk over and you can sleep in here. We'll move her to the stall next door so you can hear her."

"Oh, Rick. Thank you!" She threw her arms around him. "I could kiss you!"

"I'm surprised you haven't already." Julie's low voice came from the tack room's open doorway.

Rick eased Angelina away, looking past her to his wife, who seemed to withdraw into herself much as she'd done at the hospital when undergoing the swallow test. "I didn't expect to see you before you left with the kids this morning."

"Obviously not." Her gaze went flat. "I brought you your phone. Thought you might need it."

He checked his pockets. Sure enough, he'd left it charging by the bed, forgotten, when he'd snuck out so early this morning.

He took it from her. "Thanks. I'm sure I'll be finished in time to take you to the ENT at ten. We can get lunch out after."

She looked at Angelina. "And I assume you'll be here as well, when I return from taking our children to summer school and day camp?"

"Your husband said I could stay," Angelina answered softly.

"Yes, my husband did." Julie's voice was laced with distress.

"Let me walk you back and tell the kids bye."

He slipped past her through the door. They walked together away from the stables.

"Nothing happened in there. It's not what you think."

She'd wrapped her arms around herself. "Rachel will be late if I don't hurry."

"Julie, please. We were talking about her horse. You're hurting over something that's not true. Don't we have enough other things to worry about?"

He stopped walking, stopped talking, and watched his wife walk away from him again. Which was what he wanted, right? To avoid a confrontation?

Yet he sensed, this time it was he who'd messed up.

***

By the time Julie reached the back door, her steps had slowed as if from invisible weight, her strength had drained as if she'd carried that weight too long and too far.

She grabbed the knob. In the past, anger had often been her fuel. She'd been energized by it, and she realized, had depended on it to propel her over hurdles of exhaustion when Ben was an infant. Through red tape when dealing with insurance companies and physicians. Into new routines like learning sign language and coordinating treatments and surgeries with various specialists.

She all but stumbled to her room. Closed the door and sank to sit on the bed, her breathing shallow. Yes, there'd been long periods of time she'd lived on anger. Now she saw she couldn't afford it, or the way it made her behave toward her family.

She closed her eyes and saw them, Rick and Angelina. Her husband, being hugged by a beautiful woman who clearly wanted him. Her husband, his expression guarded as he saw her and slowly broke the embrace.

Dread bubbled in her stomach, then the pain hit, knocking what little breath she had right out of her. Anger would simply drive her husband farther away.

"Mom?" Rachel called and knocked at her door. "Mom, I can't be late for school." A pause. "Is Daddy taking me?"

Julie slowly stood. "I'll be right there. You and Ben get in my car."

Like all the times she'd been scared when Ben had stopped breathing, when they received a negative prognosis for her sweet little boy, she stuffed the pain and fear deep inside. *Later* she'd always told herself. She'd deal with it later.

But *later* had never come, had it? There had never been time. There was always a *next* thing to do. So the stress of Ben's care and the fear for her son whose early years had been such a struggle had stockpiled. The worry and hurt that she'd never get her chance at a singing career had festered. Higher and higher until there was no more room inside her. That's what had spewed out on Rachel. Her own fear and pain, frustration and hurt. Because that's what was in her heart.

How could she ever get to the roots of it all and dig them out?

And how, *how* could she reach her husband, whose withdrawal she was only beginning to understand, without pushing him straight into another woman's arms?

She lifted her purse, walked with deliberate steps to the garage. Hyper-aware as she backed out, of the car's movement and the blaring sun, she stopped at the end of their driveway, double- and triple-checked for oncoming traffic.

"Mom," Rachel huffed. "No one's coming. You'll have to drop me off first and then take Ben instead of the other way around. We'll barely make it."

She pulled onto the road. The car crawled forward.

"Mom?"

She shook herself. "I know. I'll take you first."

"But I don't want to be late either," Ben said. "Mondays the boys get snacks first."

"I'll have you there as quickly as I can." Julie repeatedly glanced in the rearview mirror until she couldn't see their home, their property.

What were Angelina and Rick doing now?

She couldn't afford to think about it. She had to concentrate to drive safely, make the correct turns to drop the children in reverse order.

They arrived at Rachel's school with seconds to spare. She left without a word or a look. Julie stopped at a convenience store, bought Ben a bag of Skittles to keep in his pocket in case he missed snack time. She dropped him at day camp, then turned into a McDonald's drive-thru.

Pulling back onto the street, she reached into the paper bag, savored the fragrant, rising steam. She grabbed the sausage biscuit and remembered her still-bound teeth.

"What is happening to me?" she cried. "I can't even *eat* this."

Nor did she want to, she realized, as she tossed the biscuit and bag aside, then gripped the steering wheel. She'd gladly give up burgers and fries for the rest of her life to feel safe and secure again in her home, her family, in Rick's love. She'd never be able to compete with the Angelinas of this world, even if she took her mother's advice and got professional help with her appearance.

She arrived at the ENT's office an hour early, parked in the small lot. Humid heat rose in waves from the lined asphalt. She lifted her phone, considered calling Rick, and saw the blonde, Dr. Lilly, exit a nearby side door.

The physician strolled to a glossy red Corvette, which matched her flirty heels. She opened the trunk and retrieved a shiny gift bag, carried it back inside. The petite woman in a sleeveless blouse and tailored slacks looked less like a physician and more like a model, with her perfect hair, her toned arms, and flat stomach.

Julie rested her head back against the seat. Remembered the attractive and single ENT's comments about Rick when visiting Julie in the hospital. No, she wouldn't call and ask him to meet her here. She couldn't take witnessing Rick get hit on twice in one morning.

Besides, this appointment was strictly a formality. Her voice had returned on its own, which meant her vocal cords had recovered. Right?

She texted Rick that she'd driven herself to her appointment and closed her eyes.

Please, God, let this part of my day be good news.

***

A hot breeze fluttered across the pasture and over Rick's face. He read the message from Julie. *Drove myself to the ENT. Errands to run after. Be home after picking up Ben.*

He wiped sweat from his brow with a worn bandana, and felt the sting of shame like the fat splinter he'd later be digging out of his finger. He was actually thankful not to be in her company right now or later this afternoon. To be working alone along the fence line, concentrating on the task without listening for Julie's approach, without bracing for the next verbal onslaught.

He strode to the flatbed behind his tractor. Lifted an armful of slats and walked along the decaying fence line, dropping pieces as he went. He removed the old timber, slid the worn and rusted screws in the back pocket of his carpenter's pouch, and methodically replaced each piece, attaching with new screws.

The task would have been much easier, gone much faster with assistance. But he'd rejected Angelina's offer to help, assuring her the job was more than manageable. That way he could say when asked—and Julie *would* ask—he hadn't spent the day in Angelina's company.

He secured the next screw, the battery-powered drill buzzing and whining in his hand. Then, the silence of grass growing tall and ready for grazing.

Walking back to the trailer for more slats, he heard Angelina's sharp whistle echo in the metal-walled arena. Godiva's weary whinny followed.

The cell in his front shirt pocket vibrated, as he'd earlier forwarded the house phone to his cell. He checked the display, saw it was an out of area number, and let it go to voicemail. He just didn't want to talk to anyone.

He worked for another hour, until he'd used all the slats resting on the trailer. Then drove the tractor back to the stables. He entered the tack room and took his sandwich from the small refrigerator.

Angelina had left a note on his desk, another apology, and a notice she'd return tomorrow. Enjoying the soothing air conditioning, he sat at his desk, guzzled a root beer, ate, and listened to the voicemail.

"*Rick-a!*" Julie's voice coach, Carmine, had left a long message stating he was available when Julie recovered, to both prepare her and help reschedule the audition.

Rick saved the message. Hopefully, his wife was getting good news at the doctor and would cool off before coming home. He wouldn't call her. He'd give her time.

Surely in this situation like so many others, silence was best. Avoiding more conflict was smart, right?

He checked the computer for emails from clients, vets, and suppliers. An email from Sean, the first since he'd left fourteen days earlier, showed a timestamp of 11 a.m. that morning.

Hey, Dad.

This is the first chance I've had to write. I do miss home. Tell Lisa I'll call her this weekend. Tell Rachel she was right about the food, it's gross. Tell Ben and Mom I said hi.

And Dad, don't worry. I was ready for this. I keep my mouth shut, just like you always do, no matter what Mom says to you.

I'm making you proud, Dad.

Sean

Rick read the message twice, then hung his head. If Sean married Lisa, would Rick want his son to behave as he did, in his marriage?

He wanted to pray. Felt like he *should* pray. Then embarrassment mixed with shame. He'd always thought himself a quiet man, an easy-going man. What if he'd really been just plain lazy? Or a coward?

Or worse, the perfect example of a man who didn't lead his family.

Chapter Twenty-one

Julie left Dr. Lilly's office on wobbly legs. Head pounding, she slumped into her car, cranked it. While the air conditioner battled the stifling June heat, she sat in the baked interior and stared at the brick building until the mortar lines blurred before her eyes.

The petite physician with Tinkerbell features had just put her through another harrowing test, then shared devastating news.

"The nodules are still present. You have a choice to make, Mrs. Matthews."

She glanced at Dr. Lilly's shiny sports car, and thought of her mother. *It's really too late to pursue your ridiculous childhood dream.*

Not true. It couldn't be true.

She put the car in reverse, noting from the in-dash clock that she'd lost the entire morning and most of the lunch hour, her stomach was so empty she felt nauseated.

As usual, there was no time for her to absorb, to contemplate what was happening in her life. Before she picked up Ben—Amber's mom was picking up Rachel—she absolutely must go to the grocery store. Her pantry, freezer, and fridge were practically empty.

The throb in her temple became a skull-encompassing pulse. With every heartbeat it seemed a sadistic, pickax-wielding miner was hacking his way through the top of her head. Her only option for food was a smoothie, so she drove back through the McDonald's drive-thru. Sipped as she made her way to the grocery store.

She loaded her cart through the produce and dairy sections, walked through the paper products aisle and stocked up. In the canned goods aisle, she stopped to ponder the tomatoes, and couldn't for the life of her choose between whole or diced. She grabbed both and continued on.

She searched in the pharmacy section for liquid pain reliever for her headache, and after finally locating a bottle almost knelt right there in the aisle to cry.

Rick in Angelina's arms. Every corner she turned she relived rounding the tack room doorway and seeing them together. What hurt worse, though, was hearing their conversation right before she walked in. Seeing her husband extend to Angelina the kindness, concern, and gentleness he'd withheld from Julie since she'd gotten back her voice.

With one hand holding in place the contents of her loaded cart, Julie pushed to the checkout line. Fifteen minutes later her trunk was full, and she sat in the driver's seat, picking at the tamper-proof cellophane on the medicine bottle.

"Fine. I'll tear it with my teeth."

But she couldn't. Her jaw was still wired shut.

Tears stung her eyes as she tossed the bottle onto the seat and drove to Ben's day camp. She pulled into the parking lot and her cell vibrated in her purse.

"Hello."

"Julie. It's Cherise. Thank heaven I got you. Did you pick up Ben yet?"

"I'm about to go in and sign him out."

Don't ask me for anything. Please, not today.

"Wonderful! My car's been in the shop all day. I've been sitting here for hours, and they just told me they won't finish it today. They're getting me a rental, but it won't be here for another hour or two. Can you drop Bradley at home? His older sister's there."

"Sure. Um, hang on, I'll let you talk to whoever's at the check out desk."

She collected Ben and Bradley. They slid into the back seat and she got a strong whiff of them. Soggy socks and little boy sweat, in a soured and fermented kind of way. She used her driver's door controls to crack the rear windows, then cranked the air up a notch.

"I told Christopher he can't be on our team anymore," Bradley said after they'd driven a ways.

"How come?" Ben asked.

Julie turned the AC back down and glanced in the rearview mirror. Christopher was Ben's other best friend.

"Because he's stupid."

"He is?"

"Yeah. I knew he wasn't any good at soccer. But basketball week is next week and he's the shortest one in our group. So I don't want him on my team."

"But how does being short make him stupid?"

"Because. If you can't play basketball you're stupid."

"I'm not very good at basketball. And I thought Christopher was our friend."

"Then you're stupid, too," Bradley said as they pulled into his driveway.

What?

"I am?"

"Yeah. So I don't want you on my team either."

Bradley scooted out and darted into his house. Julie couldn't address this with Cherise and Bradley now, Cherise wasn't even home. And the ice cream and frozen vegetables were no doubt melting in the trunk.

Pulling back onto the street, Julie turned toward home.

"I don't want you to play with or spend time with Bradley for a while." She blinked, struggling to keep her eyes focused and on the road amidst the building migraine.

"But he's my friend."

"Not if he calls you stupid." Heavens, were all of her children walking victims, walking targets? What was happening to Sean at Basic Training?

In the rearview mirror, she saw Ben squirm. "Well, I'm not too good at basketball. I do mess up sometimes when I dribble. Bradley never messes up. So he's smart, right?"

"That's not what smart means."

"If I can't be friends with Bradley, then I can't be on his team. Mom, his team always wins."

"Winning isn't everything. And Bradley is *not* being your friend when he calls you stupid or treats you like he thinks you're stupid."

Ben leaned forward, straining against his seat belt. "He's not?"

"No," she stuttered. "You are not stupid. When we get home I need help putting away groceries."

"Okay."

She drove past familiar pastures and turned onto their street. Hit a pothole and the miner digging through her head buried his ax in her skull. She had a wonderful moment of numbness, then jolted as the pain raised to a level she hadn't known previously existed.

"But I'm not smart either," Ben said.

Where were these ideas coming from? Definitely, no more Bradley.

"Of course you're smart. You're smart about taking care of horses and all kinds of things."

"Then that means Dad's smart, too, right?"

"Yes ..." She raised a hand to her face, certain it was splitting down the center. "He's the one who taught you about taking care of horses."

"But you're not Daddy's friend."

She parked in their garage and turned around to look at his sweet face. She could see his little mind working, adding two and two, but coming up with five?

"What do you mean I'm not Daddy's friend?"

He looked at her with Rick's hazel eyes, round, and innocent, and fringed with enviably thick lashes.

"You talk to Daddy like he's stupid."

What?

"I guess it means something different if you're a girl." He shrugged. "Can I line up the cans in the cabinet any way I want?"

What did he—

"Sure. I don't care how you arrange them."

She popped the trunk. As she stood, the world tilted about twenty degrees, forcing her to hold onto the door while she blinked against spots appearing in her vision. An upset Ben was the last thing she needed.

"You think you can handle this, buddy? I need to go talk to Daddy."

Ben gave a salute. "I'm on it, Mom."

Which meant her youngest couldn't possibly think of her the way Rachel did, right?

Dialing Rick's cell, she walked carefully to the stables, each step precisely placed to avoid jarring.

Or falling over.

Or vomiting.

"Where are you?" she asked when he answered.

"I'm home. Where are you?"

"I'm almost to the tack room. Again I ask, *where* are you?"

"I'm getting off the tractor about a hundred feet from you. What's the emergency?"

"I'll tell you when you get here." She ended the call.

What had been her space was now taken by a foldout cot. Her desk had been moved into the corner, with barely enough room between it and the counter behind for her to slip into the seat.

"What's wrong?" Rick asked as he walked into the room. He stopped.

He didn't say anything else. Or move toward her. He didn't even ask about her appointment.

He doesn't care. If she lived on constant voice rest—one of two awful options she'd been given today—he'd probably be happy, as long as she continued being a workhorse for their family.

And Rachel. Rachel would be *glad* Julie didn't talk at home.

But if she didn't talk, she'd never figure out what Ben had gotten all mixed up in his head.

Rick looked from Julie to the computer and back again. "You're at the computer."

"Of course, I'm at the computer. That's what I *do*. I input data and pay bills and check emails."

Rick paled. "Sean's doing exactly what he should at Basic. I haven't written him back yet, because I need the right words."

"You heard from him? He emailed you?"

"Julie, don't."

She grabbed the mouse. Clicked. Clicked.

And read.

She stood slowly. She'd thought nothing of Rachel's journal entry about Sean's comment *No drill sergeant has* anything *on Mom. Basic will be a piece of cake.*

But now ...

Her composure snapped. She felt it and her headache explode like fireworks. Adrenaline surged through her.

"After all I've done for this family. Supporting you and your dream about the stables. Waiting for my turn. Somehow our children think I'm the bad guy and you're the good guy!"

Rick said nothing.

"Aren't you going to tell me I'm wrong? Like you did this morning when I caught you in another woman's arms?"

"That's not what happened and you know it," his voice shook as it rose.

"I've seen the way Angelina looks at you." Her head and jaw might actually shatter from the pain. "I've heard the way she talks to you. Do you think I'm blind and stupid? Is that what all this stuff with the kids is? Some plan to get rid of me, so you can trade up?"

"I have never considered *trading up*. You're the one who always had your eye on something outside this family. I knew you always wished you'd gone to New York, that I was your consolation prize. Your second choice."

"How dare you say that to me."

She shook, Dr. Lilly's words ringing in her head. *You have a choice to make, Mrs. Matthews. You can talk, normally, like the rest of us, as you live with your family every day. Or, if you still want to sing as a professional, you will pretty much have to live on permanent voice rest. But you will never again be able to do both.*

Being Rick's wife, building a family with him, she hadn't simply postponed her career. Maybe, without knowing, she'd sabotaged it.

"I've sacrificed everything for you and our family. I've given *everything*."

He stepped closer, pointed at her. "You know what? Sean's grown and gone, so we'll both have to clean up our own messes with him later. I guess Ben's always been exempt because of his medical issues. But I won't let you target Rachel anymore."

"Fine." She wiped her face and sniffed back tears. "I think we've said all there is to say."

Julie fled the tack room. Rounded the corner between the stalls and a fenced corral as Angelina parked between the barn and Julie's home. The other woman hopped out of her car.

"Julie. Please. I need to apologize for what you saw this morning."

She didn't stop. *Just keep walking.* "I can't talk about this right now."

"You have to give me a chance to explain."

But she couldn't. She didn't. She ran across the long stretch of land to her home. Winded, gasping through her bound teeth, she went straight to her room. With a quivering hand on her throat, she laid down.

Voice rest was the only option to reach her dream.

Voice rest was the only option to stop her husband and her children from misinterpreting everything she said.

Voice rest was her *only* option.

Squeezing her eyes shut against more threatening tears, Julie surrendered to the torturous headache and let sleep take her away.

***

Rachel Matthews, Mrs. Tate's English class, summer session:

Wednesday, June 18:

I haven't written in my journal in a week. Sorry, Mrs. Tate, but since you're the one who showed it to Mr. Larl in the first place, maybe you will give me a break here.

Just so you know, Mr. Larl kept his word about only showing parts of my journal to my parents. I never thought they'd hack my computer, invade my privacy, and read the whole thing. But they did.

My mother was worried about me being bullied by Britney for all of about two seconds. But her main concern, as always, is how everything affects her. She accused me of making up everything, of twisting stuff. She's all worried about what you and Mr. Larl think of her. And she's all "How could you write that stuff about me?"

She was mad that I didn't tell the truth sooner about Britney, and that I did tell the truth about her.

Then she went to church by herself. Read her Bible all afternoon, and tried to apologize to me.

She didn't start with something lame like "I'm sorry *if* I hurt you or *if* I did whatever." Apologies like that aren't really apologies, are they?

Still, I stood there thinking, *Do you even know what you're apologizing for?*

Then Monday, I got home from school after seeing my best friend Amber, and the kitchen was crammed full with all my favorite stuff. I remember the many times I went to the grocery store with her, before I was old enough to stay home by myself. Going shopping takes *hours*. You have to load everything into the buggy, then you unload the buggy for the cashier, then you load it all into the car, then you unload again at home. Then you put it all away. That's like, five times you have to touch everything just to get done. And that doesn't even include cooking it.

I stood there looking at all the food and thought, *Holy cow! Every time I grab chips from the cabinet or fruit from the fridge, it's because Mom went to the grocery store and bought it and brought it home.* I felt a little guilty.

If I ever get married, my husband is *so* doing the grocery shopping.

Monday afternoon, for the first time ever I heard my parents fighting. Really fighting. I went to the stables like I always do to check on Godiva (she's one of the horses we board, and she's pregnant). Her stall is next to the tack room.

My mom and dad were in the tack room, yelling so loud I heard everything they said. Listening to them, I realized somehow they're both right and they're both wrong. My dad's absolutely right about how my mother speaks to us. And I hate to admit it, I do, but my mother is absolutely right about everything she does for our family.

I think Mom's right about something else, too ... but I don't want her to be.

I always thought I wanted my dad to stick up for me. But hearing him finally do it didn't make me feel better. He looks sad now, and angry. He hasn't been joking and laughing with me when we muck the stalls.

My mother hasn't spoken to any of us—not Daddy, not me, not even Ben—since then. Not one single word.

I don't know which is worse: being afraid she'll say something mean, or having her say nothing at all.

Chapter Twenty-two

Rick squirmed in the driver's seat of his F-250. When Ben had asked Rachel if he could sit up front during the ride to day camp, Rick figured the boy wanted to commandeer the radio. But his son didn't reach for the dashboard controls.

"Want to pick some music, buddy?"

"No, sir."

The boy sat hunched over, a bent elbow on his thigh, his chin in his hand. Rick pulled onto the road in front of their home, scanned the pulled-cotton clouds floating in a perfect Alabama-blue sky.

"I think I see a bear's head." He waited, pointed. "There's a lizard. Two o'clock."

The boy didn't budge, but offered a weak, "Hmm."

Rick drove on. "If we keep our eyes open around the corner here, we might see the Yoda cow." They saw it most mornings on the way to day camp. Its pale skin somehow exhibited a green tint. Because of the creature's wide, baggy eyes and low, strangely-pointed ears, Ben had dubbed it "Yoda cow." He always marveled at its intense stare, and once as they'd driven past, had voiced with surety that one day he'd stare the animal down. Rick slowed slightly as they cruised beside the pasture's barbed wire fence. But Ben continued staring at the floorboard.

"Something bothering you, buddy?"

His son heaved a heavy sigh. "Dad, I think I've finally figured out girls."

Rick felt his brow shoot up. "I see. Any girl in particular?"

"No. Maybe."

He glanced in the rearview mirror. Rachel had turned away from the window and caught his eye by rolling both of hers. He gave a brief shake of his head. She offered a *whatever* eye roll, then laid her head back and put in her earbuds.

"It's like there's rules, right? Like a code. One set's for boys and another set's for girls."

"Are you talking about manners, buddy?"

"Yeah. Like how we guys are supposed to open doors for girls, and the girl always walks through first." He paused. "Unless she's bigger and she's a femmy-mist. That means she wants to open the door herself."

Rick stifled a chuckle. "That's about right."

"Then there's the part where guys don't hit girls. Not in fights, and not in sports. When just the guys play football, like sometimes at day camp, we tackle and sometimes someone gets banged up or bleeds a little, but that's okay. But if the girls play, too, we wear belts with flags and we don't tackle. We just pull off the flags. Because if a boy tackles a girl, the girl might get hurt and that's bad. Even a femmy-mist can get hurt if someone tackles her."

"I see," Rick said. "For a guy who's figured all this out, you don't look happy."

Ben wiped his nose on his sleeve. "It's the last part I'm not happy about."

The last part? Rick had no idea what the child meant. He turned into the lot at the day camp center, a converted airport hangar at the edge of a large, community park. Since they'd arrived a few minutes early, he eased to a stop in an out-of-the-way spot, shifted to PARK, and turned to look at his son.

"Dad, how old were you when you got married?"

"I was twenty."

"And Mom's your only wife, right? Like, you didn't have another one before her or anything?"

"Nope. Mom's it. I've loved her since she was fifteen."

"When did you learn the rules?" Ben asked.

"The rules?"

"Yeah. The rules of marriage, which must be different for boys and girls, and doesn't work like guys being friends with other guys."

"No," Rick said. "It doesn't work exactly like guys being friends with other guys. A husband and wife are supposed to be best friends. And—"

Rick felt a *ping*—somewhere deep inside where truth often hid, where under the right conditions certainty bloomed and blossomed like a well-tended bud—it echoed through his heart and made his soul cringe.

Ben wiped his nose on his other sleeve. "Mom said I can't be best friends with Bradley anymore, because of the way he talks to me. But she says the same kind of stuff to you that Bradley says to me. How come she gets to keep you as her friend, but I can't keep Bradley as mine? Is it like all the other rules? Is it because she's a girl?"

A vise tightened around Rick's chest. "I'll have to explain later, son. I'm sorry." For so very much. "You better go, buddy."

Ben reached for his lunch. "Okay, Dad."

The child's grief was a heavy cloak on his thin shoulders. The image chipped the edge of Rick's heart as he watched his son open the truck door and hop to the ground.

"Hey, buddy? We'll talk about girls and Bradley and stuff this weekend, all right?"

"Really? Like maybe I could still be friends with Bradley?"

"We'll see. Pick you up later."

He watched Ben's progress across the lot and into the hangar. *My little boy.* Who'd one day be a man, probably a husband. And Rick had modeled a horrible example for one of the sweetest children God had ever placed on the earth.

"Dad, can I get up front?" Rachel unlatched her seat belt.

"No." Rick put the truck in gear, and noted the time. "I'm dropping you early, too."

He'd have plenty of time to settle some things with Julie before taking her to the oral surgeon's office to have the wires removed.

"Whatever." Obviously miffed, Rachel re-buckled her belt.

His heart raced as he drove to the middle school, as he pulled up at the entrance and waited while Rachel grabbed her backpack. She exited the truck, then tapped on his window.

He lowered it. "Yeah?"

His daughter looked at him with his wife's green eyes, then seemed to look clear inside him, to the place he'd heard the *ping*.

"Has Mom spoken to you since Monday?"

"Monday?" Rick rubbed a hand over his face. "I guess not."

But Julie didn't have to say everything she thought for Rick to know the dressing down he was getting. After so many years of hearing it, he knew from the look on her face.

"She hasn't spoken to Ben or me either. You know, since you two fought."

"How do you know we fought? You weren't even home."

"After Amber's mom brought me home, I went to check on Godiva. So I kind of heard you."

"Did Ben?"

"I don't think so."

"What does *that* look mean?"

"It scared me some."

Rick jerked his head toward the school building. "You go on in. I'll pick you up later."

"Daddy, now you're scaring me. What are you going to do?"

"Something I should have done a long time ago," he said, and headed home.

***

Julie heard the truck tires screech when Rick pulled into the garage, a sound she'd often heard when Sean had driven the truck, but never Rick. She stopped mid-stroke of brushing her hair, listened, and checked the time. They weren't running late, she had almost two hours before her appointment.

The door from the garage to the house slammed. With care she lowered the brush to the bathroom vanity. Already dressed and ready to go, she stepped from their bathroom to their bedroom as Rick entered from the hall and walked straight to her. His right eyebrow was furrowed and his cheek twitched, a tic that manifested when his legendary patience stretched thin and dissolved into quiet fury. As long as she'd known him, she'd only seen Rick go ballistic a few times, and always on behalf of her or their children's welfare. Even last Monday when they'd argued over Sean's email, he hadn't been this upset.

What happened? she signed, determined to rest her voice. *Is it Ben? Rachel? Sean?*

"You know," he said, "I expected the silent treatment for a while after what happened on Monday with Angelina. I've been a little surprised you held out this long, but I expected it, and I've dealt with it pretty well, I think. Including last night when we went to bed, and before I turned out the light asked if you wanted me to take the kids this morning. Your emotionless stare confirmed you did, *and* I was still in trouble."

She clasped her hands, fighting the urge to defend herself with signed or spoken word. Wouldn't they only be misinterpreted?

"No response?" Rick asked. "Well, you're holding fast, I'll give you that much. But after this morning, I won't play along anymore."

This morning? What had happened this morning?

He walked to the bed, sat on the edge, and removed a cowboy boot. Cocked his head and peered up at her. "Curious now, aren't you?"

He pointed at her with the boot cupped in his hand. "You think I don't know you, never listen to you, don't hear what you're saying. I've heard loud and clear for years. I know exactly how you're feeling, what you're thinking. Your face shows everything."

He set the boot aside and removed the second, dropped it beside the first. Placing both hands on his knees, he simply looked at her.

In her peripheral vision, the bedside clock switched from 7:45 to 7:46 a.m. Four days, almost to the minute, since she'd walked in on Rick and Angelina in the tack room. As she straightened her shoulders and lowered her hands her mind did a second calculation. She hadn't spoken to her husband in over eighty hours. She'd thought after all the conflict between them, Rick would be grateful for her silence.

"Wow," he said. "You really are determined this time. But if you want to know what happened this morning, and it involves our children, you're going to have to ask me."

Their children. What could possibly have happened to Ben and Rachel?

He turned away. "Otherwise, I'm not talking to you either."

In years past when she'd gone on voice rest, none of her family had seemed to miss hearing her speak. So, she'd expected the unfanned tension in her family to blow over. Ben's little boy noises and giggles would once again echo through the house. Rachel and Rick would resume their endless dinner discussions about the horses and Godiva's imminent delivery. Eventually, Rick would find an excuse to kiss her cheek and tell her everything would be okay.

She hadn't expected her silence to trigger their silence as well, or that she would feel so awful and alone these last four days. But to reach them all, she'd need to use words.

The cost. Rick didn't even know about Dr. Lilly's prognosis. He hadn't asked, and Julie hadn't told him.

Just today. Only for today, she'd use her voice to get her family in order, to explain to them about the voice rest, and to establish the new "normal" caring for her voice would require.

In the future, maybe she'd allow herself one day a week to talk normally with them. Or maybe use letters and email to communicate with them. Given the recent strife in their household, the strategy might be a smart move.

She swallowed. "What's going on with Ben and Rachel?"

He didn't look at her.

"Will you please tell me about our children?"

"Where would you like me to start? With Rachel? She heard us fighting on Monday. Now she's scared of both of us. Or maybe you'd like to hear about Ben first. Who's very confused about marriage and how friendship ties into marriage, since the wife—that's you— gets away with saying less-than-kind things to her husband—that's me. Stuff no childhood friend is allowed to say. Which is something I would like to know. How *did* you train me to be such a wimp?"

He stood with his hands on his hips, looking at her much as he did when analyzing an animal. "I use clicks and kisses and clucks with horses. Angelina whistles to Godiva. What did you use to train me?"

"*Angelina.*"

Julie felt her eyes flash even as her wounded heart bled anew. "She's the one training you. To look at her. To think about her. Next she'll have you feeling sorry for her. Poor Angelina, so lonely when her husband's gone on business. She's not lonely anymore, is she? She's moved herself right into the barn."

His gaze narrowed and his tic became more pronounced. "I offered her the opportunity to be near her horse," he said in a low voice. "How can you resent an owner spending the night in the barn with her pregnant mare?"

"I see my feelings on the subject don't matter. Well, I should be used to that. I grew up being disregarded and told my needs and dreams weren't important." Just thinking about the missed opportunity in New York still stabbed so deeply. "Looks like I married my mother."

"I was going to talk to you about Angelina staying in the barn, but you deliberately misinterpreted the situation and as usual, began punishing me."

"Oh, really? But you were going to tell me after the decision was made, right? Again, just like my mother."

"I am not like your mother."

Her heart had sped up. Her hands shook. "You, you hurt me like she does."

"No. You're afraid I'm going to hurt you, afraid I'm going to hit you with my words, so you slug me with yours. When have I ever treated you like your mother does? Ridiculed you and belittled your dreams? Never. I haven't done it. I won't do it."

He stalked toward her and she couldn't stop herself from cowering.

"See what you're doing right now? You're shielding yourself because you expect me to attack. So you attack first, me and the kids."

He couldn't be right. Could he?

"I, I've never screamed or cursed at you or the children."

"Neither have I to you. Neither did your mother, according to you. But she damaged you just the same, didn't she?" He shook his head. "I'm not wasting my breath."

He strode into their bathroom, slammed the door, then jerked it open again.

"No," he said, looking at the floor. "I can't brush over this again. My heart just can't take it."

He raised his head and stared into her eyes. She watched as he unfastened his cuffs, pulled the denim work shirt out of his jeans, and unbuttoned it. He tossed it to the floor and threw his undershirt down, as well. He pointed to his left shoulder.

"Do you remember how I got this scar?"

She backed up a step and turned away. "Y-yes."

He'd gotten the wound the night of her senior prom. She'd worn a deep emerald gown with tiny silver straps. When they left the event, good old Tony Stafford, who'd accompanied one of Julie's classmates, was in the parking lot. He'd obviously been drinking. He grabbed Julie from behind and spun her around, snapping one of the straps. Julie had clutched her gown to her chest.

"Oops," Tony laughed.

"Tony, go home!" Rick yelled as they backed away from him. "Have your date drive you home."

Tony reached for Rick and stumbled, then leered at Julie. "Figured I'd see you here with Miss Centerfold. What would happen if the other strap broke, huh?"

Rick had shielded her with his body and, behind his back, handed her his keys. "Get in the car," he said over his shoulder.

"Ooh, yeah, baby," Tony said. "Get in the back seat and wait for me."

"You always did have a big mouth," Rick said to Tony. Then, "Go, Julie."

Tony charged like a bull. Rick caught him and locked both arms around Tony's chest. They wrestled to the ground. Rick punched Tony once, twice. Then Tony pulled a knife from his pocket, stabbed Rick in the shoulder, and pulled it down through the meat.

She'd spent the rest of the evening with Rick in the emergency room. He'd needed twenty-one stitches. A kind nurse had re-fastened the strap of her dress with a huge safety pin, which of course had infuriated Trudey. Rick's fishhook-shaped scar had healed well, but the skin at the bend of his shoulder would always pucker.

"What?" Rick asked behind her now. "You can't even look at it? I love you more now than I did then. I can and will protect you from every outside threat. I've even tried to protect our children from you and keep down the conflict in our marriage, by refusing to protect *my-*

self," he said. "But the one thing I can't figure out how to do, is protect *you* from yourself."

Suddenly chilled, she rubbed her hands over her arms. "I shouldn't even be talking to you."

With her back to him, she told him of Dr. Lilly's prognosis.

"What about surgery? Isn't there a procedure which could be done?"

"It's delicate surgery, there are no guarantees, and consistent voice rest would still be required. I figured you'd be happy I'll be living on voice rest."

"That's your mother talking."

She turned back to him, expecting to see the fury that had consumed him. But a single tear was sliding over his stubbled cheek. And the look in his eyes wasn't anger, it was pity. Julie had seen that look on Rick's face only one other time, while she was in the hospital after the accident, when he'd told Dr. Wyman she couldn't speak.

"I support your singing because I support you." He stepped to her. "I'd support you digging ditches if it put the same expression on your face as Sunday mornings. Carmine called Monday, but I didn't tell you, because I didn't want you to pressure yourself or rush your recovery." Wearily he shook his head.

"I. Want. My. Dream," she said.

"Oh, yeah? Well, I want my dream, too. The one we promised each other when you married me. The one that doesn't include you slicing me to bits. You know, I thought I'd gotten my old Julie back. The one I married. The one who had at least one positive thing a month to say to me. You have chewed me up and spit me out for the last time. I'm not going to take this from you anymore."

"I've never wounded you like that!" She felt her voice crack in a way she'd never before experienced.

"Just because you can't see the injury doesn't mean it's not there."

He tossed his dirty shirts in the hamper. Pulled off his socks and tossed them in, too. He stepped into their closet.

She swallowed, totally conscious of the muscles, tissue, and cords in her neck, certain something awful had just happened.

She grabbed her throat, stumbled to the bed and sat. She thought of her vocal cords, the nodules and nodes, visible wounds only if one knew where and how to look.

Just because you can't see the injury doesn't mean it's not there. The same words she'd used in the letter to her mother.

He returned, dropped a clean shirt and pair of jeans on the bed beside her. Their gazes locked and he quickly looked away.

She had a vivid flashback to the day they'd made Ben. *There's no blue like an Alabama sky,* he'd said, *but I'd rather look into your startling green eyes any moment of the day. They captured me when we were kids, but the way they shine when it's just me and you ... I'd give you the world if I could.*

Now, he didn't want to look at her or connect with her, the same way she didn't want to connect with her mother.

Could it be true that she'd hurt every one in her family? Her husband?

How long had it been since she'd said something positive to Rick? Since she'd encouraged him? Thanked him?

You have chewed me up and spit me out for the last time. In her mind, an invisible hand flashed cards showing his every flinch of the last seven years, then fanned them out before her.

And it hit her. Hadn't she asked God to show her the beam in her own eye?

"I didn't mean to," she said.

He didn't reply, and the silence stretched so long she thought he hadn't heard her.

"After Ben was born, I ... what did I do wrong?"

"A man can starve for the physical, if everything else is right, you know? But he wasn't meant to be his own best friend."

She closed her eyes. "It happened gradually, didn't it? I was exhausted—"

"Yes, you were."

"And scared and overwhelmed and totally distracted simply keeping Ben alive and caring for him."

"You saved him. Revived him more than once if you remember, when he stopped breathing."

"Yeah."

What awful moments those had been, stimulating her newborn son and hoping he'd start breathing again on his own.

"And somehow I suffocated us, suffocated you, didn't I? Why didn't you tell me?"

"I should have." He finally looked at her again. "I knew how to work, learned to stay out of your way. But I didn't know what to say to you."

"And I probably wouldn't have let you get a word in anyway."

Oh, how this hurt, finding out she'd done wrong to others exactly as wrong had been done to her.

"I mucked stalls before dropping the kids," Rick said. "I've got just enough time to take a shower before I drive you to Dr. Wyman's."

She gulped. "Rick."

The space between them was a canyon she didn't know how to reach across.

"What are we going to do?"

"I don't know."

"How do we find out?"

"I don't know that either." He walked into the bathroom, pushed the door closed. "Funny you should trust my input now."

She heard him slide back the shower curtain. Heard him turn on the water.

Julie pressed a hand to her throat, cleared it, and heard the trace of raspiness.

CHAPTER TWENTY-THREE

Lightning rent the sky. Thunder roared, roared again, then lightning struck close as Rick pulled away from the oral surgeon's office, with his drowsy wife tucked into the front seat.

"I'm sorry," Julie said with eyes closed. "I'm so sorry, Rick."

He knew she referred to their conversation at home before the procedure. She'd said little else other than to apologize ever since.

"Shh." He reached for her hair and stopped, an old habit. Always checking for her acceptance before he made contact.

"I didn't do right, either," he whispered, uncertain whether he wanted her to hear or was glad she didn't. And in the back of his mind hadn't he always known he'd already gotten what he wanted? His land, the stables, his business, his dream.

Just a few short weeks ago he'd encouraged Rachel to see life from Julie's perspective. But had he? Had he ever faced the complete death of a dream like Julie now faced?

He stopped at a red light. Turned into a drive-thru and bought himself a meal, her a milkshake, and placed it in the cup holder as Julie dozed.

The storm exploded in a dark, deafening whoosh. Wipers at full, emergency flashers on, he slowed to a snail's pace. What should have been a twenty-minute trip turned to forty, the view out his windshield shortened to less than a yard.

Finally he pulled into their garage. He carried her inside, her head on his shoulder, one arm dangling as he turned sideways to enter their room and lay her on the bed. He removed her shoes, covered her with an afghan, and closed the blinds.

Quietly he shut their bedroom door. When Dr. Wyman's nurse had given him the after-care instructions, she'd said Julie would probably sleep for a few hours. He made a sandwich, ate standing, noting the rain had slowed, then walked through mud to the stables.

The tin roof shook with each rumble of thunder. All the horses had congregated in the indoor arena, rather than stay out in the pasture during the storm. They shook their heads and snorted in complaint that their daily grazing session had been cut short. Rick walked straight to the tack room and was hit full force with the scent of Angelina's perfume and the sight of her sitting at his desk reading.

She lowered the book and looked up. "I've been avoiding you," she said. "Since Monday."

He'd forgotten she would be here. He'd been so focused on the mess that was his family, on getting Julie home, on all the answers he didn't have. On a desperate need to just be alone in his barn with his animals for two whole seconds and not think about all the mistakes he'd made.

He slicked back his hair, wiped excess water from his arms.

"You're soaked." She rose, grabbing paper towels from the counter behind her.

"It doesn't matter."

She brought them to him.

He accepted the towels, wiped his face. Grabbed an extra shirt from a nearby cabinet and quickly changed in the attached bath.

"I'm sorry," she said when he came out. "I should have apologized to Julie right away."

Rick tossed his wet shirt on the counter, glanced at his watch. He had some time before he had to pick up Rachel and Ben. If he couldn't be alone in the barn, he'd take a ride.

"I caused a problem between you and your wife."

He shook his head. "No. You didn't."

"I know I did. And I didn't mean to."

"You're not to blame." He could see she did indeed blame herself. "If it makes you feel better, apology accepted."

He donned his hat. Left her there and saddled Dutch.

No, Angelina wasn't to blame. All guilt sat squarely on Julie's shoulders. And his.

He rode out through the gate, through the pasture, over the land he loved as the now light rain misted his face. But he found no solace, no sense of security as he usually did when taking a leisurely ride across his property.

What good would it do to own all this, to leave all this as an inheritance for his children, if he'd taught them to be a victim in relationships?

God must be so disappointed with him.

"I'm too embarrassed to even talk to You, or anybody for that matter," he said. "I can't even ask You to forgive me, not yet, because the only thing I hate worse than a liar is a hypocrite. Telling You I'll change would make me both, because I have no idea how to do any different."

***

Rachel Matthews, Mrs. Tate's English class, summer session:

Sunday, June 22:

Mrs. Tate, you might not give me credit for this entry. But I have no one to talk to—my best friend is on vacation, and my father has changed, too. I kind of don't recognize him anymore.

I thought my family couldn't get any weirder. More weird?

(Sorry, I guess it's only a real comparison if I contrast two different things. But, if my family of two weeks ago counts as one, my family of this weekend is definitely the more bizarre of the two.)

First, since Friday evening when Mom woke up after having the wires removed, she's kind of wilted. There's no other way to describe it. She never looked weak before, even when her mouth was wired shut, her face was bruised, and her arm was broken.

But it's like her backbone's gone or something. She's smaller somehow, fragile-looking, which doesn't make sense.

Second, now my parents talk in low voices, the same way everyone speaks quietly at a funeral. They're solemn and acting sad. When they look at each other, it's like each is waiting for the other to speak. But it's not like a "you go first" thing, it's more a "please tell me" thing. Like someone just asked a really important question and neither of them knows the answer.

Third, this morning was the ultimate weirdness. Usually on Sundays, my mom barks orders, gives time updates, and herds us all to the car for church. But this morning Daddy simply knocked on my door, stuck his head in, and asked, "You awake?" It was up to me to get dressed, eat, and manage my time so I wouldn't make us late.

I think Daddy did the same thing to Ben, but Ben didn't do so great. He forgot to brush his teeth—I know because he insisted on telling knock knock jokes while we were both in the backseat and nuked me with his nasty breath.

He couldn't find his good sneakers, so Ben ended up wearing his grass-stained play shoes. Which wouldn't have been so bad except they stink like hundred-year-old mildew from being left out in the yard when it rained on Friday. Dad's truck will never smell the same. It needs to be detoxified or something.

So we got to church and I couldn't get out of the truck fast enough. Ben chased after me—my constant shadow since Sean's not around—and I heard Mom open her door and say, "Look at this. I'm sorry. I guess I forgot about it."

I looked back and she'd lifted a fast-food cup out of the cup carrier in the back of the fold-down console. The cup had soaked through, and an entire milkshake (I think it was a milkshake) was leaking out of the bottom, over the console, her seat, and her clothes as she got out.

Then she just stood there holding the cup. I guess she accidentally squeezed it, because what was left exploded and a big glop burst out and fell on her shoes.

My mother didn't scream. She didn't yell. She didn't even get upset. She simply stared at the goop dripping from her fingers. Either an alien has taken over her body or she is on some serious medication.

And I think my father might be taking something as well. Because he came around the truck and put his hand under both of hers and they just stood there like they'd never before seen or cleaned up a mess.

"It's my fault," he said. "I forgot it Friday after I carried you in from the truck."

My mother looked at their hands, at the gunk all over herself, at the mess behind her on the seat. Then she apologized again, which never happens.

"Daddy, do you want us to go inside?" I asked.

"What? Um, yeah," he said, like he'd forgotten Ben and me were even there.

My parents never came inside. They spent the whole service cleaning up the truck and Mom's clothes, apparently using Mom's stash of napkins from the glove compartment and the remains of an old bottled water lodged under the seat.

And they didn't fight about it. I know they didn't because when Ben and I came out and got in the truck they were still as quiet as before. But it wasn't that "I'm so mad I'm never speaking to you again" quiet. They were as silently weird as they were before the Great Milkshake Explosion.

But that's not all. We were driving home and Ben started singing this goofy song he heard in kid's church, "Father Abraham." It has motions you do with your arms and your legs. So he started singing under his breath and doing the motions, and ended up kicking the back of Mom's seat.

Mom didn't move. She didn't turn around or say a word or even notice.

Then Dad said, "Ben." And he waited. "Ben." And he waited. " Ben!"

Ben stopped.

"Turn up your hearing aid," Dad said.

"Sorry," Ben said. "I was just doing the song."

"I know, Buddy. It's one of your favorites. But what about the hearing aid? Why do you always have it turned down?"

He shrugged. "I don't. Only when I don't like the noise."

Then Dad asked, "What noise?"

He shrugged again. "When somebody's upset. Or yelling."

I couldn't stand it. "He means like what usually happens over something like the milkshake."

My mom hugged herself and kind of bent over, shaking her head. And neither of my parents said another word all the way home.

***

Rick wouldn't have felt more stressed if he were blindfolded and walking a tightrope while juggling.

Somehow he and Julie, both children, and Angelina had all ended up in the barn at the same time.

Julie was hunched over the computer in the tack room, listening to music through headphones and concentrating on inputting the last entries in the business' bookkeeping programs. Rachel was begrudgingly mucking stalls. Rick figured her woeful sighs could be heard in the next county. Ben was dutifully washing and refilling all the water buckets, but the little guy kept filling them too full, and the excess sloshing over the rims created a slippery mess of hay and mud on the concrete walkway outside the stalls.

Rick parked an empty wheelbarrow in front of the stall where Rachel worked, then grabbed a push broom hanging nearby. All he needed was for one of the owners who regularly visited the stables on Sunday evenings to slip and break an arm.

"Daddy, aren't you going to help me?" Rachel asked.

"In a minute. I'm going to sweep some and check on your mother."

At least if he were sweeping he'd actually see some results. He didn't know what to do *for* Ben, what to do *about* Rachel, or what to say *to* his wife.

If Sean were here, Rick would be a failure four times over. His only consolation was Angelina hadn't been in the tack room when his family had tromped alongside him to the stables. Rather, she'd been in the arena giving Godiva a light massage. A little distance between Julie and Angelina was surely a good thing.

He started where he stood, steadily shoving the floating slush toward the nearest walkway end, and cleared a dozen feet.

To his left, the tack room door opened.

"Rick?" Julie's voice trembled.

He went to her and laid the broom aside. "Didn't your gums bleed a little after lunch?"

She looked so weary, just like he felt. Fear gleamed in her green eyes.

"You should go back to the house," he said. "Take it easy."

"What are we going to do?"

He didn't know. He still couldn't bring himself to pray for guidance. Or even open his Bible. All he could see both in the heavens and on the pages was his failure.

And his plate was so full ...

"I depended on Sean a lot around here. Rachel's gone every day for school, and Ben's just not big enough to help with larger jobs."

"I know. Having to care for me didn't help. *I* didn't help." She closed her eyes and slowly opened them. "I'm not trying to put more pressure on you. But I know you heard Ben as well as I did this morning."

She backed into the room and motioned him inside. "I don't want them to hear us."

He followed and closed the door behind him.

"I've asked God to show me what to do next. Then I worry maybe He's just not talking to me, because of all I've done wrong. But that can't be what's happening, because that would make Him just like my mother and I know He's not like her."

She looked at him with trust, with need, depending on him for answers he didn't have. If he were honest, answers he'd never had. Even before Ben was born, before his wife had changed into the Julie who constantly sniped at him, Rick hadn't taken seriously his role as spiritual leader in the home.

A pressure built in his gut and shook his soul. Julie thought God wasn't speaking to her because of all she'd done wrong, and Rick wasn't speaking to God because he was mortified at what he'd failed to do.

"How do we fix our little boy?" she asked. "And Rachel. And Sean. And *us*."

He'd thought he was being a good parent. By giving Sean room to learn about life on his own, when Julie rode him about taking on adult responsibilities. By cutting Rachel slack when Julie nitpicked her over her attitude and schoolwork. He'd even told himself Ben had been unaffected by the atmosphere in their home.

He'd prided himself on his patience. His ability to wait and "hang in there" and approach life from a slower pace, and let Julie wear all the "bad guy" hats of discipline and planning and the tasks that came with running a household.

Yet he now saw patience was simply the label he had used to cover the truth. He'd never been engaged with his family. Never been active and intentional. Before Ben he'd coasted because life had been easy, and after Ben he'd just maintained the fringes, justifying his inaction with Julie's behavior. He'd lived reacting.

"Where do we start? With the children or with us?" She reached for his hand and he watched her twine their fingers and squeeze.

A knock sounded on the door behind him. "We'll figure it out," he said.

"Daddy?" Rachel knocked again. "Ben's done with the water buckets. Can he help me now? Since you're, you know, *not*?"

Rick opened the door and held a hand up to his daughter.

"We'll figure it out," he said again to Julie. He watched timid relief drift over her face and knew he was the world's biggest liar.

His daughter's arms were crossed, her eyebrows raised in a look so classically *Julie* his memory flashed with a series of identical images. Realization hit him like a punch to the gut—Rachel wasn't mad at him, she was asking a question because she didn't know the answer.

How many times had Julie asked a question, and because she'd sniped at him earlier about something else, he'd refused to answer, or been hurt because he'd decided she meant him harm?

"Ben can help you now."

He coached Ben, then returned to sweeping the concrete walkway, which was now a muddy stream. Behind him, the arena gate opened and closed. Boots walked across concrete.

A skid. A female yelp.

He dropped the broom, turned, offering help. Angelina slid. Rick missed catching her by inches. She landed on her hip and elbow.

Rick knelt beside her. "Are you all right?"

Her blouse was ripped at the forearm. She wasn't bleeding from her arm, but when she touched it she winced.

She shifted. "I'm more embarrassed than hurt."

"You shirt's ruined."

"It's one of many. It doesn't matter."

He sat back on his haunches. "You really should consider wearing different boots."

"These are fine. They're old and durable. I'm just clumsy."

She attempted to stand, slipped again, and Rick caught her arm.

"Ouch," she said, gaining her balance.

"Sorry. I didn't mean to hurt you."

She blinked at him. "I know that. You're the kindest, most patient and nurturing man I've ever known."

He let her go, knowing he'd fooled everyone, including her. Everyone but himself.

Chapter Twenty-four

Julie's Monday morning was not going smoothly. Sometime during the night the electricity had blinked off then back on. Not long enough to wake anyone, not long enough for the fridge to defrost, but long enough for the clocks to lose their memory. Which meant the bedside alarm did not sound when it should have.

She stood by the stove, waiting for bubbles to form on the homemade pancakes on the griddle. She should never have asked Ben what he wanted for breakfast. The child *always* requested pancakes, unless he was ill. Then it was the standard chocolate-triangle toast.

Rick had roused their daughter this morning, but Rachel hadn't yet emerged from her room. How did a parent hurry her children along without sounding angry and accusing? Julie flipped over the browning pancakes and realized she'd never learned the skill of kind correction; it had never occurred to her that she needed to.

How many other things had she either learned wrong or not learned at all, before becoming a wife and mother?

Too many, she thought, scooping batter for a second batch. Almost twenty years of marriage, most of that spent being a mother, and she didn't have a clue about something as critical as fixing a communication problem with her own children.

She wished she could call a time-out, simply stop time and freeze her family. While they were stuck she'd educate herself, study and practice what to say and how to say it. Which was a ridiculous wish and proof she was stalling and making excuses.

Every time she looked at Rachel's face, she froze. Completely petrified, a hundred times worse than the worst stage fright she'd ever had.

Ben arrived and she served him at the bar instead of the table.

"Hey, buddy. Um, think you can eat fast enough for us to leave in ten minutes, but not so fast you choke?"

That wasn't so bad. He even grinned and nodded and quickly started eating.

Then her daughter walked in. *Tell her you're sorry for hurting her. Tell her you'll try to do better—*

"Do we have any *real* maple syrup?" Rachel leaned over the bar and looked at the clock.

Say it.

Julie glanced over her shoulder. "What?"

"Forget it." Rachel wrapped several pancakes in a paper towel and grabbed a bottled water from the fridge.

Tell her what she means to you.

"I'll get my backpack and be in the car. You can sit up front, Ben. I've got homework to finish on the way to school."

Her cell buzzed, signaling an incoming text. Torn, Julie checked the screen.

"My Julie! It's Carmine!"

She glanced back at Rachel, who was already on her way to the garage.

"You must call me as soon as you get this," Carmine's message continued. "Tell me you are recovered. Tell me you are better. Thad Bartell is eager to hear you. Ciao!"

"I'm done, Mom." Ben hopped down. "I'll brush my teeth in less than forty-two seconds."

"Forty-two, huh? Go ahead and take the full minute."

He scampered off. She packed his lunch, added an extra snack. They joined Rachel in the car.

Ben chattered, barely taking a breath, all the way to day camp. Apparently this Wednesday, Thursday, and Friday would be fraught with field trips—to the local fire station, the police station, even to Benson's Hardware store downtown, which contained a huge storage basement. One fortunate child would get a ride on a forklift, and of course, Ben hoped his name was drawn.

She dropped off Ben, and suddenly had complete privacy with her daughter. The perfect opportunity, but Rachel was intently working on homework. What was the best choice here?

Too soon they reached the school and Rachel went inside. Something inside Julie wanted to catch up with her daughter, just for two minutes. But what were the right words? Truly, she didn't want to upset Rachel at the start of her school day, and she couldn't afford to waste her voice on the *wrong* words.

Julie pulled to the exit and stopped, debating. Turn left and go home, or turn right and drive to the ENT's office, on the off-chance Dr. Lilly had an open appointment slot to speak with her. Was there anything else Julie could do besides being on constant voice rest, to increase her chances of singing again?

She turned right and gunned it. She should call ahead to the doctor's office, she knew she should, but she didn't want to be told no.

She waited an hour, then another twenty minutes before being called back to Dr. Lilly's office. The prognosis was the same.

"Google Screamer's Node and Singer's Node," the specialist encouraged. "There's no sign the nodules are malignant, but if they remain they become nodes. The nodes would have to be surgically removed, which can cause permanent damage. In addition, once nodes appear, the likelihood they'll return is extremely high, which again, causes more damage."

Julie drove home. She went inside, walked to the piano bench, and stared at the black and white keys until they blurred to gray. If her silence couldn't save her voice and wouldn't save her family, what was she to do?

She went to the kitchen. Sat at the bar and called Laurie.

"Hey! Saw it was you on the caller ID," Laurie said. "I've got like, five seconds. I'm at the pediatrician's office with Hope. I just can't get her diarrhea under control. What's going on?"

"Quick question."

"Shoot."

"How do you hear God? Like how can I recognize it's Him?"

"Well, sometimes I feel a peace, then maybe, a new idea or a strong impression. Have you ever read about Elijah? When he fled from Jezebel? I or II Kings, I think."

"I don't know."

"Find it. Read it. It talks about how God speaks in the midst of trouble."

"I've got trouble, all right. Laurie, I think I've hurt Rick even more than I hurt Rachel, Sean, and Ben. I've got such a mess here, I don't even know how much damage I've done."

"Wow. You've got to pray, Julie. Like you've never prayed before. God will walk you through growth and change like He did me and Pierce, but you really have to listen and pay attention. You can't react like you have before. You can't behave like you have before."

"You mean stop and pray in the middle of a disagreement?"

"Well, yeah. Can you think of a better time? That way you don't make the mess bigger."

"Before the accident I hardly ever prayed outside of church or meals, or when asking for something I wanted to happen."

"But God wants to be close to you, Julie. You can talk to Him anytime, especially about what's most important, which is your family. I gotta run. Call me later if you need me."

"I will. And, Laurie? I'm really glad we started becoming friends last summer. Bye."

Julie hung up. She'd never thought of talking to God during a conflict. The idea somehow seemed ... wrong? Unholy? How would one even recognize His response?

She got her Bible. Sat at the bar and found the story of Elijah running from Jezebel in I Kings 19.

Wind ... earthquake ... fire. Tragedy, terror, even busyness or a heart pounding with fear—any and all could completely drown the low whisper, unless one knew what to listen for.

A *low whisper*—Julie hadn't recognized it. Exactly like her first Sunday morning back at church, when she'd been talking to Laurie and felt questions deep inside.

Would you trade them? For the life you thought you wanted, would you trade them?—meaning her family.

She hadn't known then that the soft voice could work hand-in-hand with a strong impression, that God had been speaking to her spirit.

Like the voice she'd thought she heard this morning.

God had been answering her prayer. The *I need help—I don't know what to say to my daughter* prayer she'd prayed over a week ago.

Tell her what she means to you the Voice had said.

Rick came in for lunch. "Whatchya reading?"

"A passage Laurie told me about this morning. Did you know God can speak in a low whisper?"

"Can't say I did." He gathered sandwich fixings. "You were gone a long time this morning."

"I went back to Dr. Lilly's."

He slapped bread and meat together, cut the sandwich in half, rinsed the knife, and placed it back in the knife block. "I'm guessing she didn't tell you what you wanted to hear." Slowly, he took the first bite.

"My only hope—*only* hope—of ever singing again starts with complete voice rest until the blister and nodules are gone. And that's just the beginning. Having surgery would be even worse and offers no guarantees. She assures me the nodules will come back, possibly more quickly each time. Constant voice rest will be mandatory and again, not guarantee success." She looked up at him. "Tell me what to do."

"I can't," he said.

"But I need you to."

"No way. Either way you'll blame me—"

"I won't."

"Let me finish." He set aside his sandwich. "Or *I'll* blame me. I miss the way you look when you sing, Julie. I miss how happy you were then."

His cell rang.

"Can you *not* answer that?" she asked. "Please?"

"It might be important."

He answered. She could vaguely hear a computerized voice as he listened. Then he ran out the front door.

"What's wrong?" Julie sprinted after him, her heart pounding, then stood beside him outside, following his gaze to the north. In the distance, black smoke rose into the sky like a fierce dark angel.

"The call was a recording, wasn't it? One of those new emergency recordings."

"Come on. Let's go."

He didn't have to tell her. Women's intuition had never been her strong point, but as she ran behind him back through the house and out to his truck, something inside her knew.

Rachel's school was on fire.

***

Julie lived through seven of the longest minutes of her life as they drove to the school. They crested the hill at the edge of the middle school property and shock smacked her. The fire was enormous.

Thick smoke billowed up into the heavens, black fists punching a clear blue sky and blocking the sun. The top half of the four-story main building—a structure she and her husband had visited less than two weeks ago—blazed like a freshly struck match.

The truck screeched to a stop on the slope outside the fenced campus. Julie threw open the passenger door, ran full-out toward the gate where a crowd of parents gathered.

The roar was deafening, a relentless thunder like a hundred bass drums. Four large fire trucks, other smaller emergency vehicles, several police cars, and ambulances lined the circle driveway inside the fence. Shouts echoed between the various officers.

Rick grabbed her arm. "We can't get any closer." He pointed to the officer standing inside the gate. "See that cop?"

"Stay back, folks," the officer told the group. "We'll get you information as soon as we can."

An ambulance pulled away from the building, no siren blaring, no lights flashing.

Julie's heart seized. "That means whoever's inside is already dead, doesn't it? They're not in a hurry because the person's already dead."

Her knees disappeared. Rick caught her around the waist.

"You don't know that. Maybe they're being released because they're not needed."

He led her back to their truck, lowered the tailgate, and pushed her to sit. Still standing, he checked his phone. "No new calls."

Wind blew up the hill in their direction. Ash swirled like gray confetti. Heat followed, pressing like thick fog. She felt her face warming.

Cars and trucks were lining up on the road now, the occupants exiting, running toward the inferno as Julie had done. They clumped with others at the gate where the officer stood.

"Do you know anything?" a passing man asked Rick.

Her husband motioned to the nearest police car. "They'll let us know as soon as they hear something."

High on the building, windows exploded—crashing cymbals. Glass rained down outside the incinerating structure and new flames reached for the sky. Emergency personnel ran and shouted to each other on bullhorns.

"Rick!" Julie jumped down, grabbed his hand, pressed her cheek to his shoulder, and watched the school burn.

Looking down at the disaster, she couldn't believe how loud it was. The strange gusts of wind. The water surging from the hoses and hitting the old brick building in a pounding, continuous stream, which seemed to shake the ground. The fire's rumble as it thrashed out from window frames. A portion of the flat roof bubbled and collapsed, the top brick rows of the front wall fell inward.

She closed her eyes. It was all too much to take in. And her only daughter might be trapped somewhere in there, injured and needing help. Why hadn't she taken the few extra seconds this morning to encourage Rachel? To tell her daughter how much she meant to her?

Rick pulled away. "Here comes Pastor Crane."

She opened her eyes. "Pierce is here?"

"No. His dad. Daniel. Maybe he still serves as Fire Department Chaplain."

Bible in hand, the retired preacher approached. Julie scanned the older man's face, looking for any indication she should start grieving. But he had the same kind yet mischievous expression he always did, as he pulled a pack of Juicy Fruit gum from his pocket and popped two strips in his mouth.

Several feet away, he raised a hand in greeting. "We don't know much yet, except the emergency alert was incorrectly worded. You all were supposed to go to the new high school up the street."

"Seeing the fire here, we would've stopped anyway," Rick said.

"I figured as much. I need to ask you to go to the high school, now. Proceed with caution, folks!" Daniel called out to all.

"That's where the evacuated students are," he said to Rick.

Many folks hurried to their cars. The road filled with vehicles.

"I'm heading to the high school myself," Daniel said. "They want me there. The hospital's already got a chaplain on site for parents whose kids were injured."

"Not everyone got out, did they?" Julie spoke through the dread churning its way up her throat.

Daniel looked at her and grasped her shoulders. "There was at least one fatality, a school employee, and several students have been taken to the hospital. Families are being notified first. Which is why you need to go to the school."

"We'll meet you there." Rick pulled his keys from his pocket, then looked at her. They got in the truck. A kind person let Rick out into the traffic line.

"She's okay," Rick said. "I'm sure she's okay."

As her mother, she'd feel it if Rachel were dead, wouldn't she?

Dear God, don't let her be dead. What will I do if she's dead?

The more important question is, what will you do if she's not?

Chapter Twenty-five

The snail's pace was driving Rick crazy.

They were stopped dead center—what an awful phrase—in front of the school. The flames finally seemed to be under control, or rather they'd mostly burned out. Rick knew from the way the building had caved in, even the first floor was a disastrous mess.

"Why?" Beside him, Julie whispered. "Why didn't you tell me how I was hurting our children? Hurting you? How could you let me do all this damage?" She pointed to the destroyed school. "*That* kind of damage."

Someone behind him beeped, prodding them forward a whole fifteen feet.

"I knew you were exhausted and overwhelmed with Ben's condition. Then I thought it was just a phase." He grabbed her hand. "I don't want to fight."

"Neither do I." She squeezed. "I just need to know. Did you tell me and I didn't listen? Was I really that self-absorbed?"

Rick took his foot off the brake, let the truck roll forward several yards, then stopped again.

"I guess I felt guilty," he said, and realized it was true. "We'd agreed to stop having children. The picnic that day was my idea."

"Neither of us knew the antibiotics could counteract my birth control pills."

"Yeah. But I didn't think twice about your dream being delayed again. I just chalked it up to another baby and called him a bonus. Then when he had such extensive medical needs, I let you carry most of the burden. I was wrong."

They inched forward again.

"I love Ben," Julie said. "I do."

"I know you do," he said. "That was never in question to me. I just ... I thought you blamed me for getting pregnant, for him taking over your life. I knew you weren't happy and I kept thinking, why am I not enough for her? Why isn't my love enough?"

"Oh, Rick. No."

"Wait. I'm not finished."

He reached the high school, followed a policeman's directions to park near the auditorium where Sean's graduation ceremony had taken place just weeks ago.

"I guess I kind of just took it, you know? Like some kind of stupid penance for putting you in that situation. So part of me felt like I deserved it, and another part didn't know how to argue with the facts of your life. The best idea I had was to handle Sean's and Rachel's needs, so you didn't have to. And when how you treated me wore on me, I didn't know what to say. Can you understand that?"

Tears fell from her eyes. "Yes. I understand that."

He pulled into a space, then made himself look at her. His eyes watered.

"I still don't know what to say," he said. "To myself, to you, to my children. I just hope God gives me the opportunity to hold my daughter one more time. Let's go."

They followed the throng lining up outside the auditorium. They were given instructions, printed information, then, like a miracle, Rachel was brought out to them. They embraced her, sandwiching her between them. Rick kissed his daughter's hair.

"Mr. Larl died," Rachel said as they walked to the truck.

Rick stopped. "Are you sure?"

She nodded. "Yes. The alarms sounded and he was running through the building, going room to room to get everyone out. He went back in, and was found by the firemen right after they arrived. They think he had a heart attack or maybe it was smoke inhalation."

"How do you know that? We couldn't find out anything."

"Britney's in my class, remember? A policeman took her to the hospital to be with her mom. When they were leaving I told her I was sorry for her loss."

Rick hugged her and kissed her again, then unlocked the truck.

And suddenly Rick's heart began pounding. Different than it had before every high school football game. Different than before his wedding. Different even than when he'd watched Tempo take off with Julie, or later when he'd searched for his wife, not knowing if she were dead or alive.

He knew there were crossroads in every life. Times when a fork in the path offered two choices and both were scary. Surrounded by shouts of laughter and joyous reunions across the parking lot, his heart focused on one option: talking to Daniel.

Sweat broke out on his hands. He checked his watch and handed Julie the keys.

"Take Rachel to pick up Ben and go home. He's already stayed an hour later than usual. I need to talk to Daniel."

"What? I'd rather wait for you."

"I don't know how long I'll be," he said. "They might, I don't know, need help or something." His heartbeat kicked up another notch like a goaded horse. "Go on."

He kissed Rachel's forehead one more time, then she climbed into the front seat.

"I don't want to go without you." Julie bit her lip. "I'm sorry."

"It's not about *sorry*, Julie. I'll call you soon."

He watched them drive away, then marched back to the auditorium. He found Daniel talking with a single mother Rick recognized as a familiar face from The Barn Church. She had her arm around the waist of a teenage boy twice her size. The kid had been crying and was clearly embarrassed. Daniel offered them both gum. The kid smiled and accepted a piece, then he and his mother walked away.

Rick cleared his throat. He'd never been so nervous in his life. When you're young you don't realize how important some decisions are, but when you're older ...

"Daniel. Can I talk to you?"

"Sure." Daniel walked toward him.

Ooh, it stung to be this close to asking for help, to letting one of the few people who'd known him since he was a kid see his faults. Mr. Calm and Patient, his pride was about to get a much-needed whipping.

Daniel tucked his Bible under his arm, a gesture Rick knew was second nature to the man, just like his tendency to offer gum to all around him. "I think they want to close up here. Maybe you could walk with me to my car."

Rick glanced around. Sure enough, he and Daniel were the only two left except for the janitor now sweeping the floor. "Good idea."

They emerged into the hot sunlight and traversed the mostly empty lot.

"Want some gum?"

Rick smiled. "No, thanks."

They stopped by Daniel's sedan. Rick spied a bright pink car seat in the back.

"How's the Grandpa thing going?"

"You know I love it. Can't get enough of my little Hope."

"And you're not proud."

"Not in the least. She's going to be a pistol, though. Knows just what she wants. Like her grandpa."

He gave Rick a pointed look Rick supposed came in handy as a preacher, a father, and grandfather.

"Well, I could ease in and say something like: your family's been through a lot the last couple of months. Or I could call 'em like I see 'em. Since you deal with horses I'll say, son, you look like you been rode hard and put up wet."

"That's about right." Rick grimaced.

"Spit it out, boy. Chewing cud's for cows and goats."

"You ever have God show you something about yourself, something you don't like, something you've done wrong, then kind of sit on you about it?"

Daniel belly-laughed. Rick had heard that laugh before, many times in church when Daniel told a joke during a sermon and got so tickled he'd pause and wipe his face with a handkerchief.

"More times than I can count."

Rick felt the ghost of a smile fight its way to the edge of his lips. "I'm guessing it's not that big of a deal?"

"On the contrary." Daniel slung an arm around Rick's shoulder in a quick hug. "It's a huge deal. And it means you're right where you need to be."

He told Daniel details about Julie's accident and what it meant for her dream. Pushing through a wave of embarrassment, he confided about the condition of his marriage, and the brief respite from the tension he'd experienced when Julie let him take care of her.

"I've had this feeling since she got her voice back." He shoved his hands in his pockets. "I want more. I want different. I see I was a huge part of the problem. Letting the kids believe Julie was the bad guy gave me a false perspective of her and myself."

Rick caught the stinging scent of the fire carried on a slight breeze. One wrong decision, one wrong move by anyone, and his daughter might not be safe right now.

His voice broke. "I want to lead my family, but I realize I never learned how to do it right."

"Kind of like your wife, huh? I remember when Ben surprised you all, I dedicated him, if you remember."

"I do."

Rick remembered standing in The Barn Church, Julie holding the apnea monitor with its dangling wires, attached to a soft belt around Ben's tiny chest, beneath his white suit.

Daniel leaned against his car and shrugged. "Julie didn't know how to handle the pressure and her disappointment, and you didn't know how to lead. So now you'll learn. God's got ya right where you need to be."

"It can't be that simple," Rick said. "Just learn?"

"I didn't say it was simple. I said you're in the right place, looking at yourself, your responsibilities. You're humbled and willing to change, because deep down you love God and your family."

"Your daughter-in-law told Julie about a particular scripture, God speaking in a low whisper. That's not what's happening to me. It's like He's standing inside my head banging on my skull with a hammer."

"I've had sawdust fly out of my ears a time or two myself. Listen, Rick. Don't compare yourself to Julie or anyone else. You establish your own face-to-face relationship with God. You pay attention, and you obey. Just take the next right step and you'll end up doing the right things."

"Will I feel better? Will I get some relief?" He'd never felt this ashamed or guilty in his life.

Daniel chuckled. "You know, my son—your new pastor—wanted relief from some profound discomfort about this time last year. Can't say he got quick relief, but in the end he felt better having done what God wanted him to do."

"Talking to you wasn't as hard as I thought it'd be. Give me a ride home?"

Daniel smacked his gum and grinned. "Sure thing, boy. Hop in. Retired preachers like me *love* captive audiences."

"Just use a little hammer and be gentle. Please."

***

"Mom. I need the window open." Rachel pushed the button on her door.

"Do you, um, want me to lower mine, too?" Julie asked as she drove to pick up Ben.

"No." She put her arm out the window, let her hand ride the wind. "I think I just want to feel clean air on my face. The smoky smell on my skin and clothes is kind of making me sick."

When she picked up Ben, he was full of questions. How big was the fire? Did they see fire trucks? Would they be the same fire trucks he'd get to see later that week on his field trip?

Julie answered as many as she dared, as many as she could wading through the aftermath of fear. She caught herself glancing repeatedly at Rachel, much as she'd done at Ben when he was an infant, constantly making sure the child *wasn't* choking and *was* breathing. The first year of her son's life, that was all she'd done—made sure Ben was still breathing.

She wanted to reach over. Hold her daughter's hand and say how thankful she was Rachel's life had been spared. But would Rachel welcome her touch?

"My backpack's still at the school. Everybody was told to leave their stuff. I wonder if it's soaked. If it's ruined."

"We can, um, we can buy another backpack." Julie nodded.

"There's no school tomorrow, is there? Like, I won't have to go tomorrow?"

"I'm sure classes will be postponed for a few days at least. And they'll be continued somewhere else."

Her voice didn't quite feel her own. Or maybe it was the words she was using, the tone of them, the content. When was the last time she'd talked *with* Rachel instead of *to* her? When was the last time they'd just ... talked?

When was the last time Julie had simply listened?

"If my laptop's ruined a new one'll be a lot of money." Rachel's voice softened. "Do I have to earn it?"

Julie barely heard the question, as Rachel's face was turned toward the window. Her arm bobbed against the air in a carefree gesture, a total contradiction to the meaning of her inquiry. *Earn.* The child thought Julie was keeping track of dollars spent on her, and she'd have to pay to replace something even if losing it wasn't her fault.

"No. You won't have to earn it."

During Julie's childhood, her mother had indeed noted every dollar and penny. And used them to heap guilt on Julie for every need, every want, every dream. To bargain for affection.

Dear God, help me undo the damage I've done to my relationship with my daughter. Help me show my complete, unconditional love for her, in a way she understands and can receive.

"I want a really long shower," Rachel said as Julie parked in the garage.

"You want to use my big tub, take a bubble bath?"

"What about my hair? I can't really wash it in the tub."

"Soak for a while, then use my shower."

"Really?"

Julie nodded. "Really."

"Do you remember when I was little, you'd let me turn on the jets and pretend I was a turtle swimming in the ocean?"

"I remember."

"Then I grew too big to play like that."

No, then Ben came and I forgot you were still a little girl inside, Julie thought.

"Lock the door so Daddy doesn't come home and accidentally walk in on you."

Rachel rolled her eyes. "That would be so-o-o embarrassing."

They walked inside and her cell phone rang.

"Go ahead," Julie said. "This is probably your dad." Rachel proceeded to Julie's room while Julie answered her cell.

"Hello."

"When were you going to call me?" Her mother's voice speared through the earpiece. "For heaven's sake, I was at the salon getting a mani-pedi, and there on the television was a live feed from Rachel's middle school as the whole place burned down.

"My nails were wet—I couldn't even call you—and you didn't have the decency to call me and leave a message telling me if she's okay. I was stuck there, waiting and listening to the news along with everyone else not knowing if my only granddaughter was dead or alive. Well?"

"Mom, we just got home. It was quite an ordeal."

"I'll say! But you could have called. You've obviously got your voice back; you answered the phone. Is it because I never mailed you a picture of your father? That's it. You were punishing me, letting me wonder and suffer—"

"No, I was not." Julie sighed as Ben turned on the television and started flipping channels.

"You forgot about me! Calling me didn't even occur to you." Her voice went small and whiny. "Did it?"

"Honestly, no."

Relief surged through Julie at admitting the truth. She sat at the bar and felt herself smile.

"My only concern was Rachel."

"So she's all right, I guess. Worried myself sick and aged five years for nothing."

"She's taking a bath and washing her hair. I can tell her you called."

"I'll send her something. Surprise her. I saw some sexy sunglasses at the mall earlier."

"Rachel is fourteen. She doesn't need to worry about being sexy."

"I know. I know. Oh, I'll just get her a fabulous product my stylist swears by, you know, for taming wild hair like yours. Rachel must get awfully frustrated dealing with that mane all the time. You sure did."

Because according to her mother, nothing Julie had done with her hair had been right. If she let her hair grow, it was too long and too big and required too much upkeep. If she cut it short, she looked like a topiary. There was no pleasing her mother.

" ... just one more thing you got from your dad," her mother continued. "He had thick wavy hair."

"I wouldn't know," Julie whispered.

"I'll send you a picture and you can see for yourself. You got nothing from me. Absolutely nothing."

That's what you think.

"Mom," Julie said, as her body clenched with grief.

Maybe she shouldn't try to hide her feelings like she'd had to as a child. Maybe she should just let them be what they were.

"Did you like Dad's hair?"

"Well, of course I did. What a ridiculous question. I loved everything about Big Joe Pitts and I miss him everyday. You don't know what I've been through. Don't know how I've mourned."

"No, I suppose I don't."

She'd never heard her refer to Daddy as Big Joe Pitts, never heard about the love, only about the loss.

"I'd appreciate the picture. It would mean a lot to me."

"Oh, gotta go. Someone's beeping me. Let Rachel know I called, okay? Bye!"

"Goodbye, Mother," she said to the dial tone.

She remained seated at the bar, hearing snippets from the TV as Ben ruthlessly advanced the remote. And she realized, the volume was set at a normal setting, Ben's hearing aid must be turned up as it should.

Which meant for once, her youngest son wasn't fearful of something she might say.

Julie rested her chin in her hand. She should make dinner, clean the refrigerator, check on Rachel, who was obviously thrilled at using the Jacuzzi tub.

Rest. Listen.

She closed her eyes, breathed deep for several lovely moments. Something in her home was different. Softer. Quieter. She settled back in the barstool and concentrated.

This was what the absence of tension felt like. This was how it felt when she wasn't frustrated, wasn't striving, wasn't pushing at her family because of her own unhappiness and stress and workload.

This was how it felt to enjoy her life, her children's presence and needs. If she could learn to rest like this, to live like this every day how different her life and home would be.

Content in a way she couldn't remember being before, Julie stayed right where she was and waited for her husband to come home.

Chapter Twenty-six

Rick didn't want to go home. The post-adrenaline rush from the fire and the waiting. The knee-buckling relief at finding Rachel unharmed. The uncomfortable transparency talking with Daniel required—all combined together and pushed him to run, to hide, to flee any further human interaction.

When they pulled into his driveway, Rick made himself listen to Daniel's parting advice, shake the man's hand, and maintain eye contact as he thanked Daniel one more time. But he couldn't get out of the car fast enough.

He bypassed the house, his wife, his children. He just wanted to be alone.

He headed to the stables. Early summer meant the late afternoon sun was still high in the sky, cooking the land beneath, cooking him. Why he hadn't noticed the blaring sun while he'd watched the school burn he couldn't say. But his body started to sweat profusely as if purging itself of the day's events and pressures.

If he could work, if he could be alone and work and sweat, and not think for a while, maybe he'd be able to get his bearings before taking the next steps. The fork in the road lay before him and he knew which road he wanted to take. Taking it, however, was another issue.

Noting the absence of Angelina's Escalade he knew he was indeed alone. Changing his mind about working in the stables, he turned and walked the long east side of his land.

Earlier that day he'd let Dutch, Trident, and the other males out into one of the larger pastures. He strode there, braced a heel on the bottom rung of the fence while carefully avoiding the live line across the top.

"Hey, boy. Did you show everybody who's boss?"

Dutch meandered over, stretched his neck above the fence, seeking attention. Rick rubbed and patted and found a small wound, probably a nip from Trident. The frisky mustang strutted over and batted his nose right against the electric line.

Snap! The horse jerked back, squealing and snorting.

Rick couldn't help but laugh. "No harm done. You'll learn."

And suddenly he understood. Sometimes God got one's attention through a still small voice. And other times He had to make a person extremely uncomfortable, like He was doing to Rick right now, to get the message across. Either way, God loved him enough, loved his family enough, to use whatever tactic the lesson required.

Was it any different from the way Rick trained horses, catering his approach to a specific animal's strengths and weaknesses? Each had his own personality. Some were skittish about every little thing. Others were just plain ornery and stubborn and got almost perverse enjoyment out of being a nuisance.

Like Trident. Who chose that moment to test the fence one more time.

Rick chuckled again. Pulled his phone from his pocket and dialed home as he strode to the barn.

"Hey," he said when Julie answered. "I'm back. Be working in the barn for a while. Maybe send one of the kids up with a sandwich or something later. I need to catch up from being gone all afternoon."

"Okay."

"How's Rachel?"

"She's good, I think. A little water-logged maybe. She spent almost an hour in our tub then washed her hair three times in our shower."

"You let her use our bathroom."

"It seemed like a good idea." She paused. "My mother called."

Rick passed the smallest corral outside the barn and entered the stables. "You don't sound upset."

"I don't know what I am. I'm never going to have her approval, am I? She's never going to be the mother I need her to be." Julie laughed. "How can I be almost forty years old and just now figuring this out?"

"If it makes you feel any better, I'm just now figuring some stuff out myself."

"Not about my mother."

"No. About me."

And God, he thought, but wasn't quite ready to tell her.

"You know, I think we're supposed to start your exercises later this week, if your gums aren't too sore or bleeding."

"They're still pretty tender."

"Then we wait." He felt like a kid who'd just begun learning to drive and wasn't sure how to manage all the power at his command. "For another couple of days, anyway."

"Hold on a second," Julie said.

Rick heard Rachel's voice in the background.

"Rachel wants to know if she can forego chores this evening since she's already taken a shower. And if she can come visit Godiva."

"Tell her we'll make up the chores tomorrow since she won't be in school. Have her bring me some food later. She can visit Godiva then."

"Okay, I'll send her down. Rick, before you go?"

He braced himself, an old habit. Which he usually followed by cutting the conversation short and shutting down inside. There had to be a better way.

"Just tell me, Julie. Unless you're about to tell me *our* house is burning down right now, it can't be that bad."

"Not bad, just different. Something's changed, hasn't it? Today. Between us."

"I think so," he said. "I hope so."

"I don't want to go back," she blurted. "To the way it was before."

"Neither do I." Silence stretched as he reached the tack room. "Neither do I. Don't wait up." He hung up.

He mucked the first few stalls and confessed to God his complacency before Ben's birth. Mucked several more and admitted his lack of compassion for Julie after the child's arrival.

Barn lights glaring against the coming darkness, he continued down the line and repented events, actions, and attitudes, all of which had fueled the destructive fire which had constantly flared between him and Julie. When all the stalls were clean he grabbed a push broom and started sweeping the walkway.

"There are things I should've taught my children," he told God. "Things I shouldn't have. Things I should've said to Julie. Things I shouldn't have let her say to me."

With every stroke of the broom, he felt a weight lifting.

Cleaning up, he thought, *one little nasty spot at a time.*

"Thanks for sitting on me until You got my attention."

He moved into the tack room and gathered supplements for the night feedings.

"You broke me. You had to, like I have to do with horses sometimes. Now I'm depending on You to train me right."

***

Tuck Rachel into bed tonight.

The idea came to Julie while brushing her teeth. The simple joy was still a huge pleasure after almost two months of not being able to do so. As she gently flossed, another often taken for granted luxury, the perfect thought took shape, filling her with anticipation. There might be a little friction as Rachel seldom went to bed the first or second time she was told to do so. But surely Julie could find a way to prevent a disagreement.

She looked in the mirror. Thankfully, her gums weren't bleeding. Another small step in her recovery.

She found Ben sprawled on the couch, his face smashed against a pillow. He snored in spurts and his hearing aid dangled from his ear. Really, he was too big for her to carry, so she roused him slightly then steered him to his room. He fell into bed and seemed to melt into the mattress. The child always played at full speed and slept like he was heavily sedated. She placed his hearing aid on his night stand.

Julie expected Rachel to jump at the chance to have the television and remote to herself. With Rick still at the barn, and Ben in a semi-coma, she could watch a show she might otherwise miss. But she was nowhere to be found. She wasn't in Julie's bathroom, or the hall bathroom. A quick glance showed she wasn't in the kitchen getting a snack, or in her room.

Julie stood in the hall, halfway between her children's rooms and the kitchen. She dialed Rick.

"Hey. Is Rachel there with you? I thought she was in her room. Then I brushed my teeth and put Ben to bed. Now I can't find her."

"She stayed for a while after the vet checked on Godiva, but she's gone now."

Julie heard a click. She cocked her head, walked back to her daughter's room, and eased the door open further. Light from the hallway slanted into the space, throwing shadows. Then a shadow moved as the comforter shifted and tented. She thought she heard pages rustling.

Julie stepped back. "I think I found her. Don't work too hard. Bye."

She wanted to do something sweet, something special for Rachel. A kind of offering. Within minutes she'd spooned refrigerated cookie dough onto a baking sheet and slid it into the oven.

She hunted in the china cabinet, then dug around in the buffet for a platter she'd used on special days when Rachel was small. A nubby, green turtle plate. She sat on the floor, running her fingers around the awkward shape. Rachel had always loved turtles. In the back of Julie's mind, the trace of a memory surfaced. Hadn't she once promised to get Rachel a pet turtle? But, she'd never actually done it.

The oven timer dinged softly. Julie arranged the cookies on the silly plate, poured a small glass of juice and, using a large tray, carried the surprise to Rachel's room. The door was still cracked from when she'd looked in before, so Julie sneaked in, closed it quietly behind her, squelching the light from the hallway. Her eyes quickly adjusted, and she saw the glow of Rachel's flashlight under the covers.

She walked to the edge of the bed. "Knock, knock."

Rachel didn't respond. *Earbuds*, Julie thought. She set the tray aside on the floor and gently pulled down the covers. Rachel scrambled up, her eyes wide, a look of fearful expectation on her face as she turned on her bedside lamp, off the flashlight, and pulled out her headphones.

Julie's heart twisted. "You're not in trouble."

The relief that crossed Rachel's face confirmed once again Rachel lived watching for the next verbal assault.

"I want to apologize. And I brought you a surprise."

"Oh." Rachel looked from Julie's face to the cookies, smiled, then looked back at her mother. Her smile shrank. "Okay."

How did a parent explain to a child that becoming a parent didn't magically make one omniscient? That just because you had a child, didn't mean you understood the child, or knew everything the child needed, or even how to give it to them.

Children expected adults to know, and to know better. And they lived at the mercy of adults' bad decisions, when those adults didn't. How she wanted Rachel to understand her heart, her sorrow over her own actions.

She knelt by the bed and gazed up into her daughter's face, a replica of her own as a teenager.

"I've had some very humbling, very eye-opening experiences over the last few days. A kind of … revelation you might say. I've talked with Laurie. I've read my Bible a lot. And I've prayed and prayed trying to figure out the next right thing to do."

Rachel's eyebrows winged up. "Are you becoming a missionary or something?"

"No, but I guess you could say I'm changing my life's focus."

"And?" Rachel looked at the cookies on the tray. "You want to be a baker?"

"No." Julie felt a faint chuckle tickle her throat.

"Let me start over. Rachel, I am utterly, completely, and covered-in-shame sorry for everything I've ever said that hurt you. I'm sorry for not paying attention. For being too busy. For letting you believe I don't love you and don't care about your feelings.

"I'm sorry for not even knowing you."

She took a deep breath. "I had no idea the mistakes I was making as a mother. Or as a wife for that matter. I've learned I've hurt your father in many of the same ways I've hurt you. I don't want your father to be the only one you care about seeing or talking to after you grow up and leave this house."

Her eyes brimmed with tears. "I. Am. So. Sorry. I want to change. I *will* change. I want the chance to heal our relationship."

The wariness left her daughter's face. "Has Daddy forgiven you?" A tear slid down her daughter's cheek.

"I think so. He's trying to, at least. But I know I'll have to prove myself to both of you."

An awkward silence fell. Had she said everything she needed to say? Had she said it right? She so wanted to be near Rachel. Close to her child.

"I was bullied in school," Julie said.

"You?"

"Yes. I remember being picked on all the way through middle school for my last name, Pitts, and about my size, my weight. Then when I reached high school, well, a lot of boys enjoyed making embarrassing comments about—" She glanced down at her chest. "You know."

"Yeah. I know. Britney, you know?"

"The school offered counseling for us—you, your dad, and I—about the bullying. We're thinking about it."

"Would it only be us? Not like, some big group thing?"

"I think so."

"Okay."

Julie's heart pounded. "Would you, um, tell me one thing in particular that I did which hurt you?"

Rachel was quiet for a long time, her finger worrying with a frayed thread on her comforter. More tears fell from her eyes.

"You never let me stay near you," she said. "You were always sending me away to Daddy, to my room, to do something. I never felt like you wanted me around."

Now her heart split. "I'm so sorry. I was trying to keep you occupied or give you something to do, so I could do what I needed to. It's not an excuse. It's not. I should have paid better attention to the message I was sending you."

Julie moistened her lips and squared her shoulders. "Rachel, I apologize to you for making you feel—"

Her voice broke and she had to squelch rising sobs to keep speaking.

"For making you feel like I didn't want you around. For not letting you know that just having you near was a wonderful, happy thing for me, just because you're my daughter. I am so very sorry."

"Is that how you apologized to Daddy?"

"Kind of. I have a lot of apologies to give him. And you. It's one of my new habits."

Another awkward silence fell.

Rachel looked again at the tray on the floor. "You found my turtle plate."

"Here, scoot back."

Rachel shifted on the bed and Julie set the tray in place across her lap.

"These are for you. I wanted to show you I was thinking of you and, contrary to how I've behaved, do enjoy doing things for you. I promised you a turtle once, didn't I?"

Rachel bit into a cookie. "Yeah. Right before Ben was born. You told me you'd have to spend a lot of time taking care of him, and I said I wanted something to take care of, too. So you said you'd get me a turtle."

"Right. Then I had to spend way more time taking care of him than I'd anticipated. And I forgot all about getting you a turtle."

Her daughter looked up at her. "Pretty much. Whatever Ben needed kind of controlled everything around here for a long time."

"You're right about that, and I'm sorry about the turtle, too." She leaned down, kissed her daughter's hair. Rachel's arms came around her, and Julie returned the embrace.

"You know, we never went out for pizza, just the two of us, like we'd planned on the night you got hurt."

"We did plan that, didn't we?" She looked down at Rachel. "I'll be more careful this time. I'll put it on my calendar, so I don't forget, no matter how busy I am."

"Mom. In the journal? I might have exaggerated a little. Maybe more than a little." She let go and Julie eased back.

"I love you, Rachel. Goodnight."

"Goodnight, Mom. I love you, too."

Julie turned for the door.

"Want a cookie?"

"Thank you."

Outside her daughter's room Julie leaned against the wall, eating the cookie while tears of gratitude flowed down her face.

Chapter Twenty-seven

Julie woke before sunrise with a song in her head. A phenomenon that hadn't happened for many, many years, definitely not since having Ben.

The melody flowed like a peaceful brook, steady and strong and sure. Then it built and surged at the chorus, as through rapids and around rocks.

She lay in her bed in the predawn darkness, staring toward the ceiling. Fingers splayed across her stomach and rounded as if playing the music with its various parts. She caught herself starting to hum and stifled the impulse, so Rick could get a few more minutes of sleep.

By the time he rolled over and groaned, a typical start of his day, her excitement had built. She knew she'd never get back to sleep. And she didn't want to. Though she'd almost memorized the piece, she hurried out of bed, donned a robe. She barely stopped herself from skipping to the piano as she made sure the children's bedroom doors were closed.

In the family room an early morning blush lanced through the partially closed blinds, highlighting the embarrassing dust on her old friend. With the song playing a continuous loop in her head, she quickly polished the surface of her Baby Grand, then raised the keyboard cover and folded the felt.

She sat, flexed her fingers. Softly pressed the first chord and closed her eyes.

Gratefulness swelled inside. At the discoveries, the benefits, the rich reward despite the pain of learning the truth about herself. Her heart ached with it.

And as far as her future, as a singer or not, only God who loved unconditionally could teach her how to love without conditions. No matter what she gained or lost, no matter what dreams she attained or joys she never experienced.

I want to be close to You, Lord. I want to know I'm close to You, and I'm learning how to love my family.

All the times as a child she'd dreamed of flying up to heaven and singing to God ...

You don't have to travel to meet Me. I'm right here. With you.

She felt Him smile at her, like in her dreams or when she sang in church. Before, she'd believed He smiled at her with love and approval because of the song, or her voice, or because she was singing about Him or to Him.

She realized now she'd been mistaken. He'd smiled at her because He simply loved her and wanted to be close to her as well. With or without a song, with and without a voice.

God loved Julie. The joy she sensed in Him when she approached wasn't about her offering, but about *her*.

And wasn't that what she'd started feeling yesterday afternoon toward her own children, when she'd sat in the kitchen and simply experienced the joy of having them near? Then last night with Rachel, knowing her daughter was close and safe, and for once, happy to be in her company.

Julie folded her hands in her lap and sat in the quiet of the morning, in God's presence.

Take all of me, she prayed. *Change all of me.*

Apologizing to her family wasn't enough. Stopping saying the wrong things wasn't enough. She wanted to say the right things. To rebuild everything she'd torn down.

"Out of the abundance of the heart the mouth speaks," she'd read.

She wanted her words to her family to come from a pure heart, rather than bitterness and anger. To come from His work in her rather than hurt she carried and frustration she'd hidden inside.

What she *really* wanted, was for God to give her the words to speak to her family—and anoint her words with His Spirit—as she'd always hoped He would her voice.

Change what's inside me. Change everything inside of me.

Joy took root. She could almost feel it sinking into the soil of her spirit, spreading, growing, pulsing through her and up.

A smile exploded on her face. So big, so wide her cheeks hurt. She threw her arms heavenward and wept and laughed, as the awful burden of trying to reach, trying to earn God's love vanished.

And she knew, with that burden gone, God could now fill her heart with all the wonderful things that should come out of her mouth.

***

When Rick had rolled over that morning he was surprised to find Julie's eyes open. When he left their bathroom after his shower and she was no longer in their bed, he was shocked. But finding her at the piano just after dawn with her hands raised, her face lit with a smile, well, that left him dumbfounded.

He wasn't sure what to do. Standing in the hall of his own home, he felt almost an intruder on what was obviously a very personal time between her and God.

He'd seen that expression before, every time she sang in church. But only when she was performing. He had no idea she could look that way, feel that way, have that kind of joyful experience on her own right there in their home.

She hadn't been singing, he'd have heard her. Besides, her jaw mobility was still severely limited. She couldn't open wide enough to sing.

Her face. How he loved her face, made even more beautiful with the free and overjoyed expression. How he wished he could keep this Julie forever.

She must have sensed him standing there. He saw the moment she became aware of herself, then blinked and focused on her surroundings.

Their eyes met. He felt the same jolt he'd experienced the first time he'd asked her on a date. She smiled at him, and his heart tumbled forward in his chest, landing right on the ground between them.

He loved her. He'd always known he loved her. But he hadn't expected to fall in love with her again after so many years, so many hurts, so many areas of separation between them.

"I didn't mean to disturb you."

She looked almost shy. Almost uncertain. And younger. And happy.

"I woke with a song in my head."

"Yeah?"

"Yeah."

"That hasn't happened for a long while. Lyrics, too?"

"Just a melody." Her smile opened and filled with wonder. "A pretty one. I think I'll hear it in my head all day."

"Good for you."

He shouldn't be this unsettled. True, he was usually a man of few words, partly because that was his personality, partly because for the last eight years he seldom got a word in edgewise. Was he supposed to change that? Was *that* what he was supposed to learn first?

To say a little more. Connect a little more than was his habit.

She looked so at peace there, so at home at her piano in their home.

Her domain, he thought with sudden clarity. Rick felt his eyes narrow at the thought, at her.

She'd run the house, run him, and he'd begun to associate being home with being controlled or bruised. Which was why he hadn't wanted to come home yesterday. Why he'd beelined for his work, the horses, the barn. He knew what he was doing in the stables. There he was the expert. The boss.

The leader. He closed his eyes, fighting off pangs of guilt.

She rose from the piano bench. "Hey. Are you all right?"

"I'm fine." He avoided her gaze and proceeded to the kitchen.

He switched on lights, got out his favorite skillet, and turned on a burner. In five minutes, three if he pushed it, he could be out the door with a fried egg sandwich in hand. He set butter to sizzle, broke eggs over the pan.

"Still lots to do to catch up from yesterday. Send Rachel down as soon as she eats. I think I'll keep her with me until supper."

She'd followed him in, but stopped on the other side of the bar.

"You know, I could start cooking your breakfast in the mornings again," she said. "Our whole routine got disrupted from my injuries. But my arm's healed now and I don't need extra rest anymore to recuperate or sleep off the effects of pain medication."

He popped down toast, flipped the eggs, and laid a paper towel on the counter. He grabbed mustard from the fridge and was reaching for the tea when he felt her touch his shoulder.

"Rick." She looked up at him with those pretty green eyes as he turned with pitcher in hand.

She shouldn't have this kind of power over him. To make him feel so vulnerable. To tie his tongue in knots. To make him want to die for her if she asked.

To make him forget what he was doing and burn his stupid eggs.

He grabbed the pan just in time, snatched the toast, slid eggs to bread on the paper towel and squirted mustard. He hadn't realized she'd taken the pitcher from him until he heard her filling a glass.

And saw her filling a thermos. She hadn't done that in many years.

"If you take this with you, you won't have to come back to the house for more tea." Her eyes widened. "Not that I don't want you to come back. But I know how much work you have to do and, I'm trying too hard, aren't I?"

She looked at the floor. "Me trying to be Nancy Nurturer is overkill. I just ... Rick, where are we?"

"Did you fix me an egg sandwich, Daddy?" Rachel's arrival was a welcome distraction.

Ben wandered in behind his sister, wiping his eyes, his hair sticking up on one side. "I like egg sandwiches, too. Extra mustard just like Dad. Can I have two? I'm starving."

"I can make them." Julie reached for the bread. "If you need to go and get started."

"Stay, Daddy," Ben said. "I hardly ever get to eat breakfast with you anymore. You're always already in the barn."

"Okay, buddy. Think I need a second sandwich today, too." He lowered his voice to Julie. "Skillet's still hot. I'll do the eggs, you do the toast?"

She seemed to look clear to his soul. "Teamwork's kind of new to you and me. Think we can manage?"

"Maybe we start small. You know, today egg sandwiches. To-morrow, who knows?" It seemed a stupid thing to say, but her face lit with affirmation.

He felt like a king as he cooked for his children. A beloved father as Rachel scooted her chair closer to his at the table, as Ben matched him bite for bite and chew for chew on both sandwiches.

He watched his wife stand at the stove, cooking her oatmeal, as Rachel and Ben made pretend bets over when Godiva would deliver her foals. Julie glanced over her shoulder at him. He winked at her, she winked back, then gave the same shy, uncertain smile she had earlier when he'd found her at the piano.

Will you accept me? her eyes seemed to ask. *Do you love me?*

Love you, she mouthed.

Maybe love that took you to your knees and made you feel powerless wasn't a bad thing. Maybe when a husband and wife loved that way, it made their marriage strong. Maybe a love like that made you cling to each other and never let go.

And maybe, just maybe, it helped you hang in there when you'd both made crazy mistakes. When you realized you still had so much to learn.

"Tomorrow, your mom and I will make French toast."

Rick winked again at his wife.

***

Despite her special private prayer time this morning, despite the tenuous reconnection she hoped she'd made with Rick, and even considering her one, positive apology experience last night with Rachel, Julie could not get a foothold on how to apologize to Ben.

She pulled out of their driveway. The stage was nicely set—ample time during the drive to day camp, and he was right there beside her in the front seat. But confession seemed an easy out. Atonement, that's what was needed.

To her seven-year-old.

She wanted to. She did. But knowing she'd kind of trampled his innocence was distressing beyond words. Somehow in her mind Ben had been separate from his siblings. He was her baby. Her special-needs child. She'd had to think differently about him since his birth, which had been frustrating, but she'd never been frustrated with him.

She looked over at his bobbing feet, his untied left shoe, his already half-smashed lunch bag between them on the seat. He was systematically pressing the search button on the radio hoping to find a favorite song.

No, she was never frustrated with him, even when he couldn't settle on a radio station for more than two seconds.

Still he'd picked up on her less-than-shining moments, on the disapproval and animosity she'd displayed to Rachel, to Sean, to Rick. She'd thought him to be unaffected by her unhappiness. Perhaps, and this saddened her, he was the most affected of all.

She turned the corner by Ben's favorite cow pasture.

"Yoda cow!" Ben pointed. "That's both days this week. Ugly I am, yes, hmm?" Ben did his best Star Wars character impersonation.

"You have a trip today, buddy?"

"No. They start tomorrow."

"How come they're back-to-back like that? Wednesday, Thursday, Friday."

"Mrs. Teeger says it's because the county would only let us use the buses this week. They're all being serviced over the summer. But Mr. Whitney says we have to fit them in really fast before the end of the month. Something about points and grant money from the state."

"Oh."

"They're both wrong," he said. "Mrs. Shipman knows the real scoop. Coach Doddard has to go as a chaperone to meet the student-teacher ratio. But his wife's about to have a baby. Mrs. Shipman says she could pop at any minute. And even though he's the dad he's going on maternity leave after this week."

"So if you guys are going to take any trips, you have to take them before Coach Doddard starts his leave."

"Yep."

"How do you know all this?"

He pointed to his hearing aid. "I hear stuff."

If only she could erase some of what he'd heard her say.

"You're sure there's no trip today?"

"No trip." Ben slumped forward, resting his chin in his hand.

"Do you even want to go to day camp today?"

"I don't know. Sometimes I wish I could just stay home with you and Daddy. Other times I'm afraid of what I'll miss if I don't go."

"Two choices and neither one looks perfect, huh?"

"Yeah."

She wished she could truthfully tell him life wouldn't always be that way.

"Tell me. If you could pick anything to do today, what would it be?"

"Like go to the moon?"

She chuckled. "No, something real. Today. In our town or at home."

"*Any*thing?" The word stretched with possibilities and wonder. "Go to the Army/Navy store way far outside town."

She looked at him. "Really?" She'd never have guessed that.

"I miss Sean."

Her heart cracked. She actually felt it split for her little one whose world was missing one of its most special people.

"Me, too."

Sean wasn't even halfway through his Basic Training. She'd have to wait another month and a half to apologize in person, then she'd be talking to a young soldier. How would she prove to Sean she was changing?

"You know, when he finishes Basic Training we'll go to his graduation."

Ben's eyes flashed. "Really? Can I wear camo? And a soldier's cap? And paint my face?"

"I think we can do the camo and the cap." She checked the country road in all directions and pulled off beside the pasture. "You want to go to the Army/Navy store and buy some BDUs?"

"Now? Can we get the same kind as Sean?"

She nodded, and couldn't help reaching to brush his wayward bangs. "How about a haircut. Want to try a buzz?"

"Yes! Yes!" He was vibrating with excitement.

"Before we go." Julie swallowed back guilt, shame, and pride. "I want to tell you I'm sorry for all the times you heard unkind words from me to your sister, brother, and dad."

"Okay."

"I feel really bad about how I've behaved. I didn't realize I was doing it."

"Like a mistake."

"Yeah. Lots of mistakes."

He shrugged. "It's okay, Mom. I make mistakes all the time. The first week at day camp, I accidentally walked into the girls' bathroom. They all screamed."

She bit her lip. "You didn't tell me about it."

"I was too embarrassed. Do you ever get embarrassed?"

"All the time," she laughed.

"Then we match," he said.

"Yeah, buddy. We match."

Chapter Twenty-eight

He wanted her with him—Julie, his wife.

The longing had approached steadily, as a horse traveling a great distance. Closer and closer, stronger and stronger it became, beating as hoofs in Rick's chest. The knowledge brought perplexity and comfort.

He knew she'd planned to drop Ben, then run some errands. He knew those plans had changed. She'd called him to let him know she was keeping Ben with her today, and they'd planned a detour. He even knew when she'd return, bringing lunch.

Now, as he and Rachel left the barn driving another tractor load of horse manure to the farthest compost pile, he glanced at his daughter, sitting beside him on the front seat, for what must have been the hundredth time.

"About this time yesterday we were notified of the fire." Rick spoke around the lump in his throat.

Rachel hooked her arm through his and laid her head on his shoulder; it bounced as the tractor passed over a rut. "Were you scared, Daddy?"

"A little. Had to fight not to be." He hadn't let himself consider the worst possibility.

"I wasn't. I knew you'd come get me."

Truer words.

"How long did you stay at the school?" she asked.

"A while."

"What did you do?"

He knew she'd ask. Part of him had wanted to tell her. But he hadn't even told Julie about talking with Daniel. Why was talking about God, about faith, so hard?

"I talked with Pastor Crane for a while. You know, Pierce's dad."

"Mom's been talking to Laurie a lot. Did you know that?"

"She told me."

They stopped at a gate. Rachel hopped down and opened it, pushed it closed after he passed through. She climbed back up beside him.

"Mom apologized to me last night. For stuff she's said, for hurting me. I never thought I'd see the day." Rachel rolled her eyes and Rick stifled a chuckle. "She said you're trying to forgive her."

"She's not the only one who's done stuff wrong in this family."

"I think she's been more wrong than you."

"Maybe," he said. "Or maybe she's just been wrong in a different way, in a way you could see. I've got some changing to do myself. Still trying to wrap my head around it."

"So you're not getting a divorce or anything."

"Rachel. That was never an option."

"No way I could know that after hearing you fight, then not speak to each other for days. Looked to me like neither of you cared about being around the other, so what's the difference if you divorced or already live as if you were? How was I supposed to know if you even loved each other anymore?"

"You've got a point."

He hadn't realized they were giving that impression, or that Rachel was watching them so closely.

"I haven't been a good example of a husband and father. The boys, well, I'm gonna talk to the boys. But I worry most about you. You'll marry one day. I should be showing you what to look for in a man, in a husband. I haven't done a good job of that."

"He'll have to love horses, I know that much."

"Yeah. If he wants to snag you he'll have to love horses."

"I'm glad you and Mom are giving each other another chance. If I ever do something really bad one day, will you give me another chance?"

"Of course."

Rick steered around an outcropping of trees, up and down a small hill, then stopped beside the compost pile. Together they unloaded the manure by shovelfuls, tossing it onto the pile.

"This really smells bad. I'll need to soak in Mom's tub for an hour tonight to get the stink off. Think she'll let me?"

"She let you last night."

"Yeah. One time. Not enough to convince me she's, like, changed permanently."

Rick pitched manure and scooped up more. "Change sometimes comes in steps, don't you think?"

His words echoed in his head later as they returned to the barn to find Julie and Ben waiting with sub sandwiches. They ate together in the tack room.

During the meal Ben rubbed his hand over his scalp and giggled. "Feel it, Daddy. Pet my head."

Rick did.

"Daddy, did I do enough this morning?" Rachel asked as they finished the meal. "It's so hot out there today."

"You did enough."

She looked right at him, then at her mother. "Mom, since Daddy says I'm finished for the day, can I soak in your tub again?"

"I don't see why not."

Rachel looked at him with wide eyes. "Daddy, can I really go now?"

"I suppose."

"Come on, Ben." She jumped up, gathering everyone's trash and throwing it in the garbage can. "Race you to the house."

Then he was alone with Julie, the only sound the quiet hum of the air conditioner. He'd chosen to turn off his country music during lunch to concentrate on conversation with his family. And he thought again about changes coming in steps.

"How's your jaw feeling after chewing a sandwich?"

"I had to tear it into pretty small bites, still I'm a bit sore."

"I bet."

He wished he could turn back time. Relive their years together and do everything better, do everything right.

"Pull your chair over here," he said. "Let me show you the massages and exercises Dr. Wyman wants you to do for strength and range of motion."

She moved closer, faced him so her knees nestled between his. "We've done okay today, haven't we?"

He took her face in his hands and gently massaged with the pads of his fingers. He closed his eyes for a moment in concentration; he simply wasn't a big talker.

Maybe if he told it like directions. Like steps. Like a process he planned to follow.

He opened his eyes. "You know Daniel gave me a ride home yesterday."

"I figured." She sighed. "Just so you know that feels wonderful."

He grinned at her and sure enough, the Julie of their youth, the Julie he'd first fallen in love with, looked back at him with trust and appreciation. Courage thumped to life inside him.

"I talked to him a little. About us. About me. He gave me a lot to think about."

"I'm sorry I put you in that position."

"I'm not telling you to make you feel bad." He continued kneading the sides of her face and jaw. "I owe you as many apologies as you owe me."

She balked and he held a finger to her lips.

"You're not the only one who's got to grow and learn. But I don't think we're supposed to beat ourselves up over it anymore. I think we move forward."

Even as he said it, he felt panic in his gut. To move forward in the right direction, he'd have to lead.

"Tell me what we should do," she said.

"When I find out, I will. I think for now, we practice not hurting each other. We live carefully with each other. Kind of, give our hearts a break."

She was nodding, her eyes filling with tears. And he'd run out of words. Just plumb run out and couldn't string together another sentence if his life depended on it.

"Watch."

He demonstrated, showing her how to gently, slowly insert the knuckle of her pinkie finger between her teeth and work her way up to larger fingers, then multiple fingers, to get back full mobility.

"The progress will come in steps." He could see she understood he wasn't only talking about her recovery.

"We should give it a rest now. Vet'll be here in a minute to meet with me."

She stilled his hands. "Rick? Why didn't you tell me about Rachel having to go to summer school?"

He took a long breath and looked at her.

"Because of the way I've behaved before, you thought I'd blow up at her, at you?"

"Yeah."

He pulled his hands away and rose, walked to the doorway and looked back.

"I didn't want to throw a wrench in what we'd kind of gotten back. You know, us."

***

"Ben?" Julie tapped on the bathroom door. No answer came. She opened the door and found her son asleep in his pajamas and curled up on the floor. Passing Rachel's room, she shuffled him to bed.

She didn't want to hover, didn't want to smother her daughter. However, after spending the morning with Ben, a profound awareness of every day's precious moments was burning its way into her brain. She didn't want to forget, didn't want to ever forget that another day, another minute with loved ones was never guaranteed.

And every day that ticked by, was indeed one day closer to her children leaving home and starting their own separate lives. She had a lot of ground to reclaim in her relationship with Rachel.

Julie eased Ben's door closed. She knew Rachel was in her room, doing her nightly reading-by-flashlight routine. Whatever reason she had for pulling her covers high, hiding under there to read about the horses she loved—

She's just like me. Silly that she hadn't realized it before. Thrilling to have such a unique common ground with her daughter.

Kind, gentle, nurturing, understanding, a good listener. Dear God, help me be all the things I'm not.

Giving herself a quick cheer, Julie nudged open her daughter's bedroom door. Rachel must have been expecting her, as her head popped out and she flipped back the comforter.

"Guess it was too much to hope for cookies two nights in a row."

"Maybe tomorrow." Julie approached the bed. "Mind if I join you for a minute?"

Rachel flinched. "I don't have any contraband under here."

"You're not in trouble." That appeared to be the phrase of the week, possibly month and year where Rachel was concerned. Julie said it again more softly. "Rachel, you're not in trouble."

Clearly suspicious but trying to appear calm, Rachel shifted toward the wall. Julie slipped under the comforter, and pulled it up and over both their heads.

"Turn your flashlight back on."

Rachel's green eyes glowed with surprise, and Julie grinned with mischief.

"Your Daddy and I have always known you're a night person. You never wanted to go to bed, even when you were a baby. That doesn't mean you were bad, just, a night owl."

"I think too much at night," Rachel said. "I don't know how to explain it."

"You don't have to explain. Believe it or not, I did kind of the same thing when I was a kid." Putting her childhood in perspective this way and sharing it with her daughter felt strange, yet she was determined to open her heart to Rachel in a new and permanent way.

"I've wanted to sing professionally since I was a little girl," she continued. "All the time you spend in here at night reading your magazines and studying to one day run your own stables, that's the kind of time I spent writing songs in my head and pretending I was flying up to heaven singing to God."

Rachel made a face. "Bet that went over well with Grandma. Um, *not*."

"Pretty much. Being under my covers was kind of my safe place." She blinked and fought back tears. "I am really sorry you've needed a safe place from me like I needed from my mom."

"I don't always do it to hide from you. Most times I just like to read late. You didn't want my light on, so ..."

"Daddy gave you the flashlight."

"Yeah."

"And permission to go around me?"

"Kind of. You're not going to take it out on him, are you?"

"No. Or you either, for that matter. It's not your fault your father and I never learned to talk about things we disagreed on without creating more conflict."

"How many songs do you think you've written?"

"Well, hmm." Rachel's interest caught her a little off guard. "Dozens. Probably close to a hundred."

"Where are they?"

"I have a box in my closet. Notebooks and legal pads, mostly scribbled and slashed with rewrites."

"Can you publish them for lots of money?"

Julie chuckled. "Probably not. I was hoping to sing them myself one day."

"Like the song you did for the contest."

"Yeah. Like that one."

"You used to sing it to me. At night when you tucked me in bed."

Julie drew a stuttering breath. "Yes. I did. I'm sorry I stopped doing that. I'm sorry for a lot of things. Might take me a couple of years to apologize for them all."

"I believe you."

She exhaled with relief. She hadn't realized how much she'd been holding her breath, waiting to hear those words. *Liar. Hypocrite.* How she wanted a different reputation with her daughter.

"Thanks for saying that," Julie said. "It means a lot."

"Do you still remember the song?"

"Yes."

"Will you sing me some of it now?"

Granting the request could set her back. It was completely against doctor's orders; simply talking so much was against doctor's orders.

Yet, a fierce resolve stood alone in Julie's heart. If she gave only one performance in her life, she wanted it to be here with her daughter. Outside of God, this audience of one was and would always be the most important to her.

Julie gulped. "I'd love to," she said, then quietly sang to her daughter.

CHAPTER TWENTY-NINE

Julie's morning had been non-stop.

She'd dropped Ben at day camp, and after receiving a text from the school to pick up Rachel's belongings, swung by and retrieved her backpack and laptop. Rachel was now holed up in her room, e-mailing friends and getting the scoop on Mr. Larl's funeral, which would take place tomorrow, Friday afternoon.

The fire, it turned out, had been a byproduct of plumbing repairs; sparks from new solder had smoldered inside the walls.

Now, as she and Rick walked to the barn, she tried to sound nonchalant. "So, I haven't seen much of Angelina this week."

When Rick didn't comment, she finally had to admit to herself what she'd been scared to even think. The happy-bappy high she'd felt since bringing Rachel safely home after the fire and from all the progress she was making with her family, was starting to wane.

She'd faithfully tried sitting at the piano alone again this morning before cooking breakfast with Rick, hoping to hold on to her new-found peace and serenity. She'd even sat with them all during breakfast, gingerly eating pancakes and hoping Ben's excitement over today's field trip to the police station wouldn't make him throw them up in her car. Yet she could almost feel herself slipping into panic, into her old way of thinking.

They reached the tack room. Rick turned on the air conditioner while she booted up the computer. Once again Angelina wasn't here, neither was her designer overnight bag. But the folded cot was still shoved up under the counter, waiting for her return.

"I finished updating all the files," Julie said. "Probably after a couple mornings' practice, you'll be able to run it all without me."

She sat at the desk, Rick pulled up an extra chair. She opened the program and showed him the menu and files.

"I smell Angelina's perfume." The words popped out. "Sorry. Tracking invoices and cash flow will be very easy."

"Just show me."

She clicked open screens, straightened her shoulders. And got another big whiff of Angelina.

"Does she spray her perfume in here?"

"You know, you used to complain about the smell of hay and horse manure."

Just can't make you happy—she heard loud and clear.

"You're right," she said. "Here's the file you'll use to track payments from boarders."

"I don't want to fight."

"Neither do I."

"The last couple days," he said, "I thought we were sort of on the same page."

"Me, too."

She was trying so hard to be different, to be kind. Why did she feel like she was barely holding off a stampede of harsh words?

"Let's start again."

"Okay. Show me how to post payments made in advance. Angelina's already paid through the end of the year for Godiva and both the foals."

"Oh, really?"

"All right," he said. "That's the *post-Ben* Julie talking and I see where this is going."

"She's half in love with you, Rick. Anyone can see it on her face, hear it in how she talks to you."

He stood and walked to the door. "I don't think that's true. She's married. And I'm no more responsible for Angelina saying nice things to me, than I am for you biting my head off."

Unkind, then accusatory, then downright mean words jumped up her throat.

She pressed her lips together. Bit her tongue. Not too hard, just hard enough.

She turned away from him, clenching her fists and closing her eyes, leaning on the edge of the desk and sitting as still as she possibly could. According to Laurie, this was when she was supposed to pray, every time she felt the battle raging inside her.

Behind her, she heard Rick take one of his long nose-breaths.

One. Two. Three seconds passed.

"Julie."

She almost laughed. The mistakes in their marriage were so predictable, so formulaic, she knew exactly how this conversation could end. The two of them had wedged themselves into the self-made pattern so well, each time a conflict came, they simply slid right into their respective positions.

Julie, the Lasher, and Rick, he-who-was-lashed.

But what if Laurie was right? What if Julie asked God to be right in the middle of their conflict? Right inside her, with her, prompting her and telling her what she should and shouldn't say.

Dear God, if I don't change I'll undo what little ground I've gained. I'll lose him.

Rick exhaled heavily. "Julie? I'm walking away now. I'm not going to stand here waiting for you to do to me what you've done in the past."

"Don't go," she whispered, the words so heavy she could barely force them out.

She looked up at him. "Just stay another minute. Please? I don't want this time to be like all the others. Believe it or not, I'm praying over here."

Rick's chin dropped to a classic *yeah right* level. "Praying? About me and all my faults."

"No." She wrapped her arms around herself. "I'm asking God to change what's inside me. Please come back and sit beside me."

He hesitated, speculation on his face. Then he returned and sat, his back rigid.

"I heard you singing to Rachel the other night. Brought tears to my eyes. I always wondered how such beautiful songs came out of you on Sunday, then that beauty disappeared the rest of the week."

"I'm trying to change that. I don't want to fight about Angelina." She looked deep into his hazel eyes. Today gray flecks filled the iris. "I don't want to fight about anything anymore."

"I think you're wrong," he said.

"Well, I think you're wrong." They stared at each other, then she softened her expression. "What do we do?"

"She won't be here today, unless Godiva has a problem or starts labor. Then I'll call her."

"I see."

He took another long breath. "She's been having her bathroom remodeled and expanded. A surprise for her husband. The first plumber messed up, flooding half the top floor and ruining brand new zebra wood or some such thing. Why are we talking about her?"

Because I'm insecure, she thought. Because she realized how close she'd come to severing her bond with her husband, and how much work she had to do to strengthen it.

She raised her hands to his face, pressed her forehead to his.

"I will change. I am changing. I won't be perfect, but I'll work at it every single day."

"I never asked you to be perfect." He closed his eyes. "I asked you to be my wife."

"Maybe that's what I need to keep in mind," Julie said. "In case I haven't told you today, I love you."

He opened his mouth as if to speak, but she pressed a finger to his lips.

"No, don't say it back this time. Just this one time let me say it to you to kind of tip the scales to the good side. God knows it'll take me years to come up flush."

***

Rick kept his eyes closed. He left his forehead there against his wife's and let her words sink in. *In case I haven't told you today, I love you.*

Call him a dreamer, call him a coward. He wanted another few seconds before facing the next phase of the disagreement, before looking into his wife's eyes and seeing anger or disappointment or even a scolding.

I think you're wrong. Well, I think you're wrong. He knew he was less than a millionth of a second away from the war following the impasse.

Then she hugged him. She hugged him and held him and rested her head on his shoulder until he couldn't resist sliding his arms around her as well. They sat there, just holding each other.

His Julie. Sitting still. And calm, well, calm*er*. Not insisting she was right, not pecking him to death over every tiny discrepancy between them. Was she really changing?

"What do we do?" she asked again.

Her question made him antsy. And he realized she didn't have a plan. Julie always had a plan, a better plan. Or the Julie of the last seven years did.

He released her. "Show me the invoices and payments first. Then we'll look at the balance sheet."

"Good idea," she said, and he nearly fell over.

If they weren't at odds all the time, they could actually work together toward a goal. Which meant he better have a goal. He *was* the leader, and he best get to it instead of living as a spectator, watching her grow by leaps and bounds.

"You're doing an awful lot of talking this week."

Her hand stilled on the mouse. "I think I need to, don't you?"

"It'll set you back more, won't it?"

"You don't want me to talk?"

"That's not what I said."

She sighed. "Then as long as we're talking I need to ask you about something you said last Friday. When we had that awful fight before I had the wires removed."

"As long as you won't accuse me of anything."

He felt himself freeze, preparing for the coming hit, and was immediately disgusted with himself. What good would her changing do, if he didn't change, too? Even if she never said another unkind word, if he lived anticipating being hurt, he was still living as a victim, wasn't he?

Her brow furrowed. "Since I can't see them, what are your wounds?"

The dead-last thing he'd expected her to ask.

He swallowed. "I never knew if I was allowed to touch you. If you'd welcome it or be irritated that I wanted to."

A tear crawled down her cheek. "I'm so sorry."

"You made me feel stupid. For being a man. For wanting my wife. Everything I tried to do to help you or just be near you—I felt like I bothered you, like a sandspur in a shoe."

"I was wrong. Terribly wrong—something my mother's never said to me. I'm so sorry I turned you away. What can I do to help you heal?"

He couldn't look away from her. "Will it hurt you if I kiss you?"

"I don't think so." She stared into his eyes. "Do you want to?"

Rick nodded. Gently, he touched his lips to hers, let them linger to see who would pull back first.

She raised a hand to his chest and he thought she meant to push him away. Then her hand fisted in his shirt and she held on while he reveled in the smell of her, the nearness of her. Her acceptance of him.

For the first time Rick could remember, Julie didn't pull back first.

***

Rachel Matthews, Mrs. Tate's English class, summer session:

Friday, June 27:

Everything in my life has changed. And I do mean everything.

Mr. Larl's funeral was this morning. Mom took me. We saw Britney there and told her we were sorry for her loss. (I'd already told her the same thing the day of the fire.) She and I aren't friends or anything, just maybe no longer enemies.

Sean loves Basic Training. I got an email from him last night. Which means he won't fail and get sent home. He's probably moved out for good.

Ben—I can't believe I'm thinking this way and saying this—isn't little anymore. He got a military haircut, which somehow makes him look older and taller, and he's been initiated into the drama that is our family. I really thought he was oblivious. Turns out he was smart enough to avoid as much as he could.

My dad has always been my hero, but he's not as perfect as I thought. Which isn't really a change in him I guess. More like now I'm seeing the whole picture.

My mother is the biggest news of the year. First, she apologized for saying things that hurt me all the time. I didn't believe her. Until I found out she apologized to Ben, too.

And she keeps apologizing to Daddy over and over, even in front of me. She asked me to tell her when she says something that hurts me, so she can apologize right then.

She's been tucking me in bed at night. Not that I need to be tucked in, I am fourteen. She crawls under my covers with me and we talk. Mom even sings to me when I ask her. She hadn't sung to me since before Ben was born.

What most makes me believe she's changing is she let me sit with her at the piano. She's teaching me to play again and said I could practice anytime.

I hadn't planned on doing it. And probably if I'd thought about it, I wouldn't have. But yesterday I was sitting at the piano, just picking at the melody of one of my favorite songs and I started singing it. Softly at first, but then I guess I got louder and kind of lost myself in the song.

Mom came back from the barn. I don't know how long she stood there listening to me (I had my eyes closed. In the zone, you know?). She was crying but she was smiling. And get this—she said I have a really great voice, a cross between Bonnie Raitt and Alison Krauss. "Soulful yet smooth."

She's going to teach me everything she knows about singing. Breathing, posture, she's even gonna help me expand my range!

She sat by me at the piano and her cell phone rang. I answered. It was Carmine, Mom's vocal coach from before the accident. He's been trying to talk her into traveling somewhere to do the audition she missed.

She moved into the kitchen and said, "I can't, Carmine. Singing professionally will require me to be on permanent voice rest at home. I can't live that way, never talking to my family."

Mom never told me that. I think I wasn't supposed to know.

Then she said, "No, I really can't leave my family. I cannot leave my husband right now." She said good-bye and hung up, then came back to sit by me on the bench.

Our eyes met, and I knew another reason why Mom won't leave, even though we've never discussed a particular someone.

"Angelina's hot for Dad," I said.

Mom's hands slipped on the keys.

"What?" I asked. "Did you think I didn't *know*? Dad's the only one who doesn't see that forest for the trees."

Mom's eyes widened. "You are much smarter than I gave you credit for."

We didn't talk about it after that, but I knew both of us were still thinking about it.

Chapter Thirty

Did Rachel really see right through Angelina?

Julie finished rolling the second coat of pale mint on the guest room walls, determined to keep herself occupied and not spend the weekend in the barn keeping an eye out for Angelina's arrival. But she still couldn't get the thought out of her head.

She'd tried. Thursday while she played and Rachel sang.

Later when she picked up Ben from day camp, she listened intently as he shared every detail of his visit to Benson's Hardware. His name wasn't chosen to ride along on a forklift, but he did get to practice using a drill, a power washer, and a table saw. "I cut right on the line," Ben said. He now planned to be a building contractor when he grew up—which made her remember Angelina's contractor and plumbing problems.

She'd set the question aside again yesterday during Mr. Larl's funeral.

When she'd returned home and gone to the barn to show Rick the last few aspects of the accounting program, Rick had gotten a call. While he'd talked with someone who wanted to buy a horse, she'd done her exercises, progressing so far as to get three fingers into her mouth.

That's when Angelina and the vet arrived.

Humiliation didn't even begin to express how she'd felt—neither did mortified or embarrassed, for that matter—when they'd found her with half her hand in her mouth. Did a word even exist that meant all three, wrapped up in the fear that if Rick even accidentally compared her to Angelina and saw the differences, he'd reach for the other woman?

Julie grabbed the paint can and a brush, and started on the trim.

She'd done the only thing she could yesterday afternoon—fled home to her room. And called Laurie. She didn't tell her about Angelina, but she shamelessly asked for encouragement, a scripture to look up, anything that would help her know what to do and how to think when she and Rick didn't see eye-to-eye. Her friend suggested paying careful attention to the early verses in the small book of James, verses Julie had already been studying.

So she'd read them again. The opening lines about asking God for wisdom gave her comfort. The next to last verse about controlling one's tongue being a vital part of pure religion, held renewed conviction.

Yet the middle sections most caught her attention. First, the systematic description of how one can be drawn by temptation, caught and controlled by it.

Angelina, Julie had thought. Had Rick ever read this passage?

Second, the admonition to be "quick to hear, slow to speak, slow to anger." If there were ever a verse that should have had Julie's name on it, this would be it.

"Quick to hear," indeed. And "slow to anger"? Controlling one's anger over petty concerns was one thing. But could Julie remain calm when she knew she was right?

She *was* right about Angelina. She knew it in her bones, but didn't want to fight with Rick about it. How did a couple learn to disagree nicely, while still loving each other?

She climbed down the stepladder, surveyed and approved the transformation from Laurie's brilliant suggestion of the quiet green. If she hurried, she could take Rick another thermos of tea before hauling the children back with her for bed.

The children met her halfway, wanting to catch a television show. Thermos in hand, she found Rick clearing the largest stall of old bedding and waste.

"Looks like you could use some of this." Through the back window, stars twinkled to life in a soft navy sky. The night was hot and heavy with moisture and mosquitoes.

"Thanks. Leave it in the tack room."

"You should leave that until tomorrow." Why hadn't she noticed this before? His tenacity to complete a monotonous task. She'd overlooked so many things she should have been grateful for.

"Can't. Vet's coming to induce Godiva in about an hour."

"Tonight? You're moving her in here for delivery?"

"Yeah. Pete's wife had a death in the family. Cousin or some such. Got to travel for the funeral. Pete's afraid to let Godiva go any longer, and afraid to not be here. So we're gonna do it tonight before his family drives north in the morning."

"But you're so tired." She knew he was so, so tired.

He spread fresh hay, prepping for Angelina's mare to deliver. "Yeah. But that's not what you're worried about, is it?" He didn't cease his task.

"I don't want to fight with you. I *hate* fighting with you, but I can't be quiet about something dangerous you either *don't* or *won't* see."

He gave her a look. "Angelina's about as dangerous as the foals she's so eager to see."

Slow to anger. Slow to anger.

He lifted the laden wheelbarrow and pushed it out to the dung pile. She followed. His cell phone slipped out of the clip at his belt and they stopped; she bent to pick it up.

Be quick to hear, slow to speak, slow to anger.

Control your words. Don't hit him with them. Love him with them. Let him see the change.

She made herself maintain eye contact. She forced herself to keep her defenses down, facing him, her eyes open all the way to her soul.

"She wants you. She knows what I look like and she thinks she can lure you away from your family."

He wiped the sweat from his brow with the back of his forearm and looked at her.

"What you look like, or what you think you look like, has no effect whatsoever on what I do and don't do. I didn't marry you because of how you look. I married you because I love you, and in our entire marriage I have never given you any reason to doubt my fidelity."

She clasped her hands together to keep them from shaking. "You're right. You haven't."

But had she set the stage for him to unknowingly respond to a beautiful stranger's encouragement and praise?

"And I'm not saying you will. I'm saying this woman is dangerous." She cupped her hands as if holding precious glass. "Right now we're fragile. We have to be careful."

He dumped out the manure and turned to her. "I don't have to be anything. I'm not weak, and I won't break my promise to you, ever."

She stepped toward him and raised a tentative hand to his forearm. "You're right. Again, you're absolutely right. But I broke my promise to you."

The admission scorched her throat.

"I didn't cherish you. I didn't honor you with my words or my actions." Her voice became a whisper. "Many times I wasn't even a good friend, let alone a good wife."

She watched him process, as the origin of every nick, every scar, was traced back to her, his wife and his worst critic. She saw him stop at the point of decision and found herself wishing that this time, he *would* take a little more time, debate a little longer before choosing a path.

God, please, please help me say this right. Please give me the words.

"I'm sorry," she said. "Those two words aren't enough, I know, but they're all I have. Rick, I'm so sorry."

"I appreciate them. But I reserve the right to not agree with you on everything."

In her hand his cell phone chimed. A text from Angelina. Julie passed it to Rick.

His expression didn't change as he read and texted back.

"Angelina and the vet will be here within the hour. She wants to be here."

Julie stepped back. "Of course. It's her right, her horse."

He looked at her with those steady eyes. "You could stay, you know. Or come back after you tell the kids what's going on—I don't want them here in case something goes wrong. And no, I'm not saying that because I'm afraid to be alone with Angelina."

He removed his filthy gloves, shoved them in his back pocket, and rubbed a clean hand over his dirty chin.

"You hardly ever said yes to me, Julie, for years. Say yes this time. Come back and spend the night with me and a horse."

She pressed her fingers to her own lips.

He shook his head. "I know what you're thinking. You, me, and another woman. She's not. She's an owner. A client." He pulled her fingers down. "Come back this time, Julie. Be my friend and my wife."

Rick didn't wait for her answer. He pushed the wheelbarrow to its place and retrieved Godiva from the arena, walked her to the clean stall.

He's so gentle, Julie thought. *I took advantage of that.*

And at the same time, she'd resented when that gentleness wasn't aimed at her.

"Yes," she whispered. "I'm saying *yes*, Rick."

***

They were the prettiest colts Rick had ever seen. Two beige boys with blond manes just like their mama's.

Outwardly, they had nothing of their chestnut-colored father. But Trident's personality was evident in both, especially in the youngest and smallest who'd emerged at two-thirds the size of his brother. Zeus may have been the oldest of Godiva's sons, but Apollo was indeed a fighter, as Angelina had hoped him to be.

From where he sat on the soiled bedding, Rick extended a hand to his friend, Pete. "I'm really glad you were here."

"Seemed the safest thing all around. Usually I'd stay through the first 24 hours. But I can't this time."

"We'll be fine."

Rick stayed where he was, watching Zeus nurse on wobbly legs, while Angelina fed Apollo from a bottle. The baby wasn't quite strong enough to stand on his own yet, but with round-the-clock care for the next few days, he would be. Despite the odds, he'd been born whole.

Pete packed his things while giving Angelina detailed instructions. Rick already knew the drill, but figured she needed to hear it from Pete.

He scooted back to where Julie sat leaning against the wall.

"It's amazing every time." Her words slurred with exhaustion.

"Yeah, it is."

"Their labor is so quick compared to humans. You know they're hurting, you can see it in their eyes. But they know what to do, they just trust the process."

"Think you could stand doing this more often? Maybe not nighttime inductions, but stick with me for births?"

She turned to look at him. "Why?"

"Nate Jordan and I are kicking around the idea of breeding and selling. He wants to stud Trident. I figure we breed, train, and sell, split the profits."

"Rachel would love that."

"You should go on to the house. Shower and bed." They were both smeared with blood and amniotic fluid. "I'll get Rachel in a couple hours. She can take the early morning shift with Apollo."

He could see on her face that she didn't want to leave. She looked at him, but she didn't argue. And for once, the look she gave wasn't one a general would give an idiot subordinate.

She stood. "You're right about the shower and bed. Eat something when you come get Rachel, okay? You can't stay up all night, not sleep and not eat."

"I'll be fine." He reached for her hand. She grasped his fingers, squeezed and released.

"Good night, Angelina. Congratulations," Julie said and left.

Pete made them promise to call if any problems arose, said his goodbyes.

Rick shook his head against sleep-deprived double vision. Pushed himself up from the floor.

"I'm going to wash up in the tack room, grab a bottled water. You want one?"

She looked up at him from her place on the floor. "I'll get one when he's finished. Second bottle's going down good. He's a hungry thing." She smiled up at him with tears in her eyes. "I'm so relieved they're both all right."

"So am I."

In the bathroom, Rick peeled off his soaked shirt and washed his torso, arms, and face in the sink. He toweled dry, ran wet hands through his hair, then rummaged the tack room cabinets searching for a clean t-shirt. He straightened and pulled the shirt over his head.

Angelina entered. "I think I'll do the same." She pulled her fancy overnight case from beside the folded up cot and carried it into the bathroom.

Rick leaned against the counter, downed one water and started a second. Angelina returned wearing clean clothes and got herself a water.

She twisted the cap. "No music playing?"

"Didn't figure it a good idea through the night. The birth was enough disruption for the horses."

"What time is it?"

He squinted at the tiny clock in the corner. "2:30? No, 3:30."

"It's 4:30 in the afternoon in Japan. Nicholas should be landing there any minute."

"He's gone again?"

"No. He never came home. Went straight from Seattle to Tokyo."

"Does he speak Japanese?"

She laughed. "Right now I feel like I'm speaking Japanese." She ran a hand through and down her long hair.

"Get your plumbing issues worked out?"

"Plumbing's done. New flooring's being shipped in on Monday. How much you want to bet, when Nicholas finally comes home he won't even notice the changes."

Rick wasn't sure what she meant.

"He doesn't care about the house. Doesn't even see it, really. Doesn't see me either. I'm very easy to leave."

"I'm sure that's not true."

"I guess some people just aren't cut out to be married and settle down. They're restless. Goals take them other places, you know? Every woman wants a man who loves them the way you love Julie. I thought Nicholas loved me like that, but he doesn't."

She started to weep. Clearly embarrassed, she put both hands over her face and sobbed.

"He used to tell me I was beautiful. He used to say I was the most important thing in his world."

"You're certainly beautiful," Rick said and squeezed her shoulder. "Hey. I'm sure Nicholas loves you, he just—"

"Forgets me. Doesn't need me. Doesn't want me." She looked up at him, at his mouth. "Do you?"

Their gazes locked, and he saw the yearning and invitation in her eyes. He shook his head and stepped away.

Julie had been right.

"I shouldn't have reached for you that way. I'm sorry," she said behind his back.

"Apology accepted."

And he hoped, he sincerely hoped, his would be accepted elsewhere.

"You won't have any more trouble from me. I'll move Godiva and the colts as soon as I can."

Rick wiped a hand across his mouth and turned to her.

"You don't have to move your horses. Just hear me when I tell you, no one can fix your marriage but you. And God. When Nicholas comes home you should tell him he's hurting you. Take it from me, for whatever reason, he might not even know."

She looked at the floor. "You're probably right."

He left the barn.

The horses whinnied, about the new colts, about the disturbances in the barn that night. Cicadas screamed, their shrieks followed him as he jogged to the back door and entered through the mud room. He shucked his work boots, filthy socks, and jeans, trotted on bare feet to their bedroom.

He caught Julie fresh from her shower, wrapped in a towel and standing at the vanity performing her nightly skincare rituals.

He hugged her. Fast and hard, then held her at arm's length, looking straight into her eyes.

"When I got here I was still a mess, so I left my filthy pants and shoes in the mud room. I didn't want to track through the house this time of night."

"Thanks for that."

"I did change shirts after you left. Alone. In the bathroom. I changed alone."

"Okay." Her eyebrows rose.

"Look. You were right about Angelina. You were right. I was wrong. And I'm sorry." He shook his head. "Some leader I am."

She didn't yell at him. She didn't hiss a rebuke. She didn't even give him a look that labeled him a failure.

"You said you were wrong." She was smiling. The most gentle, thankful smile he could ever imagine. With so much love and gratitude in her eyes it knocked him back a step. "You said you were wrong. And you're sorry."

"Yeah. And?"

"And that's the best kind of leader I could ever have."

He took her in his arms. Buried his face in her hair and breathed in her scent.

"I love you," he said. "I love how you smell, how you look, I love that we're figuring out how to talk to each other and will grow old together."

"I'm giving up my dream, Rick." She wrapped her arms around him. "I won't leave you, and I can't live not being able to tell you I love you or apologize when I need to."

She drew back and looked in his eyes. "I love you. I'll never reject you again. I'm proud to be your wife, Rick. Your wife."

She kissed his throat.

"Your friend."

She kissed his jaw.

"And your lover."

She kissed his lips.

She. Kissed. Him.

And kept kissing him.

He kissed her back. And kissed her and kissed her and kissed her.

EPILOGUE

Nine months later

The Barn Church was packed. Most churches were on Easter Sunday.

Julie had never been more nervous in her life. What if the pianist started too early? What if the choir missed their cue?

As Pastor Pierce Crane neared the close of his sermon—she recognized the ending from rehearsals—Rick leaned over to whisper in her ear. "Everything's gonna be okay."

"I know. I *know*. I just have to survive the next ten minutes."

Her whole family was lined up down the pew. Rick, Julie, Ben, Sean, her mother, and Rachel on the center aisle. Trudey had run with the Easter theme—fuchsia body suit, cobalt blue heels, and a wide-brimmed hat so big Julie knew neither Clyde nor Millie Newman sitting behind them could see a blessed thing. Thankfully, they didn't seem to care, and Julie knew it wouldn't matter anyway in about two more minutes.

Pastor Crane gave his final words. Then, "Please remain seated," he said, giving the cue for the final song of the service.

Julie took a deep breath and—

Rachel stood. She opened her mouth and with heartbreaking depth sang the first verse a capella.

"If I had watched You die that day ..."

Clear and strong, every note true.

She continued at the chorus, the piano joining her.

"If I had been at Calvary ..."

Her intonation was perfect. Her tone, exquisite. Julie knew when she wrote the song, that Rachel's voice would make it soar.

All these years, her mother had never once attended church to hear her sing. That Trudey would make the effort, would make the trip to hear Rachel, gave Julie hope that one day she and her mother might actually connect.

Rachel stepped into the aisle as she reached the second chorus. The choir on stage rose and joined in. Their voices mixed and blended, built and rose until the crowd was on its feet and clapping so loudly, Julie expected the church rafters to sway in gospel rhythm.

Her daughter could *sing*.

In a heartbeat the song was over. The crowd broke into applause, some for Rachel, Julie knew, but mostly for God because the message of the song—the Cross, Jesus' sacrifice, His unswerving determination to do exactly what God wanted Him to do—compelled listeners to see that kind of love and welcome it. Wrap it up with both arms and never let go.

Joy and celebration echoed through the room as Pastor Crane dismissed them. Julie received many hugs and accolades. But her focus was on Rachel, on the way her daughter's face had glowed with bliss while she sang.

Her mother came close. "You know, she might have a chance at a career. That must be hard, seeing such talent from her after how hard you tried."

Julie didn't let the stab go deep. "She is great, Mama."

"She's lost weight, hasn't she? Must've been leftover baby fat. Are you still drinking those pineapple smoothies?"

"Sometimes." Still she was content with her size. She'd never be petite, her hair would never be silky smooth, but as long as she could fit in Rick's arms, well, that's pretty much all she needed.

"Sorry I can't stay longer, but, well, you know."

"Yes, Mama, I do." She knew her mother had taken the quick turn around flight to maintain her frequent flyer miles as much as to hear Rachel's soloist debut.

"I left a package in the back of your truck. It's for Rachel—don't worry, it's not something that will melt—and there's a little something for you. That won't melt either." She adjusted her push-up bra straps as Mr. Newman passed by. "Well, I gotta go. Rental car's gotta go back before I catch my flight."

Julie's family of five made it home. As they ate they shared stories of Sean's continued artillery training, of Ben's newest birdhouse design, of Rachel's upcoming part in the high school's spring musical. On the bar, Rachel's pet painted turtle, Opus I, munched on an apple slice in his terrarium.

Later that evening, Julie found Rick in the indoor arena. His country music flowed through the speakers as he leveled new sand he'd had delivered yesterday.

"It's okay to take a day off now and then," she said.

"This kind of work relaxes me. You know that."

"Yes, I do. And I'd rather be near you than away from you, so ..." She left him and found another rake.

They worked side by side, smoothing the ground.

"You wrote a beautiful song, Julie. With Rachel's voice—man. 'Bout made me cry between it being your words and my baby girl's voice."

"Rachel doesn't know it, but they made a recording for me. For her. I thought we could give one to Carmine. See if he thinks it's good enough to send to Thaddeus Bartell."

"We should let her decide if she wants to send it."

"You're right," she said. "Feel like dancing with me instead of that rake?"

He flung the rake aside. She did the same, stepped into his arms, kissed him and laughed.

"What did your mom give you?"

"If you can believe it, a picture of my dad."

"You've wanted that for a long time."

"Yes, I have." She paused as they danced. "I've got four new vocal clients starting lessons next week. Might not be able to help you as much as I have been."

"Guess that'll require some really good communication on our part. We might have to spend lots of time together talking and ..." He nibbled her ear.

"We don't get much talking done when you do that."

He pulled back. "Problem?"

"No," Julie said, and meant it. "No problem at all. I even like this song."

They swayed together to Alison Krauss' "When You Say Nothing At All."

1. In the opening of the story, we see Julie and Rick as a couple, as parents, and as individuals. How would you describe the condition of their marriage? Do they appear to be of one mind regarding their children? Every marriage is made of two individuals. Discuss how a marriage can be affected when one spouse is living his/her dream, while the other waits for his/her opportunity. Have you ever had to put a dream or aspiration aside for your family? What benefits or negative results did you see in your marriage?

2. Rick has known of Julie's professional dreams since before they married. What is his opinion of how Julie's mother handled her daughter's opportunities? Do you think Rick should have done anything before now to help Julie realize her dream? Why, or why not?

3. Julie's third pregnancy was unplanned. Discuss how an unexpected event/blessing can have both a positive and a negative impact on a marriage. Has there been a "surprise" (a child, opportunity or other change) in your marriage? Do you and your mate have the same view of that surprise? What effects did it have on you? On your mate? What challenges did that surprise bring to your marriage?

4. The birth of their special needs child created a dynamic in Rick and Julie's marriage neither expected as they survived the initial crisis of keeping Ben alive. What stresses did Julie experience from Ben's special needs? How did she respond to that stress? What stresses did Rick experience? How did he respond to that stress? Discuss how coping with stress can create unhealthy habits in a marriage. What stresses have caused unhealthy habits in your marriage? What are those unhealthy habits? Do you identify more

with Rick or Julie in regard to habits and coping mechanisms?

5. By the day of Julie's accident, communication between Julie and Rick is unhealthy—full of offensive and defensive comments. What parts of their conversation show their pain and frustration? Could either of them have said anything to the other to diffuse that conflict? Why, or why not? If one of them had tried to diffuse the conflict, do you think the other would have received the gesture as it was intended? Why, or why not? In marriage, we don't always recognize negative pre-judgments we make about our spouse based on past experience and behavior—how we expect our mate to behave. At this point, what negative judgments (expectations based on pattern) do you think Rick and Julie have about each other? Discuss any negative judgments you have about your spouse, or vice versa.

6. While in recovery, Julie's nurse mentions hearing Julie sing in church, as well as seeing her family sitting together during service. Discuss how our perceptions of others, especially those who attend church, might not be based in reality. Do you think Rick or Julie would have spoken up in a Sunday School class or small group meeting regarding the state of their marriage, if they'd been asked? Why, or why not? What might you say to Julie and Rick, if you had the chance to counsel them about their marriage? Discuss how we sometimes deprive ourselves of the help and support we need by not sharing our needs with trustworthy believers.

7. Consider Rick's feelings right after Julie's accident. Discuss how it is possible to love your spouse, yet not like a particular aspect of your relationship. While Julie is in the hospital, we see more of the issues in her marriage. Which of Julie's actions appear to be based in anger but are really based in fear? What actions do you have such as: anger, impatience, indifference, sarcasm, resentment or even blaming others, which are based in fear? How are those actions affecting your marriage? Do you know the source of your fear? Can you name/articulate your fear? (e.g., fear of failure, rejection, discovery, etc.)

8. What is Julie's biggest fear? Why? Julie begs God to heal her voice. Soon she learns that the cord paralysis was a gift and helped reveal

a serious problem with her voice. Discuss how we are sometimes quick to ask God to remove or fix a symptom of a problem without knowing the root of the problem.

9. Rick obviously loves Julie, yet for some time he has withheld from Julie the tender care he demonstrates in front of the hospital nurse. Discuss how Julie feels at the nurse's comment "Wish I had one like that." What do you think is worse: doing something you shouldn't in marriage (e.g., Julie hurting her family with her words) or not doing something you should be doing (e.g., Rick not showing care for Julie on a regular basis before the accident)? When have you mirrored Julie and/or Rick's behavior? What damage did that do to your marriage?

10. During the swallow test, Julie and Rick connect in a way they haven't for a very long time. How can witnessing your spouse's suffering or struggle help you have compassion for him/her? How can sharing your own suffering or struggle help you connect with your mate? If you are hesitant to acknowledge the first or do the second (above), why are you hesitant? What do you need from God to help you overcome this barrier in your marriage?

11. After Rick finds Julie crying in the bathroom and washes her hair, their relationship improves. What part of that improvement comes from Julie not being able to speak? What part comes from him taking care of her? In a marriage, it's possible to create habits of reacting to our spouse, rather than acting on behalf of our marriage and faith. For example, *he does that, so I respond with this*—when neither action is righteous or yields positive results. So, our dysfunction feeds on itself. What behavior do you have that seems to provoke a negative response in your spouse, and vice versa? What behavior should you put in its place? What do you need from God to make that new habit?

12. Trudey's presence helps us understand why Julie thinks, feels, and behaves the way she does. What thoughts, feelings, and behavior did Julie bring to the marriage because of her history with her mother? What thoughts, feelings, and behavior have you brought to your marriage because of your family history? Are they posi-

tive or negative? What impact have they had on your marriage? Discuss how even as believers, we can have behaviors we consider "normal" or understandable, which are rooted in our pre-marriage history.

13. As the story progresses, we learn that all three of Rick and Julie's children have been affected by the condition of their parents' marriage. How is Sean affected? Rachel? Ben? Discuss that Julie "ministers" to others with her voice on Sundays, yet that same voice and her words have become a source of pain to her family. Because of this state in their family, what possible reactions could her children have to attending church or participating in faith? Discuss how our children, grandchildren, and others we influence "learn" about faith and family as they observe a marriage.

14. Rick has a habit of running interference between Julie and Rachel, and it's implied that he is a permissive parent with Rachel. Does Rick like being in this position? Who put him in that position? What would Rick need to do to stop this pattern? Discuss how sometimes to avoid an immediate conflict, we can mistakenly build toward a larger, more problematic conflict.

15. When Julie's voice returns, Rick immediately braces himself against being berated. Can you understand his behavior? Julie seeks Laurie's help when she senses Rick's withdrawal. Discuss how we can have unseen faults and habits which hurt others, as Julie does. Should Rick have told Julie when she hurt him with her words? Why, or why not? Discuss how sometimes telling someone the truth might hurt that person's feelings, but might avoid more pain for both in the future.

16. God begins dealing with Julie about her words and with Rick about his tendency of disengaging to avoid conflict and not leading his family. The school fire prompts both of them to not only stop bad behavior, but begin new positive behaviors. Julie begins by apologizing to Rachel and Ben. Do you think Rick owes his children apologies, as well? Why, or why not? Think of a time you reacted poorly to something your mate did or didn't do. Why did you react? Discuss what you could have done differently to defuse the situation.

17. What did Julie need to discover about God and feeling close to Him? Why did that truth make a difference in how Julie saw herself? Her ability to sing? Her children? When Rick finds Julie at the piano, he becomes uncomfortable. Discuss how watching one's mate change in a good way, can sometimes make us uncomfortable. In what ways does Rick feel he needs to change? If only Julie changed, do you think their marriage would benefit as much as if Rick changes, too? Why, or why not?

18. Angelina's presence highlights the communication issues between Rick and Julie. Why does her presence make changing their conflict pattern more difficult? Think of a time, past or present, when an outside influence exacerbated a problem between you and your mate. Was Julie's concern over Angelina warranted? What should Rick do long-term with regard to Angelina, now that he knows she is attracted to him? Do you think Julie and Angelina can be friends? Why, or why not?

19. Julie repairing her relationship with Rachel is key to Julie's spiritual journey. Why do you think this is? What does it say about Julie that she becomes her daughter's voice coach? How do you think this will affect Julie and Rick's relationship? Discuss how family relationships are intertwined, and how tension in one often bleeds over into others. Could Rick and Julie's marriage thrive if they didn't work to repair the damage to their children?

* If you or someone you love wants information or instruction about handling conflict in marriage, please visit my website, www. shelliearnold.com.

www.ingramcontent.com/pod-product-compliance
Lightning Source LLC
Chambersburg PA
CBHW070612300726
48975CB00006B/1798